The
WOMEN
of the
COPPER
COUNTRY

A NOVEL

MARY DORIA RUSSELL

ATRIA BOOKS

New York London Toronto Sydney New Delhi

An Imprint of Simon & Schuster, Inc.
1230 Avenue of the Americas
New York, NY 10020

First Atria Books hardcover edition August 2019

ATRIA BOOKS and colophon are trademarks of Simon & Schuster, Inc.

For information about special discounts for bulk purchases, please contact Simon & Schuster Special Sales at 1-866-506-1949 or business@simonandschuster.com.

The Simon & Schuster Speakers Bureau can bring authors to your live event. For more information or to book an event, contact the Simon & Schuster Speakers Bureau at 1-866-248-3049 or visit our website at www.simonspeakers.com.

Interior design by Jill Putorti

Manufactured in the United States of America

1 3 5 7 9 10 8 6 4 2

Library of Congress Cataloging-in-Publication Data

Names: Russell, Mary Doria, 1950– author.
Title: The women of the copper country / a novel by Mary Doria Russell.
Description: First Atria Books hardcover edition. | New York : Atria Books, 2019. | Includes bibliographical references.
Identifiers: LCCN 2018051007 | ISBN 9781982109585 (hardcover) | ISBN 9781982109592 (paperback) | ISBN 9781982109608 (ebook)
Subjects: LCSH: Clemenc, Ana K., 1888–1956—Fiction. | Copper Miners' Strike, Mich., 1913–1914—Fiction. | Women labor leaders—Michigan—Fiction. | Labor movement—Michigan—History—20th century—Fiction. | BISAC: FICTION / Historical. | FICTION / Contemporary Women. | FICTION / Biographical. | GSAFD: Historical fiction. | Biographical fiction.
Classification: LCC PS3568.U76678 W66 2019 | DDC 813/.54—dc23
LC record available at https://lccn.loc.gov/2018051007

ISBN 978-1-9821-0958-5
ISBN 978-1-9821-0960-8 (ebook)

For Agnes Shanklin and Richard Cima, of blessed memory,
and for all the union thugs who teach high school English

The laborer is worthy of his wage.

—MATTHEW 10:10

Prologue

Turn tears to fires
—Shakespeare, *Romeo and Juliet*

The dream is always simple. The memory never is.

It's an echo from 1903 when she was almost sixteen. A rare family outing down to the county fair in Houghton, Michigan.

Her father probably expected the excursion to cheer her up. There were horse races and ox pulls, all day long. A merry-go-round and a Ferris wheel. Games of chance. Vendors calling their wares. Quilts, pies, and jams vying for blue ribbons. The promise of fireworks after dark. But there were crowds as well. Strangers. People who'd never before seen the girl called Big Annie up in Calumet.

At twenty-five, Anna Klobuchar Clements would be known around the world as America's Joan of Arc. Ten thousand miners would march behind her in a wildcat strike against the richest, most powerful copper company on earth. But that day at the Houghton fair? She was just a big, gawky girl—tired to tears of being pointed at, remarked upon, ridiculed.

Being tall didn't bother her when she was five. She liked being the biggest in her kindergarten class. She liked school. She didn't mind at all when the teachers started calling her Big Annie. It never occurred to anyone that she might be embarrassed by the nickname. It was simply meant to distinguish her from another—much smaller—Annie in her class.

The tall American daughter of tall Slovenian parents, Anna Klobu-

char had topped six feet at fifteen. In a mining town increasingly popu-
lated by underfed, undersized immigrants fresh off the boat, she could
never escape the goggle-eyed notice. The endless, stupid teasing of boys
her own age was the worst. As she got taller, they began to feel dimin-
ished by her. Intimidated. Irritated by the existence of a girl who was
bigger and stronger than they were.

Her younger sister, Maritza, was already engaged. She was barely
fourteen but she would marry in a month, long before she reached her
full height and got bigger than her husband. And Annie was supposed
to be happy about it.

So. That awful county fair in 1903. Which was supposed to cheer
her up.

Everybody stared. Grown men came to a stop and demanded, "Jeez,
how tall *are* you anyways?" as though her height were both a marvel and
an affront. Women and girls shook their heads and gave silent thanks
that they themselves were dainty little things, or at least appeared so
when compared to *that* poor girl. Boys laughed and pointed, calling
out familiar taunts, along with new ones that were more hateful. Freak.
Giant. Monster. Holy cripes! Look at the size of her! Oughta be in the
sideshow with that bearded lady . . .

She stood it as long as she could. Finally, a couple of hours before
dusk, she fled toward the cornfields and cherry orchards and pastures
beyond the fair. Her sight was still blurred with tears when she heard
her father's voice, just behind her. "Anna, don't—"

She shattered into frustrated, embarrassed, angry weeping. When
the storm passed, she sucked in snot and wiped her nose on the back
of her hand and waved toward the crowds. "I'm taller than every boy in
Calumet. I'm probably taller than every boy in Michigan! Nobody will
ever marry me. Why do I have to be so tall?"

"Your mother's tall," he said. "She got me."

Which didn't help.

It was a relief to the pair of them when they were startled by the
hushed roar of a gas-fired burner behind them, just over a little hill.
They turned, and looked up, and saw a huge balloon rising. Red, white,
and blue silk, billowing.

"Let's go for a ride," he suggested. "Just us. Me and you."

Years later, she would ask herself, Where did he find the wisdom? But that day in Houghton, she wondered where he'd found the cash. Tickets were a day's pay—*each*—for a copper miner. She tried to talk him out of it. They both knew her mother would be infuriated by an indulgence like that; nevertheless her father told the balloonist, "Two," and handed him the money. Together they clambered up and over the edge of a big wicker basket and waited for the other passengers to do the same. The balloon would be tethered— "So you won't drift out over the lake!" When the basket was full of paying customers, the pilot released the moorings. There were little shrieks of excitement and fear when the basket rocked off the ground. Everyone ducked and laughed nervously when the pilot opened the burner for a fresh blast of heat. And then . . . no sound except for their own breathing as the huge balloon lifted them higher and higher, its colors aglow in the slanting sunlight.

Below them, the merry-go-round and Ferris wheel seemed like wind-up toys made of tin, and people on the fairgrounds looked like tiny flowers on a vast colorful tablecloth laid out for a picnic.

Summer evenings in Upper Michigan are often brilliant with orange and purple and golden clouds. That spectacle can become ordinary to those who live in the far north. What surprised Big Annie was how pretty the land itself was when you could see it from above: greened by the scrubby brush that grew around countless tree stumps, laced by white waves edging the stony shoreline of the Keweenaw Peninsula, surrounded by Lake Superior's blue depths.

And that is what her dream always feels like. Like floating into the silence, leaving mockery and fear and anger far below. Like soaring upward without the slightest effort and seeing an unexpectedly beautiful world stretched out in all directions . . .

In the next decade, she would more commonly awaken with her heart pounding from a different kind of dream, one in which she runs toward some urgent task, increasingly frantic because she is late and there is always an obstacle of some kind. A train blocking the road. A locked door. Knots of men standing in her way. But now and then, that dream of silent floating would come to her, like a father's blessing. And she would remember, when she woke, what her father told her that day as they floated far above the Copper Country.

"Stand up straight, Anna. Hold your head high," he told her. "That's your strength. You are tall for a reason. When your head is high, you can see farther than anyone else."

June 1913

1

Two households, both alike in dignity

—Shakespeare, *Romeo and Juliet*

The birds disappeared when the forests went underground. There is no dawn chorus, no melodious robin-song, no cheerful cardinal-chant to greet the brightening sky. It is the first pink flush of light that rouses James MacNaughton.

The windows are open, covered only by fly screens and gauzy curtains. Rolling onto his back, stretching, he fills his chest with cool, fresh air. When he breathes out, he is *awake*.

Sunrise. Early summer.

Best time of the day, he thinks. Best time of the year.

His family is at their summer house on the Lake Superior shore, but James MacNaughton is a man of iron habits; even alone, he eases out of bed as though his wife were sleeping next to him and might be disturbed if he is not careful. Drawing on a dressing gown, he slides bare feet into carpet slippers and pads noiselessly down the hallway, stopping for a moment at each child's door. The girls' beds are made and their rooms have been neatened; still, he pictures the pillowed faces and tousled hair of his two absent daughters and smiles inwardly as he continues toward the bathing room.

His morning rituals never vary. Nearing fifty, he is determined to remain fit and limber. Ten minutes of vigorous calisthenics start every working day. To accommodate this healthful habit, two small rooms formerly used by servants have been combined to create a large bathing and exercise space. The servants have been moved to a new wing at the back of the property; this change has achieved a more decorous division between family and staff, well worth the disruption endured as the house was remodeled.

Tiled in gleaming white ceramic, the bathing room is equipped with porcelain fixtures and a modern chrome-piped shower stall that was his own particular requirement. There is a clock on the wall but, like the bathtub, only the ladies of the house use it. Years of time-and-motion studies have given James MacNaughton an uncanny sense of the exact duration of any interval between a single second and a full hour.

When he reaches the ninth minute of exercise, he pauses to turn the sink tap, bringing heated water up from the boiler in the cellar. Sixty seconds later, he begins his shave, having determined that buying blades for a Gillette safety razor is more efficient and economical than wasting time and money at a public barbershop. He showers next, methodically soaping his body: center, left, right. A rotation of 360 degrees to rinse away the suds, front and back, and then he allows himself exactly one additional minute to appreciate the sensation of hot water sluicing over his shoulders.

James MacNaughton is a great believer in showers. It pleases him to have provided this sensible element of twentieth-century sanitation to those employed by the Calumet & Hecla Mining Company. Ladies like his wife and daughters might well indulge in a long soak; for hardworking men, showering away daily sweat and grime is more hygienic than sitting in murky water once a week. Accordingly, the company bathhouse has been fitted with large communal shower rooms. At the end of their shift, workers exit the mine shafts, strip off their heavy canvas work clothes, scrub with company soap, and rinse off under hot company water. Afterward, they will pass through to the lockers where their street clothes are stored, returning to company homes refreshed.

Twenty-two minutes after leaving his bed, James MacNaughton turns off the water and steps onto the bath mat. In the kitchen one flight below, coffee is percolating, its aroma rising to meet him as he rubs his skin briskly with a Turkish towel. In the adjacent dressing room, his butler is laying out clothing in the order in which it will be donned. Undergarments. Stockings and garters. A white shirt, starched and pressed. A fresh collar. Trousers, vest, suit coat, each well brushed. Shoes, buffed to a high gloss.

In the cellar, his maid has been ironing creases from newspapers: the *Boston Globe,* the *Detroit News,* and the *Chicago Tribune,* evening editions of which are delivered overnight on the Calumet & Hecla express train, arriving at the MacNaughton home by six A.M., along with the morning edition of the *Daily Mining Gazette* and the *Calumet News.* Having stacked all five papers neatly, the maid will lay them on the dining table to the left of Mr. MacNaughton's place setting. His spectacles, gently polished, will be positioned above the *Globe's* headline. This done, the maid will ascend the service stairway at the back of the house and make Mr. MacNaughton's bed, finishing that task just in time to clean the bathroom only moments after her employer has moved to the dressing room, thus forestalling the development of mold or mildew.

Meanwhile, the cook will have prepared Mr. MacNaughton's breakfast. She shares her employer's Scottish heritage as well as his conviction that hot oatmeal is the only proper start to the day, even in midsummer. And none of your fripperies like molasses or raisins—just good, plain, hot oatmeal with a little salt and some fresh, cool cream. Unlike the rest of the staff, which is in constant flux, the cook has been with Mr. MacNaughton since 1901, when he became the general manager of Calumet & Hecla and took up residence in this home. The cook was initially puzzled and not a little resentful when her employer spent two full days analyzing her work habits. She herself has always been a methodical person and took pride in explaining why she did things in a particular manner, but she was intrigued to learn that Mr. MacNaughton was a pioneer in the field of scientific industrial management who intended to run his household just as he did the world's largest copper mining company.

He adheres to a simple principle: minimize wasted time and motion to maximize efficiency and productivity. "Everything is properly stored at the point of first use," he told her. Glassware, cutlery, and dishes were relocated to new corner cabinets, custom-built for their purpose, each forty-eight inches from the dining room table. With service items out of the kitchen, space was freed for a set of logical work stations: pantry, icebox, preparation counter, stove, sink. Every pot and pan, each mixing bowl, and all the cook's tools are stored such that she need not take more than one step from station to station. She never wastes a moment looking for a rarely used item. Everything is where it ought to be.

It was the cook's own idea to time the preparation of Mr. MacNaughton's oatmeal so that it has reached the correct temperature just as he arrives at the table. He was pleased by her enthusiasm for his methods and raised her salary by a nickel a day when he noticed. It was a princely gesture and she was grateful. Twelve years ago.

Thirty-seven minutes after rising, James MacNaughton is dressed and on his way down to breakfast, but it is his custom to tarry on the broad staircase landing before descending to the dining room. Standing before the large window, he clasps his hands behind his back like a soldier at ease: shoulders straight and feet planted. He does not own the immense domain before him, but as general manager of Calumet & Hecla, he presides over it with viceregal authority.

The Copper Country, it's called—written and spoken with capital letters. So remote, it is almost a nation unto itself. On maps, it is labeled the Keweenaw Peninsula, a blade of land thrusting north by northeast into the frigid waters of Lake Superior. Running lengthwise down the peninsula's center, like the blood gutter of a bayonet, are the richest copper deposits on earth. Ancient Indians collected chunks of the red metal from streams and shallow pits: float copper so pure it hardly needed refining at all, so beautiful and malleable that it could be made into jewelry and vessels that were traded as far south as Arkansas.

The savages and the surface veins are gone now. It took Anglo-Saxons to make something useful out of the godforsaken wilderness, he thinks with pride.

With vigor and vision, men of his own kind cleared vast forests, turning pine into cordwood and maple into timber for buildings and tunnel supports. With shovels and explosives, they sank shafts and blasted out miles-long corridors and cross-cutting drifts. With hand tools and muscle, they carved out cavernous, ore-rich stopes deep within the earth. Breaking up the rock with sledgehammers, they hauled out conglomerate to be milled and smelted on the surface, where they built railways and shipyards to carry ton after ton after ton of copper ingots to factories around the globe. Copper for cooking pots and coins and buttons and candlesticks. Copper to roof buildings and sheathe the hulls of ships. Copper to alloy with tin for bronze hardware and great bronze statues; copper to alloy with zinc for brass band instruments, machinery bearings, ship fittings, and munitions. Copper for telegraph and telephone and electrical wiring, and for indoor plumbing. Copper to transform America from an agrarian backwater to a nation that will soon be more wealthy and powerful than any European empire.

Accomplishing all this in little more than half a century has been neither cheap nor easy. Mining is a lottery. How many mining companies have formed and failed since the Civil War? A hundred? Maybe more. The Keweenaw Peninsula is riddled with exploratory trenches and abandoned shafts, the landscape littered with collapsing buildings and rusting iron machinery. Today, only a dozen deep-shaft mines run in the black often enough to avoid bankruptcy; of that dozen, only three are consistently profitable. The Quincy is called Old Reliable for a reason: it has paid out every year since 1862. The Copper Range is new and benefits from modern methods and equipment. But Calumet & Hecla outshines them all, for C&H does not merely own the Keweenaw's most productive deposits. It has the immense capital, the long experience, and the extraordinary leadership required to compete with the open-pit mines of Montana and Arizona.

What lies above the ground is equally impressive. Calumet is not a mining camp or a village or even a city, but a metropolis of forty thousand residents—an asset owned in its entirety by the company. Few things are so gratifying to James MacNaughton as showing Calumet to investors when they arrive in this remote outpost for the first time. "Paris on Mars," he murmurs when jaws drop and eyes widen at the sight of the grand sandstone edifices that house professional offices, banks, elegant stores, restaurants, and hotels. A fine library provides uplifting reading material in nearly all of the thirty-some languages spoken by the miners and their families. The Civic Theater is Calumet's crown jewel. Widely acknowledged to be the most beautiful lyceum west of New York City, it is more than worthy of the luminaries who've performed there: Sarah Bernhardt and Lillian Russell, Enrico Caruso and John Philip Sousa, Douglas Fairbanks and Lon Chaney.

The thriving business district is a neat grid of paved streets lined by telephone poles, illuminated by electric lamps, and served by streetcars that run around the clock. Farther out, there are orderly ranks and files of sturdy clapboard houses, built strongly enough to withstand a century or more of winter storms. These are rented to married miners for just two days' pay per month. C&H sells the families coal, firewood, and gas at wholesale prices. Clean, clear Lake Superior water is piped into the homes for a small fee. Thus, Calumet & Hecla rewards marriage, for married men are steadier, more dependable. And James MacNaughton always draws visitors' attention to the industriousness of his employees' wives, as well. Nearly every small fenced yard boasts a vegetable garden and a fruit tree or two. Some have little smokehouses and coops for chickens and rabbits. The company charges no fee when employees' families clear fields in the outlying scrub to set up pigsties and put in stands of corn.

The cityscape is punctuated by larger buildings. Bunkhouses for the unmarried men. Shaft houses, engine houses, boiler houses; towering mill stacks reaching more than a hundred feet into the sky. In large sandstone schools, employees' daughters learn home economics. Their sons learn trades that prepare them for jobs with C&H, and no matter how benighted their immigrant origins, those boys will be able to read their contracts in English and sign them with well-formed signatures in full legal understanding of the risks they assume by accepting work underground.

It must be acknowledged: accidents are inevitable. Metal mining is a dangerous industry, but when a man is hurt at a C&H facility, he can be treated in a well-staffed hospital. Alone among American mining corporations, Calumet & Hecla matches employee contributions to the laborers' medical fund, dollar for dollar.

In return for this largess, C&H expects an honest twelve-hour day, Monday through Saturday. Workers have Sundays off, along with Christmas and the Fourth of July. Some merely drink their leisure away, playing billiards and gambling. This is regrettable, especially since the company encourages healthier recreation by sponsoring athletic teams and offering trophies. Baseball is popular during the Copper Country's short summers. Hockey is the sport of choice during the exceedingly long winters, and the company offers roller rinks and bowling alleys for indoor recreation when the Great Lakes bring blizzards and snowdrifts pile up past second-story windows.

Sunday mornings, of course, ought to be spent at worship, and many employees do attend services. Indeed, James MacNaughton was gratified when the 1910 census revealed that Calumet had more churches per capita than any other town in America. For fifty years, wave after wave of immigrants have come to the Copper Country, all of them eager to work for the world's most productive and progressive mining company. Every group has its own religious traditions; each denomination has at least one church. C&H likes its workers to be schooled in morality; the company land beneath houses of worship is, therefore, rented to the congregations at a discount. Mr. MacNaughton himself has made a point of donating generously—and anonymously—to the building campaigns for each and every new church.

Even the Catholic ones.

He is silently proud of that unheralded generosity. James Mac-Naughton is a modest man in many ways. Private and reserved. On guard, always, against ostentation.

The prior general manager of Calumet & Hecla displayed his wealth shamelessly, throwing grand parties and balls in the immense mansion he built as a surprise for his wife. With thirteen thousand square feet to fill, Tom Hoatson missed no opportunity for display. Every room: stuffed with furniture. Every floor: layered with Persian and Turkish carpets. Every tabletop: cluttered with exotic curios from the family's travels to Europe, Asia, and Africa. At the housewarming gala, Tom ushered his guests from place to place like a tour guide, insisting that they admire everything from the fifteen-foot motorized turntable in the carriage house to the silver-leafed ceiling in the music room. In the library, he made sure that they noticed that the books had all been custom-bound in ostrich leather with gilt titles. No doubt, their costly spines remain uncracked to this day; Tom was never much of a reader. In any case, the mansion is too dark for such a pastime, even with all its gaslights blazing. Dimly lit even at high noon on a sunny day, its enormous stained glass windows are half-obscured by heavy velvet drapery, its walls dark green, with fanciful murals depicting the long-gone forests that were clear-cut for the mines.

The Hoatson dining room was a special horror. A graceless baronial table shipped back from Scotland. French porcelain, English silver, Bohemian crystal . . . but just try to enjoy a meal when your host urges you take particular note of the wall-coverings: elaborate Celtic knot-work hand-painted on the tanned hides of baby elephants!

Mrs. MacNaughton refused to visit the Hoatson house again after that obligatory first dinner. Later, when she and James undertook the remodeling of their own home, Tom's tasteless monstrosity was a benchmark as they made decision after decision. "A little too Hoatson," Mary would murmur when a tradesman offered something rather too showy or pointlessly luxurious. James would always agree. An elegant sufficiency has always been their mutual aim.

The result of their collaboration is a comfortably large home furnished with tasteful restraint.

Thus, when James MacNaughton descends to the ground floor, thirty-eight minutes after rising, he enters a dining room conspicuously lacking in baby elephant skin. Its walls are covered in pale gray silk, its floors hushed with a rose du Barry carpet. Morning sunlight through its eastern windows is softened by fine linen curtains ornamented only with borders of embroidered vines. His oatmeal is served in plain white bone china, and he eats in silence with a simple silver spoon, polished to a soft shine.

He eats in blessed silence but allows his spoon to clink against the china when he is done: a signal to the maid, who appears promptly to remove his bowl with her left hand and to pour his coffee from the pot in her right. With the table cleared, he places his spectacles on the bridge of his nose, pulls the papers close, and scans the news of the day.

There has been a decisive battle in the Philippines. Black Jack Pershing has slaughtered two thousand Moros, along with their women and children. That should put an end to Moslem resistance to American rule, he thinks, and it's about time.

Kaiser Wilhelm II is celebrating the twenty-fifth anniversary of his ascension to the German throne. "These have been twenty-five years of peace," the Kaiser is quoted as saying, "and I hope there will be twenty-five more." MacNaughton grunts at that with soft cynicism. The Germans have just launched a powerful new battle cruiser. All of Europe is preparing for the next war, and so are industrialists around the world. MacNaughton himself is so sure of this, he has increased C&H production quotas. Every bullet fired and every artillery shell exploded must be encased in brass. Each ship sunk will take copper cladding and brass fittings down with her. He wants Calumet & Hecla ready to take orders as replacement armaments are manufactured.

The *Tribune* has an editorial about South Africa's new Natives Land Act. The Parliament has now defined which territories can be owned by whites and which inhabited by blacks. There's wisdom, MacNaughton thinks. Settle it with laws. Everyone will know his place. He approves of South Africa's new Immigration Act as well. More sensible to prevent trouble than to cope with hordes of Indian migrants after they arrive. Would that America's own Congress were so far-sighted!

James MacNaughton has become increasingly alarmed by the degradation of the workforce in the past thirty years. In the old days, C&H employed experienced men from Cornwall and Ulster, the inheritors of generations of mining skills. Those were fine men who took pride in the risks and hard work of their profession. Under the watchful eye of the company that employed them, they quietly and harmoniously developed into self-respecting American citizens. The new people are simply not of the same caliber.

For that distressing reality, James MacNaughton blames a long period of peace, which has permitted Europe's poor to breed beyond that continent's capacity to employ and feed them.

Swedes, Danes, Norwegians. Poles, Russians, Czechs—they're all showing up in Calumet now. Swarms of Jews and Italians are arriving at America's ports, taking over the cities. How much of the Old World's excess population can America absorb?

Admittedly, those enterprising enough to make the long trek to the Upper Peninsula of Michigan are probably the best of the lot. They work hard but they are unskilled. At best, they can put a sledgehammer to the loosened conglomerate, shovel it into tram cars, and push the loads to the collection points. And yet, they feel themselves hard done by, complaining about the conditions underground when they're lucky to have any job at all.

The Finns are the worst. And the Slavs! Croats and Slovenians. Anarchists, half of them. Socialists. Europe is gleefully exporting its wretched refuse to America. How long, he wonders, before the entire American workforce is undermined and replaced by nihilists and hoodlums? There is bloodshed every time union agitators infiltrate an industry, and what does Congress do about it? Nothing! Congress is too busy destroying American corporations. Call something a monopoly, and you can break it to pieces and tell yourself it's legal. Damned Marxists . . .

That egomaniac Roosevelt and his stooge Taft are gone now, and may trust-busting and corporate taxes go to hell with them! Wilson may not be much better. During the 1912 campaign, he was pleased to declare himself a fierce partisan of the Open Shop policy and of individual liberty, but his anti-union rhetoric began to shift as soon as he took office. Now the new president speaks of a heartless economic system in which a few men control the fate of all the rest. He talks of overthrowing the bosses and putting Wall Street in its place. There has been one strike after another since the inauguration, and Wilson has done precisely *nothing* to stem the tide of industrial strife. Every labor dispute is dealt with as though it were an isolated phenomenon. Nothing is learned from experience. There is no canon of industrial law, nothing to enshrine a property owner's sacred right to protect his factory from violent strikers.

James, his wife would soothe if she were home. *Don't upset yourself, dear. Our miners know that they're well treated. They know how lucky they are to be employed by a man like you.*

With a deep breath, he sets the newspapers aside. Stands and tugs his waistcoat down. By an act of will, he is serene again. The Western Federation of Miners will gain no foothold in the Copper Country of Michigan, he tells himself. Miners here will be loyal to Calumet & Hecla, and to James MacNaughton himself.

The butler meets him at the door with his hat and an umbrella. A year ago, the man would have said, "The weather service predicts rain, sir," but James MacNaughton put a stop to that. Unnecessary chatter annoys him almost to fury, especially in the morning. "Obviously," he observed then, "or you would not be handing me an umbrella." Now he simply accepts his hat and hooks the umbrella handle over his arm. His first words of the day are an acknowledgment of service properly rendered.

"Thank you," he says.

He will not hear the collective sigh of relief that ends the tension inside his home when the front door closes behind him. Arms full of linens, the latest chambermaid watches Mr. MacNaughton stride down the long straight sidewalk toward his office, a few blocks away.

"I bet he don't even know your name," she tells the butler.

With an attitude like that, the butler thinks, you won't last long in this household. "It is our place to know his," he tells the girl.

Like James MacNaughton, Anna Klobuchar Clements awakens before dawn; unlike him, she has no memory of birdsong. The forests were gone long before she was born. She expects only silence in the summer morning.

Her spouse, too, is missing from her bed. Mary MacNaughton won't return to Calumet until the end of the summer, but Joe Clements will be home after the night shift, and Annie has much to do before he walks in the door.

In half-darkness, she peers briefly into a small mirror, loosening the heavy braid that falls down her back, gathering the brown hair into a pile on top of her head, pinning it out of her way before washing her face in a white enamel basin. She dresses quickly: a secondhand cotton housedress, its cuffs and hemline lengthened with calico bands to accommodate her frame. Trying not to make any noise that will disturb the last minutes of rest for her three young boarders, she creeps down the creaky wooden stairs, ducks under the doorway, and slips out back to use the privy.

With the sun on the horizon, she picks dandelion greens, giving the tough outer leaves to the rabbits, collecting the tenderest in her apron pocket for Joe's salad. She scatters feed for the chickens and robs their nests while they scratch in the dirt. With the eggs cushioned by the greens in her pocket, she collects an armful of small wood for the stove and goes back inside to bring up the fire.

She's been making pasties for miners since she was six. Her hands need no attention. Flour, salt, lard, water, mixed and kneaded. Fist-sized chunks rolled out into disks. Finely minced smoked ham from last year's hog. Diced potatoes, onion, carrots, and turnips. Stir it all together. Spoon some onto each circle of dough. Fold the crusts into half-moons, crimp the edges, slit the tops to let the steam out. With the baking sheets greased, it's pasties into the oven, and while they bake, she starts the boarders' breakfast. Fried potatoes and onions, eggs, buttered bread. Tea.

She does as many chores as she can before anyone else is stirring. Five adults share this small house. Even the little Irish housewives complain, "Not enough room t'swing a cat when everyone's t'home." And it's worse for Big Annie, who takes up more space than any woman has a right to.

She admitted to six foot one when she finally married at eighteen. Joseph Clements was twelve years her senior and four inches taller, and the only man in Calumet who wasn't intimidated by a girl that huge. "He's big enough to beat her when she needs it" was the joke at their wedding party. Joe's a Slovene, too. His family name used to be Clemenc, but like all the immigrants in Calumet, he spells the name the way Americans say it. Most childless couples would have bachelor boarders of their own kind, but Annie has had three Italian immigrants in the house since March. "They're small," she tells neighbors cheerily, as though she planned it this way. "They don't need much room. We could never fit more Slovenes in here." My boys, Annie calls the Giannellis, though at twenty-five she's not much older than they are. *Bella mama*, they call her. With toothy grins and eloquent gestures, they have told her that her round, smiling face and splendid bosom remind them of the mother they left behind. This pleases her. She is made for mothering; it is a sadness to her that seven years with Joe have yet to produce so much as a hint of pregnancy.

At six-fifteen, the warning whistle rousts the Giannellis. When they first moved in, they were cheerful in the mornings and she loved the sound of their good-humored chatter, though she understood only a few words of their language. She would stand in the kitchen, smiling as sleepy murmurs turned into jokes, quick little arguments, snatches of song. A few months underground changed all that. The oldest boy is almost eighteen. He already has the miner's slump, hardening to work that overdevelops the back of the body and leaves the chest muscles cramped and shortened. The middle boy may do the same, but Annie worries about the youngest. The work takes a toll on young bones.

Exhausted even after a night's sleep, the boys are silent as they roll up old blankets and stash their pallets behind a third-hand sofa to keep the mess out of Joe's sight. They know that Joe Clements doesn't want them here; the problem is, they have no other place to go. Last winter, their uncle sent word of jobs in the Copper Country and money for their passage from Naples. They were still in New York, waiting for a train to Chicago, when Raffaello Giannelli was killed in a rockfall on the twenty-third level of the Number 4, Baltic. When they got to Calumet, a storekeeper recognized their uncle's name on the piece of paper they were showing around, but he couldn't make them understand English. As usual, the solution was "Somebody fetch Big Annie." Apprised of the difficulty, Annie took the three tired and confused boys to her friend Carla Caretto. The newcomers recognized a *paisana*, though not even Carla understood what they were saying. "Not how we talk in Sicily," she said, and she was reduced to miming the bad news, putting two hands at the side of her face, closing her eyes as if in sleep, and saying, *"È morto, povero!"*

The youngest started to cry, while the middle boy slumped in despair and the oldest spoke in tones of aggrievement and fear. Carla made out enough of what he said to guess at the rest. "He say, they don' got nothin'. Who gonna take 'em? What they gonna do?"

Brows high, Annie looked hard at Carla, hoping for an answer, but Carla shook her head and said, "Don' look at me," because Carla and her two daughters have lived with her brother-in-law and her sister, Lucia, and their five kids since Carla's husband was killed last year. So Annie brought the brothers home. "It's temporary," she assured Joe quickly, after explaining about their uncle being dead. "They're just going to stay here until they can move into a company dormitory."

It took only one look from Joe to make the boys pull off their cloth caps and bob their heads and gabble away respectfully. His hard eyes conveyed a threat that any Italian peasant could understand. Lay a finger on my wife and I'll kill you, the giant's eyes told them. You so much as *look* at her wrong, you're dead.

Three months later, the brothers are still rooming with the Clementses. Joe is used to the arrangement now and doesn't mind the extra money they bring in, even though he works nights and they're on the day shift. The boys' foreman is Joe's pal, and he makes sure the Giannelli brothers are too tired to interfere with Joe's wife when she's alone with them.

While the boys dress, Annie gets their breakfast on the table. While they eat, she takes the pasties out of the oven. Like generations of immigrants to the Copper Country, the Giannelli brothers have come to appreciate these Cornish turnovers, for pasties are a filling meal that can be eaten out of hand and will stay warm for hours underground if wrapped properly. She opens three tin lunch pails and tucks in two pasties each, adding jars of hot tea, slabs of cheese, small wrinkled apples, and *kolaches* with stewed rhubarb filling. It takes a lot of food to fuel a trammer, even ones as poorly grown as Italians. Sixteen times each day, six days a week, they shovel a ton of broken rock into a car and then push it along iron rails to the elevators. In union mines out west, mules haul the ore trams. In Michigan, immigrants are cheaper than livestock.

The Giannelli boys' sleepy silence gets heavier as they finish their breakfast. Going underground still scares them. The business streets of Calumet are lit with electric lights, but down below, it's just a few lanterns along the maze of tunnels and drifts. Skilled miners can get two and a half dollars a day, so they can afford to buy their own carbide headlamps, but trammers are paid so little, they settle for the company's allotment of three candles per man per day. If a man's candles burn out before he finishes his shift, he has to either feel his way out and lose a day's pay or try to work blind in inky darkness that no one on the surface can imagine. Just last month, a trammer fell down an open shaft. He wasn't even missed until the body started to stink. Nobody remembered his name.

"Buona fortuna," Annie says as she hands each boy a lunch pail. "Good luck. Come back safe."

It's full daylight by then. She watches them head down the street. Tonight, when their shift is over, Annie will have macaroni with canned tomato gravy for them. She learned how to cook that dish from Carla Caretto. Annie likes it herself though Joe won't touch it. "I work all night. I don't come home to dago swill, got it?" This morning, she'll take the edge off his hunger with a big bowl of vegetable soup she started last night. Then there's greens for his salad, and when he's done with that, there'll be a plateful of cabbage rolls and smoked pork sausages and fresh biscuits. Busy at the stove, she doesn't notice the time, but when the biscuits smell done, she pulls them out of the oven and glances at the kitchen clock.

Half past seven. He should be home by now.

She wraps the biscuits in flour sacking to keep them warm. Moves the frying pan to the edge of the stove top so the sausages won't burn, leaving the soup to simmer. The clock ticks and ticks, and with each passing minute, the muscles between her shoulder blades tighten. When Joe is late, the best she can hope for is that he's gone to the tavern before coming home. The worst . . .

A visit from the company man.

Your husband is dead. Clear out, union bitch.

Living in a company house was the cause of their first marital argument. Annie's father took her side: "Live here with us. We'll make room." Annie herself liked the idea of living with her parents for, to be honest, Joe has always scared her a little. He is so big, he makes *her* feel small, a thrilling novelty when he first took notice of her at a friend's wedding reception. With unsmiling command, like a prince in a fairy tale, he held out his hand, palm up, and beckoned her to join him for the *štajeriš*. Two months later, they took the center of the dance floor for their own wedding, and her eighteen-year-old self was swept away by the romance of it all.

Of course, it wasn't long before she understood that Joe had a way of going off like a mine charge when he was thwarted or annoyed. She wanted to be a good woman—a good wife—so she ended their first argument the way she would many others: by agreeing with Joe. He wanted his own place, so they put in for a front-gable house, which was only what a good worker deserved, and the company assigned one to the Clementses after a few months. Joe applied for indoor plumbing as well. Seven years on, the Clementses are still using an outhouse. Like most men, Joe doesn't understand why it's taken so long to get the pipes installed. It's the wives who get a leering visit from the housing man. It's the wives who know the price of plumbing, and Annie refuses to pay it.

Eight o'clock.

The ticking is inside her own mind now, and she flies around the house, dusting, tucking, shaking, smoothing. Her domain is no more than an attic bedroom upstairs, with a kitchen and front room down, but there is pride in ruling it. In this she is her mother's daughter: the latest in a line of good housewives receding into unrecorded time. With so many tasks, so many people's needs, so many demands pulling a woman in so many directions, her home is the one place where she can battle the forces of chaos with some hope of temporary triumph.

Eight-thirty.

Keeping an eye on Joe's supper, she decides to pull everything out of a kitchen cupboard, wipe everything down, inspect the shelves for mouse droppings, put it all back neatly, cans lined up, jars sparkling. She puts on a kettle of water for the washing up then, and sits at the table for a few minutes, nibbling a pair of hardboiled eggs, sipping at a cup of tea. How, she wonders, did I get to be so big, eating so little? She's had her fill of food twice in her life. First communion and her own wedding. Somebody always needs it more than she does. Her father, knobby with injuries and arthritis, who kept working underground six days a week until he was almost too crippled to swing a hammer. Or her mother, who always pretended she wasn't hungry, though Annie knew different. Her little sister. Her brothers, until they, too, died like their father: underground. Her husband. Her boarders.

A life lived for others is a life well lived. That's something that both Marx and Father Horvat preach. She likes even better what Moishe Glass always says: "Make one life a little easier, whole world gets better in time." That's what Annie Clements believes. Work for the common good, and a good life will become more common.

Quarter to nine.

She takes her plate and cup to the sink. Washes the boys' dishes and her own. The Giannelli brothers give her half their salary and send the rest back to the old country. Fifty cents a day barely covers their meals, let alone the labor that goes into doing their cooking and cleaning and laundry, but Annie can't bring herself to charge more. She'd be taking bread from the mouths of the family they left behind, and that's what the capitalists want: each class exploiting the next one down. Hunger is an incentive to climb, the money men say. Make life on the bottom nicer and nobody will want to do better.

Trammers like the Giannelli boys are at the bottom of the bottom. On some levels, they work knee-deep in water, and their poor feet never dry out. Their hands bleed sometimes from the shoveling, too, but they make too little to chip into the medical fund. So Annie doctors them the best she can, knowing that blisters can go bad and kill a person. She worries about that. She would like to buy the boys some decent gloves and rubber boots at least, though Joe would beat the hell out of her. She'd take the beating if she could come up with the money, but the truth is, they can't afford even that small act of charity.

Nine o'clock.

She decides to use up the last of 1912's stored apples to make a crisp: a magic charm to bring a husband home—drunk maybe, but alive and whole. She stands again, goes down to the cellar, brushes straw off the winy, withered fruit, and returns to the kitchen. She is sprinkling oatmeal, brown sugar, and butter over the sliced apples when she hears footsteps on the wooden stairway out front and goes still. Not breathing. Just listening.

There is no knock on the door before it opens.

Not widowhood, then. Not destitution. Almost faint, she turns toward her husband. When she sees the look on his face, she knows why he is late. Why he is drunk. And everything shifts within her.

Where there was dread, there is now something beyond anger or sadness. There is a rage she feels all at once, like an overstressed machine suddenly going to pieces. Piston rods snapping. Drive belts flying. Bolts and gears fracturing. Iron housing tearing itself apart.

"Who?" she asks, rocked by the recoil as her patience cracks, her tolerance ends. Not who. Whose. Whose husband? Whose father? Whose brother? Whose son? Whose funeral?

"Solomon Kivisto," Joe says. "A hanging wall came down."

"A rockfall, sir," Mr. MacNaughton's assistant is telling him down at the general offices of C&H. "Number Six, Hecla. Level sixty-one. Kivisto's head was struck. He's still alive, but the injury will be fatal."

There are thousands of miners in the Keweenaw Peninsula, each of whom bears a one in two hundred chance of being killed in any given year. Face impassive, brows slightly raised, James MacNaughton waits to be enlightened as to why this man's impending death is of sufficient importance as to be brought to his attention.

"Kivisto was one of the miners who volunteered to run a one-man drill, sir."

"Was he operating a Leyner when the accident occurred?"

"No, sir." The assistant consults the accident report. "He was helping—" There is a pause. These foreign names are so difficult to pronounce. "He was helping an Eevert Jar-ven-pa put up a support post. Jarvenpa says the roof of the stope came down during that procedure. He was also struck in the rockfall, but not badly injured."

"Both Finns," Mr. MacNaughton notes, but if Kivisto had volunteered to run a one-man drill, then he certainly wasn't a member of the Western Federation of Miners. "Is Jarvenpa a union man?"

"Not to my knowledge, sir."

Mr. MacNaughton sits unmoving, eyes narrow. He remains deep in thought for such a long time, the assistant begins to wonder if he should leave. "Was—" Mr. MacNaughton clears his throat. "Is Kivisto married?"

After consulting the employee file, the assistant says, "Yes, sir. Wife, Matilda. Three sons and a daughter."

"Age of the eldest boy?"

A pause while paperwork is shuffled. "Fifteen, sir."

"Company house?"

"Yes, sir. It's at 217 Fourth Street, sir."

"Get the deed," MacNaughton says. "Then call the real estate lawyers."

2

Younger than she are happy mothers made.
—Shakespeare, *Romeo and Juliet*

Everyone knows what it means when the school principal gathers a family's children. He always goes to the eldest first. He always says, "You must be strong. Set a good example for the little ones."

There are large windows on the outside walls of the school building, and windows line the corridors as well. The building is designed to bring as much pale winter light as possible into the classrooms. Today the early summer sunshine is brilliant and the roof vents are open to let heat escape from the interior. Sitting at long tables in the sewing room, the older girls like Eva Savicki quit pedaling their Singers, the better to watch the drama. Their teacher slams a wooden ruler down on her desk and calls for attention, but it's no use. When there's an accident, everything stops.

In the machine shop across the hallway, separated from the girls by two panes of glass and twenty feet of corridor, the boys go motionless as well. They hardly breathe as the principal approaches, and slump a little when he passes.

When he arrives at Jack Kivisto's lathe station, Eva's fingers go to her mouth and she watches Jack bow his head. His hair swings forward, straight as straw, so blond it looks white in the sunlight. His face is hard. She knows he will not cry, but her heart breaks for him.

She has been in love before. First, it was Father Horvat. Then it was John Barrymore, who visited Calumet once. Eva only saw the actor walk from the hotel to the theater, but he was so handsome, she almost fainted.

Of course, those were just stupid crushes. This is the real thing.

Jack Kivisto is in her brother Kazimir's class. Jack has never spoken to Eva, although once he punched another boy who was rude to Eva and her friends. Eva is a year younger than Kaz—still, she'll turn fourteen in a week, and lots of Calumet girls get married at that age. Annie Clements's sister was fourteen at her wedding. Maritza already has three children and her own household with dishes and chairs and curtains and everything!

The principal stops talking. Jack jerks his head high, flinging his beautiful hair out of his eyes. He looks at the boys in his class, glaring at those who stare. They turn away, ashamed to have shown pity.

Eva's brother says something to Jack, and Jack lunges at him. The principal shouts and grabs both boys by their necks, shaking them. He speaks to Jack then, putting an arm over his shoulder. Jack shrugs it off and moves toward the classroom door. He has to collect the other Kivisto kids and go home.

As he leaves the classroom, he notices Eva across the corridor and meets her eyes for the first time ever. Her heart thumps, but he is still angry about whatever her stupid brother said, so she adjusts her face to match his own resolve, ready to endure tragedy with silence. We are both strong, she tells him in her thoughts. I will be a good wife for you.

At lunchtime, she finds her brother and socks Kaz in the arm as hard as she can, pushing one knuckle out so she'll leave a mark.

"Ow! What was that for?"

"What did you say to Jack Kivisto?"

"Nothing!"

She stares.

Rubbing his arm, he says, "Just that he'll be next down the hole."

She waits, and Kazimir's eyes go cold when he says, "Maybe *now* there'll be a Kivisto in the union."

While the principal is telling the children that their father has been hurt, women are watching a figure make his way along Third Street: the angel of death in a bowler hat and a nice brown suit. In window after window, hands hold curtains aside as he approaches. Faces pinched with fear peer at him from behind the glass. Eyes close in relief when he moves on. Irish girls cross themselves and shudder. Poles murmur an Ave Maria. Finns step out onto their stoops and look down the street to see who is getting the news. When the company man arrives at the Kivisto house and walks up to the front door, more than one union man's wife gives a little snort.

"Serves you right," they mutter, before going back to their housework.

Matilda Kivisto is not surprised by the knock on her door. Sol isn't a drinker. He never goes out with the other men after work and comes straight home every morning. So she has known for almost two hours that a man in a suit would visit her. Oh, she let herself hope for a little while—accidents are not always fatal. Sometimes it's a broken bone or a massive bruise that discolors half of a man's back. That means lost salary or even the end of a job in the mine, but not a funeral.

When the clock chimed eight with no sign of her husband, she stirred the stew, put a lid on it, and moved it off the heat. Calm, silent, she set herself to the task of making her tidy house even cleaner than usual, for the company man will be the first of many visitors today. Her brother, Artur, will be next. His wife, their kids. People from church, too, though half of them will come out of austere Christian duty. The Kivistos have been all but shunned since Sol broke the boycott of the one-man drill. Sol got a little raise for the extra risk. His partner lost his job.

Sol didn't care what most people thought; still, Artur Luoma was his wife's brother, so Sol tried to reason with him. Copper was being produced by surface mines out west. C&H had to cut costs to stay competitive. Eliminate fifty percent of the workers or shut down the whole mine. That was the company's choice. "What you expect, eh? Drill's coming. Half us gonna lose jobs. I'm keeping mine. Gotta look after your own."

Artur Luoma still didn't like it, though it meant his sister and her kids were better off. Artur was a union man and the union said, "Don't work a one-man drill. Stand by your brothers." When Sol went his own way, Artur warned Matilda that there'd be a lot of bad feeling in town, and he wasn't wrong. There were catcalls and ugly remarks in stores and on the street. More than once, Jaaki has come home from school bloody.

When Matilda opens the door to the company man, he takes off his hat and asks if she is Mrs. Solomon Kivisto. She nods, and he asks if he can come in. She steps aside and waits for him to enter.

"I am very sorry to bring you this news," he says. "Your husband has been gravely injured. He is at the hospital now."

She says nothing. Her face doesn't change. *Sisu,* she is thinking.

"Mrs. Kivisto, do you speak English?" the company man asks.

She is looking down at her youngest. Pria is standing right behind her, fists gripping the fabric of her mother's skirt, peeking at the stranger.

The company man tries again: "Mrs. Kivisto, did you understand . . . ?"

"Yeah. Sure. Thanks. My boys, they know?"

These Finns! Cold as ice, the man thinks, but he says, "The principal has been informed, and he will tell them. I expect they'll be home from school soon."

She nods. He waits to see if she has anything else to say. When she looks at the door, he murmurs something polite and leaves.

Pria asks, "*Äiti?* Who him wit' a hat?"

"Company man," Matilda tells her. "Boys be home soon. They gonna stay wit' you while I go out."

"Where you goin', *Äiti?* Can I come?"

Pria is almost three. The boys were hardly talking at that age, but Pria jabbers every waking minute. On good days, Matilda lets the endless chatter slide. Today she snaps, "Pria! Shut up!"

"Why, *Äiti?*" Pria asks.

"Do what you're told!" Matilda cries. "Why you always gotta argue?"

Tears well in the little girl's eyes, but that's just too bad. Matilda can't stand the noise right now. She sits down to wait for the boys. Jaaki is old enough to work, she thinks. But Matti and Waino will just be open mouths for a long time. What I gonna do? she asks herself over and over. What I gonna do?

Pria tugs on her dress and almost gets a slap for it. Roused, Matilda hears the knocking, pulls the child into her arms, and goes to the door, muttering, "What now? He dead already?"

The last person she expects to see is Annie Clements.

Everyone in Calumet knows Big Annie by sight, but she and Matilda have never spoken. Annie is a Catholic, a Slovene, a socialist. She's not just union, she's the president of the Women's Auxiliary of the Western Federation of Miners, Local 15, and a wash of fury breaks over Matilda. Is this giant woman here to tell her that the Kivistos got what they deserved? That Sol has been punished for taking a job away from a union man?

"Mrs. Kivisto," Annie says quietly, "may I come in?"

Wary, Matilda nods. Steps aside. Shuts the door.

Annie has a wicker basket over one arm and takes it to the kitchen, unpacking it quickly. Bread. Butter. *Kolache* for the children. Sausages and preserves that whisper, *Something for the future.* No pasties. Pasties are for the mines. When there's an accident, widows don't like to think about the mine. Matilda Kivisto isn't a widow yet, but it won't be long.

Matilda stares at the bounty on her kitchen table. Annie must have emptied her own larder to bring all this.

"Go to him," Annie says, holding out her arms for little Pria. "I'll look after the kids."

3

Their death-mark'd love
—Shakespeare, *Romeo and Juliet*

When Matilda gets to the hospital, a nurse leads her to a man in a bed and tells her that it's Sol. A chunk of hanging rock came down on him, the nurse says. His skull is broken. It won't be long.

The man's head is wrapped in thick bandages. The face is cut up. Bruised and misshapen. Could be anyone, Matilda thinks, but when she leans over to examine his hands, she knows for herself who it is. Three crooked fingers on the right, broken years ago when a new man misjudged a hammer strike and came down on Sol, who was holding the steel. Two fingers missing on the left. She can't remember when that happened. One day, they were gone. Maybe she was having a baby and didn't notice at the time. Maybe Sol told her and she forgot. Maybe he never said. Men don't talk about accidents.

She sits down next to Sol's bed, takes out a bag of knitting, and settles herself to wait. The yarn and the blue bruises on her husband's face are the only color in the room, aside from her own faded calico dress. The wooden chair, the iron bedstead, the little table are all painted white. White cotton curtains separate the beds. The sheets are white as well, and so are the ghostly faces of the other men in the ward, for they live their lives more than a mile underground and see sunlight for no more than a few hours on Sunday afternoons in summer and less than that in winter. They are all hurt or sick, but they lie still. Though they have opinions about Sol Kivisto and the one-man drill, they leave his wife alone.

Strange, she thinks, how you can live with someone for years—make his meals, wash his clothes, share his bed, have his children—and still know so little about him.

Sol was a presence, right from the start. Silent, even for a Finn. Just . . . *next* to her, standing at the rail as the ship steamed away from Ostrobothnia. Away from everything they'd ever known.

She spoke first, quoting Scripture. "'So this is the great and wide sea wherein are things innumerable, both small and great beasts.'"

"Leviathan," he said. That was in the next verse. He, too, knew the Book.

"Matilda Luoma," she said, to introduce herself.

"Solomon Kivisto," he said.

There followed many days and nights on the great, wide sea without another word from Sol, but sometimes they ate at the same long table or glanced at each other in passing. And surely it was not mere chance that he appeared at her side again as land slid into view on a clear June afternoon in 1898.

Staten Island, green between a blue sea and a blue sky.

"Amerikka," she whispered. Beside her, Sol nodded.

Fear struck her then, though no good Finn would ever show it. On the ship, she'd had shelter and food. Now, like a newborn babe, she would be thrust into the unknown. No mother to care for her—just her brother, Artur, who'd sent money for her voyage. He had promised there'd be work for her, cooking and doing laundry for miners in Calumet, so she had put her trust in the Lord and her brother, and bought the ticket.

"Do you know . . . where is Michigan?" she asked Sol.

He was older. Thirty, maybe. She felt like a sapling, whipped by wind and fear. He seemed like a tree. Tall, strong, unbending.

"West," he said, lifting his chin toward the setting sun.

He meant to go to the Minnesota iron fields, but she told him about the Calumet copper mines.

My fault, she thinks. I should've let him go to Minnesota.

Now the nurse says Sol will never wake up. Never move again. Never speak. Dry-eyed, she tries to remember her husband's voice, so rarely used. Already, the memory of it is fading, but she can still listen to the sound of his breathing. She closes her eyes and pretends that she is in bed beside him.

This is a nightmare, she tells herself. Morning will come. We will wake up together, at home.

Footsteps approach. She opens her eyes and sees James MacNaughton standing at the foot of Solomon's bed. The general manager of Calumet & Hecla is not a large man, but he holds himself very erect. Impressive and impassive, he is perfectly dressed, and he has removed his bowler hat out of respect.

"Mrs. Kivisto, your husband was a man of vision," she hears him say in slow, clear English. "He understood that industry today requires new thinking and new methods. He was a man of courage who stood up to union pressure. The company is grateful. In this time of trouble, the company wants you to know that you should not worry about the future."

There is more, but she is too astonished to take it in, apart from this one fact: she and her children will always have a place to live. The company house will be their own someday. James MacNaughton himself has promised her that.

When he leaves, she sits still, dumbfounded.

Annie Clements and James MacNaughton, she thinks. Both on one day.

Without warning: tears, at last. She has been prepared for tragedy. Unexpected kindness is more than she can bear.

4

Thou detestable maw, thou womb of death
—Shakespeare, *Romeo and Juliet*

A strong man's body can keep breathing for a long time. When Solomon Kivisto dies at last, a shudder goes through Calumet, like the small earthquakes you can sometimes feel when dynamite detonates below. Standoffish in life, Sol had no friends; famous in death, his name is now on every tongue.

The miners of the Copper Country have been arguing about the union for years, but things have changed since Sol Kivisto's accident. It doesn't matter that Sol wasn't using the one-man drill when he got hurt. His death is making the others think. A one-man is lighter than the old drills, but it's still a hundred and fifty pounds. Using one is like wrestling a bear. Only the biggest men could work that weight alone, hour after hour, day after day.

With a two-man drill, you've got somebody to spell you when your arms are numbed and buzzing. If your own head-lamp goes out? Your partner's still got light, and you can finish the shift. If there's a cave-in, he can pull the rock off you and run for help, or get you to the surface for one last look at the sky.

The "widow-maker." That's what they're calling the one-man down in the dark privacy of the tunnels and drifts and stopes. And those who never considered joining the union are talking about it these days. That organizer from out west? Charlie Miller—that's his name. Gotta admit he's honest, Michigan miners are telling one another. He'll say straight out that some union bosses are as greedy and corrupt as the mine operators. He'll tell you true: Some of those bastards just want to be big shots. Some of them have run off with a union bank account. But Western Federation of Miners has elected Charlie Miller president of the union—twice! They sent him here to organize the Copper Country because they trust him with their dues and the strike fund. Because he's one of them. He's not some city boy in a suit. He understands what it's like underground. He knows with his back and his bones that mining is harder work for longer hours than you ever thought a mortal man could do. Hammering above your head into the roof of a stope. Shoveling ore on your knees. Opening a drift off a tunnel, bent over, for twelve hours a shift, day after day after day. He's heard screams echo in darkness as dense as the rock itself. He's seen hands blown off, feet crushed, thigh bones snapped like matchsticks under half a ton of rock . . .

"Stand together or die alone," Charlie says. "That's the working man's choice."

"I'm in." That's what Michigan miners are deciding—one at a time, and then in pairs, and then in threes, and fours, and fives. That's what they say when they show up at the union office—in pairs and threes and fours and fives—to talk to Charlie Miller. And in the tunnels and in the saloons and on the street corners, they're asking one another, "Which side are you on, eh? Are you with us or against us?"

The knell has rung at Bethlehem Church, summoning the congregation to aid the bereaved. The women are cooking and looking after the Kivisto kids while Matilda and her sister-in-law wash Solomon's body and dress it in his Sunday suit. The men are out back, building Sol's coffin. Planing the boards neatly. Collecting pine shavings to make a fragrant bed for the corpse. Tacking a white linen cloth to the inside of the box to conceal the curls of softwood.

There will be no funeral photograph. That much has been decided—it's a matter of expense—but there's another question. Closed or open? Open is tradition. Then again, the children shouldn't see the mashed blue-and-white face . . . Well, the oldest boy could. Not the little ones. Bad dreams.

"Let 'em see," Matilda's brother says. The believers don't drink, but Artur Luoma is *kommunisti,* and he's been at the vodka. "Let 'em see what the bosses done."

"Bosses got nothing to do with it," Eevert Jarvenpa mutters. Artur makes everything into a union fight. "Sol was helping me with a support. Roof caved, is all."

"And why'd the roof come down? Because they're taking out the stone pillars and cheating the wood. Because they're dragging the last bit of ore out of the stopes. That drift should have been closed a year ago!"

Sol's son Jaaki is staring down at the face in the box. Head down. Angry and bullish. Drunk, too, for the first time in his young life. "You're man enough to go below," his uncle Artur told him, handing him a glass. "So you're man enough to drink."

"I'll tell you why they want that drill," his uncle is saying now, jabbing a stubby half-gone finger toward Eevert Jarvenpa.

"They gotta cut costs, Art! Price of copper's going down and—"

"There's always some damn excuse, but you know the real reason? The real reason is, they want every man alone. They want every mother's son off in his own little piece of the dark where we can't talk to each other and we can't get organized!"

"Organized to pay dues for strike funds way the hell out in Colorado or Wyoming or someplace? Is that what you want? What's that got to do with us?"

"Plenty! And if you'd read a newspaper once in a while—"

"Newspapers!" Eevert snorts. "They just put ideas in fools' heads—"

"You calling me a fool, Eevert?"

As the argument gets louder, young Jaaki's silence is more noticeable. Nearly as big as his old man was, Jaak has said nothing all this time. Now he turns and goes into the house. When he comes back, Eevert and Artur are still at it, though they shut up when they see Jaaki and Matti.

Matt is ten, and he's crying: soundless, wrenching sobs that have left his face as colorful as his father's, only blotched with red instead of blue. Jaaki's got him by the shoulder, propelling him toward the coffin. With one arm, Jaak lifts the younger boy off his feet. With the other hand, he grabs Matt's neck and forces him to look at the face in the box.

"Open your eyes!" Jaaki says, low and fierce. "Open them!" When Matti does, Jaak tells him, "Me first. Then you. Then Waino."

Jaak lets the kid go and stalks off into the darkness.

"Good Finn," Eevert Jarvenpa observes, watching Jaak go. "Tough as nails."

"Matti!" his uncle Artur snaps. "Control yourself."

The little boy pulls in a shuddering breath. *"Sisu,"* he says. *"Sisu."*

Eva Savicki knows there will be no weeping at Solomon Kivisto's funeral. Finns make no display of distress in the face of hardship. *Sisu,* they call it. Guts, that means. Grit. Endurance. Not even little kids are supposed to cry.

This is a degree of self-mastery Eva Savicki admires but cannot yet claim for herself. Her family is from Poland so she'll have to learn *sisu* if she is to be Jack Kivisto's wife someday. She's working on it.

She thought she'd never stop crying when her father was buried. Then little Wanda died of diphtheria. The worst was when her mother died. Eva still has awful dreams about the blood and that stillborn baby, like a small blue doll. She and Kazimir moved in with their father's brother. Uncle Tomek was glad to get them, too, because his wife had taken their kids and left him and he'd never told the company. Because he didn't want to move into a dormitory again. Now, if anybody asks, Eva and Kaz will count as his children.

Back when Eva kept crying all the time, Uncle Tomek hit her and told her to shut up because he worked hard and didn't want to come home to all that noise. So she does her best to be a good housekeeper for him. Because she likes thinking about how she'll have her own household someday. Because she likes thinking about how she'll do these chores for Jack.

For Mr. Kivisto's funeral, she pulls her dark blue dress over her head, startled when the buttons refuse to close over her bosom. Annie Clements has explained about things happening down below, but until this moment Eva wasn't aware of just how much more she sticks out in front. I'm too old for pinafores anyways, she thinks. I should make a skirt and a couple of shirtwaists at school.

Right now, though? She has to wear *something*.

At the back of the wardrobe there's a black dress that used to be her mother's. It's the one thing every grown woman in the Copper Country has: a funeral dress. Her mother's scent still clings to the fabric, and wearing it brings back the familiar sense of stunned emptiness. She holds her breath and, this time, she does not cry. *Sisu*, she thinks.

The black dress will fit better after a few quick stitches to bring in the waist, so she takes it off and gets out the sewing basket. Of course, she doesn't really have a right to be wearing black to the Kivisto funeral. Because she's not a relative. Even so, to be perfectly honest, it's exciting to leave that schoolgirl frock on the bed, and she hopes Jack will notice. She hopes he'll understand the silent message she is sending him and the family she dreams of joining. *I have suffered loss, too. I know how you feel. I will stand by you. The union will stand by you.*

Eva will be going to the funeral with Annie Clements. Tomek Savicki may have taken his niece and nephew under his roof, but the Western Federation of Miners has enfolded Kaz into its brotherhood, and the Women's Auxiliary is Eva's family now. Big Annie makes a special point of looking after the orphans. Eva goes to every meeting, so she can help with all the projects.

Mindful of looking grown-up, she walks down Fourth Street to Annie's house as sedately as she can. Which isn't easy because her shoes are a bit too small and it's hard to walk nicely when your toes are squashed. She has a moment of dread—What if I get as big as Annie?—but Jack Kivisto is going to be tall, too. So they'll be like Mr. and Mrs. Clements, who are a handsome couple, even if Mr. Clements isn't very nice.

Mr. Clements won't be going to the funeral. He never does. There's a burial every week, and if you take a day off to attend one, your pay is docked. He doesn't go to church on Sunday, either. He's probably in bed now, Eva figures, so she sneaks around to the back door and knocks softly.

"I checked at the union office first thing this morning," she whispers when Annie appears. "Mr. Miller says that Sol Kivisto is the greatest union organizer Calumet has ever seen! Three hundred new men in the past two days! We've got almost half the miners signed up now and . . . What?"

Brown eyes serious, Annie is standing still, so tall she fills the door frame. "A man is dead, Eva. Wait until he's in the grave for talk like that."

Eva flushes, and her face gets hotter when Annie notices the black dress.

"It's Mama's. Mine doesn't fit anymore. Besides, Jack Kivisto is a schoolmate," Eva says, providing the explanation a little too quickly because she worked it out ahead of time, in case somebody asked. "I want to be kind to him. Like you were when my parents died. Maybe Jack will join the union like Kaz did. If people are kind to him. Right?"

"No union talk today, eh?" Annie says. "Tomorrow's soon enough. Let me get my coat."

To Annie Clements, Eva's little romance seems sweet but one-sided. Still, it's hard to guess what goes on in any boy's mind. With Finns like Jack Kivisto, it's even harder. How can you tell when a Finn isn't shy? the old joke asks. He stares at *your* feet, not his own. And then there's the one about the Finn who loved his wife so much, he almost told her.

They set off for the funeral together, Annie trying to shorten her stride so Eva can keep up. The second time the girl falls behind, Annie stops and looks back, taking in the ill-fitting dress and the awkward gait of a growing child whose toes are turning under.

Annie herself has had to send away to Sears Roebuck to get shoes large enough for her own feet since she was eleven. "The Auxiliary should start a shoes and clothing bank," she murmurs. "Give something, take something . . ."

"No union talk today," Eva says solemnly.

"Brat," Annie says, but she puts her arm around the girl for a quick embrace.

Bethlehem Church is already full when they get there. Some people belong to the church and piously attend any service. Some have come to support the widow and orphans. Some are there for the refreshments afterward. All of them have wordlessly divided themselves, like the families of the bride and groom at a wedding. Union on the left, behind Artur Luoma. Independents on the right, behind Sol's widow and her children.

"Go on," Annie whispers, lifting her chin toward the right. "We'll split the difference."

Alone now, settling into a pew at the back of the church, Annie tries to remember the first funeral she attended. Was she four? Five, maybe. Not much older than little Pria Kivisto. And so many since then . . .

Week after week, year after year. A thousand or more, it must be. Hard to tell them apart. But she does recall the first one she went to all by herself. She was nine. She'd heard her father talking about the dead man at supper. He was new. Inexperienced. Froze with fear and ignorance when the shout came to run. Crushed by a collapse. Annie skipped school the next morning and went to the Requiem. Trying not to be noticed, she sat in the back and wept for him. For his loneliness. For his friendless death.

"Why would you skip school?" her mother demanded when the teacher came to tell her that Annie had been truant.

Annie wasn't sure, but she answered anyway. "He deserved some tears. He didn't have anyone to cry for him. So I did."

"Ain't none of your business," her mother said, but Annie has made it her business ever since, mourning for the dead men who weren't well known: the newcomers, the greenhorn immigrants, the single men laid in company graves for lack of anyone caring to do more. Though there are always a lot of people at a union man's burial, she also attends when the miner wasn't union but left a family behind, for she knows what it is to be a wife whose husband won't join.

Her father wanted Joe to sign up before the wedding, but Joe is contrary. Suggest? He'll dig in and pull away like a mule. Push, and you'll pay. Joe likes to think of himself as management because he's a crew boss. Big and strong and skilled as he is, Joe Clements is as likely as any other miner to leave a widow behind him, and that's why a miner's wife is often willing to join the Auxiliary, even if her husband won't sign up with the union: for companionship, for purpose, and for mutual aid when the worst happens.

Bread and roses, Annie thinks. You need both. You need more than bare survival.

She has a year-old newspaper clipping—yellowed and curling—pinned to the wall next to her cupboard: a grainy, gray photograph of young women marching, banners held high, proclaiming, "WE WANT BREAD BUT ROSES, TOO!" Money men called that frivolous. Working people understood. Some in this world have more than they can ever need or use or spend or enjoy. Why shouldn't we get just a little extra, just a little more than bread alone? Massachusetts mill workers stood up to the owners and, by God, they won—because they stuck together. They formed a union, and they went on strike. It was a terrible hard winter, but after four months, the mill owners raised wages all across New England.

Why not here? Why not in the Copper Country?

Because men like her husband won't join the union. Not yet, anyway.

So Annie scrapes and scrimps, like all miners' wives. She gardens, canning the fruit and vegetables, brining pickles. She raises chickens and rabbits in the backyard. She keeps a pig in a fenced sty on the edge of town and slaughters the hog in the fall, putting up potted meat, smoking ham and sausage. When her father was killed, her mother went up to live in Copper Harbor with Maritza's family, leaving Annie to take over doing laundry and scrubbing floors for three ladies over in Laurium, where the big houses are. Even with all that—and with Joe's salary and with the Giannellis' rent—there's never enough for anything extra. The Clementses have no kids to feed, but Joe eats three times what another man might call a good meal. His boots and gloves and coveralls and clothing all cost more because she can't find anything secondhand that would fit a man so big. There's always a bill coming due—the rent, the coal, gas for the lights. There's always something broken—a tooth, an ax handle, a bone. There's always some sudden need. She's still paying off her youngest brother's casket.

"We are the two biggest, strongest people in this town," she cried when Joe complained about her household management. "I'm a workhorse. You're a crew boss. If we can't make enough money to get even a little ahead, what hope is there for anybody? It doesn't have to be this way! The union can make things change!"

"Those bastards just want the dues money" was Joe's opinion, and he wasn't alone. Even if they didn't think the union was a swindle, a lot of miners were too strapped for cash to come up with the dues, no matter how low the union set them. Many were afraid to risk retaliation by the company. Most, she suspected, were simply too tired to show up for meetings after work. But there were more funerals than meetings. The price of getting a little more rest was always a woman's grief. So a few years ago, Annie and a few friends began to talk about wives and daughters and sisters and mothers coming together to form a Women's Auxiliary, whether their men joined the union or not.

Of course, in Calumet "somebody should" often turned into "Annie will." So when the Women's Auxiliary of Local 15 of the Western Federation of Miners was officially inaugurated, the members made Annie their president. Her advantage, if you could call it that, is also her great sorrow: she doesn't have kids, and it's beginning to look like she never will. She has more time to organize things and run the meetings.

Now the Federation has sent a new organizer to Calumet. Charlie Miller has a lot of experience, and he thinks the union should wait two more years before considering a strike for safer working conditions. That's probably sensible, and yet . . .

Two years! she thinks. A hundred more miners killed. How many hands and feet crushed? How many broken arms and legs? How many more widows and orphans will there be if we wait two *years* to call a strike?

The minister enters the nave.

The congregation's murmuring quiets.

And in the silence, she comes to a decision. Somebody has to do something, she thinks, and that means it's up to me.

Like Annie, Eva sits at the back of the nave. She's Catholic, and this is her first time in a Protestant church. There are a lot of unfamiliar songs, but a very handsome young minister leads the hymns. He has a lovely voice and Eva closes her eyes, the better to imagine herself standing before him in a year's time, with Jack Kivisto at her side. She is thinking about wearing a crown of flowers in her hair when it occurs to her that Father Horvat will not approve of her being married by a Protestant. Her eyes open wide at the thought; then she tells herself that Jack doesn't seem as devout as his parents. Maybe she can get him to convert to Catholicism. And to the union.

After the service, the mourners walk the two miles to Lake View Cemetery. There are people along the route who stand on the sidewalks and watch. In town, too, you can see the way Calumet divides. Nobody yells, "Serves him right!" when the coffin wagon passes, but some faces say it plain as day. Others look away or cross themselves. There but for the grace of God . . .

Solemn and silent, Jack, Matt, and Waino stay close to their mother. As far as Eva knows, Mrs. Kivisto has not shed a tear. Stone faced, she holds her youngest child in her arms. "Why my *isä* in a box?" Pria keeps asking. "Why he *in* dere, *Äiti*?"

E-sah. Ay-tie. That must be Finnish for "papa" and "mama," Eva thinks. That's what my children will call Jack and me.

Even though there will be awful blisters on her feet, Eva goes the whole way. When they finally get to the Finnish section of the graveyard, she edges away from Annie Clements and moves up toward the Kivistos.

The hole has been prepared, the ground raw in the sunlight. There are some hymns. The coffin is lowered on ropes. That's when little Pria panics. "Don't!" she cries. "Don't put him *down* dere!" Eva wants to go to the child and comfort her, but Jack elbows Matti, who snaps, "Control yourself, Pria!" She's only little, Eva thinks. Don't be mean to her! But Pria quiets instantly, her whole body stiff with the effort. *Sisu.*

The grave is filled quickly, dirt shoveled onto the coffin by miners accustomed to clearing ore fast. Everyone drifts off to Centennial Hall for the meal. There will be a lot of fish: pickled, stuffed, and pan-fried. Black breads and pastries. Gallons of coffee, the beverage that fuels every Finn above the age of nine. Outside, behind the hall: a great deal of vodka.

During the dinner, Eva keeps an eye on Jack, hoping to get a word with him, wanting to tell him how sorry she is, but shy about it. She tries to stay near, then hesitates when she sees him leave. Maybe he needs the privy and it's not nice to notice, so she stands by a window to see where he goes and to marvel at the way the sunlight brightens his white-blond hair.

It seems at first that he means to join his uncle Artur and the union men, who are passing a bottle around, but he moves past them and keeps walking: down the street, into the wasteland beyond Calumet. Her feet are killing her now, and only a bad girl would go off with a boy by herself. Eva knows she shouldn't follow him. She does anyway. Grasshoppers whicker out of her way as she hobbles through the high, weedy grass in her too-small shoes.

Jack stops on a small rise. Both of them stand still, facing west, toward one of those blazing summer sunsets that last for hours before darkening to what she thinks must be the deepest, most beautiful blue in the whole world, though she has lived her whole life in the Copper Country and really wouldn't know.

She waits to say something, but Jack has heard her footsteps.

"Go away," he says without turning.

Eva knows what it's like to grieve for a father. "I—I just thought you shouldn't be alone."

He looks at her. "Are you stupid?" he asks, his voice rough. "I came out here because I *want* to be alone!"

"Well," she says with biblical inspiration, "it's not good for a man to be alone." I will be your helpmate, she thinks; instead she says, "I'm sorry about your father."

"I hated him when he was alive, and I hate him worse now."

She is startled, and he sees that. Belligerent, he wants to shock her, and he does. "I hate my mother, too. She made the deal, but I'm the one who's buried alive! Fifty years," he mutters. "I was going to be a machinist! I was going to get out of this shithole! Well, Matti's ten, and when it's his turn, I'm going to get on a train, and I'll never look back, and I don't care what anybody thinks. It doesn't have to be me. As long as one of us is underground, we can live in that stupid house.

After fifty years, it will be *our very own*," he says, making his voice high, like his mother's.

Eva stands there, frowning, not understanding anything except the part about him wanting to leave Calumet. Then it hits her: what "fifty years" means. She tries to think when the house will belong to Jack's mother. In 1963? Will Mrs. Kivisto even be alive then?

The solution comes to her, sudden and obvious. "Jack, you've got to join the union! You don't have to leave! We'll fight for better wages here and—"

"Go to hell! And stay away from me."

Stunned and confused, she almost cries, but controls herself.

"*Sisu,*" she whispers as the boy she loves stalks away from her. "*Sisu.*"

July 1913

1

Too rash, too unadvised, too sudden
—Shakespeare, *Romeo and Juliet*

It takes a lot to scare Charles Miller. The union organizer has been accused of everything from Marxism to murder. He has been hunted like an animal, shot at, beaten, jailed, and threatened with the rope, but he has never wavered until now. Annie Clements *scares* him.

It's not that she's so damned big. She is often merry and her smile is nice, but there is something in her eyes . . . a fierceness that worries him. She is dazzling the way the Rocky Mountains are dazzling. Glorious to look at from a distance, more dangerous than you expect once you get up close.

He doesn't know what to make of Mrs. Clements—although, in all honesty, Charlie Miller doesn't know much about women in general. He's spent nearly all of his forty-seven years in the company of men who have little experience with respectable ladies, and he counts himself among them. Motherless at two, he's been on his own since he turned fourteen and began a slow, hungry, westward drift from Iowa to the Rockies. Hoping to earn a meal, he'd muck out a stable or chop firewood for women in isolated farmhouses. Often he was driven away by hard-faced men who didn't want a good-looking boy hanging around their lonely wives and their bored, blossoming daughters. No point getting shot when all you wanted was something to eat, so he trained himself not to look at females at all until he learned that you could pay for that privilege ahead of time. By then he was sixteen and had found work on a Wyoming ranch, but no matter what Teddy Roosevelt thought, being a cowboy was awful. Freezing in the snow, baking in the heat. Filthy, lonesome, relentless labor. A couple of years of that was more than enough, and at eighteen, he decided to try his luck back in Chicago. He hoped to get a job in the stockyards and maybe find a decent girl and settle down, only things didn't work out the way he hoped. At nineteen, he did a year for robbery in the Illinois State Pen, where he learned to fear confinement at the mercy of guards with truncheons and the felons who used weaker inmates as they pleased. When his time was served, he went back west, vowing he would never again be beaten into dumb obedience. He found work at the Homestake Mine in South Dakota, and found a family for himself as well.

The Western Federation of Miners gave him brothers. Allies. Partners. Enemies, too. Mine operators hate him, and Charlie Miller is proud of that. You know you stand for something when the powerful hate you.

His first fight with a company man came when he was twenty-one. A foreman told him his pay would be docked because he had taken the time to dig out a corpse and carry that poor broken body up to daylight. He punched the foreman in the face, and kept on punching, and was cheered by the other men for his effort, though he had to leave town in a hurry then, to avoid another stretch in jail. In the years that followed, he moved from camp to camp all over the West. Telluride. Cripple Creek. Burke. Coeur d'Alene. Idaho Springs. Gold mines, silver mines, lead mines. He took jobs on the surface or below it, and everywhere he went, the mine operators played the same games. Docking wages when they pleased for whatever reason occurred to them. Firing anyone who squawked. Promising a price for ore, then lowering the bottoms of the cars so they were deeper and you had to load more for the same money. Short-weighting the trams. Calling in their paid-for sheriffs and deputized thugs to beat you bloody and run you out of town if you protested. When the price of metals went down, so did your pay, but there was never a raise when it went up. You bought your own shovels and hammers and steels and blasting powder and lamps and boots and gloves and overalls and food from the company store for whatever price the company cared to charge. You lived in company shacks and slept in lousy company bunks and paid rent for the privilege. One way or another, every penny you earned went straight into the stockholders' pocketbooks.

The law said you were free, but what did your wages buy? No more than the tools and bare subsistence that southern planters provided their slaves before the war. You went further into debt every month. Before long, you owed the operators more money than you would make in a decade, assuming you weren't killed or maimed first. And all the while, fancy-pants rich boys back in Boston and New York played polo and sailed yachts and courted girls who wore diamonds and silk. They believed their daddies' wealth was ordained by God and nature, and the Supreme Court told them they were right. A man who accepted a job was servant to a master, that's what the court said. If he took a wage, he could be treated any way that master pleased.

Well, if miners were wage slaves, then they were free to run out on their debt like escaping slaves deserved to do. Even so, running away ate at them, for they were honest, hardworking men who shouldn't have to leave dignity and decency behind just to survive. If you tried to speak against the owners' abuses and stick up for the workers, you were branded an agitator or an anarchist. Call a union meeting and company men would be there, taking names. The next day, every single union man would be run out of town by brawny boys who wore tin stars and made the world cozy for capitalists.

Was it any wonder that angry, fed-up, desperate miners began to organize underground, in the endless night where not even the crew bosses could see them? Was it any wonder that accidents began to happen down below? A foreman would fall down an open shaft, clumsy son of a bitch. A company spy would be found sprawled flat on his back, poor fella, his chest crushed by a rock so heavy it took three men to lift it. Dynamite, always common in the mines, began to bring down productive shafts. Ore cars were wrecked. Railroad bridges were blown up to keep trainloads of scabs from breaking a strike.

Recognize the union. Give us a fair deal. That was the message to the mine operators. We have brawny boys of our own these days, and we know where you bastards live.

"Without a union, you're one man alone," Charlie Miller would preach in the tunnels and the drifts and the stopes of the mines out west, though he did so at his peril. "You're as powerless as a field hand in chains." As powerless as a child in an orphanage. As powerless as a skinny boy in a prison cell. "With a union, you've got thousands of brothers! Together, we can demand something more than a slave's life!"

But Charles Miller is in Michigan now, and from the moment he stepped down onto the platform at the Calumet depot, he began to understand why all previous efforts to unionize the Copper Country had failed. Strolling along boulevards and streets in the Paris of the North, he saw for himself that this was going to take all the patience, planning, and guile he'd accumulated in twenty years of persuading men that they could stand together against an industry.

Before he calls these miners out, he wants union membership at eighty percent or better. That might take another two or three years, despite a gratifying leap in sign-up after the Kivisto funeral. They have to accumulate dues for a fund that will keep members eating while they're on strike. They'll need to stockpile tents, cots, blankets, coal, and canned goods for when the operators throw miners and their families out of company houses and dormitories. And it would be foolish to confront Calumet & Hecla directly. Even if the company benefits weren't relatively generous, C&H is too strong, too well managed, too rich. It would take a strike fund of unimaginable proportions to wait C&H out. So. Patience. Take on the less prosperous, less powerful mine operators first. It might require a year to bring even the weakest of them to the table, but once the eight-hour day is in place and the wages have been raised, C&H will have to match those conditions or lose workers to competitors.

It is a good strategy, but Charlie Miller has not reckoned on the women of the Copper Country. He has not reckoned on Annie Clements.

They are to meet this warm Sunday morning at the union office and walk together from there to the Italian Hall, where he has been invited to address a meeting of the Women's Auxiliary. The door to the office is open when he arrives. She is already there at a desk, head down, paging through stacks of papers. Making some kind of list.

He clears his throat. She glances up and smiles, then goes back to her task. "Mrs. Clements, what are you doing?" he asked her after a while.

She looks up again, but she's not seeing him.

"Everything keeps us apart," she says to herself. "Not just the languages. The churches. The cemeteries. The mines, the mills . . ." Her eyes focus, and she taps the stack of paper. "Accident reports," she says. "It's hard to get a true count. That's what they want. Just give me a few more minutes."

Soon, she gathers up a pile of papers with neat penciled columns of names and numbers. "No more waiting," she says. "Now. It's time."

Time for the meeting, he thinks.

Then he sees her eyes.

Small children in tow, members of the Women's Auxiliary stream toward the Italian Hall. Entering through tall double doors at street level, they huff a little and smile at the effort it takes to climb the steep staircase: twenty-four steps to a second-floor meeting room above the A&P grocery store and Vairo's tavern.

Charlie Miller is used to extremes of weather; even so, the summer heat of Calumet has surprised him. Despite the fact that they're far closer to the Arctic Circle than to the equator, it's warm up on the second floor, with sunlight streaming in from the big windows that line the hall. Waiting to make his entrance, he stands just out of sight, behind the curtain of a raised stage at one end of the large open room, getting a sense of the organization Annie Clements runs. There are good signs. The executive committee was on the site early. Wooden folding chairs are arranged in front of the stage. There are a few tables at the back for modest refreshments and simple decorations. Pies and coffee. Wildflowers in canning jars.

Sitting at an upright piano, an old lady is peering at sheet music, picking out a new union song by Joe Hill. In the far corner, an adolescent girl is gathering children, getting them to play with buckets of wave-smoothed agates: toys provided gratis by Lake Superior.

The girl's name is Eva Something, but he's completely forgotten the old lady's. He's been introduced to everyone in town—the names go in one ear, out the other unless he gets reminded of a name four times and embarrassment finally brands it on his brain. This is a personal failing he excuses in himself, given the collective nature of organizing, the shifting demands on his attention, the transitory population of mining camps and crews. He's good at lives. He might not remember a name but he can remember when a man joined, or who's been hurt, or how many brothers a worker has, even if the miners remain "the boys" or "the members." So it is with mixed chagrin and respect that he listens to Mrs. Clements greet several hundred women as they arrive at the top of the stairs. Each is acknowledged with a sunrise smile, a quick embrace, a question, a brief conversation. Babies are admired. Little children are joshed or tickled or asked about a new kitten or an old dog. She even knows the dogs' names! Of course, he thinks, she's lived in Calumet all her life, and the Copper Country mines are more stable than those out west. Naturally, she would know her neighbors and their children. Even so, it's impressive.

Every encounter ends with a moment of intimacy as she leans toward an ear, whispering what seems to be a request. Some shake their heads ruefully; others nod and line up at a table opposite the doorway, bending over it to write a few words on some new list she is compiling. When the bell in the clock tower rings twelve, folding chairs begin to fill. There are precisely the number required. A one hundred percent turn-out for a meeting, he realizes as the bubble and buzz of female voices quiets. The Auxiliary officers knew exactly who would come, who could be counted on.

Soon there is only the soft whoosh of cardboard fans waving at faces that glow in the heat, and a cold little wave of panic hits him. Charlie Miller has given hundreds of speeches and understands what it takes to hold a thousand men spellbound, but addressing a women's auxiliary is new to him, and he was at a loss until this very morning, when he woke up with a bold beginning for this talk. "Labor gives birth to wealth, just as women give birth to children," he plans to say. "Oh, yes, labor needs capital to get the enterprise started, just as you ladies need your husbands . . ." He will pause before he says, "But from that moment on, we all know who does the real work!" He is counting on laughter, and perhaps a little shock, though you never know until you begin how an audience will react . . .

Mrs. Clements gathers the papers from the table opposite the door and climbs three stairs up to the stage, coming to Charlie's side. She directs him toward the center, but he stands back a little and inclines his head. Though he means to give the impression that he's courteously ceding pride of place to Mrs. Clements, the skin around her eyes crinkles. Charlie Miller is lightly built and of medium height; he is not the first man to find it embarrassing to be towered over by Annie Clements.

With a quick wink, she turns to the women seated below them and begins, "On behalf of the Women's Auxiliary of the Western Federation of Miners, Local Fifteen, I would like to welcome Mr. Charles Miller— to this meeting and also to the Copper Country of Michigan." Her cadence is slow, he notes, and leaves time for native-born girls to translate for immigrant mothers. Charlie smiles and nods, acknowledging polite applause. "I am sorry to say that the mine operators of the Keweenaw Peninsula are not nearly as happy as we are to have him here," she continues, and he joins in the wry chuckles. "The operators think that we have no minds of our own. They think that we would all just sit down and be quiet"—she points an accusatory finger at Charlie himself and frowns with mock sternness—"if it weren't for the influence of *outside agitators* like Mr. Miller!"

This provokes gleeful whispering around the room, and Mrs. Clements lets a little of her own amusement show. "So the Women's Auxiliary has designed a placard with a new union slogan in your honor, Mr. Miller." She steps back and, with a flourish, pulls a tablecloth off a poster on an easel, revealing a large drawing of a one-man drill. It is emblazoned with the legend "THIS IS THE ONLY OUTSIDE AGITATOR IN CALUMET!" And with a high-pitched shout of approval, the ladies come to their feet, clapping and laughing. When they quiet, Annie goes on. "The money men say that the Copper Country will never organize. Why not? Because we all speak different languages. Because we don't talk to each other. Well, maybe that's true of our men, but we women talk. To each other, and to our husbands and sons and brothers! We speak different languages, but we always find a way to talk, don't we? And here is what we would like to say to you, Mr. Miller."

With that, she turns to Charlie Miller and hands him the sheet of paper many ladies have written on: thirty-three penciled phrases in thirty-three different hands, some educated, some barely legible.

Welcome to Michigan, Mr. Miller.

Willkommen in Michigan, Herr Miller.

Benvenuto in Michigan, Signor Miller.

Tervetuloa Michigan, Herra Miller.

Dobrodošli u Michiganu . . .

Eyes stinging, he looks out at the crowd. "Thank you," he says, his voice roughened. "Thank you very much. *Danke. Grazie! Hvala!*" he adds to cheers and applause.

"From now on," Mrs. Clements says firmly, "the Women's Auxiliary will have a committee of ladies to translate union flyers into every one of Calumet's thirty-three languages!"

Now, why didn't I think of that? Charlie Miller wonders. In any case it is his turn to speak, and he steps forward, reminding himself to match Mrs. Clements's cadence, pausing for whispered translations. Realizing at the last moment that there are children in the audience, he almost doesn't use the joke about "the real labor," but to his immense relief, the women do laugh at his first lines, and after that he relaxes into a speech he's given many times, adding thanks to the women for their devotion to the cause and flattering them: although men are the backbone of the union, women are its heart and soul. Thank you again for your warm welcome. That kind of thing.

The talk goes over well. Mrs. Clements listens intently and leads the applause, but everyone falls silent when they see the humor leave her face.

"I would like to ask a question," she says, stepping to the center of the stage. "What is the price of copper?" There is a long silence, so she repeats her question: "What is the price of copper?"

Her voice is light and easy, as though she is simply curious about the spot market, so Charlie Miller says, "Fifteen cents a pound. No! Wait . . . fifteen and a half this week."

She shakes her head and asks once more, "What is the *price* of copper?"

Silence yields to a soft murmur of confusion.

"The cost!" she says. "What does it *cost*?"

In the back of the hall, Eva Something stands ready to answer when Mrs. Clements nods to her. "My father. Witold Savicki," the girl calls out.

"Il mio sposo," a woman in the second row says. "Orlando Caretto."

"Walter Weitman!" a woman in the back declares. "My youngest son."

"My boy, too! Tony Stimac!"

"My brother! Joe Tresidder!"

The names are coming now, the voices more bitter as the roll call of the dead lengthens. Richard Runnell. Matt Reponich. Joe Paver. Isaac Moila. Felice Magnani. Andy Predovich. Mike Jabilov . . .

"My father," Annie says when silence falls at last. "George Klobuchar. And my brothers. Joe and Frank." She holds up the list she's been making since early this morning in the union office. "There are many men whose widows and orphans have moved away. They have no one left in Calumet to remember them, but I will speak their names. Gustav Capanan. Gianni Bussio. Samuel Phillips. Andy Remakka. Pete Peterson. Wilfred Lee. Thomas James. Jacob Leinonen." Like the tolling of a bell, the names go on and on and on, until at last she grips the paper, crumpling it, and holds it up. "*This* is the price of copper," she says in that clear, quiet voice. "A dead man. Every week. Month after month. Year after year. And if I made a list of the men who have been crippled underground, we'd be here until Christmas while I read their names!"

She waits and lets each woman remember their own.

"To the operators, the lives and limbs of miners are just . . ." She shrugs their indifference. "Just the cost of doing business. The names of the dead, the names of the crippled—those aren't even a line in their account books. But to *us*, each name is somebody. A husband. A father. A son. A brother."

There is weeping now, and anger.

"Without labor—without our husbands, our fathers, our sons, our brothers—the mines are only holes in the ground. Mr. Miller is right.

Capital starts things, but labor brings them into the world. Our men wouldn't have jobs without the capitalists but without labor, capital is stillborn, dead in the womb. Without labor, there is no return on investments. The money might as well be buried in the ground unless labor produces profit!"

They are with her. Following every word, their faces fierce.

"Wages are not a gift. Wages are *earned*, and our men deserve a fair share of the profits they make possible," she says. "What the union wants is simple. Eight hours for work. Eight hours for sleep. Eight hours for families to be together. A minimum of three dollars a day for *all* underground workers, even the trammers! Is that too much to ask of a few capitalists who are making *millions* from workers' labor?"

"No!" the women shout.

"And we say *no* to the one-man drill," she calls out, "not just because it will throw seven thousand men out of work, though it will! But also because the one-man drill leaves every man who uses it alone and at risk."

She waits again for quiet.

"When they're underground, our men can only see as far as their headlamps show. It's up to us women, here, up top, to see farther. It's up to us to say, No more! Not one more grave. Not one more husband! Not one more father! Not one more son! Not one more brother!"

They are chanting with her now. *Not one more! Not one more!*

"Rich men like James MacNaughton believe they've climbed to the peak of a pyramid," she says. "But that's not where they are. They're at the bottom of a spinning top. Shift the weight, girls, and over it goes!"

No! Not yet! Charlie is thinking, forgotten now, standing on that stage, gazing at the rapt faces of women who are listening only to Big Annie Clements. Cheering her. Loving her.

At the piano, Mrs. Kaisor strikes up the anthem of the Lawrence mill girls, and the room rings with hundreds of voices, singing their union sisters' song.

> *As we come marching, marching, we battle too for men,*
> *For they are women's children, and we mother them again . . .*

Charlie Miller can only listen. To call a strike now is as wrong as it can be; still, his heart rises with their voices, for who could not be moved?

> *As we come marching, marching, we bring the greater days.*
> *The rising of the women means the raising of the race.*
> *No more the drudge and idler—ten who toil while one reposes,*
> *But a sharing of life's glories: Bread and roses! Bread and roses!*

When the song is finished, Annie shouts, "Go home now! Shift the balance! Talk to your husbands, your fathers, your sons, your brothers. Tell them that the women of the union will not sacrifice one more man to the mines. Not one more!"

There are cheers and a babble of languages as the river of immigrant women and American children flows down the steep stairs of the Italian Hall. Annie Clements watches them go and turns at last to Charlie Miller, her eyes shining.

They'll strike, he is thinking, cold to his bones. My God, they'll do it.

The mine operators have a million pounds of refined copper sitting on the dock, waiting to be shipped. C&H alone has a million dollars in ready cash, waiting in its banks. The companies can sit this out for years. What has this union local got? Songs and a strike fund that might cover a few weeks off the job.

"Mrs. Clements—" he starts.

Then he sees the bright, fierce light of resolution in those level brown eyes. She knows, he thinks. She knows that she can rouse a crowd, make it rise, send it away ready to change the world. This is what every organizer feels, lives for, lives on, and the genie is out of the bottle now. He can only hope the men will follow his advice and not their wives'. Wait a year at least, or even two years. Wait until the strikes out west are settled. Wait until the Federation can rebuild the strike funds they've spent in Colorado.

"Mrs. Clements," he says again, "that was . . . inspiring."

He will argue with her later.

2

The childhood of our joy
—Shakespeare, *Romeo and Juliet*

Fourth of July, Michael Sweeney thinks. And New Year's Eve and a saint's day, all rolled together.

Leaning against a sandstone wall, he balances his big box camera against his shoulder and wraps a long, bony leg around the tripod to keep it from toppling. Hands free, he scribbles notes for the article he'll try to sell with the pictures.

15,000 on strike? Ask CM.

Slogans: No to the widow-maker! Yes to the union! A fair share for labor!

Songs, brass band. Giddy laughter. Children shrieking.

The smell: fresh popcorn and roasted peanuts sold in little paper cones.

Giggling girls hang on to one another, slyly watching boys who scramble up light poles they hang on like circus acrobats.

Strikers as far as the eye can see, filling the streets. Everyone thrilled by their own daring, amazed by their own numbers.

He himself is thrilled by the poetry of it. Men who work bent over in hard darkness are marching in bright sunshine, their full height unfurled. Half-grown sons, who'll soon go down into the mines, linking arms with fathers and uncles, with a soft breeze on their scrubbed faces. Women with children—mothers, sisters, wives, daughters—lining the parade route, laughing at the squealing toddlers who ride the shoulders of crippled grandfathers. All of them dreaming of a better life for the next generation.

I can tell this story, Michael Sweeney decides, and he asks God to bless Charlie Miller for inviting him, even if the man does persist in calling him Martin, despite three corrections. *It's going to fail in the long run*, Charlie wrote, *but maybe we can salvage some publicity from it. You can room with me.*

Charlie even got the union to pay the train fare from Denver to Chicago to Milwaukee, and then north. And north, and north. Michael half-expected to see polar bears by the time he got to Calumet, but there were no icebergs on Lake Superior, no glaciers carving rocky valleys. Just a small impressive city owned by the most powerful mining corporation in the world.

He stuffs the steno pad and stubby pencil into a pocket, grips the camera protectively, and wades into the exuberant crush, looking for the woman Charlie wrote about. Tall himself, he can easily see over the heads of little immigrant women and their children, and it's not long before he spots her. Big Annie Clements, and no mistake about it. "Six foot three if she's an inch," Charlie told him. Built like the statue of Lady Liberty in New York Harbor and five times prettier, is Michael Sweeney's judgment.

"Sweet Jesus," he whispers. Yes. Oh, *yes*. I can sell this story.

The air throbs with gusts of song in thousands of voices. *If the working class could only see / What power labor has* . . . Annie herself stands alone in front of the Italian Hall, solitary in the midst of many, her face still. Watching. Naming each man, each boy in her heart.

Behind her, Eva Savicki has eyes for only one. All vibrating electricity, she stands a few steps up the steep stairway. Hopping a little with excitement, and hoping to see Jack Kivisto among the strikers. Annie glances back at her. "Be careful, Eva! You'll fall and break your neck!"

The girl jumps down and comes to her side. "You're crying! Annie, why are you crying?"

"Union" is not just a word anymore, Annie Clements is thinking. It's something real. They can feel it now. They can hear it. They can see their power.

With a quick motion, she palms her damp cheeks. "Go on. Go march with the Auxiliary." Go find Jack, she means, but she doesn't want to embarrass the girl.

"What about you, Annie?"

Organize, you toilers! Organize your might!

"I'm going to stay here. I want to see every single one of them."

Nine thousand men voted for the strike, including all the trammers. Those who'd like to ignore the shutdown have discovered that shaft house entrances are blocked by widows armed with brooms and buckets of slops: angry, grieving women who fling filth and curses at anyone who tries to break the strike. Nobody works until the operators recognize the union. Nobody.

We will sing one song . . .

"Excuse me, ma'am. You would be Mrs. Clements, would you not?"

She turns, automatically looking down. Apart from Joe, everyone she's ever met is shorter than she is. This man is nearly as tall as Joe, though more a beanpole than a giant. She glances at his feet to see if he is standing on tiptoe to gain some inches, but he's on the level, just as she is.

And he's sizing her up the same way. Balancing a big camera on its bundled tripod, he reaches around it to offer his hand. "Michael Sweeney," he says. "I'm second-generation—like you, right?" He sweeps a hand down the length of him. "This, y'see, is what happens when you quit trying to grow Irishmen on nothing but rotten potatoes."

She laughs at that. He shakes his head in wonderment. "Perfect," he murmurs. "You have a lovely smile," he informs her. "Charlie Miller told me you were tall, but the poor blind man didn't think to mention that you are a beauty as well."

Startled, she looks away for a moment before narrowing her eyes at him. "That's what they call blarney, isn't it."

"Mrs. Clements, it is God's honest truth. And here's some more truth," he says before she can interrupt. "You've made a lot of men very angry, and not just the big bugs who run Calumet & Hecla."

She turns back to the parade. "I've heard it all before, Mr. Sweeney."

"Well, hear it again, this time from one who means you well. I've come straight from Denver. The Federation's got a big strike working in Wyoming right now, and they are not best pleased you've gone off on your own and done all this." He turns to watch the crowd marching past. "Mind you, it's a grand thing when a young lady like yourself cries, 'Lay down your tools,' and twenty mines go idle. But you know what comes next, don't you?"

"You're going to tell me."

"Troops, missy. They send in the troops. They send in the bully boys from Chicago and New York. And if that doesn't break you, the winter will, for there'll be no money from the Federation."

He goes on, repeating Charles Miller's warnings. Nine thousand miners voted for the strike, but five thousand were against it—her own husband among them. She is mortally tired of men trying to discourage her. Before she can tell Sweeney to go away, however, he produces an easy, confident smile.

"So, I am here to get America on your side, Mrs. Clements, and I'm going to do it with pictures. People know unfairness and injustice— when they *see* it. They *saw* the Lawrence mill workers and their hungry children last year, and that brought a twenty percent raise. They *saw* the burnt, broken bodies of young women on the sidewalk in front of the Triangle Shirtwaist Factory, and the laws for garment factories changed. There are plenty of others who've died for their rights, but if nobody's there to take the pictures and tell the story, those poor souls die in vain."

He comes closer, so that the both of them can look out at the parade. Gesturing toward the beautiful architecture of Calumet, he says, "Nice people don't want to see a bunch of filthy, starving West Virginia hillbillies at breakfast. They may feel bad, sure, but they just turn the page. So I'm going to show America a town they'd like to live in—not a muddy mining camp. I'm going to show them hardworking, respectable families, just like their own. People who want a decent life for themselves and their children." He lifts his chin toward the marchers. "They should be carrying flags, by the way, not just banners. A nice big flag looks good in the photos, and it says, 'We are Americans.'"

"Not some invading horde of barbarians?"

"Exactly." He turns back toward her. Tousled dirty-blond hair mashed beneath a straw boater that's seen better days. Blue eyes shining with go-getter spirit. A determination to match her own. "And that's the very nub of the problem! Labor leaders like to talk about the working class, but that just scares readers. You have to tell one person's story and let that one person stand for the rest. America needs someone to help them understand, Mrs. Clements. They need someone who'll help them believe that if they pay attention, if they *care*, things can change and this country will become a better place—"

"Who in hell are you?"

Startled, Annie steps back. Her fingers go to her mouth and she says, "Joe, no! He was just—"

Unintimidated, the photographer holds his ground and offers his hand as friendly, fluent words breeze out. "Say, now, you must be Mr. Clements! I've heard of you, sir, and it's a pleasure to meet you. Mike Sweeney's the name. I cover labor relations freelance—I sell photographs and articles to all the big newspapers and magazines. Perhaps you'll allow me to photograph you and your wife for a piece I'm preparing to send out on the A.P. wire?"

Annie can see it on Joe's face: he's not entirely sure what the A.P. wire is, but he doesn't want to ask, either. So he shrugs and nods.

Sweeney moves into a position that will put the Clements in the foreground with the strikers behind them. Eyes a little vague with drink, Joe watches the photographer flip the tripod legs apart, extend the camera bellows, adjust the focus. When he's ready to duck under the dark cloth, the photographer's brows rise in a mute, respectful question: May I?

Joe likes the swift, sure moves of a man who knows his own tools. He nods again and does not notice when Sweeney shifts the camera—just a tick—cropping the husband out of the picture.

3

A villain, that fights by the book of arithmetic
—Shakespeare, *Romeo and Juliet*

Everyone who is not in the union is worried about a riot. In stately neighborhoods, damask draperies have been drawn and heavy oaken doors are locked against looters. In the downtown business district, aproned shopkeepers frown anxiously behind plate glass, expecting a cobblestone to come through it at any moment. In grand sandstone buildings, lawyers and bankers and engineers pull out pocket watches, annoyed and impatient. Appointments have been canceled. Meetings have been postponed indefinitely. Clients fear being roughed up if they venture into town.

Perhaps alone among the better sort of Calumet's citizens, James MacNaughton remains unruffled, for the disquiet of lesser persons evokes an emotionless calm in him. In times like these, he hears his father's voice and Kipling's words. *If you can keep your head when all about you are losing theirs . . . If you can trust yourself when all men doubt you . . . If neither foes nor loving friends can hurt you . . . you'll be a Man, my son!* Just so: he stands by his office window on the second floor of the general offices of Calumet & Hecla, impassively watching the carnival of naked hatred and shameless greed on the streets below him while he speaks to his wife.

"The first day of the strike was rowdy," he admits, a candlestick telephone in one hand, the black cone of its ear-piece in the other. "Particularly in the North Range. That's passed. Here in Calumet, the parades have been . . . orderly."

"Are you sure you're safe?" Mary asks again.

It is exceedingly rare for Mary to bother him at work, but she has read newspaper reports of violence and is concerned about it all. "This will all blow over in a few days, my dear. There is not the slightest reason for concern."

"I can't believe they're striking—after all you've done for them!"

He does not confess his own dismay at that very thought. *If you can bear to hear the truth you've spoken twisted by knaves to make a trap for fools* . . . "I've already had a delegation of miners come to say they didn't want to walk out," he tells her. "They were pressured into the strike by their wives."

"It's that Clements woman, isn't it! I knew she'd be trouble. A woman like that! It's unnatural."

Mary herself is rather taller than the ideal. She is somewhat sensitive on the subject, and her embarrassment has long taken the form of a vocal dislike for the Clements girl, whose unfeminine traits serve as a lightning rod. "Don't upset yourself, Mary."

"I can't help it, James! It's outrageous. It's—it's so unfair!"

He himself has felt that same sense of injustice, though he would never say as much aloud. He has refused to read the ultimatum from the union, though he has heard from other mine operators about the letter's arrogant dictates and menacing threats of strikes and disruption of commerce. Even to open the envelope of such a ransom demand would acknowledge the union's existence. That he will never do. If they don't like the hours or the wages or the conditions, they are perfectly free to go elsewhere.

He is, of course, anxious to get the mine pumps restarted, but it won't be necessary to confront the strikers directly. A few days' patience, he tells himself. It will all be over soon.

Mary continues to fulminate, and he lets the ear-piece drift away from his head, murmuring noncommittally now and then. At last her tone changes, and he realizes she has moved on to the notion of buying a piano for the summer house " . . . because they're losing so much ground. I'd like to see them keep up their practice. Even a secondhand piano would be acceptable here."

"They'll pick it up again quickly when you're home."

"A piano would give both of them something to do. The lake is lovely, but Martha is bored. She keeps threatening to run away. Honestly, there are times when I'd pack her bags for her. You will not believe her language! I don't know who's influencing her, it's all 'golly and gosh' and 'say, don'tcha know?' So vulgar! You really must speak to her about that."

Mothers and daughters, he thinks, suppressing a sigh. "Won't dampness affect the piano's tuning?" he asks, deflecting what could become a tedious litany of complaints about their eldest.

"Yes, but we can have someone come out every few weeks to correct it."

Eventually, he promises to have a piano sent to the shore—as they both knew he would in time. Nothing is too good for their girls.

At last, the call ends. He cradles the ear-piece. On his desk, a more important matter awaits his decision. A letter arrived in the morning post, the envelope marked PERSONAL TO MR. MAC NAUGHTON. The handwriting is very good, the composition admirably straightforward, its contents a testament to the education C&H provides to its future workers. The proffer is a businesslike quid pro quo, though one that must remain confidential. Company agents are generally paid in cash, but the proposed arrangement is more interesting. The strike will be over soon, and yet . . .

James MacNaughton's professional and private life consists of planning ahead and controlling variables. He does the calculation. A mortgage paid out over a span of decades, or immediately useful intelligence? Provided gratis, no less.

A bargain.

He rises from behind his desk and goes to the large windows. A shift in the wind brings snatches of militant songs borne, undoubtedly, on nauseating gusts of garlic-and-cabbage-scented breath. But somewhere at the edge of the mob, a newborn spy is waiting for the sign. MacNaughton pulls one shade exactly two-thirds of the way down and leaves the other fully open: the deal is acceptable.

He takes a deep breath, clears his head with the exhalation, and returns to his desk, ready for the next task. Scanning the list of points he will make, he satisfies himself that his argument is complete and irrefutable.

Lifting the telephone handset, he taps the switch lever to signal the operator. "Get me Woodbridge Ferris," he says.

In newspaper editorials, Michigan's new governor is often called the Good Gray Schoolmaster. His endless harping on universal education may be tediously controversial, but there is one thing not even Republicans dispute: Woodbridge Ferris is a splendid-looking man. Blessed with a profile John Barrymore might envy. An elegant, upright bearing. A commanding gaze beneath perfectly barbered white hair that sweeps across a noble forehead. He is the sort of figure who could be rendered in bronze and standing on a plinth. Even his detractors admit that the man looks positively presidential.

He was born in a log cabin, too, which never hurts an American politician. Like Abe Lincoln, Woodbridge Ferris studied hard, determined to rise high from very modest circumstances. In youth, he taught and served as superintendent of many schools. In maturity, he personally founded a fine institution of higher learning. In an era of catastrophic bank failures, he was trusted to safeguard the hard-earned money of his fellow citizens with a watchful eye on business practices at the Big Rapids Savings Bank.

A Unitarian Universalist, the new governor of Michigan sincerely believes in the inherent worthiness and dignity of every person. He believes, as well, that human beings are responsible for the evil in the world; it follows that human beings are responsible for correcting the world's injustices and cruelties. He believes, therefore, in the use of the democratic process to bring about a world community with peace, liberty, and justice for all. For that reason and not for personal aggrandizement, he has run for office repeatedly, only to learn that high-mindedness is rarely useful in the public arena.

Thus, the political career of Woodbridge Ferris consisted of a string of honorable failures until just last year, when Teddy Roosevelt— supreme egotist that he is—invented a political party of his very own, thereby splitting the Republican vote and denying reelection to his own protégé, William Howard Taft. Suddenly offices that had been out of reach to Democrats since the Civil War came within their grasp. In March of 1913, Professor Wilson became President Wilson. Faintly astonished, Woodbridge Ferris rode into the Michigan governor's mansion on Wilson's coattails.

Idealism and intellect were, briefly, all the rage. The Good Gray Schoolmaster's inaugural address included a heartfelt promise to his constituents: "Michigan will provide education for all—for all children, for all men, and for all women! Not merely industrial training, but a genuine education that awakens students to beauty, that gives each and every person the strength and desire to live a life of service." How will you pay for it? asked the Republicans who rule the state legislature. Thus, Michigan's infant progressive era was suffocated in the cradle, just four months after the polls closed.

Now, another four months later, Governor Ferris is on the telephone with James MacNaughton, the Czar of the Copper Country, where industrial training is all workers need or deserve and talk of awakening students to lives of beauty and service is a foolish waste of effort and money.

MacNaughton's voice on the other end of the wire is calm. His words are measured. At first Ferris believes that a case is being made for a prompt settlement of the strike. All the mines are idled. As many as twenty thousand of the Keweenaw miners have been prevented from reaching their jobs. Operators risk irreversible damage to capital equipment deep underground if the pumps aren't maintained. There will be mob rule if the strike goes on for long. And then: "Of course, it's the outside agitators who are to blame for the violence—"

"Pardon me, Mr. MacNaughton. What violence? I have read reports of some ill-considered exchanges, and I know tempers flared on the first day of the strike, but—"

"Rocks and bottles and human filth were thrown, sir. There are strangers on the street whose appearance I do not like. I believe imported gunmen are leading the mobs—"

"Gunmen! Has Sheriff Cruse arrested anyone?"

"Not yet," MacNaughton admits, his voice light and reasonable, "though surely it is prudent to act before trouble can escalate beyond that level. Sheriff Cruse is, I fear, completely overwhelmed. He has asked the county supervisors for permission to deputize one hundred and fifty men, but what can they do against so many? And, to be perfectly frank," he says, as though sharing a confidence, "I do not think highly of Sheriff Cruse. He means well, but lacks enterprise and energy. I believe it is incumbent upon you to send the Michigan Guard to Calumet, Governor Ferris, before things get out of hand."

There is more. The rights of private property owners. The number of surface workers who were loyal to the company and willing to protect it. "I have," MacNaughton says, "personally asked many miners—man to man—if they were in favor of the strike. They looked me in the eye—in the eye, sir!—and told me that they were not union members and that they did not wish to be represented by the Western Federation of Miners. They wish only to do their jobs without interference."

Well, who'd say anything different to the man who controls every aspect of their lives? Ferris thinks. "Mr. MacNaughton, it seems to me that it would be in the interests of all parties if this strike ends speedily."

"I agree."

"Well, then, I will be happy to send a team of negotiators to the Copper Country. You can sit down with the union representatives—"

"Never."

The word hangs for a time, unadorned and unqualified, until MacNaughton makes his point even more clearly: "Grass will grow in the streets of Calumet before C&H recognizes the Western Federation of Miners."

Blinking, thinking quickly, Woodbridge Ferris tries again: "Mr. MacNaughton, you yourself are on the Houghton County Board of Supervisors, are you not?"

"Yes . . ."

"Well, then, you are often called upon to make decisions on behalf of the citizens, and I presume you do so without consulting everyone in the county." No response. "I myself have served on the board of a bank, and we did not consult all depositors before making decisions on their behalf."

He waits for MacNaughton to draw the obvious parallel, but there's nothing on the other end of the line. This is what Woodbridge Ferris hates most about the telephone: you cannot *see* the man to whom you are speaking. You can't judge the effect of your words as you make your argument.

"Mr. MacNaughton, it seems to me that if the shareholders of corporations can be represented by an elected board of directors, then labor can also be represented by elected spokesmen—even if not every laboring man agrees with every decision made by the union. Is this not consistent with American democracy?"

Silence continues to fill the hundreds of miles between Lansing and Calumet. When James MacNaughton speaks again, he leaves no doubt about his attitude. "Governor Ferris, I will not be held accountable for any violence that takes place in the Copper Country. I am making a direct request for the deployment of the Michigan State Guard to protect the public and to defend private property, both of which are being threatened by the union thugs who are corrupting my workforce. Will you comply?"

Ferris stifles a sigh. All his life, he has taken his time with decisions. He gathers facts. He consults with others and deliberates as long as necessary to make a sound judgment. Nevertheless, a governor's day is riddled with unwelcome interruptions and filled with demands that something be done this instant.

Which can be useful, he realizes now. "I'm very sorry, Mr. MacNaughton. I fear there is a meeting that I must attend." True enough, though the meeting is not for another two hours. "Rest assured, I shall look into the guidelines and procedures for deploying the Guard under these circumstances."

"Thank you, Governor. Have the details to me as soon as possible," MacNaughton says, as though the governor of Michigan answers to him. "And, please, convey my best wishes to Mrs. Ferris. I do hope her health is improving."

"I'm afraid not, but I will certainly let her know you asked after her."

A few additional pleasantries are exchanged, and the call ends. Feeling off-balance and vaguely disturbed, Ferris scrubs his face with both hands and presses his fingers into his eyes. He is deeply suspicious of

those who are hostile to compromise of any kind. Given his own conversation with James MacNaughton, he is inclined to be sympathetic
toward the frustration such a man's employees might feel.

He reaches out to the oak box on his desk and activates the intercom.
"Miss McCloud?"

"Sir?" a tinny voice replies.

"Can you set up a telephone call to the sheriff of Keweenaw County?"

"Not Houghton County, sir?"

"No. I'd like to consult with someone who doesn't owe his job to
James MacNaughton."

"Of course, sir." A few minutes later, the intercom comes to life again.
"Sheriff Hepting for you, sir. Line one."

"Sheriff, it's good of you to speak to me. You must be very busy with
the strikers. Tell me, has there been much violence in your jurisdiction?"

Hepting laughs. "Some shit's been thrown—pardon me sir. I guess
I should say that the contents of some slop buckets have been hurled.
We've had a lot of yelling. A few fistfights. No worse than any given
Saturday night in a mining town."

"So you would not have any need for a deployment of the Michigan
Guard in Keweenaw County?"

"Troops?" There's a snort on the other end of the line. "Hell, no! Is
that what MacNaughton's asking for?"

"Yes, he has made a . . . vigorous case. Have you heard from the mine
operators in your area?"

"Yes, I have, and I can tell you that MacNaughton doesn't speak
for all of them. Calumet & Hecla can afford to wait it out, but a lot of
the smaller operations would like to settle with the union as soon as
possible. The Federation wants an eight-hour day and a three-dollar
wage per day. From what I've heard, the small mines could go to nine
hours and maybe a two-fifty minimum, right? There's a problem with
the one-man drill, too, but C&H is the only company with the capital
to bring those in, and everybody thinks MacNaughton would like the
strike to go on until the competition goes bust."

Which does not seem unrealistic, Ferris thinks.

"You want my opinion, sir?" Hepting asks.

"Please."

"According to our county prosecutor, strikers have a constitutional right to join any organization they like and to assemble in public to air their grievances. MacNaughton thinks he rules the copper industry. Maybe he does, but I sure as hell don't want troops stirring things up in Keweenaw County. We're handling things fine right now, and our citizens are acting within the law."

"Thank you, Sheriff," Governor Ferris says. "You've given me a good deal to consider."

And yet . . .

Telegrams begin to arrive within the hour. All of them are from the businessmen of Calumet. Each has nearly identical wording. Livelihood threatened. Potential for violence. The strike must be broken. Send in the troops. We must have troops. Provide us with troops. MacNaughton's influence, no doubt. Calumet & Hecla owns the land on which they've built their businesses. Take away their leases, and they're ruined.

There is a knock on his door. Miss McCloud steps inside, holding up another flimsy yellow form. "This one is from Sheriff Cruse up in Houghton County."

"Right on cue," the governor mutters, for this orchestrated pressure is beginning to annoy him. The Houghton County sheriff serves at the pleasure of the Houghton County Board of Supervisors, James Mac-Naughton presiding; like every businessman in Calumet, James Cruse owes his livelihood to a single man.

Cruse's telegram is essentially the same as those from the merchants, though more hysterical.

GENERAL STRIKE BACKED BY WESTERN FEDERATION OF MINERS STOP ARMED RIOTERS DESTROYING PROPERTY THREATENING MEN WHO WISH TO WORK STOP SITUATION WILL BECOME WORSE WITH GREAT DESTRUCTION OF PROPERTY AND POSSIBLY LOSS OF LIFE UNLESS I RECEIVE THE AID OF STATE TROOPS STOP I REQUIRE 2000 MEN AND HEREBY ASK YOU TO CALL OUT TROOPS TO THAT NUMBER AND DETAIL THEM FOR SERVICE HERE AT ONCE FULL STOP

Two thousand troops! And for how long? If James MacNaughton has his way, they'll be there until his competitors are driven out of business and the union is crushed. And how much will that cost? Enough to gut state funding for universal education, and for the new tuberculosis sanatorium in central Michigan, and for the farm colony that would provide sheltered employment for epileptics, and for every other program Woodbridge Ferris promised the citizens of his state.

He reaches out to the oak box on his desk and activates the intercom again. "Miss McCloud, contact the hospitals in Calumet, Houghton City, and Ontonagon. Find out if any serious injuries have been reported."

This takes some time. Miss McCloud taps on his door forty-five minutes later, steno pad in hand. "The duty nurse in Calumet says there have been some cuts and bruises, sir. Ontonagon says anyone carrying a lunch pail is likely to be roughed up, but a union man in Houghton has been shot."

"Shot! By whom?"

"He told the attending doctor it was a deputy sheriff." Miss McCloud hesitates. "Sir, I took the liberty of telephoning a cousin who works for the county up in Calumet. . . . He says that Sheriff Cruse is deputizing company men and 'handing out guns and badges like candy.' His words, sir. And . . ."

"Yes?"

"My cousin has a friend—a carpenter who works for the company. He says the lathe men are turning out great numbers of baseball bats— far in excess of the local teams' needs, Governor."

"For which side?"

"He didn't say, sir. I can telephone again, if you like."

He shakes his head.

"Under the circumstances," he decides, "perhaps the best thing is to send troops to Calumet to keep the peace—no matter who is responsible for inciting violence. Find out who's in charge of the Michigan Guard, Miss McCloud."

"Major Henry Van Den Broek is the adjutant general, sir." Noting the governor's surprise at her prompt reply, she smiles modestly. "I anticipated that you might want to contact him, sir."

She is a graduate of a new secretarial school in Detroit. Excellent stenographic and typing skills. Efficient. Capable of initiative. Remarkably attractive, as well, the Good Gray Schoolmaster notes.

She is also young enough to be his daughter and he is instantly ashamed, though he supposes such feelings are only natural. His wife has been an invalid for many years.

He clears his throat, businesslike again. "Good work, Miss McCloud. Get me Major Van Den Broek right away, please."

August 1913

1

Is the law on our side?

—Shakespeare, *Romeo and Juliet*

Every morning, there are strikers' parades past all the pit heads. "If we march at dawn every working day, we show MacNaughton it's not laziness keeping miners out of the pits," Annie argued, and the men saw the logic of that. But she is organizing something different for the coming Sunday: a march past the encampment where twenty-four hundred Michigan guardsmen have pitched tents. And, on the advice of Michael Sweeney, she will lead the parade herself.

"Mrs. Clements, they have rifles and bayonets," Charlie Miller cries, trying again to reason with her. "They have artillery! They will charge you on horseback. They will beat you and jail you—"

"No," she replies, her face serene. "They won't."

Miller throws up his hands and comes to Michael Sweeney's side. "It's like arguing with a dress-store dummy," he mutters.

"Or a statue of the Virgin," Sweeney says, but he is grinning as he watches Mrs. Clements from his perch on a stool in the corner of the union office.

She is a blur. Collating stacks of flyers by language, helping the girls pack food parcels for families already running out of groceries, directing the boys to carry the boxes off to the union families. All the photographer can do is stand back and admire her energy, though after two weeks of rooming with Charles Miller, Michael Sweeney knows the union official is being driven round the bend by this woman.

Poor Charlie still has nightmares about the Colorado strikes, and

Sweeney understands that. It was all-out war at Telluride and Cripple Creek. Company men with clubs. Troops with machine guns. Midnight slayings and daylight slaughter. The operators and their politician stooges out in Colorado couldn't get Miller for telling the truth, so they arrested him for desecration of the flag. Not even a real flag, either. Just a drawing of a flag, printed on a flyer, with a plain fact on the stripes.

Martial law declared in Colorado!
Habeas corpus suspended in Colorado!
Free press throttled in Colorado!
Free speech denied in Colorado!
Wholesale arrests without warrant in Colorado!
Union men exiled from homes and families in Colorado!
Corporations corrupt and control Administration in Colorado!
Citizens' Alliance resorts to mob rule and violence in Colorado!
Militia hired by corporations to break the strike in Colorado!
IS COLORADO IN AMERICA?

Miller was released on bail and immediately jailed again. For his second arrest, they gave the usual excuse: "Military necessity." Union lawyers appealed all the way to the Supreme Court of the United States and got slapped in the face for their trouble. Justice Oliver Wendell Holmes decided that all a governor needed to say was "An insurrection exists." Three magic words were enough to legalize everything and anything done to the strikers or to Miller himself. Beat them, shoot them, jail them, deport them. Even so, Charlie and the Western Federation of Miners have clawed out concessions, year by bloody year. The union has made life in the Colorado mines less hellish, more human if not humane. But winning those concessions exacted a terrible price.

"The woman has no idea what she's up against," Charlie mutters. "I swear, Martin. She thinks you can shame the shameless!"

"It's Michael, not Martin."

"Michael! Jesus! I'm sorry!"

"I think she's magnificent," Michael admits. With her big plans and her unshakable determination, her beautiful smile and her relentless bustling, young Mrs. Clements is indeed convinced that far-away shareholders can be shamed into acting decently. You have to love that, he thinks. She hasn't been beaten down yet. She's not cynical. "She still believes in the common good, Charlie, and that's what the country needs right now."

Standing at the union office window, gazing at the street traffic, Charlie Miller ignores that remark. "Another family," he announces, "leaving for Detroit."

"Russians," old Moishe Glass tells them, a little breathless from lugging a heavy parcel up the stairway, into the union office.

"Are you Russian, Mr. Glass?" Sweeney asks.

The storekeeper glances at him, but it's Annie Clements, across the crowded little room, he addresses. "Your order," he says, letting the package thump onto a table. "Am I Russian?" he asks then. "I'm a Jew. From Vilna. The border keeps changing. So. Am I Russian?" He shrugs. "That's a debate. Out there? Those families. They are *scared* Russians. They remember 1905. They gonna run 'fore there's trouble here. They gonna run to Henry Ford and make cars. I ask 'em, where you gonna run next? Ford gonna cut your pay. He gonna tell you: Work harder, work longer, same money. What you gonna do then? Where you gonna run when Ford bring in the bully boys?"

Carefully, he unties the string around the parcel and coils it around his hand before putting it in his pocket. "I remember, too. Soldiers. Horses. Guns. The Bund—the socialists—we lost, but . . ." He shrugs again. "Losing teaches you a lot. What you do after a defeat? That matters." He taps the parcel's shipping address: *Glass Brothers General Store, Calumet, Michigan.* "Me, I ain't goin' nowhere. I make my stand here. In America. Me and my brothers, we got American store. We got American kids. When I leave Vilna, I say, 'Moishe Glass, you gonna be American, and you ain't never gonna be afraid again.'"

Carefully, reverently, the old man unfolds the brown paper and smooths the wrapping out, saving it for reuse. "Them soldiers down there?" Moishe Glass says. "You show 'em this, Annie." Gently, he slides his hands beneath the heavy folded fabric and presents an enormous American flag to Annie Clements. "You still gotta get a pole. The flag? My gift to you," Moishe says. "No charge to the union."

"A flag won't stop a bullet," Charlie Miller says.

Sweeney is smiling broadly, pleased when Mrs. Clements returns a conspiratorial grin. "You're right, Charlie," Sweeney says, clapping him on the shoulder. "It isn't armor, but it's going to do the job."

The photographer looks at the wall clock then, takes his hat off a hook by the door, and picks up a flat leather portfolio. "Well, I've an appointment to keep with Major Van Den Broek," he tells the room cheerily. "I'll just leave the camera equipment here, if you don't mind, Mrs. Clements?"

She nods and smiles again, already moving on to the next task.

Kneeling on the floor, banging brads into the lath they'll use to stiffen banners and placards for tomorrow's parade, Kazimir Savicki sits back on his heels and watches Mike Sweeney disappear down the stairs.

"Which side is he on? That's what I want to know. Is he on the level?"

A few yards away, Jack Kivisto freezes, his stick-straight, white-blond hair falling forward, obscuring his face. He is the son of a notorious anti-union man. He's joined up now, like so many others did after his father was killed, but he knows there's some suspicion. Especially from Kaz, who thinks Jack joined the union only because he likes Eva. Which is not the case. Truly. After his father died, before the strike started, Jack Kivisto worked for a couple of weeks underground. That was all it took to convince him that any plan for staying out of the mine was a good plan. Anyway, Kaz is talking about the photographer. Which is a relief.

"He's always taking pictures of the militiamen, and he's always hanging around the office here. How do we know he's not giving things away?"

"Like what?" Carrying an armload of donated clothing, Eva pauses to look at the pile of placards Jack has finished lettering. "You have such nice handwriting," she says admiringly.

Jack is pretty sure Eva likes him. Which is embarrassing. He doesn't want to encourage her, so he barely nods in response.

"He could tell them lots of things," her brother is saying. "He could tell them that Annie and Mr. Miller don't get along. Lots of things."

"Well, Annie likes Mr. Sweeney, and that's enough for me."

"And he rooms with Miller," Jack points out, regretting the remark instantly. Shut up, he tells himself. Shut up. Shut up.

"See, Kaz?" Eva says. "Annie trusts Mr. Sweeney, and Mr. Miller rooms with him, so he must be all right."

A long shadow falls over them. Standing in a shaft of light from one of the tall windows, Annie comes over to inspect the boys' handiwork. It was a gamble to invest in a heavy, stiff paper stock for placards, but fabric banners would be too heavy for the marchers in tomorrow's parade.

"Don't they look wonderful, Annie?" Eva asks.

"They do indeed," Annie agrees. "Well done, Jack. You have a good eye. All the lines are nice and level. Did you young gentlemen sand the lath down? I don't want anyone to get splinters tomorrow morning."

"Yes, ma'am," Kaz tells her, and Annie moves on.

Still hoping for conversation, Eva asks, "Jack, how is your mother doing?"

"Good, I guess."

"Isn't she worried about losing the house now that you're not working?"

He glances at Kaz Savicki and sees the question on his face. "We get help from the church," Jack tells him.

Eva shifts the pile of clothing in her arms to get a better grip. She might be waiting for Jack to jump up and help her with it, but he makes himself busy with the lettering again. "I'm so glad you're with us now, Jack! You're making a big difference."

"Thanks," he says, trying not to cringe.

"Annie," Kaz calls out, "why is Mike Sweeney hanging around with that militia officer?"

"He's taking pictures so the newspapers can't say nothing is happening up here. He's getting us *publicity*. And publicity will get us support."

"See?" Eva asks her brother.

Kaz just grunts.

*   *   *

Across town, Major Henry Van Den Broek has this much in common with a fifteen-year-old union kid. Like Kazimir Savicki, he doesn't quite know what to make of Michael Sweeney. Outwardly, the photographer has been friendly and helpful since the Guard arrived, often stopping by the commander's tent for a little chat before sauntering off to his boardinghouse, where he shares a room with the representative of the Western Federation of Miners.

"Major Van Den Broek!" Sweeney cries this afternoon, offering his hand. "I've just learned that we are colleagues! You're a correspondent for 'This Week in the World,' are you not, sir?"

Van Den Broek has not told anyone in Calumet that he contributes a column now and then for *Detroit Saturday Night,* and he must look startled, for Sweeney grins knowingly. "Ah, well, Major, we journalists are in the business of finding things out, now, aren't we! As it happens, I've just sold a photograph of you and your men to that very organization. The editor mentioned that we are pulling our oars in the same ocean and might do well to work together."

He opens a portfolio with a thick stack of clippings and hands Van Den Broek a photograph of mounted guardsmen arriving in the city. "And don't you all look splendid! Like Spanish conquistadors arriving in Mexico . . ." he says, letting Van Den Broek take in the implications. "I'm quite partial to this one, too," he adds, admiring his own work before handing the major a picture of the guardsmen's neat rows of peaked tents, with the Calumet library in the background. "That's going into next weekend's edition," he says. "Now, here's one taken last year during the Lawrence mill girls' Bread and Roses strike. And don't the bully boys look bad, threatening those sweet young things. Imagine if there had been a camera man down in Wolverine last week . . ."

"That wasn't us," Van Den Broek says, a little defensively. A Hungarian woman reportedly refused to let a deputy sheriff search her boardinghouse. She claimed she'd been making noodles when a soldier barged in, knocked her down, and dragged her out of the house by her hair. Her husband is said to have been beaten unconscious by Sheriff Cruse's men.

"I know, sir! And that's why I'm here—for the same reason you are. Both of us are—in our own ways—on the side of the angels. We're here to get the story straight and keep things from getting out of hand, are we not? You're standing between peaceful strikers and company goons with tin badges, paid to beat the hell out of them. And my photographs will show what really happens. I'm sure you wouldn't want your fine troopers to be falsely accused of brutality."

Van Den Broek follows Sweeney's gaze toward the military encampment surrounding the Calumet Armory and finds himself faintly embarrassed. Young men in khaki banter and josh and wrestle, happy to escape their daily routine in offices and stores. They are sleeping in tents, taking their meals in the open air. If it weren't for the cavalry horses and artillery, his troops would look like Scouts on a wilderness excursion. "Boy soldiers," the striking miners call them. "We served in a real army back in the old country," one tough old bird yelled when the militia arrived, "and we can fight them boy soldiers here!"

After watching the horseplay for a moment, Van Den Broek glances at Sweeney and sees the photographer's indulgent smile.

"Sure," Sweeney says, "they can be a rowdy bunch, but my money's on you to keep them in check. And I am here to promise you: it certainly won't be the union's fault if there's trouble tomorrow."

Van Den Broek looks at him sharply, but Sweeney's blue gaze is on the sky now. "Weather Bureau says no rain tomorrow, just a bit of overcast coming in from Canada. That can flatten out the pictures, although people won't be frowning menacingly into the sun, which is good . . ." His hand comes out. "I'm sure you have duties to perform, sir, so I won't trouble you longer."

Van Den Broek watches the man go—all lank, loose affability.

In his own youth, Henry Van Den Broek went to Cuba with the 31st Michigan Volunteers. Now solidly in middle age, he has the paunch of a respected Lansing businessman but he's remained active in the Michigan National Guard, even going so far as to raise and run Michigan's Battery A, First Field Artillery. One day, he believes, state militias will be called upon for service outside the United States. The Spanish Empire and its minions must be contained and beaten back. He believes that America is the nation that must do this and so, for fifteen years, he has kept himself and his men fit and ready to fight in Panama, or in the Philippines, or along the border with Mexico. He has steeled himself to face imperial armies, hostile natives, jungle heat, venomous snakes, malaria, yellow fever, typhoid . . .

"Major," his master sergeant asked him a week after they arrived in Calumet, "what in hell are we doing *here?*"

Van Den Broek took in the high blue skies and brilliant sunshine softened by a cool breeze off Lake Superior. "Beautiful day," he observed, ignoring the question because he wasn't sure he could answer it.

The entire Michigan Guard has been mobilized to battle rampaging union thugs. They have been told that life and property are at stake in the Copper Country. Their orders are to suppress riots and aid civil officers in imposing law and order. Since arriving three weeks ago, the Michigan guardsmen have patrolled the pleasant streets and impressive industrial yards of the Copper Country. A meat market burned down a few days ago. The arsonist might have been a union man, but he could just have easily been a disgruntled supplier or even a relative with a grudge. There have been no other fires. Nothing has come of rumors that someone might dynamite a fancy social club where mining officials meet for supper and cigars. The union parades have been peaceful. Almost joyous. Thus far, casualties among the guardsmen have been limited to some infected blackfly bites, a sprained ankle, and several cases of severe hay fever.

To date, he has found nothing he can turn into an article for *Detroit Saturday Night*, and yet . . .

He has an uneasy feeling that this may change tomorrow.

It certainly won't be the union's fault if there's trouble . . .

2

O, she doth teach the torches to burn bright!
—Shakespeare, *Romeo and Juliet*

It's nearly sundown when Annie Clements hears footsteps climbing the staircase to the union office. "Mrs. Clements!" Michael Sweeney says, surprised to find her alone at her desk. "Is anything wrong?"

"No. Why would you think that? What are you doing here?"

"I've been out walking the parade route. Getting a read on the light and some vantage points. I want to be sure the camera's ready. What about you? Are you ready for tomorrow?"

"Of course."

She can feel his eyes on her, taking in the lines of her face, the curve of her cheeks, the light and shadow, the background. Ordinarily she would never stay in the office by herself. Like any good woman, she is careful about her behavior with men. Scabs are calling her the union's whore, and she does not wish to provide anything that might be used against her or the Women's Auxiliary. Even so, when Joe's drinking, it's better to stay out of his sight. . . .

Obscurely grateful that Sweeney does not press her on the explanation, she offers one anyway. "I just . . . I have some paperwork to catch up on."

He goes to the corner, fusses with the camera for a few minutes, and heads for the stairs. She returns her attention to the letter she's composing: a report to the Federation, asking again for more support. The Calumet strike is unauthorized, but surely they can see how determined Local 15 is. If she explains—

"What makes a woman like you?"

She looks up. Michael Sweeney is still standing there, frowning thoughtfully, so she says, "Well, my parents were both tall, and—"

He makes a face. "Not that! I mean—all this." He sweeps his hand past the stacks of flyers, the piles of placards, the cabinets. The boxes of canned goods. The mounds of sorted dresses and shirts donated to the new clothing bank. Every square foot of this place holds evidence of something she has put into motion. "How does a young woman in the north end of nowhere get to be so sure? So capable. So . . . different."

She gives a short, startled laugh. "I'm different, all right!"

He crosses his arms over his chest. "I'm serious."

It's not something she's ever really thought about. Her height was part of it, most likely. "I guess . . . even when I was little, I was big. I was taller than my teachers by the time I was ten. They counted on me to help them in the classroom. And . . ." She works it through. "They expected me to act like an adult."

"To have an adult's maturity to match an adult's size," he suggests.

"Yes. Exactly. I suppose it was unreasonable, wasn't it."

That gives him pause. "But if you're bright and responsible, you like living up to expectations."

She tilts her head and considers this. "For the most part."

"And the union?"

"Born to it. My father was one of the early organizers."

"So you're carrying on the family tradition. I haven't met your parents. Are they still living?"

She shakes her head. "My mother died last winter. My father was killed years ago. A cave-in. That's what the company says, anyway."

"You don't believe it."

"Hard to tell the difference between being hit by a falling rock and being beaten with one. Both brothers died underground, too. They were troublemakers."

"Like you," Sweeney observes. "So. Getting a little of your own back?"

"Maybe. Probably. Yes."

"And you want to make the world a better place."

She snorts. "Not the whole world. Just Calumet, Michigan." Uncomfortable with all this talk about herself, she sits back in her chair. "What about you? How did you end up here? In the north end of nowhere."

He sits down across from her, leaving the paper-cluttered expanse of the battered oak desk between them. "Have you ever read *How the Other Half Lives?*" he asks, tossing his hat onto the desk and running his fingers through his snarled mop of curls.

She shakes her head, then says what she thought the first time she saw him: "You need a haircut."

A short laugh, after which he grows serious again. "When I was about five, a photographer named Jacob Riis started hanging around the Bend. The 'foul core of New York's slums'—that's what our neighborhood was called. Riis was a police reporter for the *New-York Tribune*. Police headquarters was on Mulberry Street, right in the center of the stinking pigsty we called home. Trash everywhere. People sleeping ten to a room. Micks, wops, kikes. And every one of us filthy, no matter how hard the women worked. One water pump and one privy for the lot of us . . ." He shudders at the memory. "Riis couldn't get over how bad things were, and he decided to *show* the uptown swells how the other half was living. Let them *see* the conditions immigrants lived in."

"'People know unfairness and injustice,'" she says, "'when they *see* it.'"

He smiles and claps once and points at her, delighted that she's remembered what he told her the first day they met. Serious again, he goes on. "Now, in the beginning, his photographs went into the papers. A few years later, he collected them for a book. Read the chapter titles sometime—they tell my family's story. 'The Reign of Rum.' 'The Wrecks and the Waste.' 'The Street Arabs.' My dad was a coal-heaver. I saw him knifed dead on a saloon floor. He's buried in a trench in potter's field. There's a photo of that sorry place in Riis's book, too."

He slumps in his chair. "So. Ma had eight of us brats to raise on her own, poor woman. She did her best, bless her, but after a time, she gave up on the enterprise. Five of us died in her arms, one way and another. Those of us still among the living had to watch her drink herself into a stupor most nights, and how she got the money for grog, I do not like to think . . ." He sits up. "Anyway, she signed the three of us over to the Children's Aid, and away we went to the Wild West on one of

Mr. Brace's Orphan Trains!" He says that cheerily, as though it were an adventure, but when he speaks again, his voice is hard. "My sisters got pulled off early on. Pretty girls, you know . . . God help them."

He looks away, staring out the office window, where the sky has begun its nightly shift from blue to lavender to cobalt. "I was last to be picked, but the luckiest," he says, standing and going closer to the window. "Didn't seem like it at the time. At every depot, us kids got herded onto the platform and stood waiting for somebody to pluck us out of the crowd. I was such a skinny little thing, nobody thought I'd be worth a damn on the business end of a shovel. Most of the bastards who took kids in were just looking for a cheap little slave they could put to work on their hardscrabble farms out in the middle of damn-all."

Suddenly Annie understands why he was so impressed by the workers' housing and the neat, clean streets of Calumet. He glances back then and sees the look on her face: sympathy for him, and also a little shame that she is not as grateful for the conditions of her life as James MacNaughton thought the people of Calumet ought to be. "It's the conditions below ground, not the city—" she begins.

"No, no! Don't misunderstand me. Just because someone has it even worse is no reason to settle for bad! That's what my foster mother taught me." He comes back to his chair, and when he speaks again, his eyes are soft. "Ah, now, that woman! She was a dear. Frances Logan. A Kansas temperance lady—but temperate even about temperance, and willing to sip a small beer now and then. A widow, no children of her own. She had a little bit of money and a big need for someone to love. Every night, she would tell me, 'You are all my hopes and dreams. You're going places, Michael. Stay away from hard liquor, and you'll make your mark.' I felt guilty that I was luckier than so many others on the train. And I worried about my sisters. I didn't know where they were, and there was nothing I could do. 'You can't save them,' Miss Frances told me, 'but you can help others, Michael. Raise your sights and see how you can make life more decent for more people.'"

Annie smiles, understanding now, at least partly. "Ah. So that explains working for unions. And photography?"

"Well, you see, she had me out in Kansas for ten years, but all those years, I never forgot the man with the camera back in the city. That big bang and the flash and the way dark alleys lit up for one blinding moment! So, one day, Miss Frances takes me into town and we go to one of Mr. Carnegie's fine, new free libraries. And what do we see on the shelf but a book with Jacob Riis's name on it! And I was in it! Right there, in a picture with my littlest sister on my lap in the alley . . . We signed the book out and we looked through every page, over and over. And Miss Frances says to me, she says, 'Your Mr. Riis woke a lot of folks up with his pictures. He made the world a little more fair, a little less harsh. You could, too.' Well, I wanted my name on a book. And I wanted that dear lady to be proud of me."

Restless, he stands again, stretching out his back, staring at nothing Annie can see. "I was seventeen when Miss Frances died, but before the consumption took her, she gave me a stash of money she'd been saving for when I was grown and went off on my own. Forty-two dollars." Walking to the corner of the office where his camera leans on its tripod, he pats it as though it were the head of a child. "Just enough for a secondhand Gundlach Korona V, with big glass plates and a pneumatic shutter—the best camera you could buy when it was made! And every time I take a picture, I think of Miss Frances— up there somewhere, smiling. And when I sell one to the papers, she busts her celestial buttons with pride!"

Annie laughs, and Mike returns to sit across the desk from her.

"I haven't made my mark yet, not really, but I mean to do it here in Calumet, Michigan." He's all business again. "What do you remember from the suffragist demonstration—the one in Washington last March? Thousands of women in the streets, demanding the right to vote, but what do you *remember*?"

"There was a woman on a horse . . ."

"Exactly. One person caught your eye. That was Inez Milholland. Did you know she's a labor lawyer?"

Annie shakes her head, half-ashamed.

"But you *do* remember a lovely young woman dressed all in white, riding a beautiful white horse! Her photograph was in all the papers. You see? That's what a good picture can do: it can give people a memory that lasts longer than words. It can sum up something important and offer people a way to think about it. And that's what I want people to remember about tomorrow: a lovely young woman, dressed all in white, carrying an American flag. We don't want them to read 'union' and 'strike' and think 'roustabouts, roughnecks, thugs'—"

"And immigrants."

"Exactly! Union men are an anonymous crowd, don't you see, but the robber barons? The rich men who are doing the real harm? They're individuals. We know each name. Rockefeller. Vanderbilt. Gould. Fisk. Society pages have photographs of their wives and their daughters and their fancy houses and parties. Business pages tell the world what each of those fellas think, one at a time . . ."

He sits gazing at her for longer than is entirely comfortable, and chuckles when she waves her hand in front of her face as though swatting at a fly. "Mrs. Clements," he declares, "I am going to make you America's Joan of Arc!"

"Blarney," she says.

"God's own truth," he replies. "Calumet needs one name to represent all the decent people who just want decent lives for decent families. You are a beauty, inside and out, and I am going to make America see what I see."

She awakens early the next morning and lies in bed for a time: eyes open, back in Calumet after floating high above the Houghton fairgrounds.

The dream is a sign, she thinks. Things will go well today.

Joe snores next to her. He has gotten used to sleeping at night, no longer at the beck and call of steam whistles squealing the shift changes.

He follows her to meetings: protective, vigilant. He is suspicious of the attention she's shown by men like Charlie Miller and Mike Sweeney. Fearing what Joe might do to anyone who makes advances, Annie is careful not to give any reason for him to doubt her.

Between her caution and his impatience with endless discussion and blather of union democracy, he usually feels free to drift off to a bar by noon. He comes home after she does. Too late to complain about her hours at the union office. Too drunk to do much more than stagger upstairs and fall asleep, often without undressing first. He seems content with that state of affairs, and as much as she worries about his drinking, Annie is relieved.

She eases out of bed and goes to the washstand, gently pouring water into the chipped enamel bowl so the splashing doesn't wake Joe. Usually she rushes through her morning rituals, but today after she washes up, she takes her time with her hair, plaiting it into two neat, thick braids, twisting them over the top of her head, pinning them in place. She dresses carefully, all in white, as the photographer has instructed all the women to do, and pauses to study herself in the small mirror.

Level brown eyes beneath an abundance of heavy brown hair. A round Slavic face, with high broad cheekbones. A rather sweet nose, now that she looks at it. And yes—a nice smile with good even teeth.

She has been called many things. Freakish. Gigantic. Grotesque. No one but Michael Sweeney has ever called her a beauty. She is willing to concede that she has pretty features, but . . . A beauty, she thinks, trying the word out, hearing it in his voice. Hearing as well what his foster mother said. *You are all my hopes and dreams.* No one has ever said anything like that to her, either. Not even when she was small. The thought makes her sad for a moment, before she dismisses it as foolishness. Even so, she thinks, if I ever have a baby, I will tell that child what Frances Logan told Michael Sweeney: you are all my hopes and dreams.

She does not yet allow herself to think of who the father of such a baby might be, but she knows—all at once, wordlessly—that if Joe Clements were to die underground or leave her for a more compliant woman, she would not grieve. It is a shock, this knowledge. And it is the truth.

Joe's life has made him what he is. She wants to believe that he would be a better, kinder man if his life had been better and kinder. She tells herself that she is fighting for a better, kinder life for men like Joe and for workers not yet born. So she has spent her days rushing from task to task, pouring her energy into making life easier for her mother, for her teachers, for her friends, her neighbors, the union. It is just like Michael said: If you're bright and responsible, you like living up to expectations.

And her own life? What did she expect of that?

She has never allowed herself to ask the question, not in so many words. Calumet girls become wives. Calumet boys become miners. Even now, she pushes the question away, afraid of the answer. Afraid of what it will mean. Afraid of what it will cost.

"Joe?" she whispers. "Joe! Are you coming to the parade?"

He rouses slightly, grunts, and rolls over. She doesn't argue with him.

The orders have come down from the general offices of Calumet & Hecla. A show of force. A line drawn—if not in the sand, then on the street that leads past the encampment. There are rumors everywhere. The strikers will leave Calumet and march to Laurium, where the managers and lawyers and engineers live. The Marxists intend to terrorize the bourgeoisie, to attack them in their own homes and burn those mansions to the ground. Mounted troops are waiting six abreast, blocking the road to Laurium. Horses snort their boredom, shaking their bridles, neck muscles shivering. The street is lined by company security men and sheriff's deputies—most of whom are non-union miners.

Michael Sweeney has his camera set up on the sidewalk, ready to record whatever happens along the line of confrontation. And Major Henry Van Den Broek stands next to him, for Sweeney's position is also the best situated to spot trouble and to react as necessary.

They hear the marchers before they can see them. Snatches of song in the distance. *Sweet land of liberty . . . Let freedom ring . . .* Sopranos. All sopranos. Maybe it's the distance, Van Den Broek thinks. High notes carry better.

The marchers turn a corner then. A river of white, gleaming in the sunshine. A woman carrying an American flag leads what seems at first to be a procession of children, but as the parade comes closer, Van Den Broek realizes that the flag is enormous, and that the woman carrying it is very tall, and that she is followed not only by children but by other grown women, young and old. Dressed in fresh white shirtwaists, the ladies are surrounded by little boys in short pants and pressed white shirts and by little girls in white pinafores. The children look like angels in a Christmas pageant.

Many wear black armbands and march behind a street-spanning banner bordered in black: "BLESSED ARE THEY WHO MOURN THEIR MARTYRED DEAD!" Those not in mourning follow behind another banner: "8 HOURS FOR WORK, 8 HOURS FOR SLEEP, 8 HOURS FOR OUR FAMILIES!" Little girls carry placards that proclaim, "PAPA IS STRIKING FOR US!" Young boys carry neatly lettered placards: "WE ARE STRONG FOR THE UNION!" Sturdy adolescents carry poles that hold up banners: "BLESSED ARE THEY WHO DO BATTLE AGAINST INJUSTICE!" "WE SHALL BE CALLED THE CHILDREN OF LIBERTY!" "BLESSED ARE THEY WHO HUNGER AND THIRST AFTER JUSTICE!"

"And what a grand sight that is!" Sweeney murmurs, busily capturing the scene before glancing at Major Van Den Broek. "That's Annie Clements out in front—the one with the flag. God love her, all she needs is a white horse to ride and a suit of shining armor!"

The marchers are belting out an old Civil War song as they approach, only now the chorus has new meaning. *The union forever! Hurrah, boys, hurrah!* For a time, the singing drowns out taunts from the company men and deputies who line the street, but when the marchers are within fifty feet, Henry Van Den Broek walks to the center of the pavement and takes his stand between his troops and the tallest woman he has ever seen.

For all her size, she is young enough to be his daughter, and the flag she carries is immense, its colors lit by the summer sun. Her face is shining, moist with sweat. Is that fear? he wonders. Or merely the effort of carrying something so heavy as that flag?

Ten feet away, she lowers the butt of the twelve-foot flagstaff on the cobbled paving and balances it with one raised hand, like Lady Liberty with a torch. Face to face, they wait silently, listening to the chorus. *We will rally round the flag, boys, rally round the flag! We know there's power in the union!*

As the song ends, taunts and jeers are plain to hear, but so are the answers coming from the women.

"Go back where you came from, immigrant scum!"

"I was born right here, jackass! You're just a scab with a badge!"

"Union bitch!"

"Company coward!"

The tall woman surveys the mounted troops before her. "Bayonets?" she asks the major quietly. When his eyes flick away, she pitches her voice to carry and asks his troops, "Bayonets, gentlemen? Sabers?"

The breeze lifts the flag overhead. It is mere chance when it drifts over her shoulders. Nevertheless, she reaches toward the silken banner with her free hand and pulls it over her bosom.

"Well, then, go ahead," she calls to the militiamen. "Use your weapons on me! But you'll have to go through this flag first. If this flag won't protect me, I'll die with it—right here, right now!"

"Madam," Van Den Broek says firmly, "I will allow no violence here—"

"I am pleased to hear it," she says, speaking now only to him. "Because we are Americans, Major. We have the right to assemble peacefully, and we have the right to speak our minds."

"What kind of women are out walking in the streets?" a deputy is yelling. "I'll tell you what kind!"

"Come over here, Annie!" another shouts. "I'll show you what you're good for!"

From somewhere among the marchers, a woman yells, "You think she'd even notice a little shit like you?"

There are shrieks of laughter from the women and startled guffaws from some of the soldiers. Henry Van Den Broek winces at the language before addressing the woman with the flag. "Madam, I am sure you don't want these children hearing such language—"

"Get off the streets!" a man hollers. "Go home and take care of your kids!"

"We are *all* Annie's children!" a girl cries. "And she *is* taking care of us!"

At the sound of Eva Savicki's voice, cheers break out among the marchers, and Annie Clements turns toward them. Her face is still and her eyes glisten, but her head is high enough and her sight is clear enough and her heart is open enough for her to understand something fully in that moment. Yes, she is thinking. This is what my life is for. Not for my own children but for these children, for these women. For this fight.

She turns again, back toward the troopers, and now the flag is fully wrapped around her. With her eyes on Henry Van Den Broek's, she raises her voice, for her words are meant to be heard by the women and children behind her, and by all the men who surround them. Men in uniform or out of it. Men who work for the company and men who work for the state. Men who want women to cook and to clean and to bear sons who'll grow up and accept whatever pittance is tossed their way and be grateful for it. Women who have buried the dead and nursed the cripples. Women who now refuse to tell another generation of children, This is all you can hope for. This is all your labor is worth. This is all your *lives* are worth.

"It's for these children that we are marching!" Annie shouts. "And if you want to stop us, if you want to turn us back, you will have to kill me. Right here, right now!"

Behind her, the marchers cheer and all who hear them understand that these women and children, too, have had a moment of clarity and understanding. This fearless twenty-five-year-old woman is not just one of their own. She is their leader, their princess, their warrior. They intend to follow Big Annie down this street, around this town, to hell and back, and no one will get in their way.

"Union!" Eva Savicki shouts. "Union! Union! Union!" And thousands take up the chant, marching in place, stamping twice after the word, their feet like drumbeats on the cobbles. "Union! Union! Union!"

Annie Clements's gaze remains steadily on Henry Van Den Broek as she pulls the enormous flag free of her shoulders and grips its staff with hands large enough to grasp a two-inch pole and shoulders strong enough to raise this heavy burden above the cobblestones of Calumet. She glances up and sees red and white and blue silk, billowing in the breeze.

When she speaks again, her voice is pitched to reach Van Den Broek alone. "This is our country, Major. This is our flag. Yours and mine. This is not Russia, Major. We are not serfs. You are not soldiers of the czar. You can let us pass. Or you can fight us. But *you* must decide. Right here. Right now."

Van Den Broek glances to his left, where Michael Sweeney has set up his camera in anticipation of this very moment. It is the photographer who now meets the major's eyes, and they both know what is at stake. The photographs will be in black and white and shades of gray. But if trouble starts? Film will show the whole world the dark red blood of women and children splashed on clean, bleached cotton, under the clear blue skies of Michigan.

3

What is mine shall never do thee good.
—Shakespeare, *Romeo and Juliet*

On Monday morning, Henry Van Den Broek is summoned to James MacNaughton's office in the main administrative building of Calumet & Hecla. He expects to be vilified. He expects accusations. He expects shouting. He has spent a sleepless night preparing himself to respond to intimidation. There is, instead, a brief, disarming exchange of courteous murmurs before MacNaughton folds his hands on a desktop that is large enough to accommodate Annie Clements's flag laid out like a tablecloth.

"Major Van Den Broek, I believe in giving credit where credit is due," MacNaughton begins. "I have already written to Governor Ferris praising your evenhandedness during the past weeks. The presence of your troops has undoubtedly contributed to the peaceful conditions on the streets of my city, and I am grateful."

"I was just doing my duty, sir. And, in all honesty, there's been no real indication that the strikers are inclined to violence. Personally, I don't believe the militia is required any longer. I have also been in communication with the governor. He is very concerned about the cost of this mission to Michigan taxpayers and about the price the guardsmen themselves are paying for their service. They are separated from their farms and businesses and jobs, and from their families as well."

"I understand these concerns, Major. I must, however, point out that you are new to the problems faced by mine operators in the Copper Country, as is Governor Ferris. If the Guard leaves prematurely, the violence and unrest of the first days of this unpleasantry will reemerge. Now. I'm sure you will recall that what I requested from Governor Ferris was a show of overwhelming strength to reinforce the hopelessness of the strike and get the miners back to work. That was what he promised he would deliver, and I will remind you that he mobilized the Guard with that in mind."

"Sir . . . that is not entirely accurate. The governor received reports that it was Sheriff Cruse's men who attacked strikers with wooden bats—"

"Sheriff Cruse and his men are sworn officers of the law, Major. They are paid to take whatever steps are necessary to protect persons and property. We cannot judge them by the same standards as anarchists and agitators who have come from far and wide to corrupt my miners—"

"Mr. MacNaughton, the marchers live here! And in my observation, the daily parades have been orderly and peaceful. Perhaps the strikers are misguided, but those ladies were—"

"Ladies? *Ladies!* Those harridans have beaten non-union miners with brooms and smeared them with human waste! And why? Because those men are loyal to the company that has given them so much. Because those men wanted to go to work as they always have! Those *females* are not ladies worthy of deference, Major! They are capable of using language so coarse—so *vulgar*—that even your troopers must have blushed to hear it!"

"Vulgarity was plentiful on both sides, sir, and I don't believe the First Amendment is restricted simply because the bounds of feminine propriety have been crossed."

"Don't be flippant with me, Major. The sacred Constitution of this nation was not meant to protect profane and ignorant immigrant harridans who do not know what it means to be good Americans! They are not miners, Major. They have no standing in this dispute!"

"They are the wives and mothers of miners. And yesterday more than half the marchers were the children of miners. Children, sir. Surely you did not expect us to charge them on horseback!"

"I expected you to break up that mob and clear the streets—streets that this company *owns*. I'm afraid you do not understand that every inch of this city belongs to Calumet & Hecla—"

"And yet, despite all the wealth of that company, you still rely on the taxpayers to pay for your refusal to negotiate the reasonable demands of—"

"Reasonable? Reasonable! Here is my wallet, sir!" MacNaughton says, rising to remove it from his pocket, slamming it onto the vast oak desk he stands behind. "This is *mine*. The money in it is *my money*. I do not negotiate with those who wish to tell me how to spend that money. Nor do the stockholders of Calumet & Hecla negotiate with those who wish to make demands on *their* wallets. This is America, sir. The mines are private property, and private property is sacred."

Van Den Broek stares at his feet, breathing shallowly, getting a grip on his emotions before he speaks. He wants to shout, Yes, this is America! It's not Russia, and you are not the czar, and the Michigan Guard is not a troop of Cossacks, but . . . Rather than use Mrs. Clements's words, he takes a different line of attack. "Your family is from Canada, is it not? You were born there, I believe."

MacNaughton's eyes narrow. "Who told you that?"

"Do you deny it?"

"I have lived in Michigan since I was three months old."

"But . . . still an immigrant," Van Den Broek points out, his voice calm. "My own family has been here since 1643. My ancestors fought King George for their rights. And more recently, both of my grandfathers fought in the Civil War. On the side of the Union."

Against the secessionists, he means. Against men who considered human beings to be private property. Against men who insisted that private property was sacred.

"Keep your wallet out, sir," Van Den Broek advises on his way out the door. "I don't think the state of Michigan will be paying your bills much longer."

"Again?" Joe Clements cries as he sees his wife getting ready to leave the house. "You said it would just be that once!"

"The idea is to have the flag out front for every parade. Nobody else is big enough to carry it. Unless you want to do it . . . ?"

He grunts. "I don't know what good it does, all this parading around like a circus coming to town."

"It shows MacNaughton we aren't giving up," his wife tells him. "It keeps the members feeling strong—seeing how many of us there are." She stoops down to inspect her reflection in the kitchen window, settling that big wagon-wheel hat on her head. "I'll be back in time to make your lunch."

He looks at her for a long time, trying to think of why he should object. She's done all her chores. Breakfast is on the table. The wash is out on the line, drying in the early morning sun. But there's that damned Irishman, sniffing around her all the time.

"I'll meet you at the office," he warns her.

And so he does. Sitting in a corner, arms crossed. Waiting for her when she comes up the stairs. A good thing, too, he thinks, because that photographer always has some excuse for being in the office when she's working.

He's there again this morning, moving a pile of donated clothing, clearing a place against a wall. Setting up his camera. Fussing with the height of the tripod. Fiddling with the lens.

"Ah! Mr. Clements!" Sweeney cries when he notices Joe staring. "I try to have the focus ready when I'm doing a portrait," he explains. "The Associated Press is clamoring for a photo of your wife, sir, and if you could make her stand still for two minutes when she gets back from this morning's march, I would take it as a personal favor."

Out on the staircase, they can hear her footsteps. The furled flag precedes her through the doorway at the top of the stairs, and then there's a certain amount of maneuvering the pole around the landing and into the office. Sweeney glances at Joe: Are you going to help?

"She can manage," Joe says. "She ain't no china doll."

Everybody waits until she gets the pole inside the office. "And I didn't break a window!" she says with mock pride.

"Getting chilly out there, mornings," Sweeney notes, "but doesn't your wife look nice with her rosy cheeks, Mr. Clements."

"He needs a picture," Joe tells her.

"My hair's a mess! It's windy this morning and—"

Sweeney looks to Joe for help, and gets it.

"Do as you're told," Joe says, lifting his chin toward the back of the office where the Irishman's camera stands. "Shut up about your hair."

"Your hair's fine," Sweeney tells her. "Right over here, if you please. "No, don't take off your coat yet. The wool makes a nice contrast with the flag's fabric." He moves behind his camera to check the image, frowning. "Flag's wrong . . . loosen the fabric more. Wait—try leaning it against the wall behind you. Mr. Clements, look right through here and tell me what you think. Would the flag be better with her holding it or as a background?"

Joe comes over and peers through the viewfinder. The image is upside down, and he doesn't really have an opinion. "Maybe holding it," he says. "I guess."

"I think you're right," Sweeney says. "You have a good eye, sir."

"Pick it up again," Joe tells her.

"Maybe just drape the stripes over her shoulder," Sweeney suggests, "if you would be so kind, Mr. Clements."

Joe does so, but carelessly. Embarrassed to be monkeying around with cloth like this, he walks back to his chair and picks up a copy of the *Mining Gazette*.

Checking the image again, the photographer mutters, "Mrs. Clements, move back, just a little. There! Right there . . . no. Not quite . . ." He glances at Joe, and so does Annie. Joe is already absorbed by the newspaper that hides them from his gaze. Making no noise with his footsteps, the photographer comes so close that Annie must lift her head and look over his shoulder to avoid his lips. He lifts the edge of the flag over her shoulder, adjusting the drape of the shiny silk on the woolly texture of her jacket. Nodding to himself, he says, "Good. Very nice contrast. One more little change."

Reaching out, he rearranges a few strands of her hair. Then, all business, he returns to his camera and declares for the room to hear, "There now! That's what I want. Joan of Arc, just back from the battle!"

She does not laugh aloud, but he likes what he sees: warm eyes, that lovely smile. The flash goes off and he declares, "That's for the papers!"

Blinking, she relaxes and starts to leave but he says, "No! Wait there. One more, for luck."

She squeezes her eyes shut and braces herself for another explosion of light while he goes through the rigmarole of sliding the light-proof shield over the exposed film and flipping the holder around for a second shot.

"Mother of God, but that flag is a monster!" he says conversationally. "How long do you think you can keep carrying it?"

Her face loses its serene sweetness. "Forever," she says, and the flash goes off again, just as a look of stubborn resolution appears.

"And that's the one for the history books," he murmurs.

September 1913

1

They are but beggars that can count their worth.
—Shakespeare, *Romeo and Juliet*

Twenty years of organizing, and Charlie Miller has never seen a strike like this one. The copper companies haven't give an inch, but a holiday atmosphere persists as the weather cools.

The company schools are attended only by the children of strike-breakers; after the morning parades, he notices union kids leaving town. Wearing thick-knit sweaters against the early chill, older boys head off on their own, carrying fishing poles and tin cans full of worms, or follow their fathers into the scrubby wasteland beyond the town to check traps or hunt ducks. Younger boys prospect along the railroad tracks and come home—filthy and grinning—with old flour bags filled with coal that's fallen by the wayside when a sloppy fireman tossed a shovelful toward the engine. Girls carrying buckets slog into the scrubby vegetation around town. Thimbleberries and blackberries have gone past. Raspberries are ripening now.

By noon, the sun has burned off the fog, and it's hard to believe that it was ever chilly. Sweating and shirtless in the warmth of September's afternoons, men will gut the fish and butcher the game for smoking while women boil glass jars in big enamel kettles and supervise the older girls in cooking up preserves for the winter.

It gets dark noticeably earlier in September, and the air goes crisp again as the sun goes down. Courting couples, who might only have exchanged glances at church once a week in ordinary times, now have

the freedom to attend union picnics and dances organized by Annie
Clements to keep morale high. Their evenings are often spent sitting side by side on porch stoops or taking long walks together. They
are, of course, relentlessly dogged by the giggling sisters and teasing
brothers who have been ordered to act as chaperones by their middle-
aged parents—who are, Charlie suspects, luxuriating in the sensation
of being well rested and unexpectedly eager to get the kids out of
the house for a little while. The men grouse that it will be a misery
to redevelop their calluses when they go back to work, but Charlie
overhears enough from the women who work in the food and clothing banks to know that they're happy. "And his hands are so soft now!"
is greeted with knowing laughter that becomes more raucous when
someone solemnly chants the union slogan with slightly different em-
phasis: "Eight hours to work and eight hours to sleep and eight hours
for *what we please!*"

Undoubtedly, a few wives are already counting out the months.
Soon more husbands will roll their eyes as they tell commiserating
friends, "The next one's coming in May." Or June. Or July. Yes, they
admit, it will be another mouth to feed, but the union is going to get
us an extra dollar a day, and that will make all the difference. Even the
more reluctant strikers have begun to believe that all this might turn
out well after all.

And now, this very morning, old Moishe Glass arrives in the union
office with a bottle of vodka and news. Tents are being folded and
equipment is being packed up over on the Armory grounds. The
Michigan Guard is being pulled out—some of it, at least. Some troops
will remain in case violence reoccurs. If not, they'll be going home
soon, too.

Jubilation erupts. Glasses are brought out. The vodka is poured.
Even the three kids Charlie thinks of as Mrs. Clements's ducklings are
allowed to join the toasts to Governor Ferris. He won't toady to James
MacNaughton much longer, union members declare, clinking glasses.
Soon, they tell themselves. Soon, all this will be settled.

They think the militia's retreat is the union's victory. Sitting behind a
desk piled high with finance reports from around the Copper Country,

Charlie Miller knows different and so does Moishe Glass, although they let the celebration in the union office go on for a little while. Nobody wants to be cast as the mustachioed villain, but in the face of Annie Clements's persistent, cheerful ignorance, it's often Charlie Miller's task to make the others understand what they're up against, and Moishe Glass is right beside him.

"MacNaughton isn't giving up," Charlie warns when the celebration dies down.

"Things gonna get worse now," Moishe affirms.

"A cloud around every silver lining," Annie Clements murmurs to Eva. She sits up straight. "Well, then. Out with it! What do you gentlemen have to darken our day?"

Moishe hands Annie a letter. On Calumet & Hecla stationery, it is carefully phrased, designed to cloak its threat with swaths of "in these difficult and challenging times" verbiage. Sobered, she hands it to Eva, and the boys read over her shoulder.

"That went to every businessman in town," Moishe says. "My place is safe. I'm just outside the city because MacNaughton didn't want a Jew store in Calumet. But most businesses? They lease land from the company."

"And they'll be evicted if they don't join the Citizens' Alliance," Charlie says, and Moishe nods. "Standard tactic. Completely predictable."

"What does that mean?" Eva asks. "What's the Citizens' Alliance?"

"It's an anti-union group that will toe MacNaughton's line," Charlie says. "Stop doing business with the union. Refuse credit to members. That kind of thing." Charlie shrugs and drops the next rock on them: "The landlord just gave the union notice. He wants us out of the building."

There are gasps. The kids look at one another, stricken. Even Annie blinks.

"Me, I gonna take my chances," Moishe Glass says. "I got good customers ain't miners. MacNaughton's cook—even she orders from me! Other big shots, too. I ain't giving up."

"Mr. Glass, you need to think of your own future," Miller tells him. The Glass Brothers General Store has let union families run tabs all summer. If the strike fails, he'll never get paid back.

Moishe's mouth turns down as his shoulders come up in a resigned shrug. "I come to America with nothing. So? Maybe I end up with nothing again. Or? Maybe union wins, and we all better off!"

Over in his corner chair, arms crossed, a faint sneer on his face, Joe Clements shakes his head and mutters, "Sucker."

"You know what I don't understand?" Kazimir Savicki says suddenly. "Why hasn't MacNaughton kicked all of us out of the company houses? The papers say the coal miners down in West Virginia got thrown out right away. They've been living in tents for months!"

To everyone's surprise, Jack Kivisto breaks his habitual silence to answer. "Strike fund money pays the rent. The cash goes right back to the company."

Looking at Annie, Joe says, "I told you so."

Charlie Miller sits back in his chair and decides it's time to share the full burden of knowledge. "You may as well learn it all," he says, tapping the account books he's been working on. "As of this morning, Local Fifteen has eighteen hundred and twenty-seven dollars left. I don't know how long the Federation can continue to prop us up. They're borrowing money from other unions now, trying to keep three strikes going. They might be able to send us another few grand, but barring a miracle, we'll be broke by the end of September."

"Well, then," Eva Savicki says stubbornly, "we're going to have to get ourselves a miracle."

Miller smiles at the girl, though there is no mirth left in his eyes when they shift to Annie Clements. She knows what he's thinking. He doesn't need to say it aloud, for her own husband already has. *I told you so.*

The truth is, while the strike has been more effective than Charlie Miller believed it could be, it has also gone on longer than Annie Clements expected. She thought a week or ten days would bring MacNaughton and the other mine operators to the table. It's been over two months now. In her weakest moments, she finds it difficult to ignore what Miller calls realism.

Still, to come so far and give up now? Unthinkable.

And she has reason to hope. Every morning after the strikers' parade, she sorts through the morning mail. Crumpled dollar bills and a few coins have begun to arrive, donations from children and housewives and workers in other towns around Michigan. The tally is rarely more than ten dollars a day and won't make much of a difference to the strikers, but it is a sign that people outside the Copper Country are paying attention to what's going on here.

They have support nearby as well. The ladies in Laurium have continued to employ strikers' wives and daughters to do laundry and cleaning; they occasionally slip a little extra into a rough and reddened hand, or leave a package of leftover food in the broom closet to be found and taken home without the knowledge of anyone's husband—union or management.

And the backyard gardens and the outlying fields are yielding produce now. There are beans, carrots, and beets to can and pickle. Onions to be hung from rafters. White potatoes, sweet potatoes, parsnips, squash. Cabbage and apples will come in soon, to be packed up with straw down in cellar storage rooms.

An awful thought occurs to Annie: maybe MacNaughton is simply waiting to evict everyone until just before the gardens' best crops are harvested, right before winter sets in. In ordinary times, in households where nothing is ever wasted, they need all the food they can grow or gather in the summer to stretch wages out and keep the family fed in the winter when store-bought food is far too expensive for the miners' wives to buy. And these are not ordinary times . . .

And we are no ordinary people, she tells herself firmly. We are going to see this through, and we are going to win.

Lips compressed, back straight, she finishes opening the morning mail, counts out the bills and the little piles of change, and brings the money with her to Charlie Miller's desk. Head high, she waits for him to sigh and look up from his account books.

"Fifteen donations," she declares with determined cheer. "Eleven dollars and thirty-eight cents!"

She turns on her heel and goes back to her desk, just as Mike Sweeney comes pounding up the staircase.

"Ladies and gentlemen," he announces, spreading a stack of newspapers on Annie's desk, "the women's parade is news around the country."

Eva drops a pile of children's trousers and shrieks when she sees the headline of the article on the top of the stack. "'Anna Clements, an American Joan of Arc!'" she reads. "'With the American flag wrapped around her, Mrs. Clements declared, '"If this flag does not shield me, then let it be my shroud!"'"

"I *never* said that!" Annie cries. "Mr. Sweeney, did you . . . ?"

"Of course! That, madam, is my job!" He leans over and points out a paragraph. "Look! This one calls you Lady Liberty."

Eva squeals again. "Listen to this! 'One miner's wife is worth a thousand MacNaughtons. When facing cavalrymen with sabers, the woman in white refused to back down and won the day.'"

Joe stands.

Everyone falls silent.

"I need a drink," he says, starting toward the staircase.

"I'll have supper for you at six," Annie calls. "Joe? Did you hear me?"

There's no response, apart from the slamming of the door downstairs. For a time it is as though Joe Clements has taken all the air in the office with him.

"It's hard on him," Charlie Miller says. Annie opens her mouth, about to defend herself, but Miller continues: "It's not just him, Mrs. Clements. It's hard on all the men. Sitting around. Waiting."

It's only then that Mike Sweeney remembers his other errand. Digging into his pocket, he pulls out the special delivery letter the mailman handed him on his way up the stairs to the office. "This just came," he tells Charlie.

Bracing himself for more bad news, Miller slits the envelope and unfolds the letter. It is short, and astonishing. He falls back against his chair and murmurs, "I'll be damned."

Annie comes to his side and he looks up at her, mouth open, offering up the letter. She gasps, her face a mixture of amazement and vindication.

"What?" Eva demands. "Annie, what is it?"

"The Federation is wiring us more money!"

The room erupts: Kazimir and Eva Savicki hugging, Jack Kivisto smiling, Sweeney doing a little jig, Moishe Glass holding his palms upward toward heaven. Charlie Miller can hardly move. "They said they couldn't do anything! I've been begging them for months—"

"It's the pictures!" Sweeney cries. "I knew that parade would work! How much are they sending?"

"A thousand dollars," Annie says, awestruck.

Miller says, "Divided among seven thousand union men still on strike."

"It's something," Annie insists stubbornly. "It'll buy us a few more days . . ."

"Hours," Miller says, every bit as stubbornly.

"Damn you, Charlie!" Sweeney cries. "Why do you always—"

"Because *somebody* in this town has to be realistic!"

"Oh, for the love of God! Just let the happiness live for a moment before you strangle it in the cradle!"

"Every day that passes makes us weaker and the operators stronger!"

Eva bursts into tears. Kaz and Jack glare at Charlie.

"Gentlemen!" Annie Clements shouts, holding the sobbing girl in her arms. "Mr. Miller, please!"

He throws up his hands and walks to the office window, getting his anger under control. She means well. All the women do. The Auxiliary has done wonders to keep up morale and ease the burden on their men, but they just don't understand what's happening among the miners.

No matter what Mike Sweeney thinks—Charlie *has* tried to let their hope persist. They don't realize how many men have defected. Some say they're going to Detroit, to make automobiles. Some have quietly gone back to work in the mines, despite the contempt and resistance of relatives and neighbors, and they've sent a delegation to MacNaughton, offering to form a union independent of the Western Federation of Miners. They even promised they wouldn't even ask for formal recognition if the CEO was willing to negotiate wages and working conditions with them.

Of course, MacNaughton turned them down. He knows what Charlie Miller has known from the start. When men like Joe Clements sit and wait for other people to decide their fate, it eats at them. It grinds them down in a way the labor itself doesn't. All MacNaughton has to do is wait.

2

Art thou a man?
—Shakespeare, *Romeo and Juliet*

She's queen of the May, Joe Clements is thinking as he stalks toward the nearest saloon. She writes handbills. She runs a clothing drive. She plans a goddamn picnic. She marches down a street. And now she's Joan of Arc. She's worth a thousand MacNaughtons! Christ.

I've got a meeting, she says. I have to get to the union office, she says. What about me? he fumes. Everybody thinks she works so hard. She hasn't got any idea what hard work is. I'd like to see her last one day in a mine. One goddamn day.

You get up, you dress, you eat, you walk to the change house. You clock in and climb down flight after flight of slippery cut-stone stairs before a hike through miles of tunnels—just to start the day's work. It's cold underground. It's wet. It smells of rock. Beyond that dim little funnel of light from your headlamp, there's a hellish nothing, and Christ, the noise! After a few weeks, you're half-deaf from the pounding of the drills. So you listen hard all the time to the crunch and scrape of shoveling, the squeal of tram wheels grating on rusty rails, because a few seconds can make all the difference when a wall starts to come down. And then there's the dynamite. When you hear the warning call, you hustle half a mile away and wait for the muffled *WHUMP* of the explosion. A rush of air makes your ears pop, but you don't move, not yet. You wait again, listening again. Listening to the creak of long-dead trees trying to hold up the world, or the groan of rock settling, or the crack of a support pillar giving way, or the rumble of a stope sliding. Or the scream of a man being crushed.

A good day in the mine is a day when nobody gets killed or crippled. Or if somebody does, at least it's not you. At the end of a shift, if you're lucky—still alive, still on your feet—you trudge back through tunnels that seem a lot longer than they did thirteen hours ago, and you climb back up those cut-stone stairs on rubbery legs. Everything hurts. Shoulders, arms, back—everything is cramped and aching. Dislocating a finger is so ordinary, you just grit your teeth and yank it back where it belongs. Without even knowing it, you've been scared all day and you're tired, tired, tired. Filthy, but almost too tired to clean up. Hungry, but almost too tired to eat.

When you walk in the door, maybe you glance at a crippled-up father, if he's still alive. Maybe he meets your eye and maybe there's a nod, for fathers harden sons to this life, and only another miner can really understand. It's a Christ-awful way to live, and you're proud of that, even when you fall into bed knowing that you'll get up and do it all again the next day, and the next, and the next, and the next. . . . You've made your peace with it. Because that's what a real man does. And you want some goddamn respect for it! Is that too much to ask?

He shoves open the door to the Truro Pub, and a silence settles as everyone turns to look at him.

"Hey, Joe," the boldest barfly says. "I saw your wife in the papers!"

"You must be real proud, eh?" someone else says.

The laughter is general and mocking.

Joe Clements sits at the bar and taps the walnut surface. "*Šlivovitz.*"

"I've got vodka," the bartender tells him.

The big man nods, and Owen Lloyd pours him the first of many shots, while hoping for the best.

The conversation returns to its usual rumbling buzz, but Owen is more alert to his saloon's clientele than usual. He is the fourth of his family to own the Truro Pub in Calumet, an establishment passed down from Lloyd to Lloyd since 1863. That was when word of the glorious

Michigan copper deposits reached destitute villages above Cornwall's played-out mines. That was when his great-grandparents immigrated to the Upper Peninsula with little more than this nugget of familial wisdom: the only way to make money in a mining camp is to mine the miners.

In Calumet, as in the old country, Lloyds have slaked the thirst of generations of Cornish miners whose ancient ancestors once prized flint from the ground with picks made from deer antlers. As for copper, Cornishmen have worked it since Merlin's beard was short, and they've done it in conditions none of these soft-handed immigrant bastards could stand for more than half a shift. So they have no truck with the union that's idling the pits. "Their wives made 'em do it" is the sneering observation, always followed by grunted agreement: "Women! Meddlin' in men's affairs . . ." And who's the worst of the wives? Annie Clements. That's what every man of them will tell you.

Even if Big Annie were the sweetest little lady that a man could go home to, Joe Clements has no business here in the Truro Pub, and that's what worries Owen Lloyd. In Calumet, Slavs drink with Slavs. Finns drink with Finns. Eye-tyes drink with Eye-tyes. Each to his own. Those are the rules of the city, and always have been, until the union began dividing the town in a new way. Most of Calumet's Cornishmen are loyal to the company, but there are others—old stock, but ones who'd not say no to another dollar if it were to come their way. They drink here, too, and it makes for a bad mix. Too many men spending the long, idle days together. Bored. Drunk. Looking for trouble.

And some of those fools have decided that Joe Clements might be fun to bullyrag.

Saloonkeepers talk, and Clements has a reputation. A man who fills a doorway side to side and top to bottom, he has an immense capacity for drink. He's good for a fight under the best of circumstances, and in Owen Lloyd's professional opinion, Big Joe Clements is going to tolerate perhaps one more remark before he takes an opportunity to flatten someone.

"Last one's on the house, Joe," Owen says quietly, shoving a shot glass across the bar.

That's when one of the Clementses' dago boarders peers through the window. The little wop has sense enough to hesitate before coming inside a Cornish pub. When he finally screws up his courage and approaches Joe, he pulls his cloth cap off respectfully and the room falls silent in gleeful anticipation.

"Meester Clemens, sir, Mees Clemens she say you supper ready."

Joe lifts the glass and tosses the slug back without a shudder before turning ever so slowly toward the wop. "I want you and your brothers out of my house by Friday," he says. "And I want you out of my sight *now*."

The little dago bobs his head and backs away. Joe watches him leave and taps the shot glass. "Another."

"Hey, Clements," someone calls, "your food's getting cold."

"Not to mention your wife!"

Owen groans, "No, no, no . . ."

"Hey, Joe! Better hurry. That photographer fella'll eat your dinner!"

"Take it outside!" Owen pleads, but it's too late.

The first idiot goes down, and then another in no more than the time it takes Owen Lloyd to grab the cricket bat he keeps behind the bar for occasions just such as this.

Loretta Devlin has set herself a mission. It has taken her a long time to screw her courage up to the sticking place, but today is the day she will leave the MacNaughton mansion. Today is the day she'll make her way to Big Annie Clements, for Loretta has a story to tell about what a nameless maid can hear when a heedless boss doesn't deign to notice her and today, by God, is the day she will tell it.

The master has gone down to Houghton for a meeting with the other mine bosses. He won't be back until late tonight. The cook goes out shopping for groceries every morning. The butler has bought Loretta's phony story about going to the pharmacy for headache powder. "Finish the ironing first," he said. All you have to do is hint that a malady is some sort of woman trouble. Men will shudder and wave you away.

She has timed her escape: the cook will be back in forty-five minutes. Forty-five minutes! Loretta thinks with a snort, annoyed that she's keeping track of time like MacNaughton: in minutes, not hours or days, like a normal person. Folding laundry by the back window, she watches for the moment when the strikers' parade rounds the corner, ready to make her dash. Only wouldn't you know it, the tall woman is missing and it takes three others to hold that giant flag by its upper edge, off its pole but spanning half the street.

"Shite, shite, shite," she mutters.

She spots a friendly-looking girl she's seen at Mass and tells herself, Now or never. Thumping a neatly folded sheet onto the ironed linen, she throws a coat on over the black-and-white uniform MacNaughton makes her wear, plunks a felt hat over her braided ginger hair, and eases into the parade.

"Seen you at church," she tells the other girl by way of introduction. "Where's herself, then?"

The girl makes a face. "Did you hear about the brawl at Truro's?"

"Sure, didn't everyone?"

"Well, that was Mr. Clements. Annie's husband. She hasn't been marching since. She's probably home nursing him. That's what I hope, anyway. I'm Eva. Eva Savicki."

"Loretta. Loretta Devlin."

They march along side by side for a block. Fish or cut bait, Loretta thinks. "Look, I work for Old Man MacNaughton, and he's a hard, cold bastard if ever I met one. I've got something might be useful to them as fights him. Can you take me to someone? It's gotta be quick. I can't be gone very long."

They stop, taking each other's measure as the marchers split around them like a stream around rocks.

"What do you know?" Eva asks.

"Plenty," Loretta says, and when she's done telling it, Eva nods.

"You're right," she says. "Mr. Miller and the others should hear this."

The union office is a shambles. Two boys, both a little older than Eva and Loretta, are packing up boxes of papers. Furniture is shoved to one side of the room, though the walls are still papered with posters and newspaper clippings with photos of Annie Clements.

"The landlord threw the union out, so we're moving the office," Eva explains. "Moishe Glass offered us part of his storeroom. It's even more crowded than this, and Mr. Miller is afraid Sheriff Cruse will find an excuse to wreck the store or set fire to it or something, but we don't have a choice. Mr. Miller? This is Loretta Devlin. She works for Mac-Naughton."

Charlie, too, listens to the girl's story, and she has only just finished when they hear footsteps on the stairway. Everyone goes quiet, expecting a direct attack on the union's officers. The two boys grab hammers and stand, ready to fight whoever appears. Loretta shrinks into a corner, thinking, Oh, Lord, I'm for it now! But, it's Annie Clements who appears at the door, without Joe in tow.

"Oh, Annie," Eva cries softly, and Loretta tsks sympathetically when she sees the swollen jaw and the blackened eye, though they both know it's not nice to notice a wife's bruises.

"Good morning," Annie murmurs around a fat lip. She hangs up her hat and coat, sitting at her desk to sort through the pile of mail that's accumulated in her absence. She looks up only when Charlie Miller comes over with a new girl. Gorgeous red hair, pert snub nose, and a charming freckled face. Kaz's age or thereabouts, which has not gone unnoticed by that young man.

"Mrs. Clements, this is Loretta Devlin," Charlie says softly. "Loretta is a maid who works in James MacNaughton's house."

"And he is a hard, cold bastard if I ever met one," Loretta's story starts again. Annie Clements is now the third person she's told it to, and Loretta has been working on the recitation in resentful silence for months. "I've been a maid for that family a whole year now, and he has never even learned my name. His wife and daughters are no better. They all just call me Bridget, like all Irish maids are the same—"

"Tell her what you told me, Miss Devlin," Miller says. "About the union."

"Well, now, y'see, I hear things," Loretta confides. "There's dinners for the big bugs, and I serve, and nobody notices me, but I listen."

Some of it, they knew already. Enough company men have stayed on or gone back to work to keep the pumps going on the lower levels and prevent damage to the equipment. Governor Ferris is pulling out the rest of the Michigan guardsmen. The company will be bringing in men from a private security firm that advertises itself as "staffed by the very finest strikebreakers from Chicago and New York."

"But Mr. MacNaughton, he doesn't think they'll need to bust too many heads," Loretta Devlin says now. "Last night, he had all the other mine operators to the house for a fancy dinner party, and I heard him tell them—all full of himself he was—he says, 'Time is on our side. The longer the strike goes on, the more pressure there is for the miners to go back to work.'"

"Tell her the rest," Miller says. "His *exact words*."

"He told them others, 'The union has eighteen hundred and twenty-seven dollars left in the strike fund.' He said, 'It'll take a miracle for the union to get past the end of September.'"

Annie's mouth drops open. She looks at Charlie and asks Loretta Devlin, "He said that? Those were his exact words?"

"Yes, ma'am," Loretta confirms, though she doesn't know why this news has had such a remarkable effect on her listeners. She herself thought the part about the governor was the most interesting gossip she had on offer. "Now, begging your pardon, I should be getting back to the house before that bitch of a cook marks me gone."

"Kaz?" Annie calls. "Walk Miss Devlin home. It's not safe on the streets anymore."

Eva giggles. "I'll come, too, Loretta. My brother is a terrible flirt. You'll need a chaperone! C'mon, Jack! We need to watch out for Miss Devlin!"

Kaz socks his sister in the arm for her trouble, but he grabs his coat and hat, as do Eva and Jack, and the four of them clatter down the staircase.

Miller pulls up a chair across from Annie, his face impassive, waiting for her to say what they're both thinking.

"The exact amount," she whispers. "How could MacNaughton know the exact amount we had left . . ."

Miller lets her work it out.

"Somebody told him," Annie says. "Somebody from this office."

He waits.

"Who was here when you said that?" she asks. Still he waits, and she begins to tick off the names. "You, me, the kids. Moishe . . . not him, surely!"

"Well, he's been taking a lot of chances and doesn't seem too worried about the store getting burned out."

She shakes her head. "I won't believe that. It has to be somebody else. . . . Who would do such a thing? Not Michael! Was he even in the office when you said that?"

"No. I don't think so."

Charlie Miller is not shocked by her bruises. Men beat women. It's the way of the world. Big Annie can defend herself better than most, and he wonders if she's put Joe into the hospital with a frying pan to the head. Serves the bastard right if she did, he thinks, and it is with a certain satisfaction that he sees the penny drop.

Battered face in her hands, she slumps over her desk. "Joe was there," she says, looking up. "And he . . . *Bože moi*, what if it was Joe."

3

Under love's heavy burden do I sink.
—Shakespeare, *Romeo and Juliet*

Sisu keeps his mother silent, but every morning, Jaak Kivisto can hear what she doesn't say. We got no money. You ain't down in the mine. We gonna lose the house. Company man gonna come throw us out.

"Don't worry about the rent," he tells her when he sees that look on her face this morning. "I'm paying."

"How, Jaaki? You stealin'?"

She always thinks the worst. He makes a face: Don't be stupid.

Then how? her worried eyes ask.

"The union," he tells her.

That doesn't help. She was afraid of the union even before the strike. She knows that everybody in town is angry, but she doesn't understand why, though she's aware that her own widowhood is somehow part of the problem. People say things when she goes out, though she doesn't understand the remarks. She has always kept to herself. Now she won't go outside at all if she can help it, and she keeps the smaller children in as much as she can. She knows that Jaak goes away every morning, but not to the mines. Sometimes he brings home a bundle of food. Sometimes he takes his younger brothers and little sister out, and when they come back, they're wearing somebody else's clothes. She asks questions, and when he can't or won't explain it, she keeps asking and he yells at her and she cries.

Jack understands all that, but he is fifteen. The effort of producing a single sentence in any language can feel overwhelming. Her English is bad, his Finnish isn't good. Explaining things to her is just too much.

Besides, it's his load to carry, and her worry annoys him almost beyond bearing. She has to trust him. She and the younger kids depend on him. He's all they have. And he hates that. So he flicks her concerns away with a wave of his hand. You wouldn't understand, that wave says. You don't understand anything.

He himself sees things more clearly than anyone he knows.

Eva talks like being a miner will be fine if the pay is better and the hours are shorter—that's because she doesn't know anything. None of the women do. He was only underground a couple of weeks before the strike, but that's two weeks more than any girl. With every jolt of the shovel into the ore, with every swing of it heaving rock into the tram, Jaak Kivisto felt the awful weight of his family's future on his bony, pimply shoulders. Every time he wiped away the sweat that blurred his vision, he saw the dark snarl of tunnels and drifts that would lead him nowhere. If he stayed down there, he would become just like the men around him: blind, stupid mules whose sense of duty and responsibility keeps them in Calumet, like their blind, stupid fathers.

So he didn't eat with the others. Would not talk to them. Like his father before him, he kept his distance from the miners who tried to befriend him. Especially if they were union.

When it came, the strike was as welcome to him as it was to the union men, just for different reasons. Like them, he laid down his tools and climbed back out of the guts of the earth, and blinked at the sunshine. He shared this much with them: he could sense change coming. This was an ending. This was a beginning. There was a future where everything would be different.

Every morning for months now, he has gone to the parades. He's been welcomed by men whose pace he matches, whose voices he joins as they began to chant, "Union! Union! Union!" He stamps his feet with them, and keeps their cadence, only the words he hears in his mind are those he thought, hour after hour, when he was underground: *Not me. Not me. Not me.*

Every morning, he wishes that his mother would stop talking to him, stop looking at him with her big worried eyes. He wishes the union men in the parades would ignore him. He just wants to be left alone. He doesn't want any friends. And he certainly doesn't want a girlfriend.

He groans when he opens the door to leave and sees Eva Savicki out there on the sidewalk. Waiting for him. All prettied up. Without even her brother, Kaz, to glower at her and get in between.

Jaak grabs his cap and jacket, hoping to be gone before his mother can notice the girl, but it's too late.

"Who she is?" his mother asks, smiling timidly.

"Nobody."

"Nice girl? She look nice."

"Jesus!" he cries. "Just . . . just leave me *alone!*"

Scowling, Jack pulls the door closed behind himself and clumps down five tall stairs to the summertime street level. "I told you not to wait where my mother can see you."

"I know," Eva says quickly, "and I'm sorry, but Kaz went in early this morning to help Annie hand out the new banners. So he told me to wait right here. So you could walk with me. Because he doesn't want me to walk to the office alone. Because of all the strangers around."

Kaz thinks Jack doesn't want his mother to see them together because Mr. Kivisto was against the union, so probably Mrs. Kivisto is, too. Or maybe Jack's afraid his mother won't like Eva because she's Polish. And Catholic.

But Mrs. Kivisto is looking out from behind the curtain in the front room, and she's smiling a little. So Eva smiles back and they exchange a little wave. So that must mean she doesn't mind too much that her son is seeing Eva. And anyway, Eva really doesn't have a choice, does she? Because Kaz told her to wait in front of the Kivistos' place and let Jack walk her to work. So, it's not being too forward, right? Because her brother told her to. And that must mean Kaz is warming up to Jack a little, too.

"I don't know why Kaz doesn't trust Jack," Eva told Annie once. "Jack is a nice boy! He's very polite with me, and he's at the union hall every day to pitch in. All Kaz says is 'I just have a feeling about him.'" Eva rolled her eyes. "I *know* Jack likes me, Annie! I can tell! But he's so shy, and Kaz watches us like a hawk!"

"He's your brother!" Annie pointed out. "Brothers are supposed to look out for their sisters."

That's more true now than ever. The Michigan militiamen are mostly decent, but they're being sent home, and now knots of hard-looking men stand on street corners, chewing toothpicks and smoking cigars. Sheriff Cruse has sworn them in and handed out cheap tin badges, so now they're deputies, though as Michael Sweeney said, "These gentlemen don't appear to be as well schooled in the nuances of constitutional law as our Major Van Den Broek." The new men work for Waddell-Mahon, which calls itself a private security company but really just rents out thugs from New York and Chicago to companies like Calumet & Hecla. They carry guns and billy clubs, and say awful things to women and girls who try to pass them on the sidewalks. When Annie leads the morning parades, they call her "whore" and "bitch," and another word that Eva had never heard before but is so terrible that Kaz wouldn't tell her what it meant when she asked, and made her promise she would never say it again.

Eva stays quiet for two blocks before she breaks the silence. "Brrrr," she says, shivering. "Getting cold! Do you like my new coat? I got it from the clothing bank." She steps out in front of Jack, twirling once to show him, then waiting for him to say something before she gets out of his way.

"It's good, I guess."

"I'm glad you like it! Did those trousers I picked out for your brothers fit?"

"Yeah," he says, and after a time, he adds, "The dress for Pria did, too."

Progress, she thinks. "You could bring your mother in sometime, too. There are some dresses and some . . . other things . . . that a nice lady in Laurium donated. Like this coat. And I think your mother might enjoy the Auxiliary meetings. She must be lonely at home all by herself. I could introduce her around."

Jack grunts and waves his hand in front of his face to signal that she's talking too much. He's usually grumpy in the morning. Kaz and Uncle Tomek are both snarly when they wake up, so she tries not to talk right away, but it's hard. Eva herself loves the mornings. "Look at the colors in that sky! I can't decide if I like sunrise or sunset best."

There's no response. Still, when she accidentally stumbles over a place where the pavement is uneven, Jack catches her by the arm and it definitely seems like maybe he holds on a little longer than he really has to, though she doesn't try to hold his hand or anything after that. Because that would definitely be too forward.

"Thank you!" she says. "I'm so clumsy in these new shoes! They're a little too big, I think. I might exchange them when we get to the office. I think the union should keep the clothing exchange going after the strike, don't you? It's fun! You just bring something in and swap it for something new. Well . . . something that's new to you, anyway. Still, it makes a nice change and saves a lot of money. I like the food bank, too. Instead of eating the same thing day after day, you can try new things."

There's another small noise of acknowledgment. He's shy, she tells herself again, but he also ate a whole plateful of her pierogies at the last union supper and even danced with her once.

"Kaz and I are moving out of my uncle's house. He's getting married again, and his new wife doesn't want us around. We're going to move in with Annie! Because those nice Italian boys have moved out now. Kaz and I can help Annie with her chores and things. I'll do her housework and Kaz will take care of the outside, so she can do more for the union, and Mr. Clements won't get mad. I'm a little scared of Mr. Clements," she admits. "Annie says if he gets drunk and she's not there, we should go next door and stay with the Carettos. They're really nice and the children are so beautiful. Those big dark eyes! I'm learning to cook some new things, like macaroni with cheese. Do you like Italian food?"

Jack shrugs a kind of assent, so she burbles on until they reach the corner where the day's parade is forming up.

"I'll see you after," Eva calls, waving cheerily as they split up and take their places among the marchers.

He nods again and feels the blood rise in his face when an older man nudges him in the ribs and says, "Lucky fella! That Eva—she's a good'un."

4

This bud of love . . . may prove a beauteous flower.
—Shakespeare, *Romeo and Juliet*

Drums begin the cadence. The marchers begin to move, shuffling at first, then striding, until the parade stretches out behind the huge flag that Annie Clements carries: red and white and blue, flapping in a stiff breeze that pushes Lake Superior's chill across the peninsula. With more and more strikebreakers showing up in town, the Women's Auxiliary and their children now march in the middle of the column, with union men forming a protective shield all around them.

Eva always marches beside Annie, despite the danger. Jack Kivisto is somewhere behind them with the men. If this is a courtship, Annie thinks, it's an odd one. The boy barely speaks, and yet, after every parade, he walks Eva to the church and waits in the baptistery while she goes inside to pray for whatever it is she prays for each morning. A wedding most likely.

Annie herself has become uneasy about the couple. It's not a good match. Eva's full of life and enthusiasm. Jack is too silent, too broody. Annie fears they'll come to hate each other before their first anniversary. Shifting the weight of the enormous flag in its leather holster and bracing it against the freshening breeze, she lets her mind go silent for a moment and the questions come to her unbidden.

Did I ever really love Joe? Did I change? Did he?

Things might have been different if she could have given him children. She might not have had so much time for the union. He might have had the kind of wife he expected.

She glances at Eva. Maybe I should say something, Annie thinks. What you want when you're so young . . . it changes. I was just like you when I was fourteen. I wanted my life to start. You change when you're older. You want different things. You meet other people.

Of course, nobody wants to hear that when they're young and in love. . . . And infatuations can burn out as quickly as they flare up.

Maybe, Annie thinks, this will take care of itself. And so, she holds her peace.

Father Albin Horvat is also concerned about young Eva Savicki. He has known her since she was a babe in arms. He married her parents and baptized their six children and buried four of them. He gave First Communion to Kazimir and Eva, and later on said the Requiem for their parents when Kazimir and Eva were orphaned.

Kaz was an altar boy when he was small; since then, he has fallen away somewhat. Of course, he was sad after his father was killed—something children in Calumet almost expect—but he remains bitter about his mother's death. Kazimir blames God for taking her while James MacNaughton lives on in luxury. Eva, by contrast, has been consistently devout and still attends Mass on Sundays and feast days. Lately she's also been showing up for Mass every morning after the parade. Before she leaves, she lights a candle, kneels again, and prays and prays and prays, hands clasped, eyes tight shut, her chestnut hair often tumbling sideways a bit, for she has only recently begun putting it up into a grown woman's pompadour.

Watching unobserved from the sacristy, Albin Horvat wonders if perhaps the girl has a vocation to the religious life. Except . . . There is always a blond boy waiting for her in the back of St. Joseph's. A Finn by the looks of him. Protestant, no doubt. Is Eva trying to discourage his devotion by demonstrating to him the sincerity of her intent to become a bride of Christ? Or is she trying to convert the boy so they can marry in the Church? She's all alone, apart from her brother. Maybe that's why the girl is in such a hurry to grow up. She wants a family again.

"Father?"

The unexpected voice behind the priest makes him jump. "Kazimir! You startled me!"

"Sorry, Father. I just . . ." The boy lifts his chin toward his sister. "I think you should know something. About Eva."

The blond boy, Horvat thinks, expecting to be told of the need for a hurried wedding.

Kazimir says, "She's praying for a miracle."

The priest is not relieved by that. This sort of thing is always dangerous territory for the faithful. "A miracle," he repeats neutrally.

"Yes, Father. She thinks Saint Catherine will help because that's the saint who talked to Joan of Arc."

"And . . . what sort of miracle does Eva pray for? Do you know?"

"She wants three miracles, really, but I know only one of them. The union is being thrown out of the office. MacNaughton made the landlord throw us out. Mr. Glass is letting us put our boxes in his storeroom, but it's not big enough for the desks. And there's nowhere to put the food bank and to do the clothing collections or to paint banners for the parades, and we can't do that stuff at home because company houses are all too small anyway, and everybody's afraid MacNaughton's spies will find out and get them evicted. So Eva's praying that the landlord will change his mind or something. But God helps those who help themselves, right? That's what it says in the Gospels, doesn't it?"

"Well," Albin Horvat says kindly, "I believe that was something Ben Franklin said . . ."

Kaz shrugs: It's all the same to me. "Anyway, that's why I decided to talk to you instead of Saint Catherine. My sister can pray for the other miracles, but I think you can do this one."

The priest listens silently to Kazimir Savicki's plan, although he's halfway there before Kaz has finished. No need to bother Saint Catherine with this, he thinks.

He even knows what he will say when Pharaoh's heart is hardened.

On September 29, with one day left on the union's lease, the strikers' parade does not circle the city of Calumet. Instead, union members and their families converge by the hundreds on the street outside the office. Box after box is handed from Charlie Miller to Michael Sweeney to Kazimir Savicki to Jack Kivisto, moving down the staircase, in a kind of bucket brigade. Out on the street, strikers carry the boxes through town to St. Joseph's Roman Catholic Church, where they are greeted by Father Albin Horvat and a beaming Eva Savicki. Then it's through the carved oaken doors and downstairs to the parish hall, where the Women's Auxiliary awaits.

There is more space in this big rectangular room than the union has ever had before, and the ladies mean to do things properly this time. The big wooden desks and chairs were hauled down the street the night before; those were placed at the near end of the hall, close to the doors, so they didn't have to be lugged any farther than necessary. Tall metal filing cabinets are already in place. Long tables on folding legs—meant for parish weddings and baptisms and first communions and funerals—await. Food donations will go on the tables nearest the parish kitchen, at the far end of the room. Clothing will be along the sides. Down the center aisle, another set of tables will soon serve as a staging area where donations can be unpacked and sorted for distribution. For now those tables are left clear.

It's close to sundown when the last carton has been delivered, its contents unpacked and deployed. Only then are those central tables put to work as the women begin ferrying baked beans and piles of pasties and jars of pickles and dozens of fruit pies from the kitchen.

The room is noisy with shreds of song, and shouts, and raucous laughter, but when Father Horvat steps to the center of the hall and raises his hands, quiet gradually settles in anticipation of a prayer of thanksgiving after the meal.

Having duly delivered it, the priest once again raises his hands for attention and asks, "Are there any Baptists or Methodists here?"

Already the Catholics are grinning, but the Protestants look around, not sure what to make of this.

"No Dutch Reformed either?" Horvat asks. "Mormons? Mohammedans?"

He waits a moment, brows raised, as though he really expected an answer.

"No? Well, then! Mr. Glass?" he calls, looking toward the doorway. "I believe your grandsons can bring in *my* delivery now."

Grinning, the Glass boys troop into the parish hall, each carrying a heavy crate, and the laughter starts when bottles are heard rattling inside. Growlers of beer and bottles of wine join jugs of homemade vodka and *šlivovitz* that have already begun to appear from under a pile of children's outgrown coats. An accordion comes out. A fiddle. A *tamburica*. Tables are shoved to the periphery, and to grinning anticipation, Joe Clements steps to the center of the room, for everyone in Calumet knows that this is how Joe Clements wooed young Anna Klobuchar, and they all look back on those days fondly.

The space around him empties. The music begins. The crowd chants, "Annie! Annie! Annie!" Wiping her hands on a dishrag, she comes to the kitchen doorway, her apron spattered, strands of hair loosened around her face. She shakes her head, blushing, smiling, eyes on the floor, while neighbors and friends clap to the stately rhythm of the music, calling, "Go on, Annie! Dance with him!"

Annie pulls her apron off, lifts her head, and straightens her back, waiting in the kitchen doorway for Joe to make the first move as is his right. Unsmiling, dignified, regal, he puts one hand behind his back and extends the other toward her in what is both a command and an invitation. With a deep breath, she meets his eyes and walks forward in time with the music, joining him, placing her hand in his. For a moment, they both stand still. And then the dance begins.

It is a sort of waltz, stately and solemn, with increasingly complex figures as the two dancers step apart and together, first right, then left, retreat and approach: a pantomime of feminine reluctance and masculine insistence.

At the priest's side, Michael Sweeney watches the pair of them, his face unreadable. "This is a *štajeriš*," Father Horvat tells him, as though it were the dance that has caught Sweeney's interest, and not the couple themselves. "The first dance at a Slovene wedding. The bride is young and inexperienced," the priest explains as Annie backs away and Joe stamps ceremonially. "The groom must teach her, you see."

Annie returns and Joe takes both her hands, now lifting them high above their heads. As tall as Annie is, she passes easily beneath the arch their arms make, twisting and turning, but no longer breaking contact, coming closer, lingering a moment longer each time in Joe's protective, proprietary, increasingly erotic embrace.

The rhythm picks up. A circle of men forms around the couple, and a circle of women around them. As they turn and turn, Annie's gaze sweeps past the Irishman, unfocused, vague, while Joe's hard eyes return again and again to the photographer.

"You see?" Horvat says gently. "How the community supports the couple?"

"No escape," Mike Sweeney murmurs. "What God hath joined together . . ."

"Let no man put asunder," the priest confirms. "Annie means a great deal to this town," he continues, "and she is Joe's wife."

The *štajeriš* gives way to a Finnish *humppa* and then to a Polish polka. For a time, the priest simply rests a benign gaze on the celebration, which is getting louder by the minute, but he and Michael Sweeney do notice when Joe gets Annie's coat and the couple leaves without farewells: as a shy bride and an eager groom might sneak away from a wedding party.

Carrying a beer, Charlie Miller makes his way to Sweeney and the priest, standing at the edge of the twirling, stamping crowd. After the three unattached men clink glasses, Miller says, "I'm sure that liquor wasn't paid for by the union, because we're dead broke."

"And I certainly hope it didn't come out of the poor box," Sweeney says piously.

"My sister is a lovely soul," the priest replies serenely. "Very pretty, too, if I say so myself. A few years back, she caught the eye of a rich man . . ."

There are only two likely outcomes from such a revelation, and Miller takes the more optimistic guess. "She married well."

"Define 'well,'" Mike murmurs.

Horvat grunts. "My brother-in-law is a very successful businessman. A decent person in his own way, but to tell the truth," the priest confides, "I never really liked him."

"And it is harder for a rich man to get into heaven . . ." Miller suggests.

"Yes. So my sister makes sure that their prosperity is shared with the less fortunate."

Mike Sweeney nearly drains his glass before he can make his face merry. "I imagine your brother-in-law would be dismayed by the way you've spent his wife's donation."

"From what I hear," Horvat says lightly, "even the happiest of couples have secrets from each other."

"And the unhappy ones?" Mike asks then.

"Nothing stays secret forever."

Charlie Miller clears his throat and changes the subject. "Father, you know MacNaughton will come after you for taking the union in."

"Oh, yes," Horvat replies serenely. "A lawyer visited me at the rectory this afternoon. He informed me that union activities are not an approved use of church property."

"And you said?"

"I thanked him for his interest in St. Joseph's charitable work and pointed out that many are suffering in these unusual times. The parish is now sponsoring a food pantry and a clothing bank—for the poor and the needy, no matter who they may be. A number of parishioners have volunteered to assist me. Certainly there is nothing wrong with that?"

"Nicely done, Father." Sweeney holds up his glass again, and the priest meets it with his own.

"How did the lawyer take it?" Miller asks.

"There was a certain amount of sputtering. He threatened to go to the bishop about it."

Sweeney laughs. Miller frowns his confusion. He is not a Catholic.

"Mr. Miller, I'm a Jesuit," Horvat explains. "That means I don't answer to the bishop."

"Did you give that lawyer the pope's address?" Mike Sweeney asks.

The priest takes another sip of beer. "And I invited him to make a donation to the poor box on his way out the door."

*   *   *

Overnight, the exuberance of the celebration dissolves in a steady, chilly rain. Fewer than half the usual number of marchers assemble at St. Joseph's on the last day of September.

Understandable, Annie thinks. It's only to be expected that so many, warm in bed, would hear the rain drumming on the roof, feel the cold seeping through the walls, and think, Not today. Just this one time, I'll stay home. Men like Joe, remembering wedding nights and wanting more in the morning. Women, though never Annie herself, waking to a familiar sickness. Children, up too late, sleeping heavily, sweetly. Footsore grandparents with arthritis that's more miserable in bad weather, groaning at the thought of moving across the room, let alone marching in the rain around the city.

This morning's bad weather provides Annie with an exact count of how many will still show up no matter what: a third of those who voted for the strike. Close to three thousand marchers have converged on the church by seven in the morning, their umbrellas making a black, dimpled roof over their heads and the street outside the church. She is heartened by their determination, their stubbornness, even as she is aware of cracks developing in the summer's solidarity. Women now come to her, often in quiet pairs, their arms linked as though they need support to approach her with their doubts. Annie, do you think the parades are doing any good? Annie, my husband, he say we never gonna make back the money after the strike. Annie, how long can we keep going?

"If we quit now, it will all be for nothing," she tells them. "We are going to keep going until the union is recognized."

Nobody says it, but this in itself is an admission that the strike will not win all they hoped for. Recognize the union: that's the irreducible demand. The rest is negotiable.

There have been hints of progress. A small company up in Copper Harbor sent feelers to Charlie Miller about a settlement. They're willing to talk about reduced hours and some kind of raise. Charlie and the Local 15 officers were quietly jubilant and made plans to start direct negotiations. They were careful not to discuss any of this in front of Joe Clements. MacNaughton still got wind of it somehow. Maybe someone up in Copper Harbor told him. Either way, he killed the deal before it could be made.

One man, Annie thinks. How can one man dictate the lives of so many? One man with one word: never. Just refuse, refuse, refuse. I will outlast you—that's his only message to the union. The weather will get worse. The parades will get harder. Your strike fund will run dry again. No one will bail you out the next time. The company can absorb the losses indefinitely. Give up. If you don't like the work, leave. It's the only sensible thing to do.

And then there's Joe. Every now and then, he looks up from the *Mining Gazette* and announces, "Calumet & Hecla's still turning a profit." Still selling copper piled high in the warehouses—just like Charlie told her they would.

There are days when Annie herself would quit, if not for the specter of Charlie Miller's satisfaction. She'd march to the North Pole rather than listen to him say, "I told you so."

"What is the price of copper?" she asked when all this started, and the voices of the women answered: My father. My husband. My son. My brother. . . . Hands. Arms. Legs. Backs ruined. Skulls cracked. Coffins filled. "Don't lose hope now," Annie tells herself and anyone else who shows signs of wavering. "The strike is for your children. It's for their future, not just ours. Don't let them down."

A tall figure comes around the corner, stalking toward the marchers on long legs, secondhand coat pulled tight, battered fedora crammed low over damp curls, umbrella streaming drips all around him. Michael Sweeney has taken to walking the route at dawn, before the marchers set off. Reporting back. Suggesting alterations in their course if the company has set up roadblocks.

"You're screwing that mick, aren't you!" Joe shouted, mean with drink after the brawl at the Truro Pub, looking for a way to unload an anger too big to carry. "What is going on?" "Nothing!" Annie told him over and over, and it was the truth, but it only made Joe madder. "Do you think I'm stupid? Do you think I can't see it? What *is* he to you?"

She had no answer for him then, and took that beating as though it were a fall on the ice, or a chest-rattling cold, or some other force of nature that had to be endured. She has an answer now, though it's one that Joe would scoff at. Michael Sweeney is a partner. He is someone who doesn't need her failure to prove him right and doesn't need her sympathy to keep him going. He doesn't resent her strength or try to own it. She's not a beast of burden to him. And no matter what he writes for the papers, she's not a heroine to him, either. He is an equal. Whatever he says to her is said plain and true. No vinegar, no sugar. No blarney. Just truth. And that makes his friendship precious.

"The headquarters is surrounded by hired goons wearing badges," he tells her when he's close. "Not locals. Bowery lads, from the sound of them. They're carrying guns."

His warning is passed back through the marchers, rank upon rank, as is Annie's command: "Best behavior, everyone! Don't give them any excuses! Don't answer back." Then she hoists the flag pole into the cross-chest holster Michael got for her from Major Van Den Broek, and calls out the morning's slogan: "Come to the table, MacNaughton!"

Thousands of voices, rank upon rank, take up that demand. They keep it going all the way to the company's General Office Building, where they pause for a quarter of an hour, shouting loud enough to drown out catcalls and obnoxious remarks from the "deputies" outside MacNaughton's fortress. There is no sign that anyone inside hears them. There never is, but they keep it up until Annie wrestles the flag into its holster again and leads the way back toward the center of town.

In front of St. Joseph's, the marchers disperse, soaked and shivering. Annie rolls the sopping wet flag around its pole and lugs it down to what she is careful to think of as the parish hall, not the union office. The flag will mildew if it's not hung out to dry, so she brings it to the kitchen and wrings the rainwater out of it, twisting it like a rich lady's freshly washed bedsheet and spreading it out to dry near a radiator.

Joe comes down the stairs with the mail and his newspaper tucked into his jacket to keep the rain off. He's been nicer since the last beating and lately he's been going to the post office when she's out marching. That's his way of apologizing: he picks up the mail and delivers it to the union office. Then he stakes out a chair by the coffee table and reads the *Mining Gazette*. No one bothers him.

She squeezes past the crowd of women that already surrounds her desk. Questions pummel her before she can even sit down. Annie, can we get more ink to print the flyers? Annie, is this the right translation for that word? Annie, I finished with the pantry. What should I do next? Annie, did the Houghton Auxiliary give us a date for that meeting? Annie, I need a signature for this. Who should sign it?

She deals with each problem, aware that her patience is fraying. Old Moishe Glass has lectured her about this failing. "Why you trying to do it all? Give others responsibility! You're an organizer! So organize!" Good advice, but sometimes the morning just comes at Annie so quickly, she doesn't have time to think about who might help her. It's usually faster to do it all herself.

She has, at least, managed to take Mr. Glass's suggestion about making Carla Caretto the Auxiliary's treasurer. "She's honest," he told Annie. "I know this. Sometimes I send a kid home with the wrong change. An extra nickel, maybe. Carla, she send that kid straight back with the nickel. And she's a widow. Could use a little salary, right?" He was right, of course. Carla is a neighbor, a friend, and a willing worker with a good head for figures—as much a partner now as Michael Sweeney.

With questions answered and tasks apportioned, she kicks off her wet shoes, shoves cold feet into the slippers she leaves at the office, and glances at her husband. Joe's concentration on the *Gazette* is as much a camouflage as a genuine interest in the industry news. Does he realize that nobody talks to him anymore? Maybe, though it's not much of a change. He was always against the strike and has been a loud skeptic since it began.

That's part of our problem, she thinks. MacNaughton is one man with one decision and one strategy. We've been fragmented from the start. There were those like Solomon Kivisto who wanted no part of the union, and those like Joe who voted against the strike. There are those who want to go back to work now, just to cut their losses and be done with it, and those who want to hold out but only to a certain point. And then there are those who would rather die than let Mac-Naughton win.

"How long do you think you can keep carrying that flag?" Michael

Sweeney asked her once. When was that? Two months ago? "Forever," she told him then, but . . .

She was working as hard as she could before the strike started. She still does laundry for two ladies in Laurium. This afternoon, she's got her own laundry to do. There's applesauce to cook and can. It's almost time to butcher the hog. And on top of the usual grind of marches and meetings, in addition to all the begging letters and all the reports she writes, they had to move the office! All that packing, labeling, carrying, unpacking! All the decisions and reorganization—put this here and that there—and then cooking for the party, and then Joe proving who's boss.

Stop, she tells herself. It was a late night, that's all. You're tired and you need to catch up on sleep. Sunday. You can sleep in on Sunday. Just do the work in front of you, she tells herself. Right here. Right now.

The morning settles into quiet busyness. Eva Savicki sits on the floor with a ring of little kids around her, teaching them the alphabet song. A dozen women rummage through the racks of clothing: some organizing the donations, others looking for something that might fit the growing children who squirm nearby. Others are in the parish kitchen, sorting jars of thimbleberry preserves and pickled eggs, arguing over whether the Auxiliary should try to store things like onions and potatoes and cabbage here or just let everybody keep their produce at home and bring some in when someone asks for groceries. "Who gonna ask if they need?" Carla Caretto demands. "You know they too proud! We should just send the boys out with baskets. Regular, every week, so nobody gotta beg."

Charlie Miller has a knot of serious-looking men around his desk, discussing what to do about the goons. "We might be able to get an injunction against them if they block the marches," he's saying as quietly as he can, "but we can't afford a lawyer. There's nothing left in the strike fund now. Boys, I think we have to settle with C&H. If we can just get one smaller company to recognize the union, we can start negotiations again after we—"

"What did you say?" Annie cries.

The men are staring at her. Frowning. There she goes again, their faces say. Sticking her nose into our business. They can see that she is shocked, but what startles her is not their willingness to discuss capitulation. It's the abrupt collapse of her own determination. The shattering relief she feels at the thought that all this responsibility will be taken out of her hands. The possibility that she'll soon be done with all this bucking up and soldiering on.

Shamed by how close she is to giving up, she shakes her head and waves their attention off. "I— Never mind. Sorry for the interruption."

Pretending she does not hear the rest of their conversation, she goes back to sorting the mail. Carla Caretto will get the bills. Michael Sweeney will get the queries from newspapers about articles. The Federation has sent them a sample flyer to adapt for local use. She herself tallies the small donations and sets aside letters of encouragement from other unions to be printed in the union newspaper. There's really nothing out of the ordinary until one envelope that catches her attention when she notices who it's addressed to. Not to Copper Union Lady or Mrs. Clements or, absurdly, to Joan of Arc, but to Miss Eva Lucyna Savicki.

"Eva," she calls. "There's something here for you."

Eva scrambles to her feet. "Keep practicing your letters," she tells the little kids, and makes her way to Annie's desk. "Who would write to me?" she wonders aloud and takes the envelope; but when she sees the West Virginia postmark, a small moan escapes her.

"Eva! What's wrong?" Annie asks. "What is it?"

Hands trembling, Eva breaks the seal; she pulls out a single sheet of paper and closes her eyes before unfolding the note. It might just say, Sorry, I'm too busy. It might be a flat no. Solve your own problems. Or, The Upper Peninsula is too far, too remote. You're practically Canada, for Lord's sake.

She considers going upstairs to say a whole rosary before she reads it, but with all her faith, not even Eva Savicki believes prayer can change words inked on paper.

Over in the kitchen, Carla Caretto is telling the other women, "Like a pasty, kinda. Yeah! Italian pasty! What you got? Little flour, little salt, some water, make a dough. Roll it out. Few tomato. Some . . . *funghi*.

How you say? Musharoom! Maybe *little* bit meat, if you got it. Some cheese. All together, you got a nice supper."

"But you leave the dough flat?" someone asks, and Carla is about to answer when Eva Savicki screams.

And screams again, and bends in half, and straightens up, and finds that everyone's eyes are upon her, and their faces are full of anxiety. Kaz is pushing through to her, calling, "Eva! Eva! Eva!" and it's only then that she realizes that she is his last person on earth, and she's sorry for scaring him, but she still can't speak and only shakes her head as if to say, *There's nothing wrong*. Because this is not a tragedy or a disaster, and everyone can see that now as she hops up and down holding the letter high. She wants to be like Annie—serene, confident, resolute—but what she has to say comes out in a fourteen-year-old girl's high-pitched breathless rush: "She's coming! I wrote to her and told her about Annie and the strike and all of us, and I asked her to come and help, and I prayed and prayed to Saint Catherine, and she's coming!"

Annie's brow wrinkles. "Saint Catherine?"

"No!" Eva shouts with exasperated excitement. "*Mother Jones!* Mother Jones is coming to Calumet! I told you, Kaz! I prayed so hard, and it happened!"

There is astonishment among the grown-ups at first, and then the cheering starts, and the kindergarten kids are jumping up and down with excitement, and her brother is bewildered. Because she only told Kaz *that* she was praying but not *what for,* and he had no idea that this is what his own little sister was trying to do.

And then she sees Jack Kivisto, at the edge of the crowd, a little apart, as he always is even when surrounded by people.

His eyes meet hers. She waits, squealing when he smiles a little and shakes his head, for she did indeed tell Jack what she was praying for and asked him to stay with her in the church while she did so. Because she wanted him to see what true faith could accomplish.

Jack stands still, trying to decide what he thinks about what Eva has done. He certainly does not believe that dead Catholic ladies can make God do things, no matter how sincerely a girl in Calumet, Michigan, asks for their "intercession." Whatever that is. Besides which, his father used to say that Mother Jones is a socialist rabble-rouser who'd show up at any strike. So by that standard, this is not much of a miracle, and yet . . .

At least for the moment, his habitual wariness retreats and in its place comes . . . what?

Something he has not felt before. Something that goes beyond toleration of this giggly girl, whose habitual enthusiasm is wearying and whose devotion he has found bewildering and burdensome, for his family's future depends on him, and that alone is almost more than he can carry. Even so, at least for the moment, he allows himself to feel something new.

Respect. And maybe even . . . a glimmer of reflected joy.

Without a decision, he finds that his arms have opened to her and she rushes to him, and the shock of touching a girl—this girl—feels like nothing he's ever experienced before. He tells himself that this is just like taking his little sister into his arms when she runs toward him at the end of the day, but Eva is not a bony little girl. She is a grown woman, nearly, and her body fits his with soft and startling ease.

There is a sort of shift within him, like the hanging wall of a stope crumbling all at once into a drift, like the breaking up of ice on the lake. He steps back, away from Eva as she weeps and laughs and hugs him again, for this feeling is something he will need to retreat from and think about when he is alone again. It is something he will have to remember and reconsider.

And that, perhaps, is as close to a miracle as anything Saint Catherine might provide to a fifteen-year-old Finn.

October 1913

1

Thou sober-suited matron, all in black

—Shakespeare, *Romeo and Juliet*

The Miners' Angel, union men call her. Mary Harris Jones would be the first to admit she never displayed otherworldly purity, not even in the freshness of youth. Now seventy-six, she is short, stout, plain-faced, and foul-mouthed. And nothing in life gives her more pleasure than knowing what the mine operators call her: the most dangerous woman in America.

She's been fighting those bastards for decades. They've harried her from state to state and have thrown her in jail dozens of times, but they have never beaten her—not in any way that counts. Her whole long life has been a fight, and she'll go down into the earth with both hands fisted.

She left Cork during the Great Famine and survived a voyage across the Atlantic in a filthy, overloaded boat. Coffin ships, they were called, owned by sons of bitches who packed the boats to the edges with little thought as to food or medicine, and told their captains to throw the corpses overboard. Odds against, she found a good man in America, and survived four pregnancies to birth three daughters and a son, only to hold her husband and their children in her arms as yellow fever carried them off, one after another: five hearts stopped, in a matter of hours, and her own near to breaking.

A woman alone in Chicago, she clawed out a living as a dressmaker, only to lose her home and business alike in the Great Fire. So she rolled up her sleeves and went to work beside the laborers who rebuilt that city.

She was often the only woman on the job, but she proved her toughness to herself and to her comrades.

That was when she learned how the money boys operated. They'd hire by the day, smirking with contempt each morning as they listened to desperate, homeless men who shouted out how little they'd take for twelve or thirteen or fourteen hours of labor. Sometimes bosses would have a little fun with you, promising good wages only to look you straight in the eye when you came for your packet and say, "Never saw you before." If somebody got hurt on the job and asked for a little advance so his family had something to live on while he recovered, they'd shrug and tell you, "That's not my concern."

When conditions got bad enough, laborers went on wildcat strikes, but the owners controlled the courts and the politicians, and judges always ruled for the company. The last straw for Mary Harris Jones came when her own parish priest began to preach that the strikers should go back to work, for their reward would be in heaven.

"And you can go to hell" was her shout from the last pew she'd ever sit in. "I'm damned if I'll eat shite on earth, praying for pie in the sky when I'm dead."

Woman or not, she became a union organizer. For forty years, she's led picket lines, protested child labor, and demanded better pay, shorter hours, and safer working conditions—anywhere and everywhere. Cursed by capitalists as an outside agitator, she wears their label proudly: "I'll speak my truth wherever I please. Try to stop me." In all these years, she has no fixed abode and once informed a census taker, "My address is like my shoes—it travels with me." Told she ought to be hanged, she snapped back, "If you want to hang me, go ahead. I will shout from the scaffold, 'Pray for the dead and fight like hell for the living!'"

Fight like hell, that's her motto. Forty years of fight, that's her story.

She fought for mill girls in New England. She fought for bottle washers in Milwaukee breweries, and for streetcar operators in El Paso, and for garment workers in Chicago, but everyone knows: it's the miners who have her deep affection. My boys. That's what she calls the men who go into the black depths of the earth and pay with their bodies and souls for the pleasant lives of those who live up on the surface, out in the sunshine.

When miners finally stand up for themselves, they need someone to give them heart, for there comes a time when a strike begins to feel worse than the miserable conditions they worked in before they organized. She wants them to take courage for their own fight from her tireless efforts on their behalf and made a deliberate decision back in 1882 to allow herself to seem a little feeble in public. "If old Mother Jones can do it," she wanted strikers to say, "well, by God, so can I!" At first she was merely playing a role. Now—within spitting distance of eighty—she has caught up to her own mythology. Her knees are arthritic. Her ankles are always swollen. If she simply sits for any length of time, she creaks and groans when she stands. Just last week, she took a bad fall. Stepped on a damned acorn. Her feet flew out from under her and she went down like a baggy-pants vaudevillian. Lucky she didn't break a hip; still, at her age, even bruises take forever to fade.

The long, complicated train trip from West Virginia to Upper Michigan is a trial. Often hungry, always tired, she snatches naps in chairs and on benches. When she finally gets to Calumet, her bed will be a cot, or a sofa, or a sagging, smelly mattress. Whatever it is, she knows it will be the best the strikers can offer. While she's there, she will be vilified and very likely driven out of town by the men who run the mines. Fine with her. The boys in Michigan need someone to buck them up. And Mother Jones, by God, is coming.

"How many would you estimate?" James MacNaughton asks, standing behind the large office windows.

The train depot is surrounded, and the streets of Calumet are jammed with people. "Fifteen thousand is a fair guess, sir," Sheriff Cruse says.

"Is it."

"Yes, sir, counting the ones from Houghton and the other towns."

"And we have . . . ?"

A tiny place in James Cruse's soul cringes at that "we." He is a county official, and it sometimes grates on him that Calumet & Hecla's general manager treats him like an employee. In a small act of rebellion, he dares to use the pronouns he prefers. "I have a hundred from the county, and

I've deputized eleven hundred of your company's men, along with fifty volunteers from the Citizens' Alliance. Another fifty from Waddell-Mahon, and more on the way, I understand."

"Round numbers are never accurate."

Having just been called a liar, Cruse amends his statement. "We've got enough to shut that old bitch up, sir."

MacNaughton turns away from the window and fixes the sheriff with a silent stare of disapproval. Bust their heads, Cruse thinks, but heavens to Betsy, don't use a rude word. "What I mean is: I certainly have enough deputies to do the job."

A window-rattling cheer penetrates the double glazing. Hats and handkerchiefs and banners wave when a stout little woman in black appears between two third-class cars and pauses before stepping down onto the platform.

Returning his gaze to the depot and the crowds that fill the streets of Calumet, James MacNaughton takes a deep breath, not unlike the one with which he starts his mornings. Mind clear, he weighs his assets and his options. His own estimate is twenty-two thousand union support-ers, with only a tenth that number to counter then. There are still two hundred and fifty-seven Michigan militiamen deployed in the Copper Country, but only a third of them are still in Calumet, and they seem to sympathize with the very troublemakers they've been called upon to control.

Newspapers from around the country have sent journalists here to cover the strike, and more have undoubtedly arrived on the train with the Jones woman, who is always good for a lurid quote or two. Best not to feed the jackals, he decides, and addresses Sheriff Cruse. "Stay alert, but take no action without my order. Understood?"

Cruse sighs inwardly, and reminds himself that the pay is good and the job is secure. "Yes, sir," he says. "Of course, sir. Whatever you say, sir."

He is a toady, MacNaughton thinks as the sheriff leaves the office, albeit a useful one, as long as he doesn't forget when to shut up and take an order.

*   *   *

Down at the depot, Mary Harris Jones gathers herself to use the most powerful tool she has: a voice that can carry a thousand yards. She has iron vocal cords, a deep chest, and she has taken private lessons in projection from a sympathetic opera diva, but these days, hobbling down the aisle of a third-class car is enough to make her breathless. So she pauses on the vestibule to grin and wave at the assembled crowd, and to give her rattly old ticker time to stop racing within her.

There's a lot of press waiting with the strikers. A tall, curly-haired photographer catches her eye, and she holds her pose long enough for him to get his picture without blur. When the flash goes off, she is ready to make her voice reach the back of the crowd as she cocks a thumb at a large sandstone building. "Don't look now, but I think we're being watched by that tightwad MacNaughton!" she cries, and there is a joyful roar when she makes a rude gesture toward the figure who stands behind the large windows on the third floor.

Strong young men reach out to take her old carpetbag, and to help her climb down from the train, and to show her the way to a truck, and to give her a boost onto the flatbed. Though she has been known to walk twenty miles in West Virginia coal country to get to a rally, she is grateful that Calumet Local 15 has provided her with a ride to the place where she'll talk today—and grateful, as well, for the folded crescent of filled pastry someone hands her, promising that she'll have a chance to sit down to a meal after the rally.

Fifteen minutes later, the party arrives at a makeshift dais in a weedy field north of town. Someone offers Mother Jones a steadying hand as she climbs wooden stairs banged together from packing crates. When she gets to the platform, she is greeted by a welcoming committee of union officials. She recognizes Charlie Miller and hugs him, though she will have some tart things to say later on. She smiles at the Local 15 officials: Ben Goggia, Yanko Tersich, Peter Jedda. "I got you some cash. We'll talk later," she says for their ears only. "Right now it's time to put on a show."

The photographer is setting up his camera and winks at her when he's ready. Like a referee presenting two fighters at a boxing match, she lifts the hands of Charlie and the Local president above her, holding the pose during the cheers. When the photographer gets his shot, he looses a charming grin and she winks back at him, one pro to another.

"Now, where's the little girl who wrote me a letter?" she demands.

"Eva! Eva! Eva!" the crowd chants. Cheers go up as the girl emerges from the crowd and climbs the rickety stairs. She is trembling so hard that the bouquet of wild Queen Anne's lace shakes violently as she approaches the legendary labor crusader.

Mother Jones takes the flowers and cries, "God love you, child, give an old woman a kiss!" When they are very close, she whispers into the girl's ear, "Don't be scared, darlin'. I only bite strikebreakers." That old joke gets a fresh laugh from the child, who will never forget it, and Mother Jones turns toward the crowd. "Let's thank this slip of a girl who had the guts and brains to believe there are others in the world who want justice for the Copper Country!" She pauses for the applause. "And Miss Eva was right, for I am here to tell you that the United Mine Workers is sending twenty thousand dollars to the Western Federation—to support your strike!"

The cheers are deafening, and before the noise can die, she beckons to the tall young woman standing behind the men, dwarfing them all, her flag catching the breeze now and then. "And this must be Big Annie!" Mother Jones declares. Then she looks out over the throng and makes a sly face. "Now, how did I guess that?"

Laughter rolls like a tide through the crowd. The breeze will take her words away, but she knows to wait while her remarks are passed to those too far away to hear her firsthand. After decades of public speaking, Mother Jones has the timing of a vaudeville comic. She never steps on her own lines while the audience is reacting.

"Bend your neck down here and let a midget hug you!" she cries, and as soon as Annie has finished the embrace, she shouts, "Now *never bend again*! You stand up tall! All of you, stand up tall!" She points toward the deputies that hover around the edges of the crowd and hollers, "Make the scabs and company bastards look up to you!"

There is a thunderous reaction, for everyone knows that Mother Jones minces no words, and they love that about her. While the cheers persist, she hands Eva's bouquet to Big Annie Clements and says, "Hold these while I get to work."

And that she does, for two hours or more. Each rousing line has been honed and sharpened by practice, but those who listen and shout and cheer would swear in court that she's making it up as she goes, carried along on the emotion of these boys and their families.

"Yes," she shouts. "Bastards! That's what I called 'em. And, yes, I have a mouth on me! *Nice* people—nice people, who *mean well*—they tell me, Mother Jones, don't be so crude! They tell me, Be sweet and ladylike. They tell me, You'd catch more flies with honey than with vinegar."

She pulls a face, miming perplexity. "Now, what on God's green earth would I want to catch flies for?"

The laughter goes on for long enough that she can turn back toward the little table that's been provided, along with a carafe and a glass. She pours herself a drink and lifts it to her lips. Looking startled, she gags on it, with a vaudevillian explosion of spit. "Christ!" she cries. "What is that? *Water?*" Laughter. "And here was me, expecting something worth drinking!"

Everyone applauds as half a dozen flasks make their way to the dais. She uncaps one and brings it to her mouth, careful to dam the flow with her tongue. Tipping her head back, she takes what seems to be a long pull, then shudders and mimes her satisfaction before passing it down to a waiting hand.

"You'd catch more flies with honey," she repeats, shaking her head. "Well, I don't want flies! And I don't want men who'll creep one by one into the boss's august presence and doff their caps and tug their forelocks and say"—she makes her voice high and deferential—"'Oh, please, Mr. High-and-Mighty Mine Operator, would you please grant me a few more pennies in my pay so I might provide a better life for my wee kiddies? And maybe safer working conditions down below, if you please, sir, so I don't get killed and orphan them? And perhaps a few more minutes of the day to spend with them? No? Well, thankee anyway, sir. I'll just be patient and wait for Jesus to come back and bring a nicer world with him!'"

She pauses to judge the reaction in this church-ridden town; they're still with her, so she continues, emboldened: "No, I don't want to catch flies, and I don't want craven cowards like that. I want men. I want *men*!

Men who'll stand together and stand up for themselves and their families! I want strong men who will join the union and stick with it and *not back down.*"

She lets the wave of cheers break over her, and this time she doesn't wait for the noise to die. "And you women! I don't want shrinking little flowers who'll droop and swoon when somebody calls them names. Let me tell you something, girls: the bosses fight men for the sake of their wallets, but they fight *you* for the sake of their balls!"

There are screams of laughter at that.

"Men with fat wallets will tell you girls that you're unnatural and ungodly. They'll tell you to be obedient and know your place! Be womanly, they'll tell you. Be feminine. Be quiet. Shut up and go away, that's what they mean! Let the men attend to politics—you stay home and play Pretty Polly! Well, you can guess what I'd say to that!" A roar from the women gives her time to take a sip of water before going on. "And it's not just men who'll tell you to be nice. There are some ladies who'll tell you that until women have the vote, we'll have no rights and no influence. I want the vote, too. Men will make us crawl over broken glass to get it, and they'll take it away from us if ever they can, but let me tell you something: I've raised hell all over this country! You don't have to wait for the vote to raise hell! You just need convictions and courage and a voice!"

This time she lets a silence settle, for she means to turn the mood. She points toward the cityscape behind her, and her voice—though still carrying—becomes conversational, as if she were across the kitchen table from each person there and not in front of an enormous crowd. "I'll admit it," she says reasonably. "This is the prettiest town I ever saw a mine company build. I'll grant Calumet & Hecla this much: you're not living in shacks or tents."

Someone yells, "Because we'd all freeze to death!"

There's laughter at that. "That's right!" she says. "The company can't get copper out of the ground with miners who are frozen solid!"

She waves to the man with the flask and takes another pull. This time she allows herself a real one, and this time her shudder is genuine, for it tastes like kerosene and burns all the way down.

"Yes," she continues, "Calumet is a fine town. Big, impressive office buildings. Big, beautiful stores. Big, fancy houses—in some neighborhoods!" As though merely curious, she asks, "Have any of you been inside one of those big, fancy houses?"

Sure enough a woman in the crowd yells, "I have! To wash the damn floors!"

Another shouts, "Me, too—to do their dirty laundry!"

"That's right!" Mother Jones says. "You're always welcome to do Her Ladyship's scut work—as long as you go in the back door and get the hell out before you steal something, right?"

She pauses for another drink, welcoming the warmth, and this time there's no shudder afterward. "Yes, indeed, I'll admit it. Calumet is impressive. But who are those impressive buildings and fancy houses for? Who shops in those fancy stores? Whose money is in that great stone bank? Not yours! And who among the bosses would change places with a single man of you? Who among them would send their own dear kiddies to a school where all they learn is how to drudge away for another generation in the mines? Would Mr. High-and-Mighty James Mac-Naughton be content to send a son of his into the pits to work at your son's side?"

"No!"

"Would he be proud to see his daughters learn nothing more than cooking and cleaning and sewing?"

"NO!"

"And would he be happy to see his girls marry one of you lot?"

"*NO!*"

"And that's the truth of it! You aren't on strike so your children can have a better life, you're fighting so that they can have a *good* life! You aren't on strike for a better wage, you're fighting for a *good* wage—a living wage! You aren't on strike for *less* danger in the pits, you're fighting for safe working conditions!"

She lets the joyful, angry shouting go on until she can be heard again.

"And when you join the union, you're fighting for a decent life, side by side with your brothers. When you stagger and want to fall, there will be a man next to you to pick you up. When you lose heart, I want you to look into the eyes of your sons and your daughters and know this: you are fighting for them, and for your grandchildren. You are fighting for all the generations of workers who come after you!"

The cheering is ferocious now, and she gathers herself for the finish.

"And we aren't going to wait around for the Second Coming, are we! We won't wait for Jesus to come back and make things right. We aren't going to beg for a decent life, a good life, a healthy life. We are going to *demand* those things—for ourselves! For our neighbors! For our children! And for all the working stiffs who come after us!"

She stands still, letting the noise envelop her, for she is no longer an arthritic, exhausted, elderly woman who could use a meal and a quiet night in a bed without bugs. She is Mother Jones: ageless and tireless, fighting for her boys and their families.

"And I'll tell you when our fight is done! When every worker, around the world, has a decent life, a good life, a healthy life. That's when our fight is done! And then we'll welcome Jesus back to earth and each one of us who's fought to make this world a fair and decent place—each one of us can look him in the eye and tell him, *'I did my part!'* Are you ready to do your part?" she shouts. "Every one of you—are you ready?"

They are screaming now, all of them, men, women, and children—all a part of something huge and powerful and unstoppable.

"Make those bastards hear it!" Mother Jones shouts, pointing back toward the headquarters of Calumet & Hecla. "Let them hear it all over the Copper Country, and all over America, and all over the world!"

The roar is deafening, and the chant begins: "Union! Union! Union!"

She turns on the dais and beckons: to the Local 15 officials, to Charlie Miller, to the little girl who wrote the letter, and to Big Annie Clements. They face the crowd and stand shoulder to shoulder, and she takes the hands of those nearest to her and they all do the same. Once again, she lifts the hands and keeps them up, holding the pose, waiting for the flash. Then she pulls them all as close as possible to get her round little arms as far around them as she can.

Eyes sparkling, she makes her voice low and intimate: "And *that*, children, is how you by-God raise some hell!"

2

Too rude, too boisterous

—Shakespeare, *Romeo and Juliet*

Mary MacNaughton and the girls had been back from the summer house for only a few days when James began to show signs of distress.

When the girls were younger, their father's stern presence and their mother's moderating guidance were enough to keep the morning rituals moving with smooth efficiency. Martha and Molly were awakened eighteen minutes apart. Bathroom time was allotted accordingly. Teeth were brushed, faces and nails scrubbed, hair attended to, dresses donned. By then James was downstairs at the table, ready to inspect their hands. And even now, when she was very nearly a grown woman, Martha's are given particular attention.

"I cannot understand why you persist in this habit," James says irritably. "You managed to stop biting your nails this summer. Why have you started it up again?"

"Perhaps it has something to do with being treated like a child again," Martha mutters.

"Martha . . ." her mother warns.

James pretends that he has not heard the remark, choosing instead to remind his eldest, "The condition of a lady's hands are a sign of her position in society."

Before things can get out of hand, so to speak, Mary makes a small sign to the kitchen, and the maid brings in their breakfasts. Loretta Devlin's appearance with the tray is the signal for silence to descend, though Martha is sullen and Molly smirks. When the girls finish their oatmeal, they ask to be excused. Calm returns as their parents read the papers. When James leaves for the office, normal household noise can be tolerated again. This autumn, however, the mines have been half-idled, and James MacNaughton along with them.

He does not share business affairs with his family, but Mary can read her husband's demeanor as well as the newspapers. He has been forced to explain to the stockholders why confident projections about a quick return to work have repeatedly proved inaccurate. The strikers remain intransigent, stirred up and given false hope by that awful Jones woman's radical rhetoric. Their funds have been replenished with money from other unions, along with donations from foolish, interfering do-gooders all over the country. And in the meantime, open-pit copper mines out west are capturing more and more of the market.

Worst of all—for the MacNaughton household, at least—the pater-familias has found himself adrift. He cannot plan. He is forced to waste time, and this disruption of productive activity makes him peevish. He cannot be seen to have nothing to do at the office—and does not wish to be subjected to hours of chanted abuse when the strikers surround the headquarters—so he stays at home until after lunch, only to find the girls' squabbling infuriating. An ankle is maliciously kicked. Milk is spilled deliberately into a lap. Sugar has been replaced with salt, simply to get a rise out of a sister.

"Why can't you control them?" he asks his wife when hostilities break out. "What they argue about is so—so *trivial*!"

"Mother, she stole my blouse!" was a typical complaint.

"I did not! Mother! She called me a thief! Besides, it's the maid's fault. She put that blouse in my closet! I thought it was mine."

"Likely story, you little sneak! Take it off, Molly. Mother, make her give it back!"

"You're worse than Daddy, Martha! You're not the boss of the world, you know!"

That particular remark was undoubtedly hurtful, though James chose to focus on the laundry as the argument devolved into more strident accusations and outraged weeping. "Why does this keep happening?" James demanded. "What is wrong with that Irish girl? If she can't do something as simple as keep their clothing organized, Mary, you should find someone who can!"

Mary MacNaughton settled that particular argument by offering to take both girls shopping in Chicago. The promise of a trip to Marshall Field's dried the tears, but James was still rattled fifteen minutes later. "More clothing will not address the recurring problem. Fire that maid and get someone competent."

Mary MacNaughton does not wish to lose Loretta Devlin or any of the other servants. These days, keeping them from quitting en masse takes all the oil she can spread on troubled waters, for without secretaries, accountants, and copper mines to supervise, James uses his half-days away from his office to follow the domestic staff around with his stopwatch. After taking notes and analyzing each motion, he leaves typed notes labeled "Revised Schedule" tacked to their duty boards.

The cook, in particular, is near the breaking point, having been informed that "Food particles are best dislodged from cooking pots and dirty dishes with a series of three clockwise swirls of the scrub brush followed by three counter-clockwise swirls, repeated as necessary until the object is free of detritus."

"Can't you stop him, Missus?" Mrs. Aiken whispered desperately after bringing that little note to Mary. "Next he'll be telling me how to boil water!"

Mary suspects that the butler is on the verge of giving his two weeks' notice as well, and she despairs of finding a good replacement for Mr. Morris. There is so much ill will among the lower classes these days! Only the little Irish maid seems to have escaped the mood of smoldering resentment in the household. Young Loretta has been remarkably patient with Mr. MacNaughton's notes about how she makes the beds, and cleans the bathroom, and how the linens should be washed, ironed, folded, and stored. Her sunny disposition would be sorely missed, so later—and in private—Mrs. MacNaughton approaches the girl with a suggestion.

"Loretta, dear, now that Molly is almost grown, she's wearing the same size as Martha, and I imagine it must be difficult to keep their things sorted correctly. I think it might help if the girls' clothing were marked the way a Chinese laundry might do. Perhaps a small X embroidered on an inside seam in a different color for each. Pink for Molly, green for Martha?"

"Do you know what she said then?" Mary asks James that night in bed.

"Of course I don't," he snaps. Unnecessary questions with obvious answers always annoy him.

"She said, 'I think Mr. MacNaughton would say that it is more efficient to mark only one girl's things. Molly's things would be marked, and Martha's are whatever has no mark.' You see, dear? You've made a time-and-motion convert, darling! She has learned your methods."

James grunts, "Well, she should have taken it on herself to implement the improvement without being told."

That requires no response. Mary lets him lie there silently for a while before making a suggestion she's been working on all day. "You know, I think we might do better for the girls than a shopping trip to Marshall Field's. At her age, Martha should be engaged at least, but there is precious little opportunity to meet an appropriate young gentleman here in Calumet," she points out. "I think this might be an opportune time to take the girls to Europe, don't you? Molly's not paying much attention to her tutor anyway. She would learn a great deal more from travel. And it's so unpleasant here in the winter, especially with all this ugliness over the strike."

"Yes," James says after a time. "Yes. Perhaps you're right."

With characteristic alacrity, James makes the arrangements for the trip. The voyage must be sooner rather than later, for autumn storms can make an Atlantic crossing dangerous. Much thought is given to their route upon arrival as well. Paris first, to buy new clothes that Europeans will not sneer at. Berlin and Vienna next, before the weather deteriorates. Rome and Florence over the winter, and London in the spring.

Packing and planning are a splendid distraction for the girls, and whenever they begin to argue, their squabble can be silenced with a question. "If you two can't get along here at home, how can we expect you to comport yourselves as ladies in Europe?"

At last, the day of departure arrives. The staff lines up outside to see them off: the butler in an impeccable suit, the cook and maid spruce in their starched uniforms. All three are doing their best to look as though they are sorry to see the girls go, although Mary MacNaughton suspects that they will welcome the restoration of order as devoutly as her husband.

The girls are hardly able to contain themselves as the chauffeur loads their steamer trunks into the back of the Pierce-Arrow. Martha behaves herself, though Molly bounces on her toes waiting for the driver to finish with the luggage and come around to open the automobile's doors for them.

"Write to me every day," James calls as the car rolls off toward the train depot at a stately fifteen miles an hour.

Waving and blowing kisses to their father, they promise they will, and while they chatter and argue, Mary MacNaughton allows herself to relax into the leather upholstery. James likes to call Calumet the Paris of the North, but she knows it doesn't hold a candle to the real thing.

Two days after his family's departure, a telegram awaits, laid atop the neatly ironed newspapers, just beneath his polished spectacles. JOURNEY WELL BEGUN, it reads. LEAVING CHICAGO ON TIME STOP MISS YOU ALREADY FULL STOP.

The actions of others often bewilder James MacNaughton. If Mary and the girls had missed a connection and required him to make different travel arrangements on their behalf, he would have seen the point of this telegram, whereas this information requires no action on his part and seems a waste of time and money. He has, however, learned over the years that the expected response is to reply in time for his wife and daughters' arrival at their hotel in New York: *Travel safely. You are missed as well.*

Breakfast the next morning feels strangely quiet. Probing his own mind, he finds that he does miss Mary and the girls, at least this early in their absence. Sometimes, watching that Clements woman lead parades of union brats, he wonders if perhaps he and his wife shouldn't have had more children. It is a thought he has had before. The Italians, Irish, Slavs, and Jews are breeding like rabbits, while well-educated Americans of good stock are hardly replacing themselves in the population. Surely that is racial suicide. Even Martha has spoken of wishing to become a modern woman "with a career." She wanted to study business, of all things. Of course, he stopped that nonsense in its tracks. "The most useful role for an upper-class woman is not to imitate men," he told her. "Your duty is to marry well and raise racially superior children."

The maid appears with his oatmeal then. He wonders how many brats this Irish girl will produce. He has begun to believe that—in the national interest—immigrants should be sterilized. It is a radical idea, but it might be necessary—at least until good Americans can replenish their own numbers.

Difficult to implement, he thinks, tucking into his oatmeal gloomily. Too difficult for feckless politicians to implement. Not enough doctors to perform the procedures, they'll say. Too expensive. So no one will do anything about the problem, and everything real Americans have accomplished will disappear into the next dark age.

Communists believe that history is a river that carries mankind to a utopia: a golden age of *liberté, égalité, fraternité*. History, however, teaches a different lesson to men like James MacNaughton. To live in harmony—to maintain order and productivity—people *must* know their place. They must submit to tradition and to God and to their employers, as children submit to their fathers. The French rejected this truth, and what was the result? A bloodbath. An orgy of killing. The destruction of their civilization. Centuries of cultural and intellectual development, swept away.

It can happen here, too, he thinks with a strangely exhilarating despair. It *will* happen here, unless men like me are willing to do what is necessary to stop the rot—

"Mr. MacNaughton?" the butler says softly. "I'm sorry to disturb you, sir, but there is a . . . gentleman here to see you. A Mr. Fisher. He wishes to speak to you about your contract with Waddell-Mahon and claims he has an appointment. I told him to go to your office downtown this afternoon, but he said it couldn't wait. He is very insistent."

James MacNaughton hesitates, shocked by his own lackadaisical response, which is to think, Why not? It's something to pass the time.

Horrified by how quickly his work ethic has been eroded by leisure, he makes a snap decision. "Tell him to wait in the study. I'll join him in seventeen minutes."

Thomas Fisher puts a good deal of thought into the conveyance of his own importance to big shots like MacNaughton. He knows that he is not impressive at first glance. A redhead as a kid, he was glad when his freckles faded, but not when his hair thinned. He is short and running to fat in his late thirties, though still solidly built, so he wears an expensive suit tailored to cover a developing paunch.

He displays his attitude with a chin that juts upward at the same angle as the cigar he chews with a blithe indifference as to where the ash might fall. Cock of the walk, you are invited to think. A man who gives orders to the likes of Kid Libby, Tommy Stone, Weasel Jack Eller, Stinkfoot McVey, Punk Brady, and Hump Perry. A man who is obeyed by murderers and boxers and street toughs of all kinds. They are happy to do as he tells them, for Tommy Fisher is the rising star of the strike-breaking industry, and they hope to cash in on his climb to power.

MacNaughton stands in the doorway, his eyes as cold and steady as Fisher's. Without rising, Fisher lets a moment pass before unbuttoning his suit coat to pull a heavy gold watch from the pocket of a brocade vest. "Seventeen minutes—on the dot!" He returns the watch to its place and half-stands to offer his hand. "Tommy Fisher," he says. "Pleasure to meet you, Mr. MacNaughton."

MacNaughton looks at the short, thick fingers and turns away, moving behind a huge rosewood desk. Unhurried, he sits before he asks, "You come to my home wearing a pistol?"

Fisher's smile quickly becomes ingratiating, and he pats the gun in his shoulder holster. "I figured I'd be going to work right after our little conflab."

"Confab."

Fisher frowns.

"It's 'confabulation,'" MacNaughton informs him. "Hence: confab, not con*flab*."

Fisher's lips pull downward into the sneer of a small-mouth bass. "Well, who gives a shit? Confab. Chitchat. Palaver. *Business meeting,*" Fisher says, enunciating like a college kid.

"Sheriff Cruse is handling personnel issues. Why have you come to me?"

"Cruse is a tool. I always go to the top when I'm dealing with clients."

"Clients," MacNaughton repeats. "Mr. Fisher, my company's contract was negotiated with Waddell-Mahon and the Ascher Detective Agency."

Fisher makes a noise with his lips. "They're finished. Too soft. Them, and all those old guys."

"And you are . . . ?"

"The best goddamn strikebreaker in the goddamn country, and make no mistake," he says around the well-chewed end of the cigar between his teeth. He sits back, making himself more comfortable. "Seventeen minutes. On the dot!" he repeats. "I like that. I like doing business with men who keep their word. It's important. Do what you say you'll do. That's my policy. And that's why I hate these union bastards. You say you're going to work for a dollar a day? Well, that's what you by-God *do.* None of this bullshit about—" His voice becomes high and whiny. "Oh, it's too hard. Oh, I'm too tired. Oh, my kids are hungry." He snorts and waves the cigar in the general direction of Detroit. "You don't like it? Ford's hiring. Get lost, you lazy bastard. Fucking immigrants—those foreign sons of bitches want everything handed to them on a golden platter. Americans gotta draw the line somewhere, and I'm the man to do it!"

He stands then and buttons his coat, pulling himself to his full height. "Mr. MacNaughton, I fear neither God nor man. I serve America and American industry. I've broken railroad strikes, dock strikes, transit strikes, and textile strikes. I've broken unions in New York, Chicago, and Cuba. My men don't waste time pussyfooting around, and there's plenty of demand for my services. So shit or get off the pot. You in or you out?"

MacNaughton sits back in his chair, arms crossed over his chest, eyes narrowed and considering. "Calumet & Hecla's contract," he repeats, "is with Waddell-Mahon and the Ascher Detective Agency."

"Did you sign anything with them or only negotiate the rate?"

MacNaughton says nothing.

Fisher grins and lets out a satisfied chuckle, sitting down again and sprawling in the chair. "Stupid bastards never nail anything down. Well, sir, you show me their terms and I will cut their rate by five percent and you will have my word: I will break the union and have those lazy damn foreigners back to work before the end of the year."

The negotiations are swiftly concluded. Fisher stands once more, offering a thick, scarred hand.

This time MacNaughton appears to consider shaking it, but he pauses. "There is a photographer. An Irish anarchist."

"Making you look bad, eh?" Fisher chuckles and with heavy irony says, "It'll be a pity about his camera . . ."

"And a storekeeper. A Jew. Give him an opportunity to join the Citizens' Alliance first."

Fisher grins. "And if he doesn't?"

James MacNaughton's voice is light. "People have to learn. There is a price to pay when you bite the hand that feeds you."

"Count on me," Fisher says, offering his hand once more.

This time James MacNaughton takes it.

3

"I've seen it over and over," Mary Harris Jones says late that night in Annie Clements's kitchen. "The only difference in Calumet is that the troops came before the private armies. MacNaughton thought he could wreck the union on the cheap. You're fortunate in your governor— Woodbridge Ferris isn't in the mine operators' pockets. But with the troops gone? MacNaughton will pull out all the stops. He means to break you."

It is the last night of her short time in Calumet. Mike Sweeney and Charlie Miller have left for their boardinghouse. The Local 15 officers have gone home. Joe Clements is snoring upstairs. Eva and Kaz Savicki have fallen asleep on their cots in the front room, where the Clements' broken-backed sofa is made up and waiting for Mother Jones.

Tired though she is, this is the first opportunity she's had to sit and talk to the young woman who put all this in motion. Fingers wrapped around little glasses of Slovenian *šlivovitz*, they sit at Annie's battered kitchen table, alone apart from the yawning, white-haired Finnish boy who sits silently in the corner. On the table are the remains of a cream cake sent to them by his mother, the crumbs of which can still be seen on plates of thick, chipped china.

Mother Jones takes another sip of the fierce plum brandy and shudders. "Christ, but that does warm an old body!" she cries quietly. "So. Here's what happens next. When MacNaughton has enough bully boys to feel safe, he'll unleash 'em. The strikebreakers always start the fights, but they know damn well miners will always fight back. So be ready. There will be bloodshed."

"Bandages. Splints . . ."

"And coffins," Mother Jones says bluntly. "They'll blame me for the first riot. They'll say I'm an outside agitator who caused all the trouble in their little paradise, and I'm proud to wear their label! But you're the one who has to stay here, and you are everything that frightens the poor wee souls."

Annie shifts uneasily in her chair.

"Yes, you're bigger and stronger than those little men—and I don't just mean you're tall and they're short! You have done something huge here, my girl. You have made a difference in the wide world, and that's something few men dare to think of, whether they work in an office or in a mine. You rallied the families and lit a fire under thousands of miners. You've kept their spirits up and organized the living daylights out of this town. The translation work, the kitchen, the pantry, the union school, the clothing exchange—"

Annie shakes her head. "No. It wasn't just me. The Women's Auxiliary did most of that, and the union was getting stronger anyway. Charlie was signing up dozens every day before the strike." Glancing at young Jack Kivisto, sitting in the corner, she says, "It was the one-man drill that started the trouble, and Sol Kivisto's death that changed everything—"

"Don't you dare!" Mother Jones cries. "Don't you dare deny what you and the other women have done! Yes, Charlie Miller is a fine, sensible organizer, and the local has done yeoman labor here in Calumet. And I'm not saying there's no good men here. There's good men everywhere. The trouble is, their goodness is usually to keep their heads down and go to work and call it victory if the kids don't starve and their family isn't living on the streets."

"It *is* a victory!" Jack mutters, standing.

Startled by his voice, the old woman swivels on the wobbly wooden chair to face the white-haired boy glaring down at her.

"I didn't understand it when I was a kid," he says, "but I do now. A man does what he has to. He keeps a roof over his family's heads, no matter what it takes. He puts food on the table. He does what he has to, and he don't apologize to nobody for that!"

"Oh, sweetheart! I'm sorry! I didn't mean—"

His face twists with contempt and anger and frustration. "You don't understand!" he snarls, pulling on his coat and cap, jerking the back door open. "Women don't understand. Not you, not my mother! Not Eva. None of you!"

The door slams behind him. The rush of cold air is cut off, but the chill of his outrage lingers. Eva appears in the open kitchen doorway, a quilt pulled tight around her shoulders. "What happened? Is everything all right?"

"Yes, everything is fine. Go back to sleep," Annie says.

Mother Jones has her face in her hands. When she looks up, she says, "No, child. Sit down, Eva. Learn from us." Looking distraught, she casts her eyes toward the back door. "I was trying to buck Annie up, don't you see? It wasn't meant to insult the boy!"

"What happened?" Eva asks again. "What did you say?"

"Nothing," Annie lies. "Just . . . something he took wrong."

"No," Mother Jones says, "he was right. And you're right, too, Annie. The Auxiliary has been grand, and I didn't mean to belittle what good men do, but . . . There's no progress in the world if we all just keep our heads down and only do what's good and proper in our tiny corner of it! That's what the money men count on, my dears! Good workers, good fathers, good sons—showing up on time, working their hearts out, killing themselves day by day, and saying thankee kindly for whatever pittance they're tossed from on high. You put a stop to that, Annie. At least for a little while, you and the women of the union made those good men straighten their backs and demand more from the company and from their lives."

Annie turns away, staring beyond the cracked kitchen window, into the darkness. We just lost Jack, she is thinking. We've lost a lot of men. "Mother, we're all grateful that you came. All of us. But even if we can get more money—"

"I'll plead your case to the Federation and the UMW. And I can get

Ella Bloor on your side. She's working with a big strike in Schenectady. She'll come as soon as she can. And she'll bring cash. She always does, bless her. Ella has a way with the finances."

Annie isn't listening. "I'm afraid, Mother," she says, voice trembling. "I'm afraid that . . . I'm afraid I've made a terrible mistake and talked everyone into something that will leave us all worse off instead of better."

Eva drops her quilt and comes close to put her arms around Annie's broad shoulders, her eyes on Mother Jones.

"Nonsense," the old woman snaps. "Don't flatter yourself, girl. You made some speeches—good ones, too, as I hear it—but the union is a democracy. In the end, it was fifteen thousand men took a vote, and a majority voted to strike."

"And now we're going to lose," Annie says, her voice threadbare. "We *can't* win. Can we?"

"Win. Win what? An eight-hour day? A five-day week? Safe working conditions in a dangerous job? A decent living wage for every worker?" Mother Jones shrugs. "No. Not all at once. Not this time, anyway. But don't you dare cry! Stop that. Right now."

The old woman reaches across the table. Her fingers are knobby with arthritis; the skin of her hands is almost transparent, roped with purple veins and blotched with bruises. Annie's bones are long and straight, her skin cracked from washing laundry and floors, marred with small cuts and burns from kitchen work. For a few moments, they grip each other, both fighting tears. Then Mother Jones lets go and flops back against the wooden chair, her rheumy eyes hard.

"When this is over, Annie is going to get the blame," she warns Eva. "You have to be ready for that, child. It won't just be the bosses, either. The press will turn on her. Even the union men will blame her—all of them. Here, out west, down south. They'll say she went off half-cocked with no strike fund. They'll say she was foolish, trying to win a war with little children carrying flags and banners—and, oh, now isn't that just like a woman! She should have listened to the good counsel of the men who've played this game for a long time and know how to win it. But really? They'll blame her because she made them feel ashamed."

She leans over the table and whispers fiercely, "Do you know what really brought young Joan of Arc to that stake in the end? They burned her because that girl *succeeded*, if only for a little while, where all those fine, noble aristocratic generals had failed. And let that be a lesson to you, my dears, for I'm damned if I can name a single union leader who hasn't led a strike that failed. When yours does, too, every one of them will be thinking, Thanks be to God! Somebody else can take the blame for Calumet." She jabs a finger at the table and says, "Well, here's the truth of it. There is *never* a good time to strike. The cards are *always* stacked against us. The odds are *always* with the house. If you'd waited like Charlie Miller told you to—if you were sweet little ladies and did nothing but make coffee for the boys and run bake sales for the strike fund—the copper bosses would still have the cash and the power and the courts and the Congress, no matter how long or how patiently you waited for the right time."

Annie is weeping now. Sobbing, really. Mother Jones pushes herself upright against the edge of the table and comes close, pulling Annie's head toward her cushiony, black-clad bosom, cooing, "No, no, no. Don't cry, child. Don't! To hell with them. To hell with all of them and their doubts and their caution and their blame and their anger and their fear! You just listen to *me*." She lifts Annie's chin with one hand and digs into her pocket with the other, bringing out a handkerchief of dubious cleanliness. "You took on the most powerful mining operation in the world. You struck them hard and you struck them fast, and you put Calumet copper miners on the front pages of newspapers in Europe and Australia, by God! You got good men to think about their dignity and worth, and you gave bosses all over the country a chance to examine their black souls and contemplate eternity in Satan's pit."

Annie takes the handkerchief and blows her nose. "I thought you didn't believe in heaven and hell."

"Just a manner of speaking."

Clutching the handkerchief, Annie's hands fall into her lap, and she shrugs helplessly. "I'm just . . . so tired, Mother."

"Well, of course you are! And getting all this hoopla together for the likes of me piled more on a plate that was too full to start. You need someone to look after you, but you're always the strong one, aren't you? You need to let others carry as much as they can," she says, looking at Eva. "Right, child?"

Eva, stricken, bobs her head. "We can do more, Annie. All of us can!"

"How are your feet holding up?" Mother asks, to change the subject a little. "You have to take care of them, or you'll end up an old wreck like me. Get some flat shoes. Men's work boots are best."

"What will I do?" Annie asks. "After this is over?"

"Find another fight," Mother Jones tells her firmly. "Raise more hell."

"Is it worth it?"

"Maybe not for us. Maybe not even for anyone alive today." She shifts her gaze then and adds, "Maybe not even for you, Eva, young as you are. But we plant the seeds of justice, and justice will rise out of all this muck someday. I believe that. I believe in the future. I do. One day life will be better for the ones who come after us."

She gives a little snort—equal parts resignation and irony—before she adds, "Not that any of the ungrateful little shites'll thank us for it!" She goes still then, struck by a thought. "That's what I should have said! Why does it always come to us after the moment passes?"

With that, she trundles off toward the sofa; in midstride, she stops and turns and points at Eva. "You just make sure that young man of yours is at the depot tomorrow!"

The good weather holds to the end of October, and bright sunshine makes the farewells easier. Thousands of strikers come to Annie Clements's house to escort Mother Jones to the depot, where Eva presents her with another blowsy bouquet of the season's last wildflowers, crisp with morning frost.

Standing on the platform, the little old lady in black shakes hands with the men and hugs the women, and then listens smilingly to the union song that five hundred little kids shout out unmelodiously. She would like to get inside the train and stake out a place near the third-class coal stove on the way down to Milwaukee, but she knows her part in the drama. When the song is done, she will address Local 15 of the

Western Federation of Miners one last time, exhorting them to stay together, to stay strong, to fight like hell! Although she's said all that a thousand times, this morning she has something else to tell them, and when she says it, she will look into the eyes of the gangly, sullen Finnish boy who stands next to Eva Savicki.

"Nothing will ever be given to us," she is going to say. "We will have to fight for every penny, for every bit of justice, every scrap of dignity, every tiny little improvement in the lives of the working class. But we will change things. Maybe the change will come little by little, like a river wears down granite. Or maybe change will come all at once, like a landslide. Those of us alive and fighting today may never get whole for what strikes cost in blood and money. You know that now. And I'll tell you the plain bitter truth of it: we will win battles, but this war will never be over. The money men will do their damnedest to claw it all back."

There will be sober silence then as private fears are spoken publicly by Mary Harris Jones, and then she will go on.

"Let them try! Yes, they will try to break us, to divide us, to fool us. We will not surrender. We won't give up. We can't. Because we're fighting for something much bigger than our own little lives. We are fighting for those who come after us—for those who'll be born long after you and I are dead and forgotten."

She will find Eva's young man in the crowd and look straight at him, and speak then with respect and apology in her eyes.

"Those who come after us will never understand how hard it is for us now. That doesn't concern me, and you shouldn't care, either. You and I—and unions around the world—we do what's right because it's *right*, and not because we expect a lick of gratitude. And one day, because of our sacrifices and our courage and our determination, the world will be a better place for the children of the children who are with us today."

All that is what she will say in a few moments. For now, she listens to the sons and daughters of Calumet copper miners who are singing about something they don't understand.

And in the midst of them, gripping the heavy pole of a huge American flag, stands Annie Clements. Back straight, head high, surrounded by the future.

Early November, 1913

1

Like fire and powder
—Shakespeare, *Romeo and Juliet*

In the far north along the Canadian border, every casual conversation has begun with the same sentiment: "Awful lucky with the weather, eh?"

Few can remember an autumn so mild for so long. At this latitude, summer is over by the end of August, and 1913 has been no exception. September and October were not unusual. Cool mornings, warmish afternoons, chilly nights. By the first week of November, however, it should be well and truly cold. Rain should be snow and the snow should keep piling up until sometime next April. Instead, November's short days have been pleasant, with golden sunlight slanting in from the south. Sweater weather. Enjoyable, but odd and a little unsettling.

Out on the Great Lakes, there are vessels in the water that would have docked weeks ago for winter repairs and refits, in an ordinary year. Shipping companies have urged skippers up and down the Great Lakes to round out an excellent season with one last cruise, one last shipment. Bulk carriers are still being loaded with iron ore and Canadian wheat. Copper ingots, smelted months earlier, are still being sent to market despite the strike. Passenger ships and ferries are still running.

Late-season passengers have been delighted by the clear skies, flat water, and spectacular sunsets. The crews, by contrast, are wary. November can be tricky. The lakes kick up some real screamers with almost no warning, especially Superior. Gales come roaring in from the west, pushing mountains of water east until they smash against Michigan's rocky shores. Waves get bigger and bigger as mere hours pass: sixty, seventy, eighty feet high, with troughs between them that can catch a ship wrong. Hogging it. Snapping its spine. Sucking it into the deep.

By law, passenger ships are required to have radios these days. Captains on bulk carriers, however, have been reluctant to install them. If a gale is bad enough to endanger a vessel, the conditions will be too rough for those little Coast Guard lifeboats to come to anyone's aid. What's the point of a distress call if there's no hope of help? More to the point, ship-to-shore contact would just encourage company men back on land to interfere with a skipper's judgment. It's his responsibility to balance the owners' interests against the safety of his boat and his men, and it's a poor captain who tolerates anyone second-guessing a decision.

Once on the water, he'll rely on the ship's barometer and anemometer, and on his own experience. Temperature? Go out on deck as the sun sets, and judge for yourself how cold it's likely to get that night. Wind direction? Suck on a finger and hold it up above your head. Wind velocity? Is your hat blown off? That's generally all you need to know.

Even so, skippers go through the motions of consulting the Weather Bureau's forecast before leaving port, and this week they've been concerned about warnings of a big storm in the Aleutians that's headed east. Now there's another big one moving up the Mississippi valley from out of the Gulf. Either of those could be trouble. Still, systems coming in from Alaska usually dip south toward Chicago or vault north toward Ontario. The ones coming up from the Gulf usually turn northeast and bury New England.

Usually.

Skippers of the big lakers are weighing the risks and the rewards. Do we try for another voyage before the season is over? The weather is still mild. Will it hold until we can get to the next port? It's a gamble, either way.

Some don't like the look of the sky. Others decide it's a risk worth taking.

In Calumet, a sealed envelope is delivered to the hotel room of Tommy Fisher. The note inside is handwritten. No letterhead, no signature. *Heavy snow expected tomorrow, per Weather Bureau forecast. Proceed.*

Fisher goes to a window and pulls the curtain aside. Dark already, he notes. Starlight. No clouds. No sign of a storm that he can see, at least looking out a window on the east side of the hotel. He shrugs and lets the curtain drop.

Snow or no snow, his guys are ready to go.

The next morning, housewives—always up first—take note of the change. Only yesterday, laundry could be hung out on clotheslines to dry in the sunshine. Overnight, the wind has picked up and the temperature has dropped. Pulling on sweaters, they welcome the chill. When the mud freezes, floors stay cleaner.

Overnight, clouds have settled in, though the cold still hovers just a degree or two above freezing as breakfasts are prepared. Crusty-eyed children are roused, bundled up, and sent outside into a nasty spitting rain to empty chamber pots and bring in wood or coal for the stove. Husbands are shouted at: It's time to get up.

Men roll out of bed, peer out a window, and grunt at the white dust on the ground, for the sleety rain has turned to flurries. Winter, they think, pulling on trousers, looping suspenders over their shoulders. 'Bout time, some think, glad of the change. Marching in the snow won't be near as bad as getting wet. But others go back to bed.

Downtown, Albin Horvat opens the church doors and turns on the basement lights. A dozen volunteers from the Women's Auxiliary arrive minutes later to get vats of coffee started and make breakfast for the unmarried union men who'll need something to eat when they converge on the church. By seven, the marchers are assembling in front of the church, hands thrust into pockets, feet stamping in what is now a raw chill, with winter coats and scarves and hats drawn close around their ears. You always feel the cold more in the first few weeks of winter.

Chins lift and eyes glance at the sky. Not too bad now, though everyone agrees: it'll be snowing good and proper by this afternoon.

A modest cheer goes up when Annie Clements arrives with Kaz and

Eva, who are still yawning and blinking. Annie goes downstairs for the flag, and the kids bring up the banners.

Clamping his arms over his cassock, hunched against the wind, Father Horvat joins Annie outside. Jerking his head toward the marchers, he asks, "What do you think? Fifteen hundred this morning, eh?"

She looks over her shoulder. "Probably closer to a thousand," she admits. "Enough to make a decent showing."

"And I doubt that very many company men are dedicated enough to come out in the snow to shout insults. That said, we might need a different tactic this winter."

She smiles at his "we." "Get inside, Father! You'll catch your death!"

"Until later," he says, hurrying back into the church.

She watches him go. He's right, of course. Lake Superior is giving them fair warning today. You can't march through snowdrifts fifteen feet high. You can't stay outside for two hours when it's thirty below zero.

What next? she asks herself. What should we do next?

She tries to calculate how many parades she has organized since that first giddy day in July. Ninety? No. More. Must be closer to a hundred now. It feels like a million, with nothing to show for it.

With every passing day, the hope and determination supplied by Mother Jones's visit has become harder to summon up. Union membership is eroding. Charlie Miller showed her the rolls: they are down to half of the men they had when the strike started. Some have slunk back to work. Taking their chances with the one-man drills. Doing more work for the same money. Eating crow in their pasties. Others have left Calumet, migrating south to factories where they can work indoors and make more money than a copper miner will ever be paid. Many are wondering if that's the only sensible thing to do. Leave. Find something better, somewhere else.

Annie herself has suggested as much to Joe. "I know how hard the strike has been for you. Maybe we should think about a different place . . ."

He stared at her, brows closing over his nose. "I'm a miner! That's all I know. I don't want to leave. I want to go back to work, is all."

In her weakest moments, at night, when Joe is done with her, she allows herself to think about what she'd do if she weren't married, if she were free to start over and to make different choices. It is no longer possible to ignore the extent to which Michael Sweeney occupies her thoughts. He is always polite. Always correct. Always careful not to give Joe reason to doubt, and yet . . . It's in his eyes. It's in the secret brush of his hand against hers: a choice. A different life.

Grow up, she tells herself now, brushing the thought off like the snowflakes on her shoulders. You're not a child, spinning romance out of air. She looks around for Eva. "Where's Jack?" Annie asks, turning her attention to someone else's fairy tale.

"His family's sick," Eva says, her voice muffled by the crocheted scarf wrapped around her face. "His mother needs him to stay home and help today."

Kaz rolls his eyes, Eva bristles, and they square off.

"I just don't trust him," Kaz begins, as he always does.

"Why not?" Eva always demands.

"I don't know," Kaz says. "There's just something about him!"

And it always escalates from there, so this time, Annie cuts off the squabble before it can get worse. "Jack's a good boy!" she says, giving a warning to Kaz with her eyes.

She almost adds, "He'll be a good husband to Eva," but decides against it. Stay out of this, she tells herself. Let nature take its course. It's not like you've got room to give advice.

The marchers are about to set off when Michael Sweeney arrives, layered thick with borrowed sweaters. "There's a train coming in slow from Houghton," he reports. "Immigrants, is what I've heard. Scabs from New York, right off the boat. Fisher's goons are just having breakfast as usual, but there are company men over at the Armory. Maybe the weather will keep them off the streets."

Her reply is resolute: "But not us!"

She turns her face away from the wind, away from him, but it doesn't matter to Michael Sweeney. He knows every curve and line. Standing alone in the little portable darkroom he's set up in the boardinghouse, he has transferred her image from negative to paper a hundred times and watched her features emerge beneath the chemical bath. Lately, he's spent a lot of time dodging the prints: lightening the dark smudges below the tired eyes, smoothing out the new lines etched between and around them. Even in the flat, unflattering light of an early winter morning, he finds her beautiful. Still, the months have changed her. She is the fuel that keeps the hope of thousands burning, and it's using her up.

"I'm going to leave the camera down in the parish hall. I'm not sure how film will react to this cold." He hesitates then, not wanting to insult her. His offer is whispered when he nods at the flag. "Mrs. Clements, let me carry that for you."

Somehow, she produces a sunburst smile, albeit one that doesn't light up her face as much as it used to. "Perhaps one day, Mr. Sweeney. But not today." With a soft grunt of effort, she lifts that enormous banner over their heads: red and white and blue against slate-gray skies.

Its edges have begun to fray.

"Jesus Christ, it's cold!" Tommy Fisher mutters, burrowing deeper into his cashmere topcoat. Nevertheless, he can't help feeling elated. Today's the day, and he loves this part of his job.

There's a special satisfaction in watching a carefully considered plan come alive with what he expects will be clockwork precision. Downtown, every loyal businessman and professional has been given a company-printed card proclaiming the establishment's proprietor to be a member of the Citizens' Alliance, to be displayed in street-level windows and doorways. For the past week, Fisher has gone over plat maps of the city with his most trusted men, walked with them along the blocks of company houses, pointing out which are union and leaving a discreet chalk mark above the doors of those who are loyal.

"And this one?" he told them, lifting his chin toward one house. "Don't go inside. Maybe just break a window or something, so it don't stand out."

Down in Houghton, an immigrant train has been sidelined, its crew waiting for Fisher's telegram. Used to be, Tommy's brother collected strikebreakers in Pittsburgh and Chicago, but there's union bastards all over the train depots now, handing out flyers. "Anybody hired for Michigan is a scab." That kind of thing. So this time, Tommy had his brother get immigrants straight off the boat in New York and make the whole trip from the coast as miserable as possible. Tommy wants five hundred greenhorns cold, confused, hungry, and crowded so they'll be ready to fight when they climb down out of those freight cars. And to be doubly sure, his men will board the train in Houghton to hand out bottles during the last hour of travel—getting the immigrants liquored up for the festivities.

Wooden truncheons turned on Calumet & Hecla lathes have been cached in crates over at the Armory: ready to be distributed and put to good use. The railroad guys have been briefed. Three blasts on the steam whistle when the train's about fifteen minutes from Calumet. Two more blasts when the train pulls in. That's the signal for four hundred company men to show up at the station. The greenhorns will be kept on board until the strikers' parade is halfway around its route, which always passes by the train depot. The doors will be opened when Fisher himself gives them the nod.

He glances toward the headquarters of C&H and sees MacNaughton standing at his office window. Ozy goddamn Mandias, waiting to see how the morning plays out.

Watch and learn, Tom Fisher thinks, for he understands a lot more about keeping guys happy than big bugs like MacNaughton do. It's simple, really. You gotta take good care of them. You pay top dollar, you get top people! Oh, not the poor chumps you bring in at the end to break heads. Skimp all you want on those foreign bastards, but you have to let the cream rise. You have to watch and see who really gets it—who thinks on his feet, who takes pride and pleasure in his work. Those are the guys you work with, job after job, the ones who carry out the plans and use their own judgment and find ways to do the job better. You don't tell them every little thing to do and how to do it. You don't try to make them into machines. You give them some room to maneuver, some authority over their own work. You give them respect, and that's what you get back. Respect.

And today, that's what Tom Fisher is going to get from Mr. High-and-Mighty James MacNaughton. Respect.

Call me a thug, Fisher thinks with bitter pride. Look at me with contempt. Sneer at my *manners*. I don't give a good goddamn. Today, you will stand up there and admire me. Tonight you're going to admit that I did what I said I'd do, and I did it faster, smarter, and better than anyone else in the business.

And you better juice the fee you thought was such a bargain. One word from me, and my guys'll turn on you like rabid dogs.

In the restaurant of the hotel they've taken over, Fisher's thirty-man executive committee is finishing breakfast—steak and eggs and hash browns and toast and coffee. They are not just well-fed, they are well-dressed, for their nice suits give them pride in their employment and distinguish them from union supporters, as do the heavy woolen top-coats Fisher had sent up from Chicago for their work here in the north.

Sheriff Cruse and his local boys have been told to stay in bed this morning.

"So who's gonna arrest the big bitch?" Jersey asks.

Half a dozen men shout their willingness to take her on.

"One of yiz, or the whole bunch?" Pittsburgh sneers, to raucous laughter.

They gesture to the waiters for more coffee and call each other "deputy," sniggering at the cheap tin badges they got from that stooge Cruse. Waiting for the operation to begin, they discuss whether their shoulder holsters should be over or under their topcoats.

The debate ends when they hear the signal: three whistle blasts from the C&H train. They wipe their mouths on the backs of their hands, get to their feet, button coats and settle hats, and head for the hotel's front door. Time to go punch a few tickets.

"Holy shit!" someone cries when they can see outside through the lobby windows. "Holy shit, look at the snow! When the hell did that start?"

The wind has picked up, too, but they've got a job to do and they enjoy doing it, unlike those lazy union bastards. Four guys—Ulstermen from Northern Ireland—head for the Catholic church. Ten others fan out along the alleys behind houses without a chalk mark above the back doors. The rest squint into the snow and move off to take their posts along the main business street and at the train depot. There they bide their time, stamping their feet in the cold, waiting for the parade to arrive.

"You know what?" Jersey says. "We should get into this union racket. Work both sides of the street! Skim the top off their dues and get paid for busting their heads, too!"

Two blasts on the train whistle, and the immigrants inside the freight cars feel the train slow and stop. The big side doors roll open. Blinking into the gray light, drunk on the unfamiliar liquor their keepers provided this morning, bad-tempered after days and nights of confinement and crowding, they try not to fall as they're prodded to jump down onto the platform.

They are met by enormous men, beefy beneath their impressive woolen coats. These are men whose lives have been hard—you can see that from their crooked noses and hard eyes. But look at their coats! Such nice coats!

Despite being dressed like grandees, the hard-faced men are breaking open boxes with pry bars. The immigrants nudge one another and smile, buoyed by the thought that they, too, might soon be wearing nice warm clothes like these Americans. Confusion returns when the well-dressed men begin emptying the crates of their contents: some kind of tool. Ax handles maybe? Except there are no trees to be seen . . .

A short, solidly built man takes up a position in front of them. He is clearly in charge, and their hopes rise again, for they can see a family resemblance to the smiling, friendly American who met them on the dock in New York—who promised them work and gave them good food and a decent place to sleep before they began the long, terrible train trip to a place they had never heard of: Calumet.

In front of each immigrant car, a wooden crate is flipped over to make a little platform for five well-dressed gentlemen to stand on. In the distance, a parade is approaching, led by someone carrying an American flag. There is singing, too, and someone cries, "They are welcoming us! The Americans are coming to welcome us!"

"Do you want to work?" the stocky man shouts, and his question is repeated in Italian, Magyar, Polish, and Russian by the other men standing on the upturned crates. Well, yes, of course! That's why they all signed up with the friendly American back in New York: to work! So the answer is shouted in Italian, Magyar, Polish, and Russian: *Sì! Igen! Tak! Da!*

"You came here to work, right?"

Sì! Igen! Tak! Da!

"You suffered to get to America, right?"

Sì! Igen! Tak! Da!

"You left everyone and everything to come to America!"

Sì! Igen! Tak! Da!

"Why?"

"To work!" comes the answer in Italian, Magyar, Polish, and Russian.

Within himself, Tom Fisher smiles serenely. It's almost too easy. Promise these morons something they want. Let them believe in it. Then take it away. And tell them who's to blame.

"That's where the work is!" he shouts, waving his arm toward the shaft houses, the engine houses, the boiler houses, the towering mill stacks reaching more than a hundred feet into the sky. "That's where you can get a dollar every day! American cash money!"

There are cheers now, led by company loyalists who have bellied in behind the throng of immigrants.

"But you can't have those jobs," Tom Fisher tells them, waiting for this to be repeated in Italian, Hungarian, Polish, and Russian. Waiting for confusion and muttering turns to anger. "There isn't any work!" he shouts, pointing toward the strikers' march, now just a block away. "Why not? Because those bastards have shut this business down! They don't want you to get jobs!"

There is a roar of fury now, mostly from company loyalists, although the greenhorns, too, are swept up in the emotion of the moment, ready to be set off like a bomb. Still pointing at the marchers, Tom shouts, "They don't want you to work for a dollar a day!" And he loves that line because it's true. "They don't want you to work at all! Your jobs have been stolen! And who did it?"

"The union!" the loyalist scabs shout, with new wooden clubs or last summer's baseball bats lifted into the slate-gray sky. "The union!"

"Who stole your jobs?" Tom asks again.

"The union!" everyone shouts, even the ones who don't know what the word means.

"Well, what're you gonna do about it?" Tom asks, nodding at the railroad signalman.

A blast of the train whistle—

And it's all happening at once.

Fisher's men shoot into the air. A convulsion of startled fear roils the immigrants and the marchers. In a dozen languages, on both sides, men are yelling, "They're shooting at us! The bastards are shooting at us!"

Roaring, the company men push forward, herding the immigrants toward the strikers' parade.

A block away, outraged union men barrel straight into the strike-breakers—just as Tommy Fisher knew they would, for the strikers have kept their tempers and stayed within the law for months and months, and now—at long last—they can make someone pay for every insult, every humiliation, every broken bone and broken heart.

The huge flag goes down, trampled in the panic as women and children rush to the side streets. That big bitch is hauled away by three men. The curly-haired man goes after one of them. A girl jumps on another's back, pounding on his shoulders. A scrawny boy comes at the third, all stupid bravery and righteous anger, but he goes down like a dropped doll when one of Fisher's men clocks him.

Lumps of copper ore go flying through the windows of any shop or office window that does not bear a Citizens' Alliance placard. The Jew's shop is ransacked. From one side of the city to the other, there are screams of fury and fear. Men are kicking in the alleyway doors of union houses, pushing into kitchens, opening pantries and cupboards, smashing whatever comes to hand before they go on to the next house. Ropes of sausages and sides of bacon hanging from the smokehouse rafters are tossed outside, where company loyalists wait to catch them. Sacks of flour and cornmeal and dried beans are dumped on the ground to be blown away or trampled into the mud. A summer's worth of preserves is smashed to the floor.

In St. Joseph's parish hall, tables and desks are tipped over. Papers in filing cabinets are pulled out and tossed into the air. Wooden clubs flatten pots and pans into useless lumps of metal as women shriek. A big camera is smashed, its tripod put to work on the union boss and the priest. Donated clothing is torn to pieces. The petty cash box is stolen.

On the streets, no one will yield. More shots are fired. The gunmen are aiming chest-high now. And at the very hour that two mobs have been hurled together on the streets of Calumet, the cold front that started in the Arctic two thousand miles to the west smashes into the mass of warm, wet air that's traveled up the Mississippi valley from the Gulf of Mexico.

On water and on land, men are beginning to die.

"Will there be anything else, sir?" the butler asks late that evening.

Wrapped in a quilted velvet robe, James MacNaughton looks up from *Rob Roy*. Although the furnace in the cellar is cranking out heat, he is reading by firelight, indulging in nostalgia for the long winter nights when his father would regale the family with a chapter by Walter Scott, while the windows rattled and the oil lamps flickered.

His father always read in dialect, so that the MacNaughton children would grow up with a memory of Scotland, even if their father didn't agree with the author's politics. Now, with a finger to mark his place, James MacNaughton holds up the book and quietly recites, "'Nane were keener than the Glasgow folks, wi' their rabblings and their risings, and their mobs, as the' ca' them now-a-days. But it's an ill wind blaws naebody gude.'" The gale freshens, making the whole house shudder, and he listens to the windows rattling. "We have enough coal to get us through, do we not?"

"Yes, sir, I believe so. Although it will depend on how long this storm lasts. There is also firewood in the garage, if needed."

"Well, then. Until the morning . . ."

"Yes, sir. Good night, sir."

MacNaughton smiles. "Yes," he says. "Yes, it is."

2

More dark and dark are our woes.
—Shakespeare, *Romeo and Juliet*

Four days later, and exactly thirty-seven minutes after rising, when he has left his dressing room and started down to breakfast, the general manager of Calumet & Hecla tarries on the broad staircase landing before descending to the dining room. As is his daily custom, he stands at ease before the large window, hands clasped behind his back, and takes stock of his city.

It is a satisfying exercise, for Calumet is quite likely the best municipality in the world at coping with a massive snowfall. The main streets have already cleared. Downtown, business as usual will resume soon. All evidence of the riot has been removed, apart from boarded-up windows.

When he arrives in the dining room, his step slows imperceptibly. For the first time since the storm began, newspapers have been delivered—four days' worth of neatly stacked special editions of the *Boston Globe*, the *Detroit News*, and the *Chicago Tribune*, along with this morning's *Calumet News* and the *Daily Mining Gazette*.

He sits, as usual, but to the maid's silent astonishment, he waves his oatmeal off, places his spectacles on his nose, and pulls the newspapers toward him. Scanning the front pages of all five newspapers before beginning to read, he restacks them, with the latest on the bottom, and begins to read the oldest so he can understand the sequence of events.

Two weather systems combined to create an unprecedented, immense, and deadly snowstorm that covered a third of the continent. The first reports warned that anyone caught outside would be in grave danger. Trolley cars and trains were stopped on their tracks, trapping riders. Tree limbs were bringing down electric lines. Telephone and telegraph wires sagged under the ice, dragged their poles over, and snapped. There was no way to call for help.

Twenty-four hours later, the blizzard had intensified. Ambulances could no longer negotiate the snow-clogged streets. Bodies had to remain where they lay. Not even those sheltering inside could be considered safe. Windows were blown in. Roofs collapsed. Vertical surfaces perpendicular to the gale collected twenty-foot drifts; mortar crumbled under the lateral load, and brick walls toppled.

By the third day, roads and long-haul railways were impassable throughout the Midwest. Cities had become islands in a sea of snow; neither food nor fuel could get through. Candles were lit, and knocked over; houses burned as firemen worked frantically to dig their stations out. In Cleveland and Detroit, tap water turned brown when untreated sewage and lake-bottom sludge were sucked into city intake pipes along the Great Lakes shores. Health officers knew what to recommend: put a pinch of alum in each pint of water; boil all drinking and cooking water. Only there was no way to tell anyone. The death toll was rising. Frantic public health departments advised hospitals and morgues to brace for a spike in typhoid cases.

Messages from the Great Lakes shippers began to come in, reporting hurricane-force winds, torrential rain, a plummeting temperature that quickly broke below zero and kept dropping. Within minutes, ice coated every surface of the vessels, followed by a heavy, wet snow. Even ships built to withstand the worst weather on record have gone down. The *Leafield,* the *Henry B. Smith,* the *Plymouth,* the *Argus,* the *James Carruthers,* the *Hydrus,* the *John A. McGean,* the *Charles S. Price,* the *Regina,* the *Isaac M. Scott,* the *Wexford,* and *Lightship No. 82,* all reported lost. A dozen other vessels have been blown against rocky shores and wrecked. The death toll so far: two hundred and thirty-eight drowned. More still missing.

The worst blizzard in recorded history, was the U.S. Weather Service's declaration. By the time it is over, the agency predicted, the final tally will be staggering. Many millions of dollars in damage, many thousands of deaths.

Four days after its start, the storm still dominates the latest news, though the threat of famine and food riots has receded. Factual news has devolved into dozens of "human interest" stories. The storm was no respecter of persons. John D. Rockefeller's estate lost power, so he sent his employees out to buy candles; there were none to be found, so the tycoon went to bed early. Helen Keller, on a lecture tour, was escorted back to her hotel room; blind and deaf, she could nevertheless feel the power of the wind. "The storm waves were not deterred by stone walls and plate glass windows," she told a reporter. The British comedienne Marie Lloyd and the famous actor Richard Bennett spent uncomfortable days stranded between cities when their trains hit impassable snowdrifts. There are heartwarming tales of valiant nobodies as well. A young man who helped a group of elderly women off a trolley and carried them on his back, one by one, to safety. A nameless person dug an unconscious man out of a snowbank and dragged him to shelter, undoubtedly saving a life. A shivering, howling dog refused to leave the side of his stricken master's frozen body.

Government buildings, taverns, movie houses, and concert halls are still sheltering anyone who needs a place to stay. Boy Scouts have taken up shovels to clear fire hydrants and city sidewalks. Dairies are beginning to make deliveries as they did in the old days: on sleds pulled by horses. People without children are asked to refrain from buying that milk so that it can be sold to those who need it most . . .

It is only when James MacNaughton gets to the local papers that his heartbeat slows and his inner calm returns, for the only newspaper that mentions the Calumet riot is the *Daily Mining Gazette,* and even the *Gazette*'s account is scant on detail. Violent labor demonstration. Union agitators arrested.

With a deep breath of satisfaction, James MacNaughton sets the pile of newspapers aside. Providence, he thinks, and he thanks God for the storm. America's putative Joan of Arc is in jail, along with all the union officials. And no one outside the Copper Country is any the wiser.

"I'll have that oatmeal now," he calls out to the kitchen.

It is the first time any of them have ever heard him speak before his breakfast. And he sounds . . . cheerful.

His good mood persists even after the butler announces that Tom Fisher is waiting for him in the study.

"Kinda pretty, now," Fisher remarks, standing at the window. The sky has cleared to a brilliant blue, as it often does in the days after a storm has passed, but the cold remains so intense that moisture in the air freezes into glittering crystals that float like a fog of diamonds. "That was a hell of a storm. Never saw anything like it! Anyways, how'd you like our little party? My boys and I know what we're doing, eh? Nice touch, having them scatter rocks and bottles around, right? Made it look like the strikers came ready for a brawl!"

MacNaughton inclines his head.

"And now all you have to do is wait for winter to do the rest!" Fisher continues, annoyed by the silence. "Those bastards are gonna get awful hungry before very long. Their little kiddies are gonna be boohooing by the end of the week. Am I right? Am I right?"

"Very likely," MacNaughton acknowledges neutrally.

"And you'll be back in business by the end of the year. Just like I promised."

With a deep breath, MacNaughton moves to his desk and gestures toward the chair on the other side of the polished rosewood expanse. "Sit down, Mr. Fisher. If you please."

Brows raised at the sudden courtesy, Fisher purses his lips. Then, to establish parity, he inclines his head just as MacNaughton did, and takes a seat.

"Mr. Fisher, this morning Sheriff Cruse received a telegram from Governor Ferris reminding him that Michigan state law requires all deputies to be bona fide residents of the county in which the appointment is made for at least three months prior to their appointment. May I assume that your men do not fulfill that requirement?"

Fisher snorts.

MacNaughton opens a desk drawer, pulls out a check register, and fills out a draft. "This will cover the agreed-upon fee. I included something extra to expedite the departure of your men from the Copper Country."

Seeing the number, Fisher whistles, genuinely impressed. "Well, that's very generous of you, sir. My guys will now be happy to leave your fair city in your own good hands."

"That is the desired effect."

Something about the tone makes Fisher think MacNaughton is not quite done, so he waits, eyes level.

"Mr. Fisher, I would like you to resign your position as deputy but to stay on in Calumet . . . in an advisory capacity. Perhaps some of your most reliable men could be retained as well for irregular but important projects—ones that require discretion."

Fisher sits back. He was prepared to be shown the door and told to get out of town. Company men never like to admit that they couldn't solve a problem on their own. Many's the time he's offered his hand at the end of a contract only to have it left in the air by the snobby son of a bitch who just paid him off. "Screw you, too," he usually says, adding, "Just remember. If the check bounces? I know where you live."

This time, he merely asks, "What do you have in mind?"

"This strike is, as you know, the first in Calumet & Hecla's history. I am determined that it shall be the last, as well. The union has brought in anarchist rabble-rousers, so I see no reason why the company should not call upon individuals like yourself who have experience in increasing the pressure on strikers to go back to work. In particular, the Citizens' Alliance Council could use some guidance from you and your . . . executive committee."

"How much 'guidance' would you like to purchase? I got a dozen guys I'd keep with me. The rest are just muscle."

"Shall we say five hundred dollars a month?"

Fisher's eyes warm, but his lips pull down as though he were thinking the proposition over. "Each," he says.

MacNaughton's eyes narrow; then he nods. "Sheriff Cruse will have deputies detailed to collect badges from your nonessential employees when they leave. I can have a company train here by four this afternoon. Where would you like us to transport them?"

"Get 'em to Chicago. I'll give 'em some cash. They'll make their own way."

"And the immigrants?"

"Hell, I don't give a damn. Dump 'em in Milwaukee, I guess."

"As you wish. This, by the way, will be the last time you and I meet directly. Any further contact will be by proxy only. I will have a member of the Citizens' Alliance contact you at your hotel."

MacNaughton's tone clearly implies that they are done. Fisher, however, is enjoying this and waits for a formal farewell.

"Close the door behind you," MacNaughton says.

Deep winter in the Upper Peninsula often lasts for seven or eight months. Even in the best of times—when the men are working, when the summer has been kind—miners' wives are frugal. Every crumb of bread is saved and added to ground pork; long before the spring thaw, cabbage rolls will have more leaves than meat. As the months pass, pasty dough is rolled thinner. Soups and the children's milk are watered to fill bellies a little more, a little longer. By the time the weather breaks and new gardens can be put in, almost all the women will be skipping meals. "I'm not hungry," they'll tell their husbands and kids. "You eat it." Nursing mothers will lose weight and their breasts will dry up; babies are nearly always weaned in the spring.

This winter will be the worst in memory for union households all over the Keweenaw, and it will be worst of all in Calumet. MacNaughton's thugs have seen to that.

In the hours after the riot, union housewives use spoons to scrape the floor, scooping up the contents of broken jars of preserves. Spreading the mess out on baking sheets, setting lamps or candles off to the side, they patiently pull glittering glass shards out of the food they put up for the winter, trying not to bleed into the jams and pickles while their husbands sleep off their beatings. Kids are bundled up and sent outside to search beneath the snow for potatoes and carrots and turnips and cabbages scattered by the strikebreakers. Those vegetables can be scrubbed up and salvaged. And thank God for that small mercy, for the word is going around now: there will be no more credit from Moishe Glass's store. He, too, was beaten, and his oldest son was arrested for trying to defend him. The store was trashed, and MacNaughton's bully boys have threatened all of Moishe's suppliers: Demand cash from the Jew, or your business will get the same treatment.

After a time, company carpenters come around to board up broken windows and doors. They laugh at their own sloppy workmanship, for they have their orders: fix things just enough to keep the company houses from deteriorating but not enough to keep the renters warm. So union men, battered and aching, nail rugs over the gaps in the wood where the snow drifts in, while union women gather every quilt and blanket in the house to heap on the beds. Whole families huddle together to share their bodies' warmth during the long days and endless nights.

Without Annie's parades and meetings and dances and projects to bring them together, strikers' families are isolated in the dark, cold houses. Husbands and brothers and grown sons pass the time with cards, or drink and brood, and shout at babies whose hungry wails grate on everyone's nerves. Wives try to keep the kids quiet and the house clean. Laundry is the worst of the chores, and the worst of the laundry is scrubbing dirty diapers and menstrual rags in tubs of cold water. Hands freezing, women hang up the rectangles of shamefully stained cloth, shivering as drips run down their arms.

In the attics, the rafters groan and twist alarmingly under the weight of the snow. In the walls, mice skitter and gnaw, darting out at night to snatch any crumb that somehow escaped a housewife's attention. In the dark, under the piles of quilts and blankets and braided-rag rugs, men whisper of skipping out on the rent, of leaving town, of finding some kind of work somewhere else.

"We can't win," they are starting to say. "If we're going to give up, sooner is better than later."

At the first general meeting after the riot, nobody can predict how the union vote will go. There is anger, grief, stubbornness, despair, frustration, and no clear way forward. The Federation heard the news about the riot and telegraphed a promise to find more money. For all anybody knows, it's in the bank now, but all the local union leaders are in jail and the bank officers are so scared of MacNaughton, they won't let anybody else sign a check.

The argument goes on for hours.

The kids are hungry. The company is going to win.

Blood has been shed. Union men have died in the streets.

Blood has always been shed.

At least those guys died for the future, not for some rich bastard's greed.

In the end, a bare majority votes to continue. Frank Aaltonen is elected as president pro tem, and a delegation goes with him to the bank, where he demands that the union money be released. Alarmed by the crowd, the bank manager nods to a teller, who counts out the cash. It's not much, but it will buy them a little time.

At the end of the week, low and heavy clouds settle over the north like a blanket. The cold moderates from lethal to merely bitter. Desperate to be helpful, children go out with old flour sacks and scavenge along the train tracks for coal now deliberately tossed to them by sympathetic firemen. Sometimes the kids come home with a few pennies and proudly hand them over to their mothers.

They are begging on the streets.

"Don't tell your father," the mothers say. "It will break his heart."

Churches are the last resort. Ministers and priests are writing to congregations outside the Copper Country, asking for donations of clothing and food and money.

"Charity," the men mutter. Hating themselves. Hating MacNaughton. Hating the union. "I just want to work. I just want to go back to *work*."

Annie would know what to do, the wives think, but Annie is in jail with the rest of the union officers. No one says it aloud, though all the women are thinking it now: it will be easier to quit if Annie's gone.

3

Shut up in prison, kept without my food,
Whipped and tormented
—Shakespeare, *Romeo and Juliet*

She's heard stories about what happens in jail to women like her. Trade unionists. Suffragists. Women who don't know their place. Women who speak up. Women who make trouble.

Annie Clements is not scared. She's big. She's strong. Like most women, she's been beaten before. She thinks she's ready for what will happen after her arrest. She is wrong.

Separated from the others. Frog-marched into the jail. Slammed against the sandstone walls of an unheated cell. Kicked when she falls. Hauled upright and stripped by policemen. With her hands cuffed to a hook in the ceiling, her arms above her head, her feet reach the floor if only barely. When the beating begins, she kicks and tries to use her knees, but the cops dance out of reach and laugh because all she can do is twist and squirm, hoping to take the billy club blows to her buttocks and back. When she's too tired to fight back, they aim for her unprotected breasts and keep at it until she is sobbing and snot pours out of her nose and down into her mouth. After they've had their fun, they take the cuffs off and let her crumple, naked, to the floor. Chuckling, they lock the cell and leave. She hears them laughing again as they walk down the corridor, talking about how funny it was when she tried to protect herself.

The lights go out. She curses them, and weeps alone.

When she can gather herself, she gets up off the floor and feels along the masonry walls until she finds a wide wooden platform that is slightly warmer than the cement floor of the cell. Cold, scared, aching, alert for the sound of footsteps and keys rattling, she lies down and waits for whatever comes next. Sleep is impossible.

In the morning, a patch of sky becomes visible through a small window near the ceiling. There is a slop bucket in the corner, with a pail of cold water next to it. Her breasts are a mass of bruises. Her back aches fiercely. When she uses the bucket, she sees why: there is blood in her urine.

She will not cry. She will not cry. She will not cry.

Sitting gingerly on the plank that serves as a bed, she eases herself back down and lies flat until she hears a man's voice say, "She's in there."

Despite the pain, she springs up, ready to fight.

A middle-aged woman in uniform approaches the cell. There is no sympathy, no encouragement in the other woman's eyes.

Annie stands as straight as she can. Naked. Determined that she will not be ashamed. "I want a lawyer," she says, and her voice does not crack.

"What you want and what you'll get are two different things." The matron tosses a gray cotton dress and a faded apron through the bars. "Put that on. It's the biggest we've got. If it won't button, put the apron over your front."

"I've committed no crime. I am a political prisoner. I want my own clothing back."

The woman makes a little noise of dismissal through pursed lips. "Your hearing's in ten minutes. I'll take you to court like you are, if that's what you want."

It's a challenge Annie considers. Let the judge see what the jailers have done, she thinks. Let him see the bruises and cuts. But . . . no. He'll just assume I resisted arrest.

Bending carefully at the knees to keep her aching back straight, she reaches down for the dress on the floor. Keeping her eyes on the matron, she steps into the dress. It stinks of the last woman to wear it, but she is glad of its slight warmth and the small dignity the garment provides. The buttons won't close over her bosom, so she pulls the apron on. When her eyes are clear of the fabric, she stares defiantly at the squat, dyspeptic woman before her.

The matron shakes her head. "Jesus. They said you were a big bitch, and that was no lie." She throws Annie's own shoes and stockings through the bars. "Put those on."

"I want—"

"What you want doesn't make a bit of difference to me or anyone else in here. Put your shoes on or walk through the snow barefoot."

Sitting on the wooden shelf, Annie leans over as little as is necessary to draw up her stockings and tie the shoes, gritting her teeth against the groan she will not allow to escape. When she's done that, the matron calls for a bailiff to come and unlock the cell door.

"That way," the woman says, pointing down the corridor with a truncheon. "Try anything on me, I'll make you wish the boys still had you."

The windows of the courtroom are half-blocked by snowdrifts, and it's still snowing. Somewhere in the building, a furnace pours out waves of heat; the judge doesn't appreciate it nearly as much as the barely dressed prisoner does. Opening his robes to keep from perspiring, he looks bored and annoyed behind an imposing wooden desk.

"Union?" he asks the bailiff, who nods and shrugs.

She tries to speak, but the judge cuts in: "State your name and address."

"Anna Klobuchar Clements. I want a lawyer."

"Can you post bail?"

"No, but my lawyer—"

"How do you plead?"

"I don't know what I'm accused of! I am guilty—" She is about to say, *of nothing more than exercising the constitutional right of any American citizen,* only before she can get the words out, the judge bangs his gavel.

"Guilty plea entered," he says to the court recorder. "House of Detention. Fifteen days. Next!"

*   *   *

A scant breakfast of weak coffee and thin oatmeal is waiting for her on the plank bed in the cell. Hours pass. Eventually there are two other meals, each as meager as breakfast. The daylight fades. Aching from last night's beating, she lies on the plank and waits, trying not to panic or despair.

This is part of it, she tells herself. They're letting fear do their work.

Eventually exhaustion overcomes worry and cold. Sometime during the night, the cell door opens. Panicking, she sits abruptly, crying out from the stabbing misery in her back, but the newcomer is only a girl wearing a gray jailhouse dress. They both watch the jailer lock the cell and retreat down the dark hallway. The newcomer rubs her skinny arms briskly to get some warmth into them, and stands by the door for a few minutes while her eyes adjust to the darkness.

"Say!" she exclaims when she recognizes the tall woman on the bench. "You're Big Annie! I seen your pitcher in the papers! I'm Betty." Without missing a beat, the child turns back toward the corridor and yells, "Hey! Henry! You know damn well we get two blankets each! And there's supposed to be a mattress in here!"

To Annie's astonishment, a guard appears fairly promptly. He is holding a mattress so thin, he can feed it between the bars without opening the cell door.

"And the blankets, Henry!" the child reminds him. She winks at Annie as they wait. "You gotta know your rights, and you gotta make some noise."

"Why were you arrested?" Annie asks after a time.

"Soliciting. My dad lost both legs in a cave-in. I'm the oldest, so . . ." When Annie stares, the girl shrugs, as though prostitution to support your family is simply expected of her. Then she grins, proud of her own canniness. "Made sure I got arrested tonight, though! I knew a hooker, she froze to death last winter."

When the blankets arrive, Betty joins Annie on the filthy mattress, and they pull all four blankets over the two of them. Slowly, their shared body warmth works its way past their skin, into their muscles, and like the child she is, Betty falls asleep almost immediately, her bony young back curled against Annie's belly.

After a time, Annie rises carefully on an elbow and studies the unlined face resting on a slender arm. Fifteen, maybe? Not much older than Eva Savicki . . . A child, on the street. A girl in jail because crippled workers and their families are tossed aside like used rags.

And I am here for the same reason, she tells herself, lying down again. I am here because miners and their families are discarded when their usefulness is done.

They wake to dim light and a woman's howls, somewhere down the corridor.

Betty grabs one of the four blankets and wraps it around her shoulders. Moving to the bucket in the corner, she squats over it with nonchalant familiarity. Down the hallway, the moans and shrieks rise in pitch and volume.

"What is *wrong* with her?" Annie asks with more exasperation than compassion. "Is she having a baby?"

"Oh, that's Beatrice. Bea's a China girl. Opium, get it?" Wiping herself with a sponge left next to the bucket of water, Betty scoots back under the blankets and cuddles close. "Don't you know anybody like Beatrice?"

Annie shakes her head, and Betty seems surprised. "A lot of the miners get the habit in Houghton, after they get hurt. Sometimes their families start using, too. Me? I don't, but a good belt of whiskey helps when the johns get rough."

All day long, Beatrice screams and cries. Sometimes the iron bars clang as the poor woman beats her head against them. Betty chatters casually about her life and the other girls who work the streets and how she hopes to be hired by one of the brothels in Houghton. She gives no sign that she hears Beatrice, even though that woman's anguish—a relentless wail of insatiable, unbearable, unrelenting *need*—is the worst thing Annie has ever listened to. Worse than childbirth. Worse than cancer. Worse than a limb crushed by rock.

"The judge said I'd be sent to the House of Detention," Annie says toward evening, trying to think of something besides Beatrice. "Is this detention? Is this where we stay?"

Betty laughs. "Oh, no. The workhouse is in Marquette. They're prolly just waiting for the roads to get clear before they can send us out."

"You're coming?" Annie asks. To the workhouse, she means. Coming with me, she means. She tries not to look relieved.

"Yeah, this time I'll go," the child says ruefully. "When the weather's decent, I just do the judge a favor so's I can get out the next morning." She winks and then laughs, amused when Annie's eyes widen. "When it's this cold? I'd rather spend a week at the workhouse. My family'll miss the money, but I'm no good to them if I freeze to death out there."

The girl's voice hardens then. "'Bout time for my little sister to pay her own way. She's old enough now."

Sometime during the long black night, Beatrice falls silent. Is she dead or just asleep, Annie wonders. And she wonders, as well, which would leave the woman better off.

Two days later, there is a sudden spike in activity. While the matron trusts Betty to walk on her own, two guards come for Annie, shackling her hands behind her back, grabbing her by the arms, and half-dragging her outside.

There is no reason to drag her. They're just doing it to humiliate her, so she lets her body go limp and makes it harder for them to move her. Someone cuffs the back of her head and says, "Walk, bitch."

A small triumph: annoying her keepers.

The doors open to a high-walled, stone-cobbled yard ringed by mounds of snow too high to see over. Wearing cotton prison dresses, several other prostitutes greet Betty as one of their own. A bone-thin woman stands apart, hollow-eyed and silent. Beatrice, Annie thinks. That must be Beatrice.

For what feels like hours, the prisoners hop from foot to foot and clap their hands over their arms, trying not to freeze. "We're waiting for the Black Marias," Betty explains. "They bring us out early so we're too cold to give them a hard time about loading up."

The police van finally pulls into the yard. The back doors are flung open, and a set of rickety steps is tipped out on its hinges. The women climb inside, chatting with remarkable good humor, happy to be out of the wind swirling in the courtyard. Still shackled, Annie stumbles as she climbs in, and the guards laugh, but the other girls help her get to her feet and find a seat on one of the wooden benches.

The van is painted black inside and out. There are no windows, just a few louvers high on the walls. It would be an oven in the summer. In this weather, the closeness of their bodies provides the prisoners with a little welcome warmth.

Another long wait. Across the courtyard, a heavy door swings open, iron hinges squealing. Annie half-stands and cranes her neck to see between the van's louvers. Chained yet heavily guarded nonetheless, male prisoners shuffle outside. She recognizes several union officers: Ben Goggia, Yanko Tersich, and Peter Jedda, all of whom look as though they've been treated as badly as Annie has been. She sees Ike Glass, one of Moishe Glass's sons. He isn't even a union member! she thinks. Then her breath stops when she spots Michael Sweeney.

Although he himself is limping heavily, he has both hands around the arm of a man whose blackened eyes are swollen shut above a nose that's mashed toward his left cheek. "Two more steps," she hears Mike tell the man he's guiding, "then we're at the van."

Dear God, she thinks. That's Charlie Miller!

"Michael?" she shouts. "Michael!"

"Annie!" he calls, looking around for her.

"Michael! How many—?"

"Annie, are you all right?"

"Yes!" she lies. "How many of us—?" How many of us are in jail, she means, but he answers the question he thinks she's asking.

"Seven dead, I think. One in the hospital—"

"Dead! Who's dead?"

"Shut up, you!" one of the male guards says, jabbing Michael in the back with a billy club.

Michael gets Charlie up the steps, and they disappear into the men's Maria.

Motors are cranked and turn over. The vans ease forward and start their creaking, shuddering, skidding way toward the Marquette workhouse.

4

Beg, starve, die in the streets!
. . . I'll ne'er acknowledge thee.
—Shakespeare, *Romeo and Juliet*

In Calumet that afternoon, James MacNaughton settles himself behind the desk, ready to work through the backlog of mail that awaits him at the office. Internal memos about the number of men who've returned to work. Accumulated messages from ownership in Boston. And a plain white envelope, addressed to him in a now-familiar hand.

He opens that one with particular interest, for it is the first to arrive since the riot. It is a report on the casualties. Many strikers were hurt—cuts, bruises, broken bones. The dead are listed, but he skims over names that are impossible to pronounce, and which mean nothing to him. *Diazig Tižan, Stanko Stepić, Ivan Stimać, Aino Kallunkis, Johan Myllykangas, Yrja Aaltonen . . .*

There was another body, someone nobody seems to know. The writer has enclosed a photograph found in the dead man's pocket. MacNaughton sets the letter aside and studies the stiffly posed family portrait with mild curiosity. An elderly woman, a middle-aged couple, six stair-step children, the oldest of whom is perhaps twenty, probably the one who is dead now. MacNaughton turns the picture over and sees an awkwardly printed notation. *Ricordati di noi caro figlio Manfredi.* One of Fisher's immigrants, most likely. Who knows?

He tosses the photo into the wastebasket and returns to the spy's report. Its second page takes an offensive turn, tone changing from the spare factual rendering MacNaughton has come to respect since their correspondence began. The writer now sounds aggrieved. He complains about unnecessary damage to the church and to the workmen's houses and the union pantries. He bemoans the fact that innocent children will suffer. He hints of dissatisfaction with the agreement they made in July. He wants to renegotiate its terms, to shorten the duration of the contract.

Snorting softly at the impertinence, MacNaughton dismisses any thought he once had of employing this person after the strike ends. Have you learned nothing? he wonders. I do not negotiate.

He strikes a match, holds the letter up by one corner, and watches the words *innocent children will suffer* blacken and curl as the flame reaches them. Yes, they will, he thinks. And they will remember a lesson that will serve them well when they are old enough to work: ignore the blandishments of union organizers. You cannot win, and your own children will suffer as you did in your youth.

Shaking the last bit of flaming paper out before his fingers burn, he brushes a few stray ashes into the basket, where they settle onto the photograph. Then he takes a fresh handkerchief from his pocket and rubs a smudge of ash from his fingers before walking to the office window.

Come to your senses, he tells the rebels in his mind. I am a reasonable man. Those who denounce the union will be welcomed back. All will be as it was.

Down at the depot, the first group of Fisher's hirelings is boarding the train out of town. It comes to him: perhaps the only reason some strikers are staying in Calumet is that they can't afford to leave! Perhaps the company should offer free passage out of town for union men. Shipments of the new drills are being delivered every week. Labor requirements will be halved. Why wait for the end of the strike? Why not decrease the number of potential troublemakers as soon as possible?

Pleased by the notion, he is about to turn from the window and calculate the cost-benefit ratios when he sees two men carrying a large wooden crate into the building.

On guard, he steps away from the glass. Unions have been known to bomb the offices of companies under siege. You cannot be too careful with militants and anarchists roaming the streets. Sheriff's deputies guard the C&H property, but they really should be stationed at the homes of corporate officers as well.

Before long, however, his secretary buzzes him on the intercom. "It's here, Mr. MacNaughton! The trophy is here, and it is beautiful!"

Relieved, though perhaps a little unnerved by the anxiety he has momentarily experienced, he opens the door to the anteroom, and there it stands: the MacNaughton Cup. Three feet high. Forty pounds of handcrafted sterling silver, to be awarded annually to the regular season conference champion of the Western Collegiate Hockey Association.

Before leaving for the girls' European tour, Mary worked for weeks with a silversmith to design it. When he saw the craftsman's bid, James was taken aback; now he can see that two thousand dollars bought the perfect combination of icy gleam and tasteful ornamentation. It is breathtaking.

"Send a cable to Mrs. MacNaughton at the Plaza Athénée Paris," he tells the smiling secretary. "Tell her that the cup has been delivered and I am pleased."

With that, he returns to his office and gives his attention to the idea of adding a freight car to each train going south to export former miners who will become somebody else's headache. This evening, however, he will write to his wife personally, and include news that he is happy to share.

Order in the city shall soon be restored, he will assure Mary. *You and the girls can plan on coming home in the spring.*

Late November, 1913

1

After the gunfire, her memories are a jumble. Eva can remember shouts of surprise and roars of anger. She remembers union men rushing toward the scabs at the train depot. She remembers women screaming. She remembers trying to protect Annie, and she remembers falling to the ground when some awful man laid a club over her arm, and she remembers how that arm went numb. The bruise is the largest she's ever endured and it aches now, but she remembers not feeling the blow at the time. She remembers the bottoms of Annie's shoes as she was dragged away by thugs wearing badges. She remembers Annie's great flag twisted and trampled.

She remembers her brother's blood: brilliant red and so warm it melted the snow.

And then? There is time she can't account for.

Later, somehow, she found herself in the attic bedroom and she remembers Carla Caretto saying, "You gonna stay with us. Long's you need to, you gonna stay up here with me and the girls."

In the days since the riot, moments of that weird blank time have begun to surface. Sometimes her eyes snap open in the deep cold of starless nights and she lies still, untangling the snarl of nightmare images and genuine memories, piecing together where she is and why.

When she remembers more clearly what has happened, she feels her throat close up and her eyes sting. Warm and sweet, Carla's girls, Rose and Grace, are snuggled beside her in the narrow bed. So she cries without sound, without motion. She does not want to disturb them.

In the morning, she dresses, drinks a little tea, and hurries downtown, walking past the white crosses that have been nailed to telephone poles near where each man was killed.

There's really nothing she can do at the hospital except sit there, willing Kaz to wake up, to make fun of her, to tell her he was just teasing. Now and then, the white curtains around her brother's bed are pulled aside. Someone comes in. A nurse usually, checking his pulse or changing the bandages around his head. Once it was Mr. Glass who came to visit. His face was cut up and he was hobbling, but alive.

For a long time he just stood in the corner, turning his cap around and around in his bony hands. Then he came close to Eva and began to speak. "The old Jews, they tell us, save one life? You save a whole world. Here's what I think. Improve one life? You improve the world. So . . ." He gestured toward the bed. "Not for nothing! This is not for nothing," he told Eva fiercely, his eyes on Kazimir's motionless form. "To make the world better, even a little bit—that's something to fight for."

Other men have come, too. She doesn't remember who exactly. Union men, by ones and twos. Bundled against the cold, they pulled off knitted hats and held them in thick-fingered hands. Awkward, silent, they stood over the bed and looked down at the thin young body beneath the white linens. Before leaving, they looked at her and shrugged their sorrow helplessly. *Won't be long now,* their eyes said. They meant to comfort her. That was the best they could do.

Of course, women also came. Unlike the men, they were willing to speak to Eva, although their news was grim. Annie and the union officials are being blamed for the riot. MacNaughton's thugs started it, but they've all gone free. Dozens of strikers were hurt, they told her. Seven are already dead. Six of us, and one of them—an Italian boy by the looks of him.

The women would gaze at the body in the bed then. A man in spirit. Thin and childlike now, the face pale as a baby's, the head swaddled in white bandages. Nobody will say it; still, she can hear them thinking: *It'll be eight, soon.*

The women bring meals for her, even though they have so little at home. Eva wishes they wouldn't. Her mouth is dry. Everything tastes like . . . nothing. Like paper. Like a dishrag must taste if anyone was stupid enough to taste a dishrag. She knows it's important to the women to feel they've done something for her. So she breaks off a little piece of bread, or the edge of a small pasty. She makes herself chew and swallow. "Thank you," she says, handing it back, "but I'm not hungry. Save it for the kids."

Mrs. Kivisto has visited. The first time, she brought little Pria. Staring at Kaz's bandaged head, the child asked, "He gonna go inna box?" Mrs. Kivisto shushed her. For a time, she simply watched the shallow breathing of the boy who might have been her eldest son's brother-in-law. Then she pulled her Pria to her bosom. "Poor kids," she said in English, so Eva could understand. "They learn so young . . ."

Jack was there a lot. More than anyone else. He would slip through the curtains and sit in one of the white metal chairs, waiting for a chance to be helpful. Hopping up to fetch a nurse or a glass of water, or simply sitting at Kazimir's side when Eva had to excuse herself. He just wanted to be of use, and Eva understood that. The problem is, Kaz himself had never warmed to Jack, and Eva finds herself annoyed at the way Jack hangs around all the time.

She wants to sit quietly with her brother without being hovered over and watched. She wishes Jack would leave her alone, and . . . That is when she remembers Jack's first words to her. Go away, he said.

I just thought you shouldn't be alone, she said.

He's sorry about Kaz, she realizes.

Jack loves me, she realizes. And . . . she feels nothing.

The days pass. Kaz lingers for so long, there is time to hope that he will recover and to fear that he will remain like this forever: pale and motionless. Then one morning Eva arrives to find the curtains drawn back.

A nurse, not much older than Eva herself, has stripped the bed. There is a pile of crumpled linens on the chair, and she is making up the mattress with clean, pressed sheets. Getting it ready for the next patient.

Straightening, the nurse says, "I'm so sorry, dear. They took him away last night."

Eva stands still, staring at the empty bed.

"He passed away in his sleep," she hears the nurse say. "It was peaceful."

Half-turning to face the nurse, she is calm when she speaks. "My brother didn't pass away," she says. "He was murdered. And it wasn't peaceful. His skull was broken by a strikebreaker with a badge."

Father Horvat takes care of everything for her. A lot of people come to the funeral Mass. It's still brutally cold, so the ceremony at the grave site is brief: a couple of prayers and then the coffin is lowered into one of the many holes dug in the autumn for people who would die during the winter, when the ground is difficult to excavate.

Some people go straight home from the cemetery. Others return to St. Joseph's basement. It's been cleaned up and repaired after the vandalism. Carla Caretto has managed to pull together a little reception with small contributions from the Auxiliary. Just coffee and a few little cookies, but it's better than nothing.

Nobody stays long. They shrug into their coats and shuffle past the dry-eyed girl in black who stands at the doorway to the vestibule, accepting the murmured condolences offered to the sole surviving member of the Savicki family. "It's the shock," they tell one another as they pass her and move toward the vestibule. "Poor thing. All alone now."

Hovering near Eva, Jack Kivisto almost argues with them. *She's still got me,* he wants to say. Instead he stays quiet, following Eva and the priest up the stairs when the big room empties, waiting with her while Father Horvat locks the doors that lead down to the parish hall—an extremity deemed necessary since the day of the attacks.

"Thank you," Eva says then, "for what you said during the funeral, Father."

The priest smiles as much as the scabby split lip beneath a yellow bruised cheek will allow. "You probably won't remember anything I said," he tells her. "That's normal. Would you like Jack to walk you . . . ?"

Home, he was going to say. The word dies in his mouth. Where is home for Eva now? Parents dead. Sister dead. Brother dead. Has she gone back to her uncle? Surely the girl is not living with Joe Clements after Annie's arrest.

"It's only two blocks to the Carettos' house," Eva says. "I'll be staying with them until . . ." She, too, stops speaking, for she has no idea what comes next—in the sentence or in her life. "Father, if it's all right, I'd like to spend a little time in church. Neither of you need to stay."

"Of course," the priest says. "God bless you and keep you," he adds, pulling open one of the heavy carved doors for her. "If you need anything more, I'll be in the rectory."

"I'll wait," Jack says. "My mother wants you to come to our house for supper. She says you shouldn't be alone."

Eva seems to notice him for the first time. "No," she says. "Really. Don't wait. I'd rather be alone."

He, too, remembers the first time they spoke. It was just after his father died, and he said the same thing to her, much less kindly. He watches Eva walk up the central aisle.

The priest pats him on the shoulder, aware of the boy's hurt and shame and confusion. "She'll be all right. Sometimes, you just need some quiet after a funeral."

"Yeah," Jack says. "I know."

2

Eva hears the hushed click of the vestibule door closing behind her. As she has done so many times before, she walks toward the altar. A few rows from the back, she pauses, considering a pew, deciding against it. For a long time, she simply stands in the aisle and tries to pray without kneeling. Not a single word comes to her. She is vaguely surprised by that.

She has known the prayers since she was a small girl. Coming to Mass with her family, hearing the Gregorian chants and the Latin liturgy—those are among her earliest memories. The prayers are as familiar to her as . . .

As her brother's name.

There is only a black silence inside her, like the echoing darkness of the abandoned mines she and Kazimir used to explore. And when, at last, the words break loose, they come to her like a cave-in. Like the crushing collapse of everything she relied on. Like the loss of everything she thought was true and good.

"*Why?*" she demands, her eyes on the thin and bloody figure above the altar. "Why do you just hang there and let all this happen? Why don't you *do* something? Why do rich people keep getting everything? Why do they always win? Why isn't MacNaughton in jail? Why isn't Tom Fisher in a box in the ground?"

"All good questions."

She whirls, heart lurching in her chest, for the voice is quietly feminine, and for a panicky, crazy moment, it seems that Saint Catherine or the Holy

Mother herself might have spoken. Instead, she sees a woman standing in the doorway, dressed in ordinary street clothes, not in saintly robes.

She is in her middle years, short and plump, seemingly made entirely of circles: curly hair coiling about a round, sweet face with lively blue eyes. Coming down the aisle, she pulls off her gloves and holds out both hands to Eva. "I'm so very sorry about your brother," she says. "And forgive me for startling you. I'm Ella Bloor. Mother Jones sent me. She said, 'Ella, you get yourself up to Calumet as soon as you can and help Annie Clements.'"

"Annie's in jail."

"So I heard. We'll see what we can do about that. Mother also said I should give her very best to a girl named Eva Savicki. A boy outside on the street told me I could find you in here. What happened to your brother is a stinking shame. You have every right to be angry and shout your questions, but . . ." She lifts her eyes toward the crucifix. "That's made of wood," she says bluntly. "It won't have any answers for you."

Sliding into a nearby pew, Ella Bloor plops down abruptly and folds her hands in her lap. Her pudgy little legs don't reach the ground. Pointing her toes, she tips a hinged kneeler out so she can rest her feet on it.

"It took me a lot longer than you to ask hard questions and demand straight answers." Taking her bifocals off, she polishes the fogged-up lenses with a hankie. "Then again, I had a very nice childhood. Petit bourgeois. Nothing special really. I went to nice schools and had nice friends. We lived in a nice big house with a nice big lawn around it. But you only had to glance down the hill to see the glass factories. We'd drive in our nice carriage through town—on our way to someplace else that was nice, of course—and we'd go right past homes that were small and shabby. Paint peeling. Windows broken and boarded up. And the people weren't 'nice.' Their clothes were raggedy. Their shoes were old and misshapen." She puts her glasses on again and looks away, remembering. "Now, why didn't I just accept that, like everyone around me? I really don't know. But . . . it just didn't seem *fair* to me. I'd ask my father, 'Why do we live in such a nice house up on the hill while the people who work in the factory live in those awful little houses down below?' And he never really answered except to say, 'That's just the way things are.' I must have been about eight when I asked my mother, 'Why doesn't somebody paint the houses and fix things up?' And she told me, 'Because no one has any money—they drink it all up.'"

Ella Bloor shakes her head and smiles at Eva, who is still standing in the aisle. "Took me years before I understood that the poor don't grind up their cash and make some kind of fruit punch with it!"

The older woman pats the pew next to her, inviting her to sit. Eva does so, but it feels strange, as though a sacred place has become ordinary and human because this woman is speaking in an ordinary human voice.

"I asked our minister my questions, and he said, 'The poor will always be with us.' Even when I was a child, I knew that was no real answer! Christian complacency, that's what it is." She shrugs, and a small smile crinkles the skin around those bright blue eyes. "Mind you, I was nearly twenty before I had the nerve to say so." She cocks her head and looks side-eyed at Eva. "Personally, I like a little Old Testament fire, myself. 'Justice! Justice you shall pursue!' And even better: Mr. Percy Bysshe Shelley!"

With that, she kicks the kneeler back out of the way and heaves her little self up onto her small feet, and fills the nave with a ringing, mellow voice, trained in a hundred union halls: "'Now *rise*, like lions after slumber—in unvanquishable number! Shake your chains to earth like dew! We are many—they are few!'"

Her voice is ordinary again. "Did you know that Shelley wrote that about the Peterloo strikers?" She reaches for her gloves and pulls them back on. "I used to be a journalist, covering labor. Now I'm a socialist. I've stopped asking God questions. I just ask myself, 'What needs doing right now?'"

She beckons Eva toward the door. "Come along, my dear. You and I have work to do."

Eva retrieves her coat and hat from the church cloakroom, and when they are both bundled up, the little woman pushes the big door open and shouts into the cold, "'Once more unto the breach, dear friends!'"

The street outside the church is empty. Jack must have given up and gone home, Eva thinks, and that is a relief. Mrs. Bloor keeps up a steady patter of poetry and declarations as they march through the streets. Eva doesn't say much, but for the first time since Kaz was hurt, the constant urge to scream or weep has eased. She feels she is part of a parade of two: leaning into the knives of the Arctic wind, nose and eyes streaming, lips thickening in the cold. Then, to Eva's surprise, they stop in front of a bank.

"I'll wait out here," she says.

"Why?" Mrs. Bloor asks. "It's freezing!"

"I—I've never been inside a bank."

"First time for everything! Pay attention, child. There are lessons to be learned."

Inside, the bank is all figured marble walls, and stained glass windows, and gleaming copper gaslights. Dark wooden wainscoting, deeply carved and heavily oiled. Intricately designed mosaic floors . . .

"Fancy as a church," Ella Bloor whispers. "Just try to find a school this nice! The rich are reverent about their money. Shows you what they really care about."

Standing behind a high counter topped by a delicate-looking wrought iron fence that goes all the way up to the coffered ceiling, a row of clerks wearing green eyeshades and starched white shirts beneath gray pin-striped waistcoats attend to prosperous men in fine woolen topcoats.

"Watch this," Mrs. Bloor says with a wink, taking Eva by the elbow as though they are mother and daughter. Even though they are both dressed with notable shabbiness, Mrs. Bloor marches up to a teller's window and, with blithe confidence, leans past the gentleman at the front of that line. Her voice is firm when she says to the teller, "Young man, I'd like to see your manager immediately."

Eva expects a harsh rebuke. Indeed, the customer who was being waited on seems startled and then put out. Mrs. Bloor smiles at him and places an ingratiating hand on his sleeve. "Thank you so much," she says warmly, as though he were allowing her to do something she means to do regardless. "You are so very kind."

The gentleman blinks, then shrugs. The teller murmurs, "A moment, please," and leaves to knock on the closed door of an office behind him.

218 MARY DORIA RUSSELL

Ella Bloor glances at Eva and winks again. "Lots of tools in a woman's kit," she whispers. "Learn to use them all!"

The teller returns presently and asks them to follow him into the manager's office. An older man wearing a very nice suit rises when they enter. "How may I serve you, madam?"

"My name is Ella Bloor. I wish to make a deposit," she says, her voice sweet and unassuming. When he inclines his head with deference, she adds, "Into the account of the Western Federation of Miners' Local Fifteen."

The manager's smile fades. Mrs. Bloor's eyes do not drop. She lays a draft from the Schenectady Trust Company on his desk.

"Ah," he says, taking in all five figures. "Yes. Of course, madam. Have a seat, if you please."

The transaction goes smoothly. The manager's good manners seem a little strained toward the end; nevertheless, he shakes Mrs. Bloor's hand and ushers them out of his office, polite as you please. The teller nods to them as they pass. The gentlemen in the queues tip their hats. A boy in uniform pulls the heavy carved door open for them.

Mrs. Bloor smiles prettily at each of them in turn and takes Eva's arm to steady herself as they descend the shoveled stairway to the street. After swiveling her head in both directions, Mrs. Bloor hurries toward the nearest cross street. Before they've gone half a block, Eva feels the older woman's hand clutch her arm harder and then begin to shake. Nerves or the cold? she wonders, but soon little whines begin to escape from her companion.

"Oh, Eva!" Ella Bloor cries when they've turned the corner and are finally out of sight. "Did you see his face when I showed him that bank draft? You could practically hear him think, Well, a deposit is a deposit . . ." She starts to laugh. "And then—when he saw the number—it was, *I want that money!*"

Eva giggles and soon great gusts of laughter rock them both as Mrs. Bloor mimes the goggle-eyed greed of the bank manager, and the grumpy courtesy of the gentlemen in the queues, and the bewilderment of a teller who's never had to wait on a woman.

"Oh, my Lord!" Mrs. Bloor gasps, pressing one hand against her diaphragm. "I think I ruptured myself!" That sets Eva off again, and the effort to sober up fails twice, laughter returning like an echo, a little weaker each time. Finally, wiping away tears that are as much from breathless merriment as from the cold, Mrs. Bloor lets out a long sigh and cries, "Oh, but that felt good! Now then, where is the union office?"

"It used to be in the church hall," Eva says. "Since the riot, it's been in Frank Aaltonen's kitchen."

"Lead on, Macduff!" Mrs. Bloor cries, and when Eva looks confused, Mrs. Bloor says, "It's from Shakespeare's *Macbeth*. The correct quote is 'Lay on, Macduff,' but people have been getting it wrong forever. Now it just means 'Show me the way.'"

The paved streets and sidewalks of the shopping and banking district have been cleared to the pavement since the day after the storm. In the workmen's neighborhoods, the snow squeaks beneath their feet, for it has merely been packed down with horse-drawn rollers, the side streets lined by frozen white walls, twenty feet high.

"This is amazing!" Mrs. Bloor says. "I feel like a Hebrew crossing the Red Sea. I wonder, does it ever get cold enough in Egypt to freeze into God's miracle . . . ? How much farther?"

"Half a mile, I think."

They crunch along in silence until Mrs. Bloor asks, "What have you learned so far, my dear?"

"I—I'm not sure. . . . Banks are fancier than churches or schools?"

"And money changes everything," Mrs. Bloor says firmly. "It changes how you think of yourself, and it changes how people treat you. That's why the rich hold on to every damned penny, long past the point where they know what to do with all their money. They buy bigger and bigger houses stuffed with more and more things. They hire a little army of servants to take care of it all and to say 'yes, ma'am' and 'yes, sir.' Every Sunday, they go to church, and when Jesus tells them to give all they have to the poor, they drop a few coins on the collection plate. On Monday, they go back to their offices to make more money and complain about the cost of labor. You're allowed to ask them for charity, but if you say, 'Take less,' they'll call you an anarchist."

When they turn down Fourth Street, the MacNaughton mansion becomes visible, set apart from the city, up on a slight rise. Cocking her head at it, Mrs. Bloor says, "So, you have to wonder, don't you, why a man who lives in a fine house like that would want to change anything."

"He doesn't," Eva says. "Well, not yet."

"And he won't," Mrs. Bloor says. "Not ever. So it's up to us. We have to change things." Her tone becomes thoughtful. "It's always been like this, Eva. It used to be warlords against peasants. Now it's factory own-ers against mill girls and industrialists against unions. Who knows what comes next, but don't be fooled—we will win battles, but the war will go on. Remember, Jesus said, 'The poor you shall always have with you.' What he didn't mention is that the rich will always be there to exploit them."

Eva stops walking, exasperated. "Well, then . . . !"

Ella turns to look at her. "What's the use? Is that what you want to ask? Because in the long run, we can make things better. As Mr. Parker said, 'The arc of the moral universe is long, but it bends toward justice.' So here's what good people do: We don't give up. We will not be cowed. We will refute their lies. We will get the vote, and we will use it. We will take them to court. We will march in their streets, and we will fight for justice every damned step of the way."

It's not easy picking out the Aaltonen place along the row of identi-cal half-buried houses. It helps that there's been a lot of foot traffic to Frank's place since the riot, and after two tries, they knock on the right door.

Husky with layered sweaters, the president pro tem of Local 15 opens the door to them. He recognizes Eva of course, and they nod commiseration to each other, for Frank's brother Yrja was killed in the riot. Then he looks at the stubby little woman at Eva's side, waiting for an introduction.

"Mr. Aaltonen, this is Mrs. Bloor. She—"

His eyes light up before Eva can finish. "Mrs. Bloor! Mother Jones said you would be coming! Come in! Come in! Welcome to Calumet."

Stamping snow off her shoes, Mrs. Bloor starts to unbutton her coat. Eva shakes her head. Their breath is visible even inside the house, and it's best to stay bundled up. So they simply loosen their scarves and take off their gloves.

"I am happy to be here, Mr. Aaltonen," Mrs. Bloor says when they move toward his kitchen table. "I have come bearing cash and encouragement. We just deposited a bank draft for thirty-six thousand dollars into the union account."

He goes still. Smiling, she says archly, "I hope you don't mind my boldness . . . ?"

Stunned, Frank says, "No! Of course not! I just—I didn't expect . . . We never hoped for so much!"

"Every penny was collected for Calumet by the members of thirty-six trade unions at General Electric in Schenectady, New York, sir. A thousand dollars from each! And a message to the miners of Calumet: You are not alone."

It is impossible not to be borne along on her cheerful energy as they draw rickety chairs up close to the kitchen stove, for Ella herself is thrilled by what she has to tell them. "We were ready to go out for eighteen months or more, but G.E. settled after just one week of a general strike! Everybody went out. Nearly *twenty thousand* workers!" she cries. "Molders, metalsmiths, machinists, carpenters, electricians—almost everyone who works for a wage in Schenectady! The important thing was, we had the mayor on our side. George Lunn is a socialist and a Congregational minister, and he's committed to an industrial democracy that is accountable to the needs and desires of the working class. Union voters put George in office, and he knows it! So when a pack of company cops beat up some office girls on the picket line, I went to see him. And I took twenty-five men of the strike committee with me—big, strong boys! We told Mayor Lunn, 'The police had no call to do that. We have perfectly orderly picket lines.' And you know what he did?" She waits for them to shake their heads. "He deputized the strike committee representatives! So when the scabs showed up from Albany and Troy, union deputies ordered them to leave. When they resisted, we arrested *them*, and the mayor kept them locked up until the strike was over!"

Frank Aaltonen takes a long breath. "Mrs. Bloor, I'm afraid it doesn't work like that in Calumet. We don't have a mayor at all, let alone a socialist mayor. This town is owned body and soul by Calumet & Hecla. Nothing happens unless James MacNaughton wants it to happen."

"Yes, I understand," Mrs. Bloor says, all business now. "It's capitalism for industrialists and feudalism for the rest of us. Bend the knee and do homage or lose your job, if not your head. But the Copper Country is still part of the state of Michigan, and Governor Ferris is a good man. So here's my plan. We're going to go to Lansing and— What is it, child?"

Eva has just jumped up, a look of panic on her face. "I completely forgot! Jack's mother invited me to supper! I was supposed to go there after—I'm sorry, Mrs. Bloor, do you have a place to stay tonight?"

"Yes, dear. I have a room, thank you." She waves Eva toward the door with a plump little hand adorned only by a thread-thin wedding ring. "Off you go! I'll find you in the morning."

3

Outside, the world is blue and starlit. Free to walk at her own pace instead of matching little Mrs. Bloor's steps, Eva hurries to the end of the street where most of the Finns live. She arrives breathless from the quick, cold journey, climbs the five wooden stairs flanked by piles of snow, and knocks, prepared to apologize for her lateness.

It's only when Mrs. Kivisto answers the door—her face full of sad concern—that Eva realizes that Kazimir's burial was just this morning. It feels like forever. What is wrong with me? she wonders. How can I be so shallow? A few hours in Ella Bloor's energetic company have left her feeling exhilarated, and after so much grief . . .

"Please," Mrs. Kivisto says, ushering Eva inside.

"I'm so sorry I'm late! There was business to do for the union, and I lost track of time. I came the moment I realized—I hope I didn't spoil your supper!"

Mrs. Kivisto smiles a little and shakes her head, but it's not clear whether that means *Supper wasn't spoiled* or *You're talking so fast, I don't understand what you're saying.* Either way, she holds out her hands for Eva's things and shows her how they are stored in this household. Mittens into coat pockets; hat and scarves pulled into the sleeves; the coat on a peg near the door.

Five pairs of outdoor shoes—old, used hard, but brushed and oiled—have been neatly placed along the wall next to the door. Mrs. Kivisto smiles and nods when Eva realizes she should pull off her own boots and add them to the line, toes pointed toward the wall. Then Mrs. Kivisto makes a small gesture toward a basket of thick felted socks in various sizes, kept there for guests.

"Please," she says again. "Cold feet, no good! Use inside shoes."

Jack is standing in the corner with his brothers and Pria. Speaking for the first time, he says, "Slippers, Ma. Use good English."

Mrs. Kivisto frowns, trying to understand. "Slip? No, don't slip!"

Shooting a quick frown at Jack, Eva says, "Your English is fine, Mrs. Kivisto."

"I practice now. Matti help me."

Eva sits on a little wooden stool next to the basket to pull the socks on over her regular stockings. Smiling brightly, she stands and looks at Jack for some indication of what she's meant to do next. Little Pria knows Eva from visiting the hospital, and she comes right over to hug Eva's legs. Eva bends over to let the child kiss her on both cheeks. She is more formal with Matti and Waino, whom she barely knows, offering her hand when they come forward one by one. She glances again at Jack, who seems unsure of how to act.

What really interests her is the room she finds herself in. Miners' houses always feel crowded—tiny spaces crammed with three generations of kin and salvaged furniture that was second- or third-hand when it was bought years earlier. Walls are usually decorated with saints' pictures and catalog pages and the free calendar from Moishe Glass's general store. Each person's wooden chair is surrounded by half-done chores: sewing baskets, ironing baskets, knitting baskets; tools and shoes and clothes to be mended.

The Kivisto home is small, of course, and it's simple almost to the point of bareness, but the effect is one of quiet, calm coziness. Deerskins laid on the floor for warmth, topped by a large braided-rag rug. A painted cabinet in one corner. A scrubbed pine table surrounded by wooden chairs, each carved in a different design by the father missing from this home since the accident five months ago. On the table, a pressed linen cloth, its edges embroidered with geometric designs worked in red thread: perfectly sized and positioned so they meet in neat mitered corners.

"Your home is beautiful," Eva says.

Mrs. Kivisto nods at the compliment. "Please," she says again. "Sit."

The table is set for six. Evenly spaced down the center: a dozen or more small dishes. Three kinds of pastry. Paper-thin slices of sausage and cheese. Pickled smelt. Little rounds of rye bread.

When everyone is in place, heads are bowed, and Finnish is spoken—a grace before the meal, Eva supposes. She has been placed across from Jack but finds herself mostly paying attention to Pria, who pipes up with words like *makkara* and *pulla* and *perunapiirakka,* trying to teach Eva the names of each thing on the table.

Once the meal begins, no one seems inclined to make small talk, not even Pria. It's only after her second bite that Eva realizes she is starving, for she couldn't bear to eat before Kazimir's funeral and hasn't had a thing all day. Now, for the first time since Kaz was hurt, food tastes good again, even when it is unfamiliar and often sort of sour.

When the meal is finished, Mrs. Kivisto nods with evident satisfaction at Eva's empty plate. "Good girl," she says. "Hard to eat when you sad. I know of this." She gets up then and goes to the kitchen, bringing out coffee and small sweets.

"You have been so kind!" Eva tells her. "I can't remember when I had such a lovely meal!"

Mrs. Kivisto's face lights up at the praise, and then she steps toward the wooden cabinet and takes out three small glasses. These she fills with something that looks like water but isn't. She hands one glass each to Jaaki and Eva, signaling that they are now adults. She and Jack raise their glasses and say, *"Kippis!"* They down the drink.

Eva does the same, then chokes and coughs, gasping out *"Kippis!"* while she wipes her eyes and the smaller kids giggle.

Everyone stands. And the meal is over.

While the boys pull the wooden chairs back to their places along the wall, Mrs. Kivisto lets Eva help carry all the little dishes and glasses and cups to the kitchen. Beneath a crocheted curtain, the window over the sink is steamed up and dripping, its exterior all but covered by a snowdrift against the outside wall, blocking the drafts. The wash water simmering in a pot on the stove adds to the warmth of the vodka.

Communicating with gestures and nods and brief little smiles, Mrs. Kivisto washes and Eva dries. When they finish the dishes, Mrs. Kivisto pats Eva's arm.

"Good girl, you," she says. "Good girl."

"I'm happy to help," Eva tells her.

And she means it, even though she has become uneasy. Because—somewhere, somehow—she already knows what is bothering her. There is something about all this . . . .

Before she can put her finger on what's wrong, Mrs. Kivisto says softly, "Jaak, he gonna make good husband. Pria gonna like it when you live here. Me, too."

And there it is: what Eva Savicki has dreamed of and imagined and hoped for and planned since the spring. A little surprising—a little disappointing perhaps—that Jack's mother rather than Jack himself has brought things to a head, but still . . .

This is a moment she has waited for.

Suddenly, after so much loss, so many changes, so much uncertainty, her life is laid out before her. She will move into this cozy, calm, quiet house. Mrs. Kivisto will teach her to cook Finnish foods. She will learn to embroider perfect geometric designs and to crochet curtains. She will knit sweaters and scarves and hats and mittens and "inside shoes." Her life will be gardening and canning and doing laundry and dishes with Mrs. Kivisto and Pria and any daughters she herself has while Jack and Matt and Waino work their shifts at the mine. She will go to church—maybe even Bethlehem, the Lutheran one. She will make coffee for union meetings. She will forget that she ever wondered about succeeding Annie Clements as president of the Women's Auxiliary. She will be too busy with her own children and with the nieces and nephews to come to meetings.

She likes Mrs. Kivisto, who has been kind to her since Kaz was hurt. She is very fond of little Pria, who has not yet become a silent Finn, clutching *sisu* like a shield. Matt and Waino are schoolboy strangers, although they seem nice enough.

And Jack? Jack himself?

At the front door, the process is reversed: thick woolen slippers removed, boots tugged on, scarf snaked out of the coat sleeve, buttons fastened. Eva shakes hands with Matti and Waino. She kisses Pria and smiles warmly at Mrs. Kivisto.

Jack opens the door for her. He hovers protectively as she makes her way down the tall, slick steps, as though she is made of glass and has never walked on snow before. She feels a wash of annoyance, then tells herself that's unfair. He means well, she thinks. He's being thoughtful.

They walk in silence. Halfway to the Carettos' house, Jack takes Eva's mittened hand in his own. She does not resist.

It is what she wanted. It is what she has wanted so much.

When they get to the Caretto place, their hands pull apart. She turns toward him. He pulls off his cap, his lank hair silvery in the starlight. She realizes with a shock that it's already thinning. He's going to be bald, like his father was.

She can tell that he is trying to decide if he should kiss her good night. She sees the shyness, the hesitation, the yearning for . . . more. She recognizes all that, for it is what she has imagined over and over. And she knows she should lean forward a little bit and close her eyes. Just . . . let him kiss her, however awkwardly and chastely. It will all be settled. She will be his girl. And then, his wife. And then, the mother of his children.

And she must decide. Right here. Right now.

She smiles and reaches out to shake his hand. "Thank you for a very nice evening," she says and goes inside before he can say a word.

"Eva!" Carla Caretto says when she comes through the door. "I was starting to worry! Where you been? What! Why you crying? What happened? What!"

Choking on sobs, Eva shakes her head. Flapping her hands, she tries to assure Carla and the girls and Carla's sister and brother-in-law and their kids that it's all right, it's nothing, it's only that . . . what? She tries to tell them, but the effort dissolves again into crazy, stupid, helpless crying.

"C'mon upstairs," Carla tells her. "We get you into bed and get you warm, right? Hard day. Real hard day, eh? Time to talk a little and sleep a lot, eh?"

And Eva knows that Carla has misunderstood, that she thinks this is finally the collapse after Kazimir's funeral. Which makes Eva feel even *worse*. Because she *should* be crying about Kaz, and instead it's just this . . . *boy*. Just this ordinary boy, with ears that stick out and a too-big nose, and that ridiculous Adam's apple bobbing in his throat.

Hiccupping and snuffling, she lets Carla take her upstairs to the makeshift attic bedroom they share with Carla's daughters. Eventually she calms down enough to tell her about Jack, and it's embarrassing and shaming and awful, but it's true, and she doesn't even care that little Rosie and Grace are listening, wide-eyed, as sodden words tumble from a girl they thought was a grown-up.

"I wanted so *much* to marry him," Eva cries. "All this year, that's all I could think of! In the spring, I just *looked* at him and I fell in love. I had my wedding all planned. I was deciding on names for our children! And tonight, I just looked at him and—and felt *nothing*. Nothing at all. Just—" She makes a *pffft* noise and flicks her fingers like she's waving a fly away. "Gone."

She turns toward the girls and says, "Let this be a lesson to you. I fell in love with a boy's *hair*!" She laughs wetly. "And he'll be bald before he's thirty!" She looks at Carla then, bleakly amused at her own foolishness. "How could I be so stupid? How could I be so fickle?"

"How," Carla suggests, "could you be so *young*?"

"But girls get married at my age all the time!"

"And regret it, resta they lives." Carla sits up straight on the edge of the bed. "Not me," she assures her daughters, reaching out to stroke their cheeks. "You had a good papa and I had good husband, but . . ." She looks at Eva. "You just don't know how things gonna be. A wedding?" She shrugs. "Nothing. Just a *festa*. After? Comes life."

"How did you know? That you picked the right man?"

Carla's eyes sparkle, and she smiles at her girls. "I met you papa at your Zia Lucia's wedding. Orlando, he was a miner up in Copper Harbor. Her new husband's brother. So he comes down here for the wedding. He looked nice." She shrugs. "Not like a movie man. Just . . .

nice. Then the music start. You papa, he dance with all them fat old ladies. And with them little girls, like you two," she says. "He was a hard worker, too, but I didn't know that yet. I watch him dance and I think, He gonna be good to his wife when she get old and fat! He gonna be good to his kids."

She looks away, her eyes welling. "And he was. Never lift a hand to any of us. A good man, my Orlando. A good man . . ." She looks at her daughters. "So, two sisters, they marry two brothers, and your Zio Giuseppe, he a good man, too. He takin' care us. Now Eva, too. And it ain't been easy for him, even before the strike."

The four of them are quiet then, huddled together, blankets pulled around them. To her own surprise, Eva feels remarkably better, as though she is waking from a fever. "Carla, what did Annie see in Joe Clements?"

"I don't know," Carla admits. "She was getting older. Her little sister already had a family. Joe was tall. He wanted a wife. And he was a real good dancer. Mighta been simple as that." She shakes her head. "Love is crazy sometimes."

4

Smooth that rough touch with a tender kiss.
—Shakespeare, *Romeo and Juliet*

There is a woman waiting at the workhouse door when the union men are released. Short and stout. A round face ringed by coiling curls. Bifocals flashing in the sunlight. Easily fifty, she waves a handkerchief coquettishly and calls, "Yoo-hoo! Boys! Over here!"

Michael Sweeney looks behind himself to see if she's waving at someone else. Before he can decide whether she is confused, she cries, "Hail the conquering heroes, bloodied but unbowed!" then comes near to say, "I'm Ella Bloor, and I'm here to take care of you!" Smiling, she herds them toward two motorized cabs idling in the street behind her. "Let's get you out of this cold! I have meals and hotel rooms waiting for you in downtown Marquette."

"Can't afford it," Charlie Miller mutters around his broken teeth, balking before she can get him into a taxi. "No money."

"There is now, dear," Mrs. Bloor soothes. "You've got thirty-six thousand dollars in the bank, donated to Calumet by the General Electric strike fund. And I'm going to use part of that to get a dentist in to see you this afternoon. The goons have made a mess of your smile."

"Where's Mrs. Clements?" Mike asks. "Is she all right?"

"You're the photographer. Mr. Sweeney, am I right?" When he nods, she says, "I've seen your work. Is she as beautiful as you've portrayed her?"

"Yes," he says. "And as brave."

She gazes at him, makes an assessment, and nods. With something approaching pride, she reports, "Her sentence has been extended another two weeks. She is, I am reliably informed, *not* behaving herself inside."

With their bogus debt to society paid, the five union men, along with Moishe Glass's son Ike, are driven to a clean but simple hotel and led to three rooms on the second floor. Soup and soft rolls are delivered to the rooms while bathtubs are being carried up and filled with hot water, bucket by bucket. A barber arrives to cut their hair and shave them. A doctor comes to check them over, and a while later, a dentist appears. Charlie's nose and mouth will never be the same. Ben Goggia and Yanko Tersich have half-healed gashes in their scalps. Peter Jedda's fingers have been broken. Ike Glass's cheekbone is broken. Still, they'll all recover, barring infection.

A full meal, quite substantial, awaits them in the dining room when they look and feel more presentable. As the last man lays down his fork, Mrs. Bloor heaves herself off her chair and onto stubby legs. "Back up to your rooms now. Two to a bed, I'm afraid. We need to stretch the dollars," she says. "Get some rest. We'll talk in the morning about what comes next."

With Charlie Miller snoring away next to him, with his own belly full, feeling warm and safe, at least for the present, Michael Sweeney finally is able to think clearly enough to wonder what Annie's done to get an extended sentence. The workhouse makes prisoners wash and iron sheets for the hotel trade. Is she leading protests? Organizing a prison laundress union? Maybe even starting a hunger strike, though God knows there's little enough food given to prisoners under the best of circumstances.

He himself has been ravenous while serving out his time, shoveling snow by hand on public property. On his first morning in Marquette, he was ignorant enough to believe he was lucky to have been arrested in November, when there were only nine hours of daylight in which to work. Shoveling kept him warm until sweat soaked through his woolen underdrawers and shirt. Then the shivering began. By noon, the cold was crippling. Nose running, lips chapped and bleeding, he despaired of his fingers and toes. By the end of the day, he was numb all the way back to his elbows and knees.

And the work itself! Shoveling bent over, lifting and tossing, lifting and tossing, hour after hour after hour. The snow was heavy, and he couldn't imagine doing this with copper ore. Dear God, he thought over and over, how do the miners stand this for twelve hours a day? At least Annie Clements is inside, he'd think, by way of comforting himself.

It helps now to imagine her standing over a giant vat of steaming water, stirring sheets with a wooden paddle. She'd be tired and hungry, but warm, he thinks as he drifts off between linens she herself might have ironed. . . .

In the morning, Mrs. Bloor has arranged for a big breakfast, and when they've eaten their fill, she presents Ike Glass with a train fare back to Calumet. "The rest of you are coming with me to Lansing," she informs them. "I've spoken to Governor Ferris about negotiating an end to the strike. He's giving us an appointment on Monday afternoon."

She listens to their doubts. There is skepticism about the cost of traveling to Lansing. There is no direct rail route from the Upper Peninsula to Lower Michigan. One day there may be a bridge across the Mackinac Straits, but for now, getting to Lansing by train takes days. South, from Marquette to Milwaukee to Chicago. East, around the bottom of Lake Michigan. Then north again to the state capital. And then they'll have to make the same long trip in reverse to get back to Calumet.

"Yes, I understand," Mrs. Bloor replies serenely. "Nevertheless, I am quite convinced the journey will be worthwhile and I'm certainly not going to insult the governor of Michigan by refusing his offer. He is, by all accounts, a man capable of moral indignation. I want him to see your faces before the cuts heal and the bruises fade. In any case, the tickets are paid for. Our train leaves in an hour."

In the end, even Charlie Miller capitulates, his mouth too sore to go on arguing. When they rise from the table, Mike Sweeney hangs back. "What about Mrs. Clements?" he asks again. "How will she get home from the workhouse?"

"I've left money with the hotel clerk, and I spoke to the matron about sending Annie here when she gets out." She aims shrewd blue eyes at him. "Of course, if you were to take a photograph of her at the moment of her release, it would make for a good headline," she says. "America's Joan of Arc freed at last from unfair imprisonment!"

"The camera was wrecked, Mrs. Bloor. During the riot. They used the tripod to break Charlie's face."

"I'm sure there are camera vendors in Lansing," Ella says comfortably. "Replacing yours will be a legitimate union expense. When we're finished in Lansing, I want you to come back to Marquette. I want a picture of Annie in front of the workhouse gates on the front page of every newspaper in the country."

Days later, after a night in an inexpensive hotel, barbered, shaved, and wearing cheap but respectable new suits paid for by the unions of Schenectady, the representatives of Local 15, Western Federation of Miners, are promptly ushered into Governor Woodbridge Ferris's office, along with Ella Bloor. Smiling at them like a proud mother, her round cheeks rosy, she introduces them to the governor, who is visibly shocked by the evidence of the men's mistreatment. A few minutes' conversation demonstrates that Charlie Miller's injuries make it difficult for him to speak clearly, and that Ben Goggia, Yanko Tersich, and Peter Jedda are not entirely fluent in English. During their long journey to Lansing, the four union officials have recognized that Ella Bloor is an experienced and canny negotiator who has a way with politicians. They have agreed before the meeting that they will take a step back when she has steered the conversation to the general manager of Calumet & Hecla.

"You know, Governor Ferris," she says, "I have heard such unpleasant things about James MacNaughton! It must be difficult for you—a man of genuine importance who must serve all the people of this state—to deal with someone who is so unwilling to compromise."

"Compromise! James MacNaughton doesn't know the meaning of that word, Mrs. Bloor. He is, I am sorry to say, utterly impossible to work with. I can barely stand to speak to him," the governor admits. "And I must tell you, in my opinion, hell will freeze before he gives an inch to the union."

"Oh, my goodness! So you've given up on him? That's not very Christian of you, Governor," Ella says, peering over the top of her spectacles. "Surely anyone can be redeemed! Mr. MacNaughton may well be an awful man, but the alternatives to negotiation are not very attractive for any of us. If he is allowed to persist in his intransigence, the result will be a prolonged labor battle that will drag all of Michigan's economy down!" She leans over her round little belly then to confide, "I have it on good authority that Samuel Gompers is taking an interest in the Copper Country now. That means the American Federation of Labor will take a stand, and *that* means the copper strike could involve many other industries in the dispute. If labor sees no movement on management's side, I fear we may be forced to take up an offer from Mr. Clarence Darrow to sue Calumet & Hecla on behalf of the union . . ."

Ferris goes still. "Is that under discussion?"

She looks away, eyelashes fluttering, as though she is dismayed even to bring this up. "It is a possibility," she warns reluctantly.

After a thoughtful pause, the governor says, "Well . . . while it might be rather entertaining to see Clarence Darrow cross-examine James MacNaughton, I suppose I can send a state's attorney up to the Copper Country. We can try at least to reopen the negotiations."

"Oh, that is such good news!" Ella cries, sitting back in her chair and folding her plump little hands in her lap. "I am so very grateful to you, Governor, and I'm sure these good men can tell you what your own representative will need to know about the union's positions."

With that, she inclines her head toward the men as if to say, *My work here is done.* The discussion becomes general and, like the good gray schoolmaster that he is, the governor of Michigan makes a neat list of the miners' demands and aspirations.

Recognition of the union for collective bargaining.

A decent living wage: three dollars a day for all underground workers—trammers included.

An eight-hour day, five days a week.

Improvements in mine safety—and an end to the one-man drill.

"That was a bluff, right?" Michael Sweeney asks Mrs. Bloor when the Calumet delegation is in the hallway outside the governor's office.

"What was, dear?"

"Sam Gompers?" Yanko Tersich asks, brows high.

And Charlie Miller lisps, "Clarenth Darrow?"

With a bright smile, she continues her lively stride down the corridor, and the men follow her out of the building. Standing at the top of the stone staircase, she squints into the hazy outline of the sun behind the clouds, pulls on her gloves, and settles her hat more firmly on her head before she speaks. "Mr. Darrow has indeed made the offer to represent you," she says. "As for Mr. Gompers . . . well, he is a busy man, of course, and the Western Federation of Miners hasn't joined the A.F. of L., so—technically—I suppose you could call that a bluff."

Yanko Tersich laughs. Charlie Miller snorts, and shakes his head, and smiles around his broken teeth; his dentures will take some time to make. Ben Goggia kisses her hand. Peter Jedda tips his hat.

"Mrs. Bloor," Michael Sweeney says, "I expect you could bring about a visit from Jesus Christ if you put your mind to it."

She reaches up and puts a fond hand on his cheek. "I'd certainly do my best, dear."

Their plan now is for the delegation to split up. The union officials will return to Calumet. Mrs. Bloor will travel down to Detroit to speak to some automobile workers about more support for the miners.

"And I have a few things to do here in Lansing," Mike Sweeney tells the others. "I'll see you soon."

There are good-byes and good lucks and handshakes, after which Michael Sweeney and Mrs. Bloor stand side by side, watching the others leave.

"Now, you make sure you get that picture of Annie!" Ella commands, giving him a hug and pressing an envelope into his hand. "This is my own money. Use it to take care of any extras you incur on her behalf."

His first stop is a courtesy call on the Lansing home of Major Henry Van Den Broek. The major, it transpires, has kept up with the events in Calumet. Since he retains no warm feelings with respect to James MacNaughton, he is inclined to be helpful to the photographer: one press man to another. A few phone calls later, the major has arranged for Michael Sweeney to do a series of illustrated articles about the Calumet strike for newspapers in Lansing and Detroit. He himself provides the photographer with a small cash advance, to be repaid at some convenient date in the future.

With the major's money added to what he's received from Mrs. Bloor, Michael Sweeney goes shopping to replace his camera. It takes some searching, but that afternoon he finds it: a used Sanderson quarter-plate. Hand and stand. Excellent lenses. Exposure times from pneumatic bulb release to one-hundredth of a second. Struts to hold the bellows in a variety of positions. Brass fittings with an integrated case of polished wood. A beautiful thing, just to look at. Better technically than the one he bought with his inheritance from Frances Logan. And there is film stock that can take the cold.

By nightfall, he is on a train again, not willing to wait even one extra night in Lansing before he is on his way to Marquette, and to Annie Clements.

Mrs. Bloor has distributed liberal tips to Marquette hotel staff, and Michael Sweeney is greeted like a long-lost brother when he checks in. Every morning, he reads a stack of newspapers with his breakfast and then packs up and leaves for the women's workhouse in time for the day's prisoner release. With the camera steady on its stand, he sets the exposure and focus for two feet outside the gate, for he intends to frame America's Joan of Arc with the massive sandstone walls and that medieval-looking door. Shutter release in hand, he stands ready to take a picture that he hopes will make headlines, and considers how to give some scale to the photo. Would it be better to capture her height and strength, or will there be more sympathy if she seems smaller than she is?

Each day, his hopes rise when the workhouse doors creak on their iron hinges. Each day, his heart sinks when he sees only a small, thin woman or two emerge: prostitutes, petty thieves. Working girls, just trying to feed their families, Miss Frances would have said. Each day, the gates close, and he is left to wonder how many times Annie's sentence can be extended for bad behavior.

He attempts to pry answers from the guards, but they slam the door in his face. Increasingly anxious and angry when he returns the next morning, he has a new plan of action. if Annie doesn't come out today, he will telegraph Ella Bloor about hiring a lawyer—

Then he sees her. A tall figure in the dark just inside the door, surrounded by a gaggle of girls. He grins and waits, but when he can see her clearly in the thin winter light, his smile fades and he sets aside all thoughts of photography. Drawing back the bellows, snapping the camera into its case, collapsing the stand, he stuffs it all into its canvas carrier, and goes to her.

"Thank you," he tells the girls who are supporting her. "I'll take care of her now."

They glare at him and look to Annie.

"I know him," she says, her voice raspy. "Go. Thank you."

There are embraces and murmurs of encouragement—from the girls to the woman, not the other way around. That alone is alarming, and confirms the changes Michael Sweeney sees in a face he has studied in a thousand negatives and a hundred prints. Sparkling brown eyes, dulled and sunken. High round cheeks, hollowed out. In all the months he's known her, he's rarely seen her standing still and silent, apart from the moments when she stopped her cheerful, purposeful bustling to decide on her next task. What he recognizes now is not a thoughtful stillness. It is a kind of frightening passivity.

"Where's Joe?" she asks, her voice husky. "Why isn't he here?"

"He . . ." Not now, he tells himself. "He couldn't come."

She makes a small sound—a little snort of derision that turns white in the dry, cold air. "He went back."

"That's what the papers are saying." He doesn't tell her about the smug editorials praising a man for not being ruled by his wife. "I'm sorry."

"Don't be. I thought he would."

Camera bag in one hand, he grips her arm with the other. He can feel the bone through the wool of her coat. Hunger strike, he thinks. "Did you eat at all?"

"Eventually . . ." she says vaguely. "They make you." She winces when she swallows, her throat raw from the feeding tubes. "But then I . . ." She starts to cry. "I couldn't keep it down."

My God, he thinks. My God. "Ella Bloor has arranged a room for you at a hotel," he says. "It's not far from here."

He expected her to insist on going straight back to Calumet, straight back to the strikers. He expected an argument about the expense of the room, modest though it is. He has heard all the stories about how prison guards treat women who get above themselves, and yet . . .

Somehow, he expected Annie Clements to emerge defiant and un-changed.

She's tired, he thinks. She needs to eat. "Food first," he asks, "or bed?"

She shrugs, an almost invisible movement. So he makes decisions for her. When he has her settled into her room, he goes back down to the front desk and orders a meal. Soup. Tea. A soft roll. Not too much, or she'll vomit. He waits to carry the tray to the room himself, ashamed that he needs that time to come to grips with her condition.

There is a chair in the corner of her room, so he sits and watches while she eats: methodically at first, then with a kind of rapt atten-tion.

"Who's dead?" she asks when she is done.

He blinks, not understanding.

"Back in Houghton. Before we came here. You said . . ."

"Mrs. Clements, get some rest first."

"Who."

He tells her about the six he is sure of, stumbling over the Slavic and Finnish names. She nods at some, closes her eyes at others. He mentions an Italian-looking immigrant nobody recognized. He leaves one name off the list. There will be time later to break the news about Eva's brother.

He tells her instead about Ella Bloor. About the money from the Schenectady unions. About the negotiator Governor Ferris will send to the Upper Peninsula to talk to MacNaughton. He's not sure how much of this is getting through. She is looking at him. He can't tell if she is seeing him.

Presently, a tarnished bathtub arrives. Copper clad, of course. An irrational wave of hatred sweeps over him, for he knows the price that metal extracts from everyone who gouges it from the earth. Even so, he has it placed behind the dressing screen, and they wait silently while buckets of hot water are delivered, along with towels and soap.

"Mrs. Clements?" he asks. There's no response. "Annie? The bath is ready."

When she finally stirs, he says, "I should go . . ."

"I should go," she hears Michael say. "Annie? I should go."

She looks up then and meets his eyes.

"No," she whispers. "Stay. You should stay."

Remember this, she tells herself. It cannot happen again. Remember . . .

That first simple meal. The careful way he undressed her. His silent anger at her discolored body, the bruises now faded to yellow and green. The long, curving lines of her ribs beneath them.

The warmth of the bathwater. The scent of the soap. His hands, washing her filthy hair, rinsing it over and over. The crisp, white cleanliness of the freshly ironed sheets. Sleep that came within seconds. Waking sometime during the night. Seeing him sitting in the corner, watching over her.

In the morning, there is more for her to remember. The softness of his lips. The weight of him. The comfort. The safety.

"This can never happen again," she says. "My husband will kill us. It can never happen again."

But it does. It does. It does.

Later, much later, she will tell him what it was like in the workhouse. How prisoners were forced to work without pay—slave labor, really. How angry she was, how she protested. The punishment cells. How cold they were, how dark. The hunger strike. How the jailer would bring tea and oatmeal in the morning, leaving it there all day, just to taunt her. How she would turn her face away from the food and lie still on a straw mattress, minute by minute, hour by hour, day by day. Dazed by hunger, then feverish with it, nauseated by emptiness.

It took less than a week to kill any sense that what she was doing could possibly be worthwhile. She was alone. Nobody knew what she was doing. Would this blank, stupid, gnawing misery fill the belly of one miner's son? Would it keep one daughter off the street, or put food on the table of one family, or bring dignity to one man? In the end, there was nothing left in her mind except darkness and cold and hunger. She hardly knew who she was.

"Don't be a fool," someone told her. "Here. Take this crust. No one will know. Don't swallow. Just hold it in your mouth. Let it in slowly or you'll throw up." Who was it? Betty? Beatrice? A matron even? Somebody. Just . . . somebody.

I am not alone, she thought, sucking on that crust, crumb by crumb. Somebody is with me.

And that's what broke her.

On their last morning in Marquette, he lies behind her in bed and whispers into her ear, "Run away with me. No one will know. We can just . . . go."

"I can't," she says. "I can't let everyone down."

"You're not the only woman in the Copper Country! Let somebody else carry that damned flag. You've done enough. Come away with me."

She does not answer for a long time. He wonders if she has fallen asleep.

"Maybe," she says then. "Not yet. But soon."

December 1–23, 1913

1

I will be deaf to pleading.

—Shakespeare, *Romeo and Juliet*

"Why me?" Arthur Nolan asks the governor.

"Because you're a lawyer, and a good one," Woodbridge Ferris says in the patient, measured, schoolmasterish tone that annoys so many. "Because you're a judge, and a fair one. Because you have a reputation for getting parties to settle matters out of court. Because I've known you for thirty years and I trust you. And because I've been warned that if we can't get this matter resolved on our own, Clarence Darrow will grace our fair state with his august presence."

"Darrow! That grandstanding publicity hound—"

"The very man, and I don't want him up in Calumet turning this strike into an international cause célèbre."

"While drumming up his next spectacular case. Loves the headlines, our Mr. Darrow."

For a time there is only the soft crackle and pop of the wood fire, its warmth caught and kept near them by the high-backed wing chairs pulled close to the hearth. Not ready to make a decision, Artie Nolan buys himself some time by puffing on his cigar before he asks, "How's Mrs. Ferris doing these days?"

The governor makes a half-hearted gesture toward the fire. "A bright flame, flickering," he says, slumping into the upholstery. "We've given up on the sanatorium. She'd rather be home in Grand Rapids. The girls bring their children to see her, and she enjoys that, but . . . This miserable job keeps me from her side, just as her illness keeps her from mine, here in Lansing."

"And yet, the opportunity to do good for the citizens . . . ?"

"Is some recompense. Yes. It's what Helen wanted for me, you know. I think she was—*is*—more political than I ever was. She urged me to run for the office, but in all honesty, we never expected a Democrat to win."

"And the lovely Miss McCloud?" Nolan murmurs. "She is well?"

Ferris sits up a little straighter. "She is well. A fine secretary—a partner in my daily tasks." There is a delicate pause. "And she allows me some hope for a future that will not be entirely devoid of companionship."

"Helen has been unwell for a very long time," Arthur observes, by way of absolution.

Ferris stands and moves soundlessly across a Turkish rug to the polished rosewood sideboard. "I am still not used to all this," he admits, filling two snifters from a cut-glass decanter. "The statehouse. The staff. The deference. It's easy to forget what real life is like." He returns to the fireplace. "Artie, please," he says, offering the brandy. "Michigan needs you. The people in the Copper Country need you. I need you."

Nolan takes the glass from him. Cradling it in his palm, he gazes at the fire's glitter, seen through the deep golden glow within the crystal. Finally, he makes the decision. "All right. I'll do it."

Ferris sags with relief. "Thank you, Artie."

"Tell me about James MacNaughton. What is he like?"

In the changeable light of the fire, the governor's face is hard to read, though an entire thesaurus of descriptions is passing through his mind. *Impervious. Unreasonable. Unmovable. Uncharitable. Sanctimonious. Utterly content in his smug self-satisfaction* . . . In the end, a chest-deep chuckle escapes him, and it is as sardonic a sound as Artie Nolan has ever heard from his old friend.

"You'll find out soon enough," the governor says. Then he raises his glass and advises, "Drink up. You're going to need it."

The governor's words circle Arthur George Nolan's mind as he listens to steel wheels click over the rails. A lawyer, and a good one. A judge, and a fair one. And what transforms a good lawyer into a good judge? Their tasks are very different.

An attorney's merit is measured by a knowledge of precedent, a command of the facts, and rhetorical skill. To navigate the legal waters and deliver the client to a desired destination, the lawyer must employ the strongest elements in a client's favor: the law, the facts, the emotion of a case, an appeal for justice or a plea for mercy. It is very easy to succumb to a conviction that every client's case is good and right, and that justice is served when you prevail. You can blind yourself with your own advocacy and lose sight of fairness.

A judge, on the other hand, must not go into the courtroom convinced of anything except the sanctity of the law. He must listen carefully to each litigator's argument. He must be alert to the possibility that neither side deserves to win on the merits, and when that is the case, he must bring both advocates into chambers and open their eyes. He must show them the weaknesses of each argument, presenting them both with the possibility that neither case is as airtight as they've come to believe. Letting each of them realize that they might well lose, that the judge could rule against their clients.

Sometimes Artie Nolan lets the attorneys work it out for themselves, remaining out of the discussion, biting his tongue when necessary. And yet, his own finest moments in the profession have come when he has been able to lead two advocates toward a clever solution that provided minimal dismay and sufficient satisfaction to both sides.

His task in Calumet will be unlike anything he has tried before. There are two opposing parties, but no private chamber where their representatives can be reasoned with. There will be no judge to make a ruling, no jury to come down with a verdict. In labor disputes, a business can speak with a single loud, clear, well-paid legal voice, while each employee is alone and hardly any of them can afford the most rudimentary representation. This places employees at an almost insuperable disadvantage in any dispute with an employer. They are prevented from joining together in a single legal voice—unless and until the employer recognizes their union as a legitimate representative empowered to bargain on their behalf.

And that is the crux of the matter. That is at the base of the strike.

Gazing out at the snow-covered landscape beyond the train window, Artie Nolan knows now what he must do. He must get the copper companies to agree *in principle* to recognize the union. Then, surely, it will be possible to craft a truce that will end the strike, bring union members back to work, and return the mines to full production, *temporarily*. Two years might do it: enough time to allow passions to cool and minds to become clearer.

He will have to convince the union leaders that their wages, hours, and working conditions are all contingent on a single point: recognition of their union's legitimate capacity to negotiate for them. Exchange recognition now for a better contract later. Live to fight another day. This walkout was a noble effort, but two years will give you time to build a strike fund, to coordinate with the national union, to be better prepared to act from a position of strength.

And what might convince James MacNaughton to agree? President Wilson has just put together his Commission on Industrial Relations. There's talk of a new federal statute, one establishing the principle that unions, strikes, picketing, and boycotts are not illegal conspiracies. Don't let the government take the decisions out of your hands. You've always been good to your employees. Why not get ahead of the changes that are coming? Exchange a simple recognition of the union's right to exist for two years of labor peace.

A lot can happen in two years, Artie will murmur. When the next war breaks out in Europe—and, God help us, there's always a next war—copper will be in greater demand than ever. Larger profits will produce a bigger pie—one that can be shared more equitably. Skilled miners will be in demand. The industry will want all the workers it can hire. Win some goodwill now, and Calumet & Hecla will be the company that gets the best workers in the industry.

Yes, he thinks, beginning to relax. I can do this. I can fix this mess.

When he returns to Lansing ten days later, Arthur Nolan, too, has collected a thesaurus of terms to apply to James MacNaughton, most of which are unspeakable in polite company.

"You knew," he accuses Ferris. "You sent me up there on a fool's errand. None of the other copper companies will buck Calumet & Hecla, and you *knew* what MacNaughton is like. That trip was an utter waste of my time!"

"I suspected as much," Governor Ferris admits. "I had to try, Artie! I've only spoken to him on the telephone. I truly believed that if you could sit across the table from him and make a reasoned and reasonable case—"

"That bastard wouldn't let me into his office! He let me cool my heels in his waiting room and then canceled my appointment with no explanation! And when I got back to the hotel, *this* was waiting for me," Art says, tossing a typed statement onto the governor's desk.

The governor smooths out the crumpled note and sighs when he recognizes both the quote and the anger with which Art Nolan had crushed it.

The rights and interests of the laboring man will be protected and cared for—not by the labor agitators, but by the Christian men of property to whom God has given control of the property rights of the country.

"George Frederick Baer," Artie says. "Lawyer for the coal industry during the 1902 strike. And it took a presidential intervention to settle that one. I never had a chance!"

"Did you talk to MacNaughton at all?"

Nolan snorts. "He invited me to a hockey game. A hockey game! I swear he did that just to watch me freeze. I tried to talk about the strike, but he'd say, 'I do not negotiate.' Like the goddamn King of Siam. I made every argument I could. If you could just see the children in that town—those kids are starving! I warned MacNaughton. I told him, 'When a poor man is down to his last dime, he won't buy food. He'll eat the rich.' MacNaughton just watched that game on the ice and smiled. . . . He *smiled.* And then he asked me if I'm a socialist! 'I do not negotiate. I do not negotiate . . .' My balls were numb, but that bastard's heart was even colder. I swear to God, I will write to Clarence Darrow myself and beg him to come. I will pay his fee out of my own damn pocket!"

Woodbridge Ferris watches the other man pace and fulminate and mutter and shout. To have reduced Judge Arthur George Nolan to this state of rage . . . What chance can there be for a settlement?

He waits until Artie finally collapses into a chair, his fury spent. "I'll contact President Wilson," the governor says. "Maybe he'll be willing to do something."

Four hundred miles north as the crow flies, James MacNaughton gazes at the latest report from his spy and finds himself cheered, for the neatly written note confirms all his expectations. There will be no further bailouts from the Western Federation of Miners. The money from those Schenectady communists will be gone soon. The union leadership is split, arguing over what to do next.

Christmas, he thinks. This will all be over by Christmas.

Even more gratifying: the preliminary figures gathered by his accountants for the year-end report to stockholders. Over the past months, some of the more softheaded investors have expressed concern as the strike dragged on; now he can reassure them as to the outcome of their patience.

With a small smile of satisfaction easing across his features, he initials each page, then calls his secretary in. "These numbers look excellent. Have Finance draft the report. I'll work on the cover letter this morning. Oh, and send Mr. Fisher a letter this afternoon. Thank him for his services, which are no longer required. He and his men are to be paid until the end of the week."

"Will you be providing references for him, sir?"

"Nothing in writing."

When he is alone again, James MacNaughton removes a Mont Blanc pen and a single piece of company stationery from the middle drawer of his desk. For a moment he sits in contemplation, readying himself to compose his report. It comes to him then that there is a distinct similarity between the furious action of a hockey game and the noisy display of a strike. The point of it all is to reach a goal. A losing team can pressure the opponent, even get into the offensive zone, slap two or three good shots, and still accomplish nothing. Of course, that is too informal a metaphor to use in his letter, but Mary will appreciate it when he writes to her.

Uncapping his fountain pen, he lets the words of his report roll smoothly across the texture of the paper.

During my tenure as Chief Executive Officer, I have emphasized efficiency throughout the company. These efforts are paying off for you, the stockholders of Calumet & Hecla. The past six months have been challenging, but you will be pleased to know that we have increased productivity while driving down the cost of production without yielding to a single demand of the labor agitators. Despite their efforts to intimidate and abuse loyal workers, many of our most reliable employees have denounced the criminal and violent actions of these outsiders. A majority of our miners have already come back to work.

What did that idiot from Lansing say? Why not get ahead of the changes that are coming? Well, that is precisely what James MacNaughton has done.

2

Delights have sudden endings.
—Shakespeare, *Romeo and Juliet*

Michael Sweeney leaves Marquette first. The union men welcome him back to Calumet; he is one of them now and has paid his dues in the workhouse. There are grins when he shows off his new camera and laughter when he talks about meeting the governor in Lansing. They especially enjoy his rendition of Woodbridge Ferris's reaction when Ella Bloor mentioned Clarence Darrow, and they roar at Mike's mimicry of the governor's face twisting when Ferris said the name James Mac-Naughton.

He is invited to a meeting of the Women's Auxiliary. They have questions about Annie, of course. She is the only one of those serving time at the workhouse who has not yet returned. They, too, are proud of her "bad behavior," although concerned about how long she has been gone. Pressed, he tells them he heard she'd been released. Mrs. Bloor was there to meet her, he lies. Annie has been staying "with friends" to rest for a while before returning to Calumet.

If they ask more questions—*Who does Annie know in Marquette?*—he is prepared to make something up about Annie meeting someone in the workhouse, though he prefers not to dig a deeper hole of deception. "Mrs. Bloor says to expect Annie here on Thursday," he says to change the subject. "I'm not sure what time." Another lie, but one that won't be noticed.

"That'll be the eleven-twenty from Marquette," someone says.

He is careful to look merely mildly interested, as though he has not been counting the hours.

*   *   *

On Thursday morning, Eva surveys the room, thrilled and satisfied in equal measure. This is how Annie must feel, she thinks. Making something out of almost nothing. Imagining a result and getting others to help make it real.

It was her idea to have a celebration for Annie when she returns to Calumet. The project has filled the spaces of her mind where her brother would have been, mercifully crowding out a grief she doesn't want to believe is real. And in truth, the party has been quite an undertaking. Booking the hall with money Ella Bloor donated to the Auxiliary. Getting Mrs. Kaisor to organize a children's choir. Enlisting children to make decorations.

"Go to all the barbershops and the library. Ask for old newspapers and magazines," Eva told them. "Bring all the color comics pages and the magazine covers to me." She and the Caretto girls have made paper chains with the pretty parts, and Carla has used the rest in the woodstove. Eva also collected leftover union flyers. "Write a letter to Annie on the backs," she told the older children. "Draw a picture for her," she told the little ones.

Each union woman has donated a penny for the vat of coffee to be served at the party. "Bring your nicest cup and saucer," she told them. "With all the colors in the decorations, nothing has to match. The table will look wonderful!"

And it does. Like a spring meadow. All pinks and blues and yellows and greens. Eva herself has brought a cup her mother loved, its thin white porcelain splashed with painted forget-me-nots. A present from her father to her mother for their tenth anniversary . . . Seeing it now, on this table, the sorrow she has held at bay for so long threatens to swamp her. It is a relief when Jack Kivisto interrupts her thoughts.

"Annie will like it," he tells her. "You did good."

"Thank you," she says with a bright, impersonal smile.

He waits for something more. She busies herself with the coffee urn. Finally he leaves her side to finish arranging the folding chairs in neat rows and columns.

Jack still hasn't figured out the cool indifference she has shown him since she went to his house for supper. His mooning around really has become annoying, and she is gladder by the day that she didn't make Annie's mistake: falling in love with something stupid and getting married before she thought it through. Even so, she can't bring herself to be mean to him. And if she's honest, there is a part of her that wants him to yearn for her as hopelessly as she did him for all those months.

Old Mrs. Kaisor has begun to herd the children up onto the raised stage. While they take their places, tallest in back, shortest in front, she sits at the piano and, with gnarled fingers, runs through a difficult passage one last time. Eva checks the coffee table again, straightening the cups so the handles all go one way, and it's then that she recognizes a china plate piled high with Finnish pastries: the most generous display of baked goods on the table.

Mrs. Kivisto must have sent it, she thinks. How sweet of her.

Behind her, the older women nudge each other, taking note of her busy competence, nodding their approval. She's one of them now. Bereaved, but strong. Knocked down, but back on her feet. Outsiders might think that Eva Savicki is alone in the world, but the union has become her family, and the Women's Auxiliary is collectively proud of her.

The party for Annie has been much like planning a wedding reception. That's an experience that will come in handy someday soon, they all think, although . . . it has not escaped their attention that things have cooled between Eva and the Kivisto boy.

Not that Jack himself has noticed. He is as besotted as a Finn can be, and give him credit: he's done everything he could to help Eva get the hall ready for Annie's welcome home. Lugging the folding chairs out of storage. Draping paper chains across the stage. It was Jack's own idea to hang clotheslines corner to corner, all around the room. He's swagged embroidered tablecloths over the windows and clipped the children's pictures in between—with clothespins, no less!

"Do you suppose there's another man in Calumet who's ever once touched a clothespin?" one woman asks.

"Finnish romance," another murmurs.

A few minutes before the eleven-twenty from Marquette is due to arrive, a scrum of reporters converges on the depot to wait for Annie Clements. Steno pads ready. Pencils in gloved hands. Shivering in the Calumet cold, breath freezing into fog between their mufflers and their hats.

Somebody has alerted journalists from Houghton and Copper Harbor, and Michael Sweeney has learned that some have come all the way up from Chicago and Milwaukee. The tipster will make a few much needed bucks. The newspapers will be a market for Michael's own photographs. Even so, he hates every one of the reporters with an intensity fueled by guilt. He made Annie Clements famous. He made her America's Joan of Arc. Now she is column inches. She is a story, and newsmen will mine her for it: badgering her, scrutinizing her, goading her to say something they can print.

Tall as he is, Michael climbs onto the roof of a sidelined freight car to see over the heads in the crowd as the welcoming committee of the Women's Auxiliary approaches. The giant American flag has been washed and mended and ironed for the occasion. No one but Annie is strong enough to carry it on its pole, so Eva has recruited two other girls to help her hold it like a banner in front of the little parade. He gets a few shots of the girls, and marvels again at how much easier it is to use the new Sanderson. The roll-film advance is far quicker than changing out big format holders.

He sits on the roof and waits for the train to pull in, mentally calculating the focus depending on which car she is in. When Annie appears in the vestibule, he is all business and takes a series of shots before he allows himself to look at her directly. She seems better, he notes. Food. Sleep. Safety for a time. Love.

There are cheers from the women, and volleys of shouted questions from the reporters: idiotic, intrusive, insulting.

"Hey, toots! How tall are you anyways?"

"Very," she says.

"How many children do you have, Mrs. Clements?"

She waves her hand toward Eva and smiles at the girls holding the enormous flag. "Too many to count."

"But you're childless yourself, aren't you?"

"Are you a Sangerist, Mrs. Clements? Do you use birth control?"

"Sorry?" she asks, her face innocent. "I'm not sure what you mean, sir. Would you care to explain your question to me?"

The reporter does not, and may even have the decency to blush behind his muffler. "Watch out!" one of his colleagues yells. "She'll have you for violating the Comstock law!"

"Mrs. Clements, are you a communist, a socialist, or an anarchist?"

Eva Savicki starts a union song, and the women of the Copper Country take it up like a battle cry. When reporters shout more questions, Annie shakes her head, tapping her ear with one finger, calling back, "Sorry. Can't hear you!"

She did well, Mike thinks, climbing down gingerly, careful not to slip and damage the camera. Eva, too. Good thinking.

By the time he's at street level, the reception committee of the Women's Auxiliary of Local 15, Western Federation of Miners, is halfway down the street, determined to get Annie away from the reporters, out of the cold, inside the Italian Hall. For once, he notes, they do not let her lead the way.

The women of the Copper Country surround her, like a suit of armor.

She is different. They aren't sure how or why, but . . . she has changed.

Not a single union woman in all of Calumet has eaten her fill since the November riot, but even by that standard, Annie's round Slavic face has thinned alarmingly. And on the way up the steep staircase, she stops to catch her breath, shaking her head at her own feebleness, making a little joke about it.

On the second floor, the children of the choir are trying to be quiet, but when Annie appears at the top of the steps, they explode, yelling "Surprise!" loud enough for Old Man MacNaughton to hear it.

Annie's coat is taken, and she is seated in the front row as Mrs. Kaisor rolls through a joyful arpeggio. The children begin a program of union songs they've rehearsed for days, with special enthusiasm for a new one by Joe Hill.

That's the Rebel girl, the Rebel Girl,
To the working class she's a precious pearl!
She brings courage, pride, and joy
To the Rebel union boy,
For it's great to fight for freedom
With a Rebel Girl!

Their performance over, Eva has the children troop down the stairs in a long line. They pass in front of Annie, one by one, to give her the letter or the drawing they've prepared. Pictures of flowers and sunshine from the little ones. Simple notes from the older ones. *Welcome home, Annie. We missed you. You are very brave! Union forever. Give them hell!*

Some of these, Annie reads as they are given to her, and soon her eyes are streaming, the letters clutched in thin hands. So Eva takes the pile from Annie, stacks the papers, smoothing the crumpled ones, and places the collection in a cardboard stationery box she got from Mr. Glass.

On the top of the children's pictures and notes, she places her own letter for Annie to find later on. Eva thought hard about what she should write, and changed her mind a dozen times. In the end, she settled on something Mother Jones might have said. *You've planted seeds of justice. They will grow, and someday life will be better for people like us.*

Now she ties a ribbon around the box and looks up in time to see Marie Neimela laying her new baby in Annie's arms. "She was born during the storm last month," Marie says. "Me and Abram, we named her Little Annie."

Holding the squalling infant, Annie manages a laugh. "Well, we're both crying now! Solidarity, eh?"

"Do you gots any babies?" little Gracie Caretto asks. Her sister, Rosie, shushes her.

Annie hands the baby back to Marie, and holds out her long arms, gathering in Carla's daughters and as many of the other children as she can embrace at once.

"I have lots and lots of babies, Gracie. You are all my children," she says to the children themselves this time. "You are *all* mine." She wipes her eyes then and sits up straight, and her voice is firm when she speaks again. "Everything I've done, I did for you."

Most mothers and children go home. The Auxiliary officers stay for a brief business meeting to give Annie a report on what has happened in her absence. Michael has already told her much of it, but she contrives to look astonished when treasurer Carla Caretto tells her about the money Ella Bloor collected from the General Electric workers. Her surprise is genuine when she learns of another wire transfer from the Federation, but she nods at the warning they've received. The national union is tapped out. The strike in Colorado is getting uglier by the day. Until that's settled, there won't be anything more.

Direct donations have fallen off as well. They still get letters of encouragement, but very little money. Christmas is coming. People are looking after their own.

There is more. She can tell from their faces, from the way they look past her, around her. "What else?" she asks, bracing herself.

Gunmen have fired into union boardinghouses twice in the last week. Six dead. "Nobody saw nothing," Carla says cynically. Of course, the Citizens' Alliance is blaming the union, and that's in the papers now. MacNaughton's maid, Loretta Devlin, reported that he was telling everyone that the union hired gunmen to kill miners and make the operators look bad. The smaller copper companies have withdrawn any hope of concessions. Word is, the governor's negotiator went home empty-handed as well. The daily parades have been called off. It's too cold, and too many men think they're pointless now.

And then questions begin to come at her. Annie, how much longer do you think we can hold out? Annie, what will we do next? Annie, should we keep going?

All her life, people have looked up to her, as children do to adults. All her life, she has risen to the demands on her and she became the woman others needed her to be.

I can't, she thinks. I just can't. Not anymore.

She feels her muscles sinking back toward her bones. The tightness in her throat makes it hard to breathe.

When she loses her fight against the tears, a kind of guilty shock blankets the room. Nobody says it, but they all know now: Big Annie has come to the end of her strength. Their workhorse, their leader, their Joan seems almost fragile.

And that means they are done. If Annie can't keep going, nobody can.

Eva Savicki sits at her side. With an arm around Annie's shoulders, she tells the others what Mother Jones once said: "The union is a democracy. It's up to the men now. We've done all we can, and so has Annie."

"Right," Carla Caretto says decisively. "Let's clean up or we gonna get charged another hour rent."

While Annie pulls herself together, the others take down the decorations: folding the tablecloth "bunting," collecting the clothespins, coiling the laundry ropes, stacking the folding chairs so Jack Kivisto can lug them back into the storage room. The conversations are low and focused on each task. Here, hold this. Whose cup is that? Is the urn empty? Who brought that plate of pastry? I haven't seen anything sweet since before the riot, have you?

"Annie has an idea," Eva calls out.

Silence falls, and they turn expectantly.

"I think . . ." Annie says, "I think we should have a Christmas party. For the children. Something for them to remember when the strike is over. Little presents, maybe . . ."

The women of the Auxiliary glance at one another. Voicing their thoughts, Carla Caretto says, "Annie, we don't got money for that."

"I think," Annie says. She stops and clears her throat. "I think I know where I can get some money. I just . . ." She gets out of her chair and stands, shoulders back, head high. "I just need train fare to Houghton. I'll pay it back."

Once again, glances are exchanged, and an unspoken decision is made: if Annie Clements wants a Christmas party for the union kids, then that's what they'll do.

"Christmas carols cost nothing," old Mrs. Kaisor points out.

"Annie, Mr. Glass could give you a ride to Houghton on his delivery truck, maybe. Wouldn't need train money that way."

"You can stay with my sister. Danka's husband is union. They got a sofa."

"We'll make paper chains with colored paper again," Eva says. "The kids can collect more newspapers and magazines—"

"No! That would spoil the surprise," Annie says, some of the old energy coming back to her. "We'll do it all for them. Cut a tree. Decorate it. And make little packets of candy, maybe. With pretty paper."

With the ordinariness of planning to absorb her, Annie seems herself again. They all know there was more bad news to share with Annie. Not yet—another unspoken agreement, for nobody wants to upset her again, just as she's getting her feet back under herself. And anyway, it's Eva's place to tell her.

So they adjourn. As Eva and Annie leave, Jack Kivisto calls, "I'll lock up, Eva." There's no response from Eva, who is already halfway down the staircase at Annie Clements's side.

"Thanks, Jack," says Carla Caretto. "You a good boy."

It's only three in the afternoon when Annie and Eva leave the Italian Hall, but twilight has begun: a deepening blue hour between the astonishing fire of a Keweenaw sunset and the glowing dance of an aurora that sometimes turns the snow as green as spring grass. The packed snow squeaks beneath their shoes and their nostrils stick closed, moist breath inside freezing against the frigid air. Each alone with her secrets, they hurry through the streets of Calumet, arm in arm to steady each other against a fall. When they get to the Clementses' place—before they climb the stairs to go inside—Eva hesitates, then speaks.

"After you were arrested, MacNaughton's thugs did a lot of damage to union homes," she begins. "We cleaned up the house for you. We got the windows fixed, too, but . . . Joe won't be inside, Annie. He gave up on the strike. He's back at the mine."

"I know." It almost slips out of her: *Michael told me.* "There was a newspaper on the train," Annie says instead. "Joe never wanted to be part of it, Eva."

Eva is still looking at her, chin trembling, eyes welling. There is something else. Something worse.

"Tell me, Eva. Just say it."

"Kaz is dead! He died last month. They broke his skull. During the riot. They killed him, Annie. Kaz is dead."

"Oh, Eva! Oh, no! Oh, God . . . Oh, my sweet, dear girl. I am so sorry," Annie says over and over as the two of them cling together, tears freezing on thin cheeks. "I am so sorry. I am so sorry for it all."

3

Leap to these arms, untalk'd of and unseen.
—Shakespeare, *Romeo and Juliet*

In daylight, Annie Clements's mind is filled by the drumbeat of obligations. She has taken up her union duties again—going to meetings at Frank Aaltonen's place, writing letters pleading for help from other unions. She still has all her own housework—cooking, cleaning, washing, ironing—though the ladies she used to work for over in Laurium are sending their laundry elsewhere. They were apologetic about it. While she was gone, a new Chinese laundry opened: cheaper, better, quicker service than Annie could provide. MacNaughton has probably made threats to anyone who gives her work, but one lady still lets Annie clean her floors twice a week. For that, Annie is grateful. Earning a little cash on her own means she can sneak a bit into the strike fund without Joe knowing.

She has said nothing to Joe about him going back to work. He stands straighter now. His drinking is defiant, not belligerent. He is his own man again, with no committees to tell him how to run his life. Money is power. Work is respect. The union has been fighting to get more of each for the miners, but Joe never believed that and Annie has given up trying to change his mind. Now, at least, she knows he can't be spying on the union anymore, if indeed Joe was the one who'd given information to MacNaughton.

They fall into old patterns. Joe works nights and sleeps through the day. Every evening, when the whistle for the night shift sounds, Annie hands him his lunch pail. Watching from the window, she waves to him if he looks back over his shoulder.

Then, alone, she paces. Waiting. Watching the clock.

In the darkest hour of the night—when her husband is in the lowest level of the mine, when neighbors are in the deepest levels of sleep, when killing cold keeps everyone else inside—her lover comes to her.

"Leave him," Michael whispers every night. "Come away with me. We'll change our names, we'll disappear."

"Stop. Don't. I can't. Not yet."

When he is gone, she swears that she will not let this go on. She is ashamed. She is afraid. She fears an accident at the mine, and a knock at the door. A pump failure, a shift canceled. Discovery by a smirking mine official, or by an outraged cuckold.

The Carettos, next door, aren't fooled by Annie's sudden zeal for keeping the stairs and the walkway shoveled clean. They don't like Joe, and Italians are good at keeping secrets. *Omertà*, they call it.

How long will it be before Joe notices a stray footprint in the snow at dawn?

How long will it be before rumors circulate at the Auxiliary? Women talk. Someone will notice that something has changed between Annie and the photographer. Someone will say something, and then?

Warmth from a few. Carla and Eva will stick up for Annie, but from others? There will be coolness and suspicion and blame. She took a vow. If she will betray her husband, how can anyone trust her?

A wife will tell a husband. A husband will tell a friend. The friend, laughing, will tell somebody else at work. And Joe will overhear . . .

On December 13, Annie Clements climbs into Glass Brothers' delivery van on her way to Houghton to visit merchants there and "to raise funds for the children's party."

A day later, Michael Sweeney takes the southbound train. He is going to Milwaukee "to buy a new lens at a camera shop down there."

These are not lies. They will do these things.

*   *   *

Big Annie is known throughout the Copper Country by sight and by reputation, but storekeepers in Houghton don't hate her the way they do up in Calumet. Houghton businesses are not beholden to Mr. High-and-Mighty James MacNaughton, the way everyone in Calumet is. He can't shut them down if they don't toe his line.

The Houghton merchants have been hurt by the strike, certainly. A few have gone bankrupt, and everyone wants the damned thing settled, but they know this as well: every penny a miner earns at the Quincy Mine will be spent in Houghton on overalls, boots, work gloves, groceries, seeds, canning jars, cloth, yarn. Millions sent to stockholders do no good in Houghton—that money gets hoarded or spent in Boston and New York and Chicago.

So when Big Annie Clements comes through their doors in December, they don't curse at her and send her packing. They are inclined to be sympathetic when she asks them for small donations: "Just little things we can give to the children, sir, to make their Christmas brighter." They nod and tell her to wait, and take a look in their stockrooms for things kids might like, things that haven't sold well, things that might be a bit dusty and shopworn, but which the Women's Auxiliary can spruce up. And they put a few pennies in the parcels. New ones, minted just this year, the copper still bright and shiny.

No one recognizes the tall, curly-haired Irishman who arrives in Houghton a day later. From the depot, he goes to a café and sits alone at a table.

He's carrying a carpetbag, and the waitress figures him for a salesman of some sort. His hands are clean, and his back isn't bent into that permanent curve miners get.

She tries to engage him in conversation, for men who eat alone will often buy a meal and a dessert, just to keep talking with a girl. He is very pleasant and has a nice smile, though he seems distracted. "Just coffee, thanks" is all he says, so she gives up and simply refills his mug when it's empty.

After an hour, he finally orders a meal and eats silently, staring out the window, looking at his pocket watch.

At dusk, he pays his bill, pulls on his coat and hat and gloves, and leaves a decent tip. The waitress pockets the coin and watches him go. She isn't surprised when he heads toward the brothels out on the edge of town.

The lady of the house ushers him into the private parlor. Annie looks up, and when she sees him, her face is transformed by that glorious smile of hers. She seems almost as giddy as the youngest hooker, holding out her hand to show him a stack of crumpled bills. "Michael, look what the girls have collected for the children!"

"Thirty-two dollars and fifty cents!" one girl declares proudly. "We even got the Chinaman to give us a dollar."

"God knows he makes enough money off us," a thin woman says blearily.

Michael Sweeney has a good eye for faces and recognizes some of the girls as the ones who took care of Annie in the workhouse. They and their colleagues surround her now, sorting through the trinkets she's brought back from the Houghton shopkeepers. Most look far older than they probably are, but some are very young, and they squeal as though the hair ribbons and dolls and shiny pennies and toy trucks were meant for them.

Soon a bottle is passed around. The giggling gets more suggestive when "Annie's fella" joins them. Then the front bell starts to ring, and they disappear, one by one, down the narrow hallway.

When all her girls are busy, the madam returns to the private parlor and beckons her two guests toward her own room. It is larger than the others, and warmer, and the mattress is newer.

"The girls decorated it for you," the madam says, lifting her chin toward gauzy scarves and nearly new silk flowers. There are extra pillows, freshly laundered sheets, and the nicest blankets in the house. "Take all the time you want," she adds. "I have account books to work on."

*   *   *

It is inexpressible, unspeakable luxury: to take all the time they want. To make love and then to fall asleep, warm and sated, side by side, with no fear of discovery. To awaken and to gaze at the beloved's sleep-slack face, or to be awakened with a caress. To make love again and to linger in bed, as the dim winter dawn slowly reveals the room around them.

With fresh feeling, he says it all again: "Leave him. Come away with me. We'll change our names, we'll disappear."

"After Christmas," she says, making the decision as she speaks the words. "We can't spoil the party for the children. We'll meet here, after Christmas. And then . . ."

"Chicago!" he says. "Or New York?"

"No. I want quiet. I want peace. I'm tired of fighting the world."

"Someplace far away, then. Iowa! We'll grow corn and kids in the exact middle of absolutely nowhere."

"You need a haircut." She pulls one of his curls, wrapping it around her finger. "I want a place where everyone is tall."

He touches her cheek. "You will be the most beautiful woman in town, no matter where we go."

"Blarney," she says.

"God's own truth," he replies.

A night. A day. A night. In the morning, a curly-haired salesman with a carpetbag approaches the ticket counter at the Houghton depot and asks for a round-trip to Milwaukee. Meanwhile, an exceptionally tall woman walks swiftly to a warehouse a mile north of town. Parcels of donations from the Houghton stores have already been loaded into the back of the Glass Brothers' delivery truck.

Annie climbs in. The broad-faced Russian driver nods to her, cranks the engine, and hops into the cab.

"No snow last night," he notes with dour stoicism. "Good luck for us. No pushing truck out of ditch."

4

As is the night before some festival to an impatient child
—Shakespeare, *Romeo and Juliet*

When Annie Clements arrives in Calumet this time, she does so without fanfare. Joe is still asleep when she gets home. She starts his breakfast and begins making his pasties as soon as she's hung up her coat and hat.

"How'd it go down in Houghton?" he asks when he comes down.

She listens carefully for any edge, any hint that he might suspect. Voice light, she answers, "The Houghton merchants were generous."

He nods and sits down to eat, lifting his chin in greeting when Eva comes over from next door just before he leaves for work.

The Carettos have made her welcome since Kaz died, and Annie is glad of that, for many reasons. Carla's sister Lucia is a midwife, and Eva has begun going out with her. That's good. Learn a trade like that and you won't be dependent on a husband. While Annie hasn't made an issue of Joe handing in his union card, Eva finds it hard to be civil to him. "He's a bully and a coward" was Eva's opinion. "He's mean to you and he waited until you were in the workhouse to quit."

Which was true, though not something Annie wanted to acknowledge yet.

"I'll clean up," Eva tells Annie now. "Sit. You look tired."

Eva is not the flighty young girl she was six months ago. While she washes the dishes, she talks about a book by Elizabeth Gaskell called *Mary Barton*. "Mrs. Bloor sent it," Eva says, scouring a pasty sheet pan.

"It's about poor people in London, and it's a novel, but Mrs. Bloor said I'd learn a lot, and I have."

"How are the party plans coming?"

"I've been experimenting with the glue recipe," Eva tells her, wringing out the wash rag. "I think I've got it down to the smallest possible amount of flour that can be mixed with water to make things stick. And I've cut about a million strips of colored comics to make paper chains." Her hands stop, and she straightens. "I negotiated a lower fee for the Italian Hall," she announces proudly. "I booked the room for the early afternoon on Christmas Eve so the owner could hire it out to another party in the evening."

"Has anybody spilled the beans yet?" Annie asks, watching carefully to see if Eva catches the double meaning.

"Nope!" the girl says brightly. "Everyone's lips are sealed!"

December 23, 1913, and the secrets are all intact.

Members of the Women's Auxiliary of Local 15 of the Western Federation of Miners have waited until their children were asleep before working on the decorations and gifts. They've created half a mile of paper-link chains and a blizzard of paper snowflakes. With yarn quietly donated by a few ladies in Laurium, they've knit mountains of mittens and stockings and caps. Hundreds of little cloth bags have been sewn from clean rags and filled with trinkets Annie got in Houghton. And at the last minute, one of the local merchants snuck two big boxes of chocolate drops to the Auxiliary, warning, "You didn't get them from me, understand?" Small cash contributions have come in by mail. Added to the money Annie brought back from Houghton, the Auxiliary accumulated a grand total of $64.30 in cash, and they've spent every penny on the party: renting the hall, buying milk for the kids, and coffee for their parents, and sugar and flour and eggs for cakes that will be baked in the kitchen at the Italian Hall.

All this has been an almost unimaginable extravagance after so much austerity, but nobody regrets it. It's Christmas, after all. And in their hearts, they all know this will be a lasting memory of the strike: a party for the children of the union.

The men have been left out of these preparations until the eve of Christmas Eve. Now there are tasks requiring heavy lifting, and the muscle is to be provided by Frank Aaltonen, Michael Sweeney, and Jack Kivisto.

After dark, they load a huge old upholstered chair from the St. Joseph rectory onto a sled and haul it through the snow-packed streets to the Italian Hall.

The owner has given them a key. They unlock the two big front doors and stand still for a few minutes, catching their breath and staring at the staircase to the second floor: twenty-four steps and no landing to rest on.

"Jesus," Frank says. "Whose idea was this?"

"Eva's," Jack answers. "It's going to be a throne for Kris Kringle."

"Well, then!" Michael says, for the men know how Jack feels about the girl. "An order from on high."

"Jack, you take the top," Frank tells him. "Mike and I will get the front legs. One step at a time, right?"

Grunting and swearing, they *ca-chunk* the chair to the second floor, step by step. Drag it to the raised stage at the end of the hall. Heave it up and over the rise. Pull it back to the center of the stage.

Jack retrieves a ratty red blanket from a closet and drapes it over the chair, just like Eva told him.

"This is all going to be worth it, just to see Charlie Miller playing Saint Nick," Mike says. "He's going to wear a white paper beard and a red plaid jacket stuffed with a pillow. We could sell tickets, just for that!"

"How's he doing?" Frank asks.

"Better. Dentures help. He can eat better now, but . . . he still gets headaches, and his eyes don't focus right. The Federation wants him to go see a doctor in Chicago. I don't think he can keep working. You should probably figure on running the local permanently, Frank."

"Bastards," Frank mutters bitterly. "They just kept beating on him . . ."

"Tree next?" young Jack asks.

"Tree next," Frank agrees.

"I know where there's a good one," Jack tells them.

Frank hands around a flask of vodka, and they all take a pull to fortify themselves before towing the empty sled out to a frozen bog on the edge of town. Jack points out a spindly pine, its open branches perfect for hanging the ladies' paper snowflakes along with ten cents' worth of store-bought tinsel. After another pull on the flask, they cut the tree down, tie it to the sled, and trudge back to the Italian Hall. One last struggle up the steep staircase, hanging on to the lowest branches of the tree, hauling it upward, butt first.

Frank nails some scrap wood together, and they pound the stand into the base of the tree so they can prop it upright on the stage. It's crooked and wobbly.

Mike Sweeney fiddles with it until the best side faces the big open room. "Are we supposed to decorate it, too?" he asks Jack.

"No. Eva and I will do that tomorrow morning."

Frank sits down on the edge of the stage, legs dangling. There's enough vodka left for one swallow each, and he hands the flask to Jack, waiting for the boy to take his drink before he says, "You asked her yet?"

Jack coughs. Mike smiles and accepts the flask.

"You sound like my mother," Jack says.

"What are you waiting for?" Frank asks, taking the flask back from Mike.

"I—I . . . She . . ." He shrugs and blushes. "I need a job before I can . . ."

"Hell, if that's all that's holding you up . . . It won't be long now."

Frank looks back over his shoulder at the tree and Kris Kringle's throne. "We've done our best for the kids," he says with a finality about more than the Christmas party.

There's a silence until Jack asks, "The strike's over then?"

"Maybe," Frank says. "I don't know. Yeah. Probably. I think we're done."

December 24–31, 1913

1

That I should love a loathèd enemy!
—Shakespeare, *Romeo and Juliet*

You asked her yet? Seems like everybody in town is watching him, everyone waiting for the announcement. Every day, it's the first thing he hears, and the morning of Christmas Eve is no different.

"You ask her?" his mother asks.

"Not yet."

"She's a good girl. Ask her!" his mother urges, with a rare smile.

"Jaaki's in lo-ove," his brothers chant. "Jaaki's in lo-ove!"

"Shut up," he snaps.

"I like her," little Pria says. "When she gonna come here to live?"

How can he explain? He had a letter to write, and an answer to wait for, and plans to make, and nobody in Calumet who could advise or help him. He has just turned sixteen and the daunting truth is that he's going to have six people to support, even if everything turns out for the best. He might be able to get Matt an apprenticeship and Waino can sell newspapers, but it's still a lot of mouths to feed and he'd just about given up hope when the letter from Dayton finally arrived.

"Bring Eva here after the party," his mother says. "I have a nice supper for you."

"Why can't we go to the party?" Waino asks.

"Because it's for union kids," Matti says sullenly.

"Well, aren't we union?" Waino wants to know. "Why can't we go?"

Everybody looks at him, expecting an answer.

It's just too complicated. He doesn't want them around when he asks Eva. He doesn't want them around at all—asking questions, telling people things. He has kept two worlds separate for months. He wants to leave Calumet clean, and the kids might blab something that'll ruin it all.

His brothers are still looking up at him, expecting some kind of answer.

"Because," he says finally. "Because . . . Shut up."

"But I don't understand!" Waino persists.

"Waino!" his mother warns, for she sees in Jaak's face the look Solomon used to get before tipping the table over and beating one of the kids. Her frightened eyes fasten on Jaak's, and he flushes.

"I'll bring you something nice," he tells the kids. "After the party."

"Bring Eva," Pria says. "She's nice."

"Yeah," he says. "She is."

He pulls on his coat and hat. The letter from Dayton is in his pocket. He's rehearsed the words he'll say, imagined the look on her face, and how she'll throw her arms around him the way she did that day when they heard Mother Jones was coming. He knows what they'll tell the priest or the minister, whoever Eva picks. He knows the trains they'll take to Ohio. Everything is in readiness. It's all planned out. Today's the day.

"Jaaki's in lo-ove," his brothers chant. "Jaaki's in lo-ove!"

"Shut up!" he yells, but even he is smiling a little.

Nothing goes the way he expects it to.

She told him to come at one-thirty. He thought they'd be alone, decorating everything together. He thought he'd ask her then, and they could announce their engagement at the party. Except they're not alone. As he climbs the stairs, he hears women working in the little kitchen beneath the raised stage. Cardboard boxes filled with gift bags and chocolates have already been delivered to the hall. Paper chains loop across the ceiling. Cut-out snowflakes cover the windows. The tree is almost finished.

"Just put this on the top," Eva says, handing him a paper angel. "I can't reach."

Confused, he stretches up to pull the leader branch toward himself and sticks it under the angel's paper-cone dress. "You told me one-thirty, right?" he asks, but when he turns around, she's gone.

He goes to the kitchen door and peers inside, hoping to find her. One by one, the women stop bustling and the room gets quiet, for if the men all know what Jack means to ask, the women know what Eva is likely to answer, and they ache for the boy.

Carla Caretto nudges Eva and lifts her chin toward Jack. "He want you will notice him," she whispers. *Be kind,* her eyes say. *Don't break his heart.*

"Eva . . . I need to ask you something," he says.

She sighs and turns to face him. "Can it wait? There's so much to do!"

"Please. It'll just take a minute."

He leads her down the stairs, into the vestibule, where they can be alone. A crowd has begun to converge outside the big doors. They can hear the kids, noisy and excited, waiting on the sidewalk for the surprise that awaits within.

Eva stands on the bottom step. She seems annoyed. Later he will think, I should have known. Right then. I should have been able to tell. I should have said, "Nothing. I changed my mind." Except he'd thought about this moment for so long that it had become like a play in his head, with lines he had to speak and lines he expected her to say.

He pulls the letter from Dayton out of his pocket and hands it to her. Frowning, she reads it, amazement slowly changing her face.

"Jack," she says, looking up at him, her eyes bright. "This is wonderful!"

I've made her happy, he thinks, and his heart rises in his chest, and the words begin to tumble from him—more words than he has ever said aloud. To anyone, ever in his life.

"I wrote to Orville—to Mr. Wright—last month," he says. "I told him I was sorry to hear about his brother Wilbur's death, and I told him about my father getting killed, and about how I wanted to be above the earth, not below it—in the sunshine, not the darkness. And I said, I got good grades in school and want to be a machinist and I can already work a lathe and a punch press and I'd like to come to Dayton and learn about building airplanes from him. But then I didn't hear back, and it turns out he was traveling in Europe, so he didn't get the letter until he got back to Ohio, and then this letter came." He points to the signature at the bottom of the letter. "See? Charlie Taylor! He's their machinist. He's worked with the Wright brothers since they were making bicycles, and he's offered me an apprenticeship! I can start as soon as I get to Dayton."

"Oh, Jack!" she murmurs, looking up from the letter. "Jack, I am so happy for you!" And she means it, sincerely, for she did love him once, and she does want the best for him, and this way, there will be no hard feelings—

"Marry me," he says.

"What?"

He takes her hand. "Marry me. Any church you want. We can get married and . . . just *go*. Just get away from the mines and the union and all of this stupid mess. We can go to Dayton and—"

It's starting to sink in, and she blinks and shakes her head. "Jack! I can't . . ." Can't what? she thinks. Can't quite tell him the truth. "Jack, I can't think about this now. I have to help with the party! Annie's counting on me!"

"She's got plenty of people to help her. She doesn't need you. I need you! Please. Marry me and we'll just leave!"

"But what about your mother? She'll lose the house! Matti's too young, and one of you has to be working in the mine, or . . ." She stops, and he can see her putting it all together in her mind, all the pieces, all the little secrets underneath the big one.

How could I have missed it? she is thinking. He didn't come to the parade the day of the riot. She believed the story about his mother wanting him to stay home. And then Kaz was in the hospital. And then there was the funeral. And then Ella Bloor arrived. Then there was dinner at the Kivistos' when she might have wondered why that was the only union house the goons left alone. She might have figured it out then, if she hadn't been so caught up in how she didn't love Jack after all, and how the whole thing was just some schoolgirl crush. Then Annie came home. And two babies were born, and she herself had been so busy helping Carla and Lucia Caretto, and then . . . She simply stopped thinking about Jack.

Eyes closed now, she stands still, remembering each moment that should have given it away. When the final piece clicks into place, she bends at the waist, almost sick with it. He *told* her he wasn't going to stay in Calumet, after his father's funeral. She should have asked him why he joined the union after all, but she didn't. Because she was in love. She was a stupid girl in love with a stupid boy. And she wanted to believe in him.

"Kaz was right about you all along," she says. "You were never really one of us, were you. You were the spy. You. Not Joe. You."

"Eva, please," he says, his voice low and urgent. "Yes, I . . . It was for my family. I know now it was wrong, but I thought I was being smart. And, see, once you make a deal with MacNaughton, he won't let you loose! Eva, I . . . I never told him anything important— I just wrote letters. I swear! I never gave him anything he could really use. Eva, please! The mines are terrible. They're worse than anybody on top knows. Fifty *years*! I couldn't—And it was before—before I thought of going to Dayton. Before I had a job there. And now I don't have to go underground, and neither do Matti and Waino! The Wrights will pay enough for me to get a place in Dayton, and we can bring my mother and the kids down, too, and— Try to understand! I wanted to save my family! And—I love you. I want to marry you! I want to get all of us out of here."

Mouth agape, she stares.

"Eva, *please*," he whispers. "Try to understand."

Annie Clements goes to the top of the staircase and sees the two young people alone. Even in the dim light of the vestibule, she can make out the desperate pleading on Jack's face, the hard rejection on Eva's. Oh, dear, she thinks. He's asked, and she's said no, and he's being difficult about it, and it's going to get nasty.

"It's two o'clock! Open the doors!" she calls, to help Eva change the subject. "Make sure everyone shows a union card before you let them in!"

The girl turns toward the big street-level doors and shoves them open as if the doors themselves were the object of her anger. There's a shriek of excitement from hundreds of kids waiting outside, giddy at the prospect of something new and exciting and just for them. They are accompanied by smiling parents making half-hearted and wholly useless attempts to calm them down.

"One at a time." Eva is shouting. "Show us your union card, or you don't get in."

Annie is borne back inside by the joyful rush of the first of the children who've come running up the stairs.

Silent, side by side, Jack and Eva check union cards for nearly half an hour.

"Eva, please," Jack whispers when they are alone again.

"Go home," she says. "Go to Dayton. Go to hell. I never want to see you again."

2

All things that we ordained festival
turn . . . to black funeral
—Shakespeare, *Romeo and Juliet*

"Go home, pal," Owen Lloyd is saying a few blocks away. "You're drunk."

"Home? Home!" the stranger cries. "Not here. Not in Calumet. No home here. Just a fleabag boardinghouse . . ."

Nobody who runs a bar expects to have a good time during the holidays. On any given night, there are only a few ounces between rowdy hilarity and sullen hostility for too many drinkers. That gets worse from Christmas Eve to New Year's.

A good two-thirds of the Truro Pub clientele are old friends. Settled men with families. For generations, they've started their celebrations with song and spirits. They go home when it starts to get dark on Christmas Eve. The ones who are left behind are strangers mostly. They drift into the Truro when they hear the Cornish carols and they stay until closing. These are single men who've come to the Copper Country because they heard that jobs were easy to get. Men like that soon find out: mining is hard work. And the hours are murderous. And the pay is shit. A month later, they're too broke to leave. The closed-off conviviality of the Truro regulars makes such strangers morose, for they've nowhere better to spend Christmas Eve than an unfamiliar tavern, hunched over a shot glass, lecturing the bartender on the evils of modern society.

"You know what I hate?" this one asks.

"You're going to tell me," Owen says.

"Greenhorns. Coming here, taking jobs from good Americans. And socialists! With their goddamn strikes and their union dues . . ." He taps his glass.

"Two bits, and this is the last one," Owen warns.

"Put it on my tab."

"Two bits."

"Awright then, how much is a beer?"

"Nickel."

The man digs through his pockets and pulls out some copper coins. "Four cents. All I got." He waits, eyes pleading. "C'mon. It's Christmas Eve, for Crissakes."

Owen takes the pennies and pulls a short beer.

The muttering starts up again: "Goddamn greenhorns . . . You know what I hate? Nobody's for the guy in the middle. Nobody! The big shots? They get money from the goddamn stockholders. The greenhorns? They get money from their goddamn union. But the poor bastards in the middle? Nothing. Nobody gives us any free money. Nobody gives us nothing. I was selling hardware, you know?"

"Yeah," Owen says. "You told me."

"I made good money, too. Stockroom. You could do a little business on the side if you had to. See?" He points to the button on his collar and reads it, frowning and bleary-eyed, touching each word. "Citizens' Alliance. See? Citizens means *citizens,* right? Not some lousy greenhorn who can't speak good English. Strike starts. Damn socialists don't buy anything. Business goes to hell! Boss says to me, he says, Can't make payroll, he says. Gonna hafta let you go."

Owen Lloyd knows the owner of the hardware store. This lush must be the man Calvin fired for thieving two weeks ago.

"'Let you go . . .'" the drunk snorts. "Jew. Prolly a Jew. Let my people go!"

"Cal's Presbyterian," Owen murmurs, though he's not in the mood to argue with an idiot. "Look, you don't have to go home, but you can't stay here. We close at three on Christmas Eve."

"Goddamn Jews . . . what do they care about Christmas?"

"Last round, gentlemen!" Owen yells to the room.

*   *   *

The second floor of the Italian Hall is nearly three thousand square feet and it's crammed to the edges with families. Parents stand along the walls, jouncing babes in arms while keeping a sharp eye on the littlest kids, who've been given the best seats on the main floor. Older children have been directed up to the balcony opposite the stage, where Michael Sweeney has his camera set up on the tripod. From this vantage, he can see when the stairway has cleared, and he waves to Annie.

"Ready to go!" he yells.

She pushes through the throng toward the kitchen. "Carla, how many gift bags do we have?"

"Why? Something wrong?"

"We've got close to seven hundred kids out there! Do we have enough to go around?"

Carla nods. "We got three new babies since I counted. No bags for them. And over in Swedetown? They got sickness this week. . . . We got enough—long as it's only union kids."

"They all had union cards," Eva confirms.

"So we got enough," Carla says, with a shrug.

Annie nods and goes back out to the main room. Clearing the three steps to the stage level in one long stride, she slips behind the stage curtain. Charlie Miller is in the wings, in costume, waiting for his cue. The Women's Auxiliary choir has gathered in front of his throne to conceal it until the last moment, and Mrs. Kaisor is waiting at the piano while Frank Aaltonen snarls curses, struggling to get the theater curtain to rise.

"It was working half an hour ago," he tells Annie. "Something's snagged in the rigging."

"Start the carols," Annie tells Mrs. Kaisor. "Play as loud as you can."

Out in the hall, everyone quiets down. Suddenly whatever was wrong with the curtain is fixed, and Frank hauls it up, hand over hand, as the choir begins "Adeste Fideles" in three-part harmony.

*   *   *

Nobody takes much notice of the drunk when he leaves the pub. He is muttering and yelling, but that's a common enough occurrence, and his weaving walk is merely amusing to a bunch of half-grown boys, who nudge one another and make bets on whether he'll fall into a snowdrift or pass out in a doorway.

"I'm no thief," he yells. "I'm a citizen, see?"

"You're stewed is what you are!" the boldest of them yells back, before they get bored and move on.

He decides to head for his usual place, only that's closed, and so are the next two bars he tries. Then he sees that the lights are on at Dominic Vairo's saloon, on the first floor of the Italian Hall.

"Dominic. Ha. Dummy Nick!" The drunk giggles at his witticism, even though Dom's good people—for a dago. Or a Portagee, or whatever the hell he is. Dom knows how to help a man out. Says right on the building. *Società Mutua Beneficenza.* I need a little *beneficenza,* he'll say. Just a beer. And slice of salami, maybe. Down on my luck. Christmas Eve. Help a fella out . . .

He crosses the street to Vairo's just as someone inside locks the door and flips the sign to CLOSED.

"C'mon! I can *see* you bastards in there! C'mon, Dom, you cheap son of a bitch! Help a man out, can't you!"

Nose running from the cold, eyes watering, he kicks at the entrance, but Dom won't let him in.

"Damn Jews," he mutters, giving up. "Don't care about Christmas. Call me a thief. Let you go! Just say it, you coward. You're fired! Fire *me,* eh? *Fire* me!" he yells. "I'll show you."

It is then that he notices the carols. Ladies' voices, not men's, like back at the Truro. Ladies' voice, coming from above him.

Angels, he thinks. It's a miracle, he thinks. A Christmas miracle! There's angels in the Italian Hall!

The choir is only halfway through the program when one of the kids spots Charlie Miller in costume. A wave of fresh excitement pulses through the squirmy, chattering crowd as the rumor spreads. Annie goes backstage again.

"Mr. Miller, I think we'll skip the Mother Goose play. The kids are too restless."

He nods his understanding. Annie catches Mrs. Kaisor's attention and draws a finger across her throat: Last song. The pianist nods and passes the news on to the choir.

Charlie adjusts his paper beard and his pillow-belly and his new dentures, calling, "Merry Christmas" as he comes out onto the stage carrying a flour bag filled with a blanket to make it look full. The kids scream and clap as he settles onto his throne, and his helpers bring out shipping boxes marked with blue and pink, so that boys won't get clothespin dolls and girls won't get little trucks.

Still trying to keep things organized, Annie shouts, "The first two rows of children—line up over here, single file! You'll come up onto the stage, and Father Christmas will give each of you a present. Don't push! There are plenty of presents. Everybody will get a gift!"

The kids rush the stage anyway, but the parents take over, getting the rowdiest into line.

"No pushing!" Annie says sternly, though she's smiling as—one by one—Father Christmas hands each child a gift bag and a piece of candy wrapped in colorful foil.

Mrs. Kaisor and the choir start another round of carols, and everything is going smoothly until Carla collars one of the bigger kids. "Hey! I seen you before. You been through the line."

"The other kids are doing it," the culprit says, by way of exculpation.

"What, you wanna be a cheater like them?" Carla snatches the gift back and is about to hand it to the next kid when she notices a stranger standing in the door at the top of the staircase, shouting something and waving his arms.

"What he say?" Carla calls to Annie. "He say 'fire'?"

Annie looks around. "Fire? Did you say 'fire'?"

* * *

Who says it next? A child. Then another. And another. Suddenly the word is coming from everywhere—*"Fire!"* Screamed, shrieked, wailed, bellowed.

Up on the balcony, Michael Sweeney is waving his arms above his head, shouting, "There's no fire! I can see the whole room! There's no fire!"

It doesn't matter. The fire is in their minds now, real as real can be.

Frantic parents grip squalling babies and lunge into the crowd, reaching terrified toddlers and crying schoolchildren. Everyone is pushing toward the exit, trying to get downstairs and outside. Because they all know about the Shirtwaist Girls.

Girls burning alive in a locked factory.

Girls jumping from windows.

Girls lying dead on the sidewalk.

Girls laid out on the floor of a makeshift morgue.

Everyone has seen the pictures, and they are certain now: they're going to burn to death like the girls at the shirtwaist factory.

Seven hundred children are howling and sobbing, and no one can hear what Annie Clements is screaming over and over and over, until her voice is frayed and torn with it.

"There *is no* fire! Don't panic! There is *no fire!*"

3

There's no fire, Chief Joseph Trudell is thinking as the Sixth Street fire brigade's wagon pulls up in front of the Italian Hall. He was expecting to see a building engulfed in flames, but nothing is visible: no smoke, no fire, just a bunch of kids milling around on the sidewalk in front of the building.

Another false alarm, he thinks, for they have been common lately. Young hooligans, pulling the call box lever, just to see the firemen scramble. Of course, you have to take every alarm seriously. Christmas candles do get knocked over.

Leaving Bert Foster to secure the horses, Chief Trudell and Chris Messner jump off the wagon, settle their helmets onto their heads, and push through the crowd toward the big double doors.

"I can't smell anything," Chris yells. "You?"

The chief shakes his head. There's still no sign of trouble. It's just a lot of scared children rushing down the staircase. He is about to yell, "Stand aside!" so he can get upstairs to see what's going on when one of the kids coming down the staircase stumbles.

And falls.

Before Trudell can even think the words "Be careful! Don't run!" a second child trips over the first. Another child falls, and another and another, and nobody can get their balance, and kids keep falling, and all he can do is stand there, stupefied, as a waterfall of children pours down toward him, one little body after another.

It happened so fast. That's what he will tell himself over and over and over, for the rest of his life. There was nothing he could have done! But he will never stop seeing it. Never as long as he lives. The horror of it, going on and on. An eternity of it.

Half a minute, he will tell himself later. It can't have been more than half a minute.

Children falling. Mouths open, screaming as they tumble onto those below, crushing them. Mouths open, sucking at air that cannot get past the weight on their lungs as more children fall. Mouths open, lips turning blue as the pile above them gets higher and higher, until it reaches all the way to the second floor.

Wails within the pile become whimpers. Screams from those watching on the street become shrieks. Children are dying before their eyes. Brothers and sisters, cousins, sons, daughters . . .

"My God," Chris Messner whispers. "My God, Chief. What do we do?"

Behind them, they can hear big Bert Foster, hollering above the crowd's wails, "Chief? Chief! What's going on?"

Joseph Trudell opens his mouth, but he cannot find words for what he sees. A monkey puzzle of interlocking bodies. Fingers twitching. Little faces bleaching white. Children in a tangled heap, twenty feet high.

Moments later, Bert gets through the crowd and stops.

"Jesus," he says. "Jesus."

An instant later, Chief Trudell's stunned immobility shatters. The children at the bottom are already dead, but skinny arms stick out of the middle of the pile. "Try to pull them free!" Trudell shouts.

Bracing a hand against the side walls, Bert and Chris lean over the lowest bodies to grab whatever hand or foot they can reach without stepping on a head or chest. They tug gently at first, not wanting to hurt the children worse. When they can't pull a single body from the tangle, they get a better grip on whatever it is in their hands and heave.

"No good," Chris shouts over his shoulder. "Too much weight!"

"The angles are all wrong," Bert yells.

"There's a fire escape around back," the Chief hollers. "We'll have to get at them from the top."

Breathless, Chris and Bert stop and look at Trudell as though he is speaking Swahili. "We can't do anything down here," he insists. "Go around back to the fire escape. Try to pull them free from the top! *Go!*"

They nod then and make a dash for the corner.

Chief Trudell remains at the bottom of the stairs a few moments longer, for he has met the terrified eyes of one of the little boys. Four years old, maybe? Too far from the top to be rescued from above. Not strong enough to breathe between the weight above him and the un-yielding stair tread below him.

"Watch me, son," Joseph Trudell tells the child, his own eyes steady. "Keep looking at me. It's going to be all right," he lies. "We'll get you out. Just keep looking at me."

When James MacNaughton heard the fire bells clanging earlier that day, he barely looked up from the production report he was studying. He has forgotten the alarm entirely by the time someone knocks on the front door.

Odd, he thinks. Who could that be?

He is not expecting anyone and hopes it is not carolers. Mary and the girls are in Europe, and he himself prefers quiet solitude, especially during the holidays. With mild curiosity, he lowers the business section of the *Boston Globe* onto his lap and watches the door of his study. The butler passes by on his way to the front entry.

There is a murmur of conversation and the butler reappears, with a visitor in tow. "Sir, there's been an accident. Fire Chief Trudell needs to speak to you."

Without rising, MacNaughton frowns at Trudell, whose face is ashen but not smeared with soot.

"Yes?" MacNaughton prompts. "What was it? A cave-in? Which shaft?"

"No, sir. It was at the Italian Hall."

"Then what business is it of mine?"

"There have been fatalities."

MacNaughton lets silence repeat his question: What business is it of mine?

"I came to tell you," the chief says, blinking rapidly, "and to ask if we can use City Hall as a morgue."

The butler has returned with the cook and the maid. Together they stand just outside the sitting room, listening. MacNaughton sends a reproving glance toward his staff. He will reprimand them later. "City Hall? Don't be absurd. Notify the undertakers."

"There are too many, sir. At least sixty. We're still counting."

The maid makes a small sound, her hand at her mouth.

"Good Lord," MacNaughton says, startled. "Is the fire out?"

"There wasn't any fire, sir."

"Well, then!" MacNaughton snaps, beginning to be annoyed by this melodramatic doling out of detail. "Spit it out, man! What happened?"

"It was a Christmas party, sir. For the union children. We're trying to get the story straight, but nobody's sure. There were hundreds at the party, and everybody is— It was mostly children, sir. Little kids. Everyone's confused and upset. We think somebody yelled that there was a fire, and everyone tried to get down the stairs to the sidewalk, and then . . . a little boy tripped. I saw him—He tripped and—and . . ."

He raises his hands and then drops them: a man who saves lives, helpless to describe what that pile was made of, *who* that pile was made of.

"It was a *Christmas* party," he repeats, hardly able to believe it. "A Christmas party, for *children*."

The butler steps into the study, guiding the fire chief into a chair, then pouring him a glass of brandy. Out in the hallway, the maid is sobbing, and the cook looks horrified. The butler returns to them and puts a sheltering arm around the two women while the fire chief regains composure and tries again to explain.

"It was little children, sir, at the party," Trudell says. "One of them stumbled on the stairs, and another one fell over him, and it then . . . They just kept falling. The entire stairwell was— It was completely jammed with children's bodies, sir."

"So there was no fire?" MacNaughton asks.

"No, sir. A man yelled, 'Fire!' People panicked. That's all we could figure out."

"Who would do such a thing?"

"Nobody seems to know him. He had a Citizens' Alliance button on his coat. That's what people are saying. I've sent for the coroner."

Even James MacNaughton sits still for a moment. Then he shakes himself, remembering why he was told all this in the first place. "Telephone the janitor at City Hall," he tells the butler. "Have him open the building."

The chief doesn't seem to realize that he is finished with his task, so MacNaughton gives the man a nudge. "I'm sure you must have duties to perform, Mr. Trudell. I won't keep you longer."

Blinking, Trudell comes to himself and stands without another word. As the butler ushers him out, MacNaughton tries to remember what he was reading when all this started. Oh, yes. An article in the *Boston Globe* that he has saved for the evening, when he can pay closer attention to its news. Two hundred and thirteen banks have applied to join the new Federal Reserve System, and he needs to understand how the idiots in Washington plan to distort the markets now. They aren't even trying to conceal their plans to print money, and that will affect all metals-based currency—

The butler reappears.

"What now!" MacNaughton demands. "And why are you two still standing here?" he asks the cook and the maid. "Haven't you duties to attend to?"

"Chief Trudell would like to know, sir: Will you want a list of the dead? When they have names and a complete count?"

"No," MacNaughton says. "It's a union affair. Nothing to do with me, or the company."

The cook gasps in disbelief, and the wet-eyed maid glares.

"Don't waste your sympathy," their employer tells them sternly. "Nobody from the Citizens' Alliance did this. It was a union stunt that went wrong. They wanted newspaper stories about a Christmas party ruined by evil capitalists. This is the price they pay. Maybe now they'll come to their senses."

In the long silence that follows, he shakes out his paper and resumes reading, only to look up when he hears the maid declare, "Oh, you are a cold-hearted bastard. You are a wicked, selfish, cold-hearted bastard."

He lowers the newspaper to his lap, watching her wipe her snotty nose on the back of her hand. "And you are fired," he tells her evenly.

"Say my name," she demands, quiet and fierce. "I've worked for you for eleven months. Say my name!"

"Get your things and get out."

"Perfect," she says flatly. "Sack a girl on Christmas Eve. Aren't you just a treat? Well, my name is Loretta Bernadette Devlin, and the only reason I've put up with your high-handed, arrogant shite all these wretched months is to spy on you for the union."

She turns on her heel and stalks off toward the servants' quarters.

"You'll get no reference from me!" he shouts at the retreating footsteps.

"Nobody decent would take your word anyway!" she yells back.

"Pay her salary," he tells the butler, "prorated for the month. No Christmas bonus." He glances at the cook and asks, "Don't you have work to do?"

How many years is it for me? she is wondering as she watches the maid go. Twelve? More—almost thirteen since that single, solitary nickel raise . . . Has he ever spoken to me since then, apart from issuing an order?

"My name is Louise Hope Aiken," she says, taking off her apron and dropping it to the floor. "There's a roast in the oven," she warns as she follows Loretta to the servants' quarters. "Good luck with it."

"The same arrangement, I presume: prorated salary, no bonus." The butler waits for MacNaughton's confirming grunt before asking, "And will it be the same for me, or would you prefer my two weeks' notice?"

"*Get out!*"

"Dee-lighted!" the butler says archly, mimicking Teddy Roosevelt just to needle the man. "My name, by the way, is James Edmund Morris, and if I may say so, sir, you can go straight to hell."

4

Across town, Dr. William Fischer is in the middle of reading Clement Clarke Moore's poem to his children when there is an insistent knocking at the front door. His wife goes to answer it. He continues the story, then stops again when she returns looking dismayed.

"There's been some kind of accident at the Italian Hall," she tells him quietly. "There are fatalities." She whispers, "Children," so her own can't hear.

"In the Italian Hall?" he asks, half-rising. "What on earth could happen there?"

"Papa, no!" the children cry. "Finish the story! Please, please, please?"

"And supper is almost ready," his wife says. "An hour won't hurt. The dead can wait."

True enough, he thinks, for he is a coroner now and no longer a physician who attends to the living. So he finishes the story and sits down to dinner before leaving his family and their tree and all the wrapped and beribboned gifts. Hat pulled down, muffler pulled up, he walks swiftly toward the central city, noting how silent the streets are. Strange, he thinks. Christmas Eve, and no carolers?

It is his first indication of the scale of the event.

Two policemen are guarding the building, arms crossed against the cold, moving from foot to foot, trying to keep their toes from freezing. "The children are laid out over at City Hall," one tells him. "Nothing to see up there, Dr. Fischer."

"No relation," he says automatically, for his lack of connection to the disreputable Tom Fisher is something he feels compelled to point out these days.

Although his office is an elected one, he is a conscientious man who has read up on investigative procedures. "I'd like to see the scene of the fatalities," he tells the policemen, and they pull the big double doors open for him.

"Terrible thing," one of the officers says. "Terrible thing."

There are children's shoes and little bags of toys in the stairwell. The second floor is chaos. Hundreds of chairs tipped over. Decorations and little plates of cookies littering the floor. Coffee spilled—did someone slip in that? Some sort of panic . . .

He has almost finished his inspection when he notices Annie Clements sitting alone, crumpled on the steps of the stage.

"There was no fire," she says dully. "There was no fire. I tried to tell them. No one listened."

He attempts a few questions, but she cannot seem to focus on the answers, so he leaves her and heads over to City Hall. There he finds the people who would ordinarily have been out visiting, caroling, carousing, for the news has spread, house to house, block by block.

The entire union membership has converged on this building, forming an enormous protective ring around distraught, disbelieving, dumbfounded families, shouting questions, making demands. Attempting to be deaf and blind to the hysteria around him, William Fischer keeps his head down and moves forward steadily until he gets to the door. This one, too, is guarded by policemen who recognize the coroner and allow him to slip inside.

"Second floor," he's told. "The big meeting room."

He climbs the stairs with no expectation of shock. A mining town coroner, after all, becomes hardened to gruesome mortality. Every week, year after year, William Fischer has gazed at the body of some poor man with his head caved in, or his chest crushed, or his limbs twisted. And this is hardly the first time he has signed death certificates for children. Measles and mumps. Diphtheria and tetanus. Pneumonia. Burns. Infected cuts . . .

Nothing he has seen before could have prepared him for what he finds on the second floor of the Calumet City Hall on the night of December 24, 1913.

After a full minute of paralysis, he regains some kind of self-possession and takes shelter in bureaucracy. "Lay the bodies out for identification," he tells Bert Foster and Chris Messner. "Face-up. Sorted by sex and age. Adults closest to the door. Children in two long lines beyond them."

While they do that, the coroner interviews Joseph Trudell. The fire chief seems almost stupefied but gets enough out for Fischer to presume that the cause of death for all of them will most likely be suffocation.

"Christ," the chief whispers, looking at the bodies. "Christ! Look at them all!"

Little boys, arrayed in rough order of height, smallest to tallest. Little girls, side by side, wearing their nicest dresses. Little faces, pale and perfect, like those of William Fischer's own children, waiting for him at home. *Nestled all snug in their beds, while visions of sugar plums dance in their heads . . .*

"Why are their feet bare?"

The coroner turns toward the voice and sees Michael Sweeney, his face wet, his eyes red. His camera hangs at his side, held in one trembling hand, and he is standing in the doorway, looking at the long rows of perfect little corpses. "Why are their feet bare?" he demands again. "Where are their shoes?"

"Some of the shoes came off when they fell, and . . ." Fischer clears his throat. "There will be . . . tags put on their toes. When they've been identified."

"Jesus!" Sweeney cries, breaking down. After two quick, gasping sobs, he pulls himself together and lifts his camera.

"Surely," William Fischer says, "this is not the time for taking pictures."

"This is exactly the time," the photographer snarls. "Let the bastards see! Make them learn what the price of copper is! Let them see for themselves who pays it."

Downstairs, outside, the crowd is increasingly restive. Union members shout for the doors of City Hall to be opened. Families of the missing demand to be given the bodies of sons and daughters, brothers and sisters.

Now comes the hardest part. It is never easy to watch the bereaved identify their loved ones. And this time, the survivors will have to pass down the long rows of the dead, looking for a familiar face. Bracing himself, Dr. Fischer leaves the makeshift morgue and calls to the policemen guarding the front door: "All right. Let them in. Families only. No more than eight or ten people at a time," he warns. "We don't want another panic on a stairway."

Those who climb the steps now are acquainted with grief. Everyone, in every generation, has lost men to the mines. Everyone has seen disease carry off a whole family. Everyone has watched helplessly as small injuries turn into infections that overwhelm bodies—strong or weak, young or old. This is different. Even the Finns, who are almost inhumanly stoic in the face of loss, cannot hold back emotion tonight. Mothers collapse, screaming, weeping. Fathers roar and howl. Surviving brothers and sisters cling to parents, sobbing.

One by one, the dead are recognized and named. The coroner fills out toe tags. Ages and addresses are noted and logged on a master list. The bereaved are directed toward the town's undertakers, who have set up behind a long table at one end of the room.

Finally, the room is empty—except for the dead, and the coroner, and the undertakers, whose work is just beginning.

One of the morticians opens a flask.

Pete Madornovich takes a pull. "How many coffins do you have on hand?"

"Not enough" is Helen Kallio's bleak answer. "Not near enough."

"We're going to need small ones," Jimmy Richetta says. "Painted white."

William Fischer finishes the final census around five in the morning. Seventy-three. Fifty-seven children. Sixteen adults. Mostly mothers. One woman was pregnant. Does that make it seventy-four?

Italians, Croatians, Slovenians, Finns. Mostly Finns. The oldest: Kate Petteri, sixty-six. The youngest: Rafael Lesar, two and a half. He was brought to the party by his sister Mary, thirteen. Also dead. A lot of the children are nine, ten, or eleven years old. Young enough to get a present on Christmas Eve. Old enough to run for the staircase on their own or with a smaller sibling in tow.

The bodies are unmarked. Death came so quickly after their fall down the stairs that there was no time even for a bruise to form.

The coroner commandeers some city official's desk. Hands shaking, he lifts the handset of the telephone and rouses the operator, who places his call to the Houghton home of the *Daily Mining Gazette*'s editor.

"Jesus!" the editor says over and over as he takes down the information. "How many did you say? Jesus!"

Fischer repeats the numbers and says, "Get that out on the A.P. wire."

The editor yawns twice, seems befuddled, and will probably get some of it wrong. But at least the story will be sent out to the world, where these deaths can't be denied or lost or forgotten, like so many others. Make them see, Fischer thinks, echoing the photographer's words. They need to know what the price of copper is.

When the call ends, Fischer opens desk drawers until he finds some city stationery. Writing carefully, checking each name twice, he makes two complete lists of the dead. Then he tucks one into an envelope and calls the telegraph office for a courier.

The winter solstice is just past. It's still dark outside when the boy arrives. Fischer hands him the envelope and says, "Take this to Mac-Naughton."

"It's early, sir," the boy points out. He is barely awake himself, his uncombed hair mashed down under his cap. "You mean the mansion or his office?"

"The mansion. I want you to bang on the door as loudly as you can. Loud enough to wake the dead. And you are to put this into Mr. MacNaughton's hands directly. Don't give it to the butler, understand? I want James MacNaughton to know what happened here."

When William Fischer leaves for home, the sun is low on the southeastern horizon, sending his long shadow northwest. Church bells begin to ring. It's Christmas morning, he realizes. As he climbs the six steps to his front porch, he can hear their excited cries of "Papa! Papa! Papa!"

"They've been awake for hours," his wife tells him. "I made them wait until you got home to open the gifts." She is smiling. The children are hopping up and down, clapping their hands and squealing.

They don't know, he thinks. Nobody has told them.

His wife searches his face and shushes the children. "Papa's been up working all night. He needs sleep now. We can open the presents later."

The children look stricken. He tries to smile. "No! I'm fine," he says heartily. "Let's see what Father Christmas brought these good little girls and boys!"

He sits next to the tree and watches his wife as she lets each child in turn choose a gift. "Who is it from?" his wife asks, making a note of the donor so that thank-you letters can be written later today, while they wait for Christmas dinner. Wrapping paper is torn off, squeals of excitement are emitted, the gift is shown off, and then the next child repeats the sequence, until all the presents have been opened.

"Billy, go to bed," his wife urges, surrounded by colorful paper and ribbons. "I'll take care of all this."

"No," he says. "I . . . I have a little more to do."

He retreats to his study, closes the door, and takes out the second list of the dead. He spends the rest of Christmas filling out and signing seventy-three death certificates, one by one. When at last Dr. William Fischer goes to bed, he will stay there for three days, unable to eat.

Many years later he will admit that he could never again bear to see his children sleeping with their feet uncovered.

5

Civil blood makes civil hands unclean.
—Shakespeare, *Romeo and Juliet*

James MacNaughton awakens to darkened silence. Heavy brocade curtains block drafts through the bedroom windows, but they also block
the light—what little there is of it in December, in Calumet. He hates
this time of year. Sunrise, in midwinter, doesn't come until it's nearly
nine in the morning, and he is reduced to relying on an alarm clock to
maintain his normal routine.

The lingering smell from last night's burned roast reminds him of
a thoroughly disagreeable evening. An expensive cut of perfectly good
meat, ruined. Wasted. Still in bed, he glances at the clock. Seven forty-
three. The alarm hasn't gone off yet.

He lies still, wondering what did wake him, until he hears someone
pounding on the front door. "Answer that!" he shouts before he remembers that he is alone in the house.

The pounding is insistent. "All right! All right!" he mutters, sitting
on the side of the bed and smoothing back his sleep-disarrayed hair.
"I'm coming."

He draws his dressing gown on over his pajamas, shoves his feet into
his house slippers, and hurries down the stairs. It is in that undignified
attire that he opens the front door to a young courier.

"You're MacNaughton, right? Not the butler?" the boy asks, and
when the chief executive officer of the Calumet & Hecla Mining Company nods curtly, the urchin shoves an envelope into his hands. "Dr.
Fischer says that's for you."

He takes the delivery. The brat holds out his hand, expecting a tip. Shaking his head at the impertinence, MacNaughton looks down at the insolent little face and shuts the door without a word.

Alone again, he opens the envelope, withdraws the contents, and glances at it long enough to see that it is a list of names and ages. They are numbered, so he looks at the bottom line before dropping the pages on his desk in the study.

Hoping to resume his morning in an orderly fashion, he goes back upstairs to start his routine again. He is halfway to the bathroom when the alarm clock goes off. He returns to his bedroom, shuts the alarm off. For a time, he simply sits on the edge of his bed, calming himself before he starts over. Down the hallway to the bathroom. Ten minutes of calisthenics. A shave. A shower. Then it all goes wrong again.

What is the matter with people these days? he asks himself, rummaging through his wardrobe, opening drawers, looking for stockings and underclothes. There is no loyalty, no respect, he thinks as he dresses himself.

He will have to hire temporary help until his family returns from Europe. Mary will want to interview candidates for a permanent staff, and this time he will make sure she doesn't hire any more immigrants. Not even those from Great Britain can be relied upon.

On the landing, he pauses more briefly than usual, taking in the cityscape. There has been some snow overnight, though not enough to require the street cleaners. Streams of worshippers are leaving the churches. Calumet is quiet, and he is relieved, for he half-expected, if not a mob with pitchforks, then some sort of rumpus.

Of course, nothing has been done about his breakfast, but how difficult can it be to make oatmeal? He goes into the kitchen. Opens a window to draw off the lingering stink of the burnt roast. Finds a pot, fills it with water, and stands there watching it slowly come to a simmer.

"Does it always take this long?" he asks the empty room. "Why is this so slow?"

Once again, he hears pounding on the front door and he stalks down the hallway. "What now?" he demands, seeing that the courier is back.

The boy shoves two telegrams at him. "Want me to wait?" he asks, offering the reply forms.

MacNaughton glances at the sender's lines. "Yes," he says. Then he shuts the door and leaves the brat to learn some manners in the cold out on the porch.

The first telegram is from Mary. She and the girls have read about the occurrence in the London *Times*.

I should have expected this, he tells himself. Copper telegraph wires now connect the far north of Michigan to the rest of the world. The union has wasted no time in alerting the press, undoubtedly couching the story in the most lurid and damning terms. The second telegram is from Boston, and it reinforces his surmise. Quincy Shaw, president of Calumet & Hecla, has also seen the union version of the story and knows it must be countered, for embedded in the text is an instruction to general manager MacNaughton.

I FEEL SURE THAT EVEN WITHOUT THIS MESSAGE YOU WILL DO EVERYTHING IN COMPANYS POWER TO GIVE ASSISTANCE TO THE VICTIMS OF THIS FRIGHTFUL ACCIDENT STOP SEE SOME WAY THROUGH TO THE LOCAL PAPERS STOP CONVEY MY SYMPATHY TO THOSE FOR WHOM THE LOSS IS A PERSONAL ONE AND TO THE WHOLE COMMUNITY THAT HAS TO FACE THIS DREADFUL TRAGEDY FULL STOP

He is reaching for a reply form when, for the second time in twelve hours, he detects an awful odor coming from the kitchen. Crying, "Oh, for the love of God!" he rushes in and sees smoke rising from the pot he meant to cook the oatmeal in.

The water has boiled away. Without thinking, he snatches the pot off the stove, sears his palm on the handle, and drops the pot, hopping away from it as it clatters to the floor.

"Damnation!" he shouts in pain and frustration.

Close to tears, he is running tap water over his reddening hand when he smells something else. This time he wraps his other hand in a kitchen towel before he grips the pot handle and lifts it off the floor.

"Damnation," he mutters again, glaring at the perfectly round scorch mark on the kitchen linoleum.

The courier is banging on the door again, yelling, "I can't wait any longer!"

"Two minutes!" MacNaughton yells back.

Hurrying to his office, he lays out the reply forms. Knowing that the contents of any wire he sends is likely to be made public, he is always brief and measured in his responses, even when his writing hand is not bandaged.

He cannot manage cursive, so—slowly and with care—he prints his message to Mary: A SENSELESS TRAGEDY STOP WE ARE DOING WHAT WE CAN FULL STOP. To Shaw, he simply replies: UNDERSTOOD FULL STOP.

Given the apparent breakdown in civil society, he expects that the courier will have left by then, but the child is still on the porch, stamping his feet and slapping his arms to keep warm. He takes the replies MacNaughton hands him, then holds his palm out again.

"Tell the telegrapher to put it on Calumet & Hecla's account," MacNaughton says curtly.

Noticing the bandage on the executive's hand, the courier asks with what sounds like sympathy, "Aw, gee. Hurt yourself?"

Receiving only a glare in response, the boy shrugs and takes his leave. Halfway down the front walk, he looks over his shoulder and yells, "Serves you right!"

With that, the boy makes a dash for the street and hits a patch of ice, going down hard.

"Serves *you* right!" MacNaughton calls.

There is, he thinks, some justice in the universe.

Back in the kitchen, he dumps the oatmeal pot into the trash and finds some cheese and an apple with which to break his fast. Feeling somewhat better, he places a telephone call to his secretary's home.

"Get the office up and running," he says, and his tone makes it clear that there is no point in reminding him what day it is. "I will need to make several calls through the company switchboard."

On his way out the door, he finds a special edition of the *Daily Mining Gazette* lying on the porch. The front-page headline is huge and black, and a gross exaggeration:

80 PERISH!
CHRISTMAS EVE TRAGEDY AT CALUMET!
FALSE CRY OF "FIRE!" THE CAUSE.

Heads will roll for this, he thinks. God damn them all.

When he arrives at his office, his first call is to the editor of the *Calumet News,* a local paper run by a man who knows that loyalty to the company is paramount to his own future. "I would like you to print the following," MacNaughton tells him. Then he dictates the statement from Quincy Shaw's telegram, amending the wording slightly and leaving out the sentence about influencing the local papers.

The next call is to the home of the *Daily Mining Gazette*'s editor, down in Houghton. Listening in as his secretary speaks to the man's wife, he hears the woman call to her husband, "It's James MacNaughton, dear." Her palm over the mouthpiece isn't enough to keep MacNaughton from catching the man's complaint: "It's Christmas, for crying out loud." Nevertheless, he comes to the phone, and MacNaughton begins without preamble.

"Get your facts straight. There were seventy-three, not eighty, dead."

"Are you certain about that number, sir? Our interviews last night indicated that some of the bodies had been taken directly to private homes and—"

"I am quoting the official enumeration made by the coroner, which is the only information that should be reported. Now, then. Take this down: Sheriff Cruse will be offering a reward."

"For the man who yelled, 'Fire'?" the editor presumes, his pencil scratching. "We'll need a description—so far, all we know is that he was from the Citizens' Alliance—"

"Stop interrupting me! The so-called 'man who yelled fire' is nothing more than an unverified rumor being spread by the union. Remind your readers that Charles Miller is an outsider and a known criminal and tell them that he is attempting to use the deaths of children to benefit his illegal and violent strike. Make it clear in future editions that no one was seen wearing a Citizens' Alliance button."

There are four seconds of silence.

"Sir, the *New York Times* is already on the wire service reporting that a man wearing a Citizens' Alliance button came up the stairs and shouted, 'Fire!' And we have witnesses who said—"

"Hysterical women and children. Not reliable sources. In any case, the *New York Times* cannot possibly know what really happened yesterday in Calumet, Michigan. They are undoubtedly among the newspapers Charles Miller has contacted to spread his lies and malign the decent people of our city. You are the newspaper of record here in the Copper Country, are you not?"

"Yes, sir, I like to think so."

"Good. Now. Sheriff Cruse will offer a reward of one thousand dollars for information leading to the conviction of union thugs responsible for the recent murders in Painesdale."

Once again, the silence persists for countable seconds, and James MacNaughton can almost hear the editor thinking, *But not for the man who yelled fire?* And then reminding himself, *There was no man. No one yelled fire.*

"Yes, sir," the editor says finally. "Shall I interview Sheriff Cruse for details, or would you like to dictate them?"

"Your tone is not appreciated, young man! Sheriff Cruse will contact you after I've spoken to him. And I want no more baseless speculation or preposterous claims regarding this regrettable accident. For now, you can simply say that arrests are expected."

"Arrests. Plural, sir?"

"Yes! Plural!" MacNaughton bangs the handpiece into its cradle and curses his poor burned fingers. "Get me Cruse!" he shouts to the secretary. "And find out who's handling the inquest!"

The rest of the day is a futile exercise in controlling the publicity, for it seems to James MacNaughton that he is the only man left in the country who has any sense. He is certain that any charity given to disloyal workers will invite them to claim that it is hush money; nevertheless, the Citizens Action Council authorizes the disbursement of cash to aid the families of the dead with funeral costs. Worse yet, a telegram arrives in midafternoon from Quincy Shaw. An emergency meeting of the C&H board of directors has been held. Shaw's proposal that additional recompense be made by the company to the bereaved has passed, with three yeas, two abstentions, and one nay. Foolishness, MacNaughton thinks, but he has been given his orders and agrees to distribute the funds as soon as they are wired from Boston.

By the evening of December 26, the special editions of the *Boston Globe,* the *Detroit News,* and the *Chicago Tribune* arrive. Publishers are undoubtedly gratified to have something exciting for newsboys to yell about during the slow week between Christmas and New Year's. Front pages are dominated by a titillating photograph of dozens of barelegged little girls, and damn Tom Fisher for not killing that Fenian photographer instead of merely roughing him up! Three anonymous sources have provided stories of "General Manager MacNaughton's callous reaction to the disaster." Well, there's no question who that treacherous trio is, and James MacNaughton gives his attorney instructions to sue all former household staff members for defamation and slander. Let them pay legal fees for the rest of their miserable lives.

When he gets to the editorial page, the outrage continues. Woodrow Wilson has issued a statement lamenting that "in our rush to be great, we do not stop to count the cost of lives snuffed out, of energies overtaxed and broken, the fearful physical and spiritual cost of the men and women and children upon whom the dead weight and burden of it all has fallen pitilessly." That weasel Ferris has also expressed his mawkish sympathy, and the mayor of Detroit is reportedly sending one thousand dollars to help the union defray the burial expenses.

"Despicable," MacNaughton mutters. And he telegraphs his outrage to both politicians, lamenting their shameless effort to turn an unfortunate accident into a partisan truncheon with which to beat one of America's premier industries.

*   *   *

On December 29, the task of distributing checks to the bereaved falls to the company man whose usual job is to inform families of mining accidents. Walking from house to house, followed by a gaggle of reporters who've made the long, difficult trip north, he carries with him a list of seventy-three people, and their ages, and the addresses of their next of kin.

Shivering, he stands on the snow-packed street in front of each address. First he practices the pronunciation of each name, though he is sure to get most of them wrong. Then he does his best to make his heart as numb as his hands and feet when he approaches a home.

He rarely gets to the front door before he is noticed. Sometimes a flour-sack curtain is pulled back. Seeing the Angel of Death, those inside shout and gesture. Sometimes a man with a ravaged face flings open the door, and curses, and runs at him, yelling broken-voiced threats. Sometimes he climbs all the way up the front steps and knocks. Expecting someone else, a grieving woman appears. He speaks quickly then, hoping to get everything out before the door slams in his face.

"I have been authorized by Calumet & Hecla and by the Citizens' Alliance to offer you sympathy for your loss and a cash donation for the burial of—"

For the burial of Katarina Gregorich, age ten.

For the burial of Jenny Giacoletto, age nine.

For the burial of Sulo Rubet Lauri, age eight.

For the burial of Elisina Taipalus, age six.

For the burial of Heli Ryadilahti, age thirteen.

For the burial of Johan Myllykangas, age seven.

For the burial of Kristina, Mary, and Katarina Klarich, ages eleven, nine, and seven.

For the burial of Ina Isola, age thirty-three, and her child Tilma, age five.

For the burial of Antonia Staudohar, age seven.

On and on, he works through the list. He is told to go to hell in a variety of languages, but rage is easier to accept than the cold fury of Frank

Aaltonen, who hears him out and then asks, dead-eyed, "How much? How much are you offering for my wife and my two kids?"

The company man names the figure.

Aaltonen laughs in his face.

"Tell MacNaughton that you are authorized by Local Fifteen of the Western Federation of Miners to inform him that the union won't accept a penny of this blood money. Tell the Citizens' Alliance that we take care of our own. We feed our hungry, we clothe our naked. And we will bury our dead. We don't want *charity*. We want a living wage, an eight-hour day, and an end to the one-man drill. And we want *justice!*"

There will be no such thing, the company man thinks as he descends the icy wooden steps onto the fresh snow below. There will be no justice in Calumet, which is not a mining camp or a village or even a city but an asset owned in its entirety by the company. Nevertheless, he completes his job. Name by name. House by house. Family by family.

When he gets back to the office, he does the only thing that has made it possible for him to carry out this task. He quits.

6

Wherefore weep I then?
—Shakespeare, *Romeo and Juliet*

Public opinion is a fickle thing. It is, after all, the holiday season, and people rarely like to think about dead children for long. Journalists from out of town begin to leave, although a film crew will stay until the funeral to get footage for news reels to be shown between Lillian Gish's new Western, *An Indian's Loyalty*, and a feature film called *The Last Days of Pompeii*.

Mostly, however, the news moves on. No one who lives beyond the Copper Country takes any notice when a local jury of sorts is organized to inquire into the Christmas Eve events.

It will not be an inquest, for the coroner has written the cause of death for all seventy-three certificates: "Killed in a jam caused by a false cry of 'Fire!' by someone at present unknown, during a children's gathering at the Italian Hall." Nevertheless, attorney Anthony Lucas gathers a panel of respectable citizens. Nine men, all members of the Citizens' Alliance, will hear testimony. The inquiry will focus on the rumor that a man wearing a Citizens' Alliance button caused the panic by raising a false alarm about a fire. This, after all, is the element of the event that is still in question.

Charles Miller is called upon first, and his testimony is adamant. He was on the stage, above the crowd, facing the top of the stairway to street level. He gives a description of the man who started the panic: dark hair, a dark coat, a white Citizens' Alliance button. His testimony is corroborated by seven other eyewitnesses, despite close questioning by panel members and Mr. Lucas himself.

As the day goes on, however, the certainty of the first eight is countered by the doubts of sixty-one others, as attorney Lucas expected would be the case. The hall was crowded. Only a few people were near the doorway at the top of the stairs; fewer still were facing that door when the false alarm was said to have been raised. Many who attended the event admit under questioning that they were not in a position to see the exit door when the panic began; neither did they see a man with a white Citizens' Alliance button on his coat.

At the end of the grueling but gratifying day-long inquiry, Lucas is able to issue a brief, definitive statement to the few remaining reporters.

I have personally interviewed a great number of witnesses who claim to have been in the hall at the time the trouble started. The result of my investigation is that there is no proof that any person deliberately entered the hall and cried "Fire" for the purpose of causing a panic. I assure the public that a thorough investigation of this matter has been made and the blame must be laid at the feet of those who placed children in danger by overcrowding a party room without adequate supervision. The excitement and rowdiness of the children themselves contributed to the tragedy.

1914

1

Poor sacrifices of our enmity
—Shakespeare, *Romeo and Juliet*

In threes and fours, the required number of children's caskets are delivered by train from Chicago and Milwaukee, or by hearse from Houghton and Marquette. In Lake View Cemetery, steam shovels have dug six long trenches for the caskets to lie in, side by side. When at last the earth is ready to receive them, the adult coffins and those of larger children are loaded into the hearses. The smallest caskets, those of the littlest children, are carried in the arms of fathers, uncles, brothers. Members of the union and of the Women's Auxiliary line the streets. When the cortège has passed, they fall in behind the bereaved. No union songs echo in the streets today. The only sound is the steady beat of drums and the muffled tramp of winter boots as thousands march toward Lake View.

They are led by Frank Aaltonen, who has lost his wife, Sanna, and their two daughters, Silvia and Wilma. Behind Frank are the parents of the three little Heikkinen boys: Eino, who was ten; Elis, who was nine; and Edwin, just seven. Maria Lanto's husband walks behind her coffin, carrying the box with their five-year-old daughter, Hilja, inside.

Rank upon rank of mourners follow. Most are Finns; *sisu* rules the day. There is silence even as they pass MacNaughton's mansion, where the curtains are drawn against the sight of those hard-faced, silent mourners.

Aware of the irony, Michael Sweeney climbs a fire escape staircase onto a rooftop with a good view of the funeral route. Below him is a river of dark woolen coats and hats that will be dramatically grim against the white of fresh snow. He knows that letters to the editors of many newspapers have protested the printing of his picture of the dead girls—at Christmastime, no less. He doesn't care. That photograph did exactly what he meant it to do: it shoved the nation's face into this tragedy. It made comfortable people uncomfortable. It provoked pity, but also shame and guilt.

The response, however temporary, has been well meant. Donations have poured into Calumet. Cash from the adults. Rewrapped Christmas toys sent by children. Candy and coins. Little notes in labored handwriting.

This is my second favrite doll.
Please dont be sad.
I'm sorry for you.
I hope you feel better.

So he does his job. He changes vantage points, and focus, and framing. He seeks out the most informative and memorable image of the funeral march. And when the end of the procession is visible in the distance, the photographer packs up the camera and climbs down from his rooftop vantage. He has to get to the cemetery. He has to show the world those long rows of coffins in the trenches.

It's only then that he realizes that he has not seen Annie Clements.

"It's not your fault," Eva has told her. "It's not our fault. We gave a party. It's MacNaughton's fault, or the Citizens' Alliance. Not ours! Not yours!"

"You don't gotta do this," Carla said, and her sister Lucia added, "It's too far. You don't wanna take a chance so early—unless . . . that's what you want?"

Eva noticed that, but it was so unthinkable, she didn't realize until later what the midwife was talking about. And anyway, Annie insisted that she had to be there with the mourners. Marching at the very end of the mile-long procession, carrying no flag, wanting no attention. Just . . . walking, head down, with Eva and Carla and Lucia and all the Caretto cousins around her.

We got out alive. That's what Eva has reminded herself over and over: We got out alive.

Carla has been quiet all week, hating to leave the house, at a loss for what to say when she meets those who've lost children in the disaster. She's been having nightmares so bad, she dreads sleep. Eva hears her at night, pacing, pacing, pacing. Carla won't admit how upset she is. With so much raw grief around her, how can she speak of simple nightmares?

Gracie is almost mute and Rosie wakes up screaming—still, at least Carla's children are alive. What must it be like for the families . . . ? Worse. So much worse.

Eva herself has hardly spoken. In the bed with Rosie and Grace, she pretends to be asleep as she listens to Carla's footsteps. Trying not to wake the girls, she concentrates on her own body, struggling to calm the great storms of wordless emotion that shake her for five minutes at a time and then mysteriously drain away.

Even in daylight, she has had waking visions of her own few moments of horror. She hears Carla, clutching Gracie, screaming, "Eva! Stop her! Get Rosie!" She feels her own heart go off like a dynamite charge in her chest. Feels herself chase after the little girl. Feels herself reaching out, gripping the child's collar, leaning away from the momentum of Rosie's terrified flight from the hall. A week has passed, and even now there are moments when she reels, feeling herself teetering at the top of the staircase . . .

She has not forgotten what Jack told her just before the party began, but she has kept that secret. There's been a lot of bitter, angry talk since Christmas Eve. She fears that someone will take Jack's treachery out on Mrs. Kivisto and the kids. She doesn't want any more children to suffer. Anyway, Jack's leaving town soon, and good riddance to him. So she holds her tongue.

Sisu, sisu, sisu, she tells herself over and over, until the word loses all meaning and simply takes on the cadence of the funeral drums.

The cemetery is two miles from the center of town. In numbing cold, mourners listen to prayers in several languages. There are no hymns. No one can sing. Only when the caskets are being lowered into the ground, one by one, does all that silent suffering become wailing heartbreak, shouted pain, and the low, growling moan of despair.

Afterward, the crowd disperses to homes and taverns. There will be no funeral dinner.

That night, in bed, there are quiet questions, some whispered, some only thought. How can we go on living here? Where else can we go? The copper mines in Arizona? The automobile factories in Detroit? What next? What next? What next? Let's just go. MacNaughton is giving train fare to anyone who wants to go. Let's just get out of here.

And so, families pack up. They leave town with no good-byes, for how can survivors face the bereaved? How can the bereaved face the sadness of farewells? They just go. They just get out of Calumet.

They are determined to put it all behind them.

Years will pass, but they will never escape the Italian Hall. No matter how far they travel. No matter how often they hide themselves and weep alone. No matter how much they drink. No matter how hard they beat the children who did not die on Christmas Eve. No matter how many times they ask themselves, Why didn't I catch him? How could I let her hand go? No matter how often they curse God and ask, Why her? Why not me?

They will never be able to explain their dark moods and sudden furies as each Christmas approaches. Decades will pass, and yet every holiday, every wedding, every baby born, every milestone will stand in a shadow. When a daughter walks down the aisle of a church, they will see her brother, who did not live to carry on the family name. When they see a grandchild's face, sweet in sleep, they will remember the still and perfect face of a sister who never grew up, never married, never had babies like this one. Each joy will be a reminder of someone who is not there to share it.

Someday, when they are very old, someone in the family—a daughter, a grandson—might put it all together and ask, "Were you there that day? At the Italian Hall? Did you see what happened?"

"It was a long time ago," they'll answer. "Let's talk about something else."

2

For those who stay in Calumet, the winter grinds on in serene indifference. The union still exists, although its men seem stunned during the meetings, unable to come to any decision about the strike.

The women of the Copper Country have more immediate concerns, as always. The next meal, the next pile of laundry, the next crying kid. And in the crowded Caretto household, the gloom is sometimes punctuated by news of an impending birth and a rush to a mother's bedside.

Apprenticed to Lucia Caretto, Eva now goes with the midwife on every call. Her tasks are mostly fetching and carrying. She heats water and soaks rags to press comfortingly into the laboring woman's bottom. "Makes 'em warm, see?" Lucia says. "So she don' be so tight like this," she says, balling her hands into fists.

"It's wonderful," Eva tells Annie one night when they are sitting around the table with Lucia and Carla. "It's scary, but then when the baby is born, everybody is crying and laughing, and it's just so *wonderful*."

Lucia says, "Not too many right now. April, May, June? We gonna have a lotta strike babies. Glad I got some help for that." She inclines her head at Eva. "She pretty good! Nice an' calm!"

There is an odd silence then. Annie smiles briefly, but working with the midwife has gotten Eva into the habit of detecting distress in other woman so she can do something for them. Annie had begun putting on weight when she got back from the workhouse. Now she's as bony as she was after her hunger strike. She is pale, too. Of course, it's midwinter in Calumet. Everyone is as colorless as a day-shift miner. Still, there's something wrong here. Eva can tell.

"Annie, you wanna stay with us?" Carla asks. "Till you know what you gonna do?"

Annie shakes her head. "I'm all right. But thank you."

"You know you welcome, eh?" Carla says.

"My husban', he say the same," Lucia says. "We make room."

"Thank you. I'll come next door if I need anything."

"Annie . . . you think Joe, he suspect?" Carla whispers, leaning over the table.

"He always suspects." Annie puts her head in her hands, fighting nausea. "Eight years we've been married. Almost nine. All that time, he always suspected. I never gave him any reason, but he expected it."

"Wait," Eva says. "What? Wait. You mean you're . . . ?"

Lucia nods, then shakes her head: Yes, but stay out of this.

"Maybe you're wrong," Annie says. "Maybe I'm just late."

Lucia shrugs eloquently: It's early, but I'm not wrong.

"Joe gonna find out soon," Carla says. "What you gonna do?"

"I don't know yet. Something. I have to do something."

"Annie," Lucia says cautiously, "if you don't want—I can . . . you know."

Eva looks around, astonished. "Annie, why would you . . . ? You always wanted children! Why wouldn't you . . . ?" They all just look at her, waiting for her to figure it out.

"Oh," Eva says. "Oh, dear. It's not Joe's. It's . . . Michael's?"

Annie freezes, then gets up so abruptly, her chair tips over. She pushes Carla aside and vomits into the sink. For a time, she stands still, hands on the rim of the sink. "I'm sorry," she manages to say before the nausea hits again.

"Sit," Carla tells Annie. "I clean up." She hands Annie a soda cracker, then drains the boiling water from a pot of macaroni into the sink, swirling it to wash the puke away. Filling a bowl with the noodles, she grates a little donated cheese she got from the Auxiliary over the top.

"Take this next door," she tells Eva, giving her a look that warns, *Be careful what you say.* "Joe gonna want his breakfast."

"He'll need lunch, too," Annie says, despairing.

"Go lie down. I figure something out," Lucia says. "Eva, get over there now. If he ask, you say him: 'Annie's sick. She gonna stay here a little. Till she feel better.'"

The warning whistle for the night shift shrieks. The mines are running with managers, and scabs, and men like Joe Clements, who have renounced the union and gone back to work. Holding the macaroni dish close, Eva scuttles across the twenty feet between the two houses and climbs up the tall stairs to the Clementses' back door.

Joe opens it, and she almost falls off the little landing when he does. Standing above her, he looks like every giant in every fairy tale. Six foot six, shoulders that all but fill the doorway. Glowering as though he'd eat her. *Fee fie foe fum* . . .

"What do *you* want? Where's my wife?"

"Annie's sick," Eva tells him. "Carla sent this over." She lifts the bowl of macaroni up toward him, like a supplicant. Here, Giant, please don't eat me.

He glares down at it and grumbles, "Dago slop." Eyes narrowed, he looks at her sideways. "I'm night shift. I need a lunch, too."

"I know. Carla's making something. I'll bring it over in a few minutes."

"What kind of sickness?" he calls as she starts back to the Caretto's.

She hesitates for just a moment, and when she turns to him, he can tell that she's thinking up a lie. Because she is.

"Nothing you can get," she says with sudden inspiration.

And that's the truth.

There are no dancing green ribbons in the sky that night. Just a black blanket of heavy cloud above the Copper Country.

More snow coming, Michael Sweeney thinks, watching the weather beyond the window. Have to be careful about leaving footsteps up to the house.

The great bronze bell in the Civic Theater clock tower tolls twelve. The sound is faint, noticeable chiefly because he has been listening for it. He pushes himself out of the broken-spring chair in the corner of the room he shares with Charlie Miller.

"This is crazy," Charlie says, watching him pull on his coat. "You're crazy."

"Go to hell," Mike says genially.

"Keep this up, and you'll get there first," Charlie replies.

"Most likely," Mike admits. It is a stupid risk, for so many reasons.

"Leave," Charlie urges. "Get out of this town while you can."

"That is the plan, but I'm not going until she agrees to come with me, and she wouldn't leave until after the . . . After Christmas." Mike pulls an anonymous-looking knit cap low over his ears. "You know Annie."

"It's like arguing with a dress-store dummy."

"Or a statue of the Virgin."

Gloves on, Mike lifts his chin in farewell. "See you later."

He pulls the door closed behind himself and starts down the corridor. Usually the boardinghouse is quiet at this time of night, so he slows when he hears the landlady's voice insisting, "Come back in the morning!"

Heavy footsteps. Several men pounding up the wooden stairway. His instinct is to hide. He has no wish to explain to anyone where he's going or why. Stepping backward, he shrinks into a little hallway that leads to the fire escape, intending to wait this out.

The footsteps pass by; a moment later, he realizes they're headed for the end of the corridor. Damn it, he thinks. They're going to arrest Charlie again. There were rumors. A big sweep. MacNaughton's deputized army, making life miserable again.

He hears the voices, if not all the words. A demand, a defiant response.

Charlie or Annie. Stay or go. He has to decide. Right here. Right now.

Annie, he decides. He's sent a note. He can't disappoint her.

Then he hears the gunshots.

*   *   *

She has heard women talk about utter exhaustion and a dull mind in the early months. The funeral march was probably a mistake, but she had to see it through. Soul-sick, gut-sick, heart-sick, she had to bear witness. To do penance.

Think, she tells herself. Think. You have to decide.

Lucia has given her a choice. She can make everything go back to the way it was before or turn away from everything she ever thought she was. A good woman, a good wife, a good person.

She and Michael have not met since . . . since before. Now the time has come. Tonight, she thinks. I'll tell him tonight. Then I'll decide what to do.

By midnight, the snow has tapered off. There is no noise apart from the wind against the clapboards, the ticking of the clock, the tapping of her own fingers on the table. The clock ticks and ticks, and with each passing minute, she is more frantic, the muscles between her shoulder blades tightening with that old, familiar sensation of worry and dread.

He's not coming, she thinks. He's guessed. He's run away. What will Joe do? What is it like—to end it before anyone else knows?

At last, exhausted, she climbs the stairs and falls into bed, fully expecting another of the long, awful dreams she has had so often lately: running and running and running from something that hasn't caught up with her. She awakens with a start, not knowing why, but in those first few moments, she lies still, remembering the dream.

Not running. Floating. Looking up at red and white and blue silk billowing in the clear sky above the Copper Country. And in those first few moments, the decision is made. She will hold her head up. She will have this baby, and be damned to those who damn her.

A daughter, she thinks. Please, God: a little girl who'll be a tall woman who will stand up straight and see beyond the place where she is born, wherever that may be—

Someone bangs on the back door. Louder, faster, more insistently than the first attempt. Realizing now why she woke up, she waits, eyes wide.

She can see no sign of dawn through the burlap curtain on the little gable window. It can't be Joe, home early. He wouldn't knock on the door. He'd come straight in. Michael. It must be Michael.

Fighting nausea, she hurries down the stairs. Hair wild, in her nightgown and wearing a blanket as a shawl, she pulls open the back door and with a rush of heedless certainty and unrepentant joy, she tells him, "I'm pregnant. It's yours. It's ours. It's mine. I want this baby. You can do as you please, but I . . ."

Except it's not Michael. It's Father Horvat.

For a moment, they are speechless, both startled by what has just been revealed and to whom.

"Mrs. Clements—Annie," the priest amends, for this is surely not the time for specious courtesy. "Let me in. Michael isn't coming tonight. Something's happened. He came to me. Read this."

She can't move. She just stands there, like Lot's wife. Turned into a pillar. The priest knocks snow off his boots against the door jamb outside and pushes past her into the kitchen. She closes the door and takes the note he holds out to her.

She recognizes the handwriting. She has seen it before on the backs of photographic prints. Usually the neat, regular letters are nearly as nice as Jack Kivisto's; this is a hasty scrawl. *Cruse came with six goons. Told Charlie to recant his testimony about the CA man. Charlie refused and they shot him. He died a few minutes later. I was with him. I have to leave now. Come to me.*

She puts out a hand, steadying herself against the kitchen sink as the walls reel and the floor rises toward her. The priest catches her arm and tells her to sit, but she shakes her head and looks again at the note. There is an address at the bottom. She memorizes it.

"I have to get dressed," she says. "I have to go—"

"Annie, wait!" Albin Horvat orders in a low and steady voice. "MacNaughton's men are all over town. Deputies are watching the depot and the road to Houghton. They don't expect anyone to go north. I can get Michael up to Copper Harbor. He can wait a few days and then catch a freight south. When he gets to Wisconsin, he'll be safe, I think."

She nods, only half-hearing him. Smoothing out the note in her hand, she reads the address again, making sure of it before she opens the stove door. A flame flares up in the oven, and she watches Michael's words become ash. Then she vomits into the sink. When it's over, she rattles through the confessional prayer, not meeting the priest's eyes. "Bless me, Father, for I have sinned. . . . I—we—Michael and I—I never meant for—"

Albin Horvat waves a cross at her and murmurs, "*Ego te absolvo*. Does Joe know?"

"No. I—I'm afraid of what he'll do." She starts to cry. "He'll hate me. He'll hate the child. He'll kill Michael!"

"Do you want me to tell Mike? He's a good man, Annie. I think he'll do the right thing. Should I tell him?"

She shakes her head, snuffling in snot decisively. "I want to talk to him. I want to tell him."

"Annie, no! They'll see you come to the church, and they'll suspect. You need to stay out of sight. I'll find a way to get you out of town, too, but you have to wait. There are goons everywhere. They've already killed Charlie Miller and—"

She straightens, wiping her nose on the back of her hand, finally able to think past her own crisis. "I have to get word to the union officers. I have to warn them. Everyone is in danger now, Father. I have to—"

"No! You can't go out there. They'll be looking for you, too." The priest holds up a hand while he thinks. "Annie, does Lucia Caretto know? About . . ." He glances at her belly, and Annie nods. "All right. Priests and midwives can be out at night with no one asking questions. I'll rouse Lucia and Carla and we'll raise the alarm."

"I'll make a list. You have to know who they'll come for—"

"Annie! I know who to tell! You've done all you can. You've done more than anyone could ask of you. It's our turn now. Let someone else carry the flag."

She goes back to bed but does not sleep, listening for the sound of gunshots and shouting. When at last the steam whistle blasts end of shift, she swings her legs out of bed, groans, and lunges for the chamber pot, puking neatly into the enamel bowl.

You are all my hopes and dreams, she tells the child in her mind and in her belly. Still, it would be nice if you didn't make me sick.

When her stomach settles, she opens the window to air out the bedroom. Gathers her hair into a loose pile on top of her head and pins it out of her way. Washes her face in the basin on the bureau and spits the sour taste from her mouth. She puts on a secondhand woolen dress, its cuffs and hemline lengthened with corduroy bands to accommodate her frame, arranging its folds over her middle to hide the slight swelling below her waist.

Pulling on a thick knitted cardigan, she carries the chamber pot downstairs and pukes again. She leaves the back door open when she trudges through the snow to dump its contents into the privy.

The cold air does her good. She goes back inside, scrubs the pot with salt and vinegar, and wipes every surface in the kitchen thoroughly. She feels a draft on her wet hands. She's left the window open upstairs. That is easily dealt with, although panic threatens as she straightens the bed. What else would give her away? She has to make this nightmare into an ordinary morning. Joe must not see anything amiss. He must not suspect anything.

She gets his supper started. He expects a good meal now that he's bringing in a salary again. She can't bear the thought of meat, so she dices turnips, carrots, and potatoes for a soup. No cabbage. Nothing with a strong odor that could make her throw up again. When at last she sits at the table and looks at the clock, she is sure that all is in readiness, but Joe is late. There was a time when she would have worried. Now, unbidden, it comes to her: if he's killed, it would make everything easier.

A little past nine, he arrives at last, smelling of liquor. "Big doings in town," he reports. "Word is Cruse is arresting union men, left, right, and center."

She waits, but he says nothing about Charlie. Or Michael. Or Father Horvat. "On what charge?" she asks, letting indignation rule her voice.

"Interfering with loyal workers."

Loyal workers. Like you, she thinks. Like my own husband. "I'll have to call an Auxiliary meeting," she says neutrally.

"Oh, for Crissakes, Annie. It's over! You *lost*."

She waits, as though thinking about it. Sighing, she shrugs her defeat. "I suppose you're right. Sit down. Your soup is getting cold."

This will be over soon, she tells herself. One way or another, it will all be over soon.

3

No better term than this: thou art a villain.
—Shakespeare, *Romeo and Juliet*

In the general offices of Calumet & Hecla, James MacNaughton is entirely satisfied with the events of the past twenty-four hours. At four-fifteen yesterday afternoon, a grand jury quietly issued fifty-four indictments. Sheriff Cruse's deputies have fanned out overnight to arrest agitators and troublemakers on suspicion of plotting an attack against C&H employees. Anyone resisting arrest has been dealt with, and those who've eluded capture are being pursued with vigor. The whole matter will be wrapped up soon.

Mont Blanc pen in hand, a fresh sheet of stationery before him, he sits still and gathers his thoughts regarding the composition of a report to be delivered at the stockholders' meeting in Boston.

It will be best, he decides, to begin with an admission of what everyone will know when they walk into the conference room.

As you are all aware, 1913 has been a challenge. The worldwide price of copper has fallen under pressure from the open-pit mines in Montana and Arizona, where the cost of production is much lower. It must be recognized that Calumet & Hecla mines are at a structural disadvantage in this competition; Michigan's remaining deposits, while rich, are now very deep underground, requiring ever more complex and costly infrastructure dedicated to ore extraction.

That is the bad news. Happily, he can continue on a note of optimism: *Despite the inflammatory headlines of the past year, Calumet & Hecla remains profitable.*

Just barely, he thinks. No need to make that plain. Investors can study the numbers themselves if they care to go over the charts. And while, admittedly, the company's losses have mounted up, the Western Federation of Miners is bankrupt after spending eight hundred thousand dollars on the Michigan strike, a third of which was borrowed from other unions' treasuries.

No doubt, sympathy and donations made directly to the Calumet miners will wither as editorials in the better newspapers nurture doubts and confusion about the issues. His favorite example of the genre was sent to him by a shareholder in Scarsdale; the clipping from the *New York World* noted, "Houghton County is not a community of self-governing American citizens. It is one chiefly of aliens brought thither to serve the copper monopoly, ruled from Boston in defiance of the law and in spite of democratic institutions."

Shrugging off the insult to the company, James MacNaughton was pleased, for he knows that readers will simply mumble, "A plague on both your houses." Soon they'll turn their attention to other headlines. Suffragettes have bombed a church in London. The Marines have taken Vera Cruz after heavy fighting, killing two hundred with only twenty-four U.S. casualties. Joe Jeannette has defeated the French boxing champ Georges Carpentier; Joe's from New Jersey, but he's a Negro, so does it really count?

That's what really interests the American public, James MacNaughton thinks. Not some obscure industrial squabble in Michigan.

I am gratified to report that the phase-in of the Leyner-Ingersoll drill has continued to increase efficiency. We have already cut the workforce nearly in half with a concomitant decrease in production costs. It can be anticipated that this trend will continue. Automation is the future of industry around the world, and you can be proud to know that Calumet & Hecla is leading the way in mining technology.

He pauses there, listening to the ten forty-seven freight whistling its imminent arrival. Every week, northbound trains deliver another shipment of one-man drills. Every week, southbound trains carry the infection of trade unionism away from Calumet. The workforce is being cleansed of socialists and anarchist criminals. Every disillusioned union member who leaves Calumet is another item crossed off the company's liabilities: a salary that can be eliminated, a house that can be sold off or razed. All done with minimal disruption.

He ends his report with a promise he means to keep:

> *The stockholders of Calumet & Hecla have my personal assurance that we have seen the end of labor unrest here in the Copper Country. Every employee who remains will be a man who is willing to do the work for the posted pay—without complaint. The workers of Calumet won't soon forget this winter's lessons.*
>
> *Your company's officers will, with resolution and integrity, turn the worst of times into the best of times. Those who hold stock in Calumet & Hecla may expect that returns on your investment will reward your patience.*
>
> *Sincerely yours,*
> *James MacNaughton*
> *General Manager, Calumet & Hecla Mining Corporation*

For a few weeks more, the remaining union members persist in their refusal to bow their heads and bend their knees.

Nothing justifies their stubbornness. Congressional committees end their investigations without coming to much of a conclusion regarding wrongdoing by the copper companies. Houghton County officials have absolved the Citizens' Alliance of any responsibility for the Italian Hall disaster.

The killing blow comes on April 4, when a brief letter to Local 15 arrives from the president of the Western Federation of Miners. "After fighting a most determined battle," it instructs, "striking miners of the Michigan Copper Country should return to their employment under such terms as they are able to secure." On April 12, 1914—Easter Sunday—the union votes to end the nine-month strike.

As the meeting breaks up, one or two grim jokes about resurrection are made. No one laughs.

The next morning, Calumet & Hecla issues an announcement: anyone who worked through the strike will keep his job. Strikers may reapply for employment; they will, however, lose seniority if they are hired. They must also hand in their union cards and sign a company ledger confirming that they have renounced the Western Federation of Miners. Finally, so that the company can be absolutely certain of their loyalties, any man wishing to return to work now must also contribute five cents to a fund for the purpose of buying a fine gold watch to be inscribed with these words:

> *For James MacNaughton from the grateful employees of C&H.*
> *Due to your attitude of NO COMPROMISE,*
> *the Copper Country is not afflicted with the presence*
> *of the Western Federation of Miners.*

At the presentation ceremony, Calumet & Hecla rewards Mr. James MacNaughton with a substantial raise in salary in recognition of his steadfast opposition to the strike. Having returned from their tour of Europe, his wife, Mary, and their two daughters are there for a quiet, tasteful celebration of his success.

The following morning, as he descends the stairs to the dining room, he tarries, as always, to gaze at the town over which he rules with vice-regal authority. Mind and conscience clear, he hears his father's voice and Kipling's words: "Yours is the Earth and everything that's in it. You are a man, my son!"

4

Consequences yet hanging in the stars
—Shakespeare, *Romeo and Juliet*

Even on the Keweenaw Peninsula, winter does not last forever. Mountains of dirty snow erode and melt in the sun. Patches of weedy grass appear. When the temperature climbs even a little above freezing, children refuse to put on coats and hats and boots, insisting, "It's warm, Ma!" as they dash outside. "You'll catch your death!" their mothers shout, and regret the phrase as the words die in their mouths.

Even the little kids know not to flaunt their lively spirits near families with black ribbons on the doors, so they spend their hours of freedom roaming the town's outskirts, searching for mushrooms and wild asparagus shoots, or collecting chunks of coal along the tracks, or picking through the wreckage of bulldozed company houses, hoping to find a button or a hair ribbon or a broken plate. The boldest prowl around recently emptied homes. Peeking in the windows. Daring one another to try to go inside and see what's left. Company watchmen patrol the neighborhoods to keep them out. At night, a big searchlight sweeps the streets to discourage looters. MacNaughton's Eye, they call it.

The town is hollowing out. Down in Detroit, the Ford Motor Company is offering five dollars a day with a bonus plan for those who sign on to build the Model T. Even non-union miners are leaving on those southbound trains; Michigan copper companies are finding it difficult to hire workers with the skill and stamina needed to replace experienced men underground. Up and down the fine streets of the Paris of the North, storefronts are emptied out and boarded up.

Nominally independent businesses that made it through the strike are now shuttered, for one-man drills don't buy groceries or lunch pails, or heavy jackets and boots and gloves, or bolts of cloth and children's shoes. Sales are down by half. Time to cut losses, businessmen are thinking. It's all going to get worse. Michigan is being underpriced by new open-pit mines out west. Copper's not dead, but this town is.

There is only this to provide cold comfort to Calumet: down in West Virginia, the coal strike has gotten worse than anything that happened in Michigan. Miners in West Virginia have been machine-gunned by American troops sent to protect the property rights of men who live far from the coal fields. The newspapers are calling it a labor war.

Too bad for them, the cynics mutter. Strikes are a big damn mistake. You're worse off than before it started. "And I'd tell that to Annie Clements's face!" they declare, though they don't know where she is. Not for sure.

There are plenty of rumors about her and that photographer fella. Some snicker that Big Annie finally found herself a man who could get her pregnant. Some think maybe Joe Clements killed her and Mike. In the bars, they razz him about it and Joe snarls at them, though in all honesty, he seems more like a bereft husband left behind than an enraged murderer who strangled his wife for cheating.

The women of the Copper Country know more about Annie and Mike than their husbands and brothers and sons. Not everything, but enough to keep their hopes up for a time. Quietly informed about the baby by Carla Caretto, a majority voted to empty the Auxiliary's meager coffers and give the proceeds to Annie.

They didn't dare go to her house with the cash. They didn't dare visit to say good-bye before she slipped out of town. Anything out of the ordinary might have made Joe suspicious. It might have given MacNaughton the excuse he needed to have her arrested and sent back to the workhouse. So they brought the money to Father Horvat, who brought it to Moishe Glass, who was going to hide Annie in his delivery van and get her south to Wisconsin, someplace beyond even James MacNaughton's long reach.

"Give her this envelope," Albin Horvat told Moishe. "Tell her it's from the Auxiliary. Tell her she can write to me when she finds a safe harbor, and I will pass the word."

"Eva, she'd write if she could," Carla says when months have passed with no news of Annie Clements. "This ain't no fairy story, *cara mia*. The goons mighta got her, *cara*. She might be dead. Michael, too. Annie's gone and she ain't coming back."

Gone. All right. Eva is willing to accept that much, but she refuses to believe that Annie Clements is dead. Although Joan of Arc came to a bad end. And she won't believe that Michael Sweeney is dead, either. Because she liked Mike, and she doesn't want to think of Annie alone, penniless and pregnant, fending for herself and her baby. So she decides that Annie and Mike have become like Mother Jones: going from mine to mine, giving people hope and bucking them up.

Except they're doing it secretly, maybe.

Eva knows that's probably not true. Still, that's what she decides to believe. Because she is tired of feeling sad about everything. She wants to believe that someday, she'll see a photograph by Michael Sweeney on the front page of a newspaper. A picture of Big Annie leading a picket line, head high and carrying an enormous American flag. Or . . .

Maybe they're safe up in some little town in Canada, making a new life for themselves and their child. That notion makes Eva feel better about everything for a while. In the end, though, Eva decides to believe they've gone to Chicago. Because that's where Eva wants to go. To Chicago. Of course, most people say Chicago is the worst place in the country—violent, loud, lawless, ugly, stinking—but Eva has been in love with the idea of going there ever since Ella Bloor sent her a copy of a book by Jane Addams.

Twenty Years at Hull-House is the most thrilling thing Eva Savicki has ever read. Better than a love story, better than a made-up tale of adventure. It tells about how Miss Addams and a few of her friends took over a big old derelict house in a scary Chicago neighborhood where immigrants and the poorest of the poor lived. Miss Addams talked rich people into donating money to fix up the old Hull mansion so they could make it a place for a food bank and do clothing drives and so on, but the project grew and grew. First, Miss Addams took in a little baby who was born with a harelip because his defect made him unwelcome, even to his own family. After that, she sheltered a forlorn little Italian bride of fifteen, trying to escape her husband because she didn't want to be married to an old man who beat her.

All kinds of people began to come to the Hull-House door. A poor young German whose tuberculosis was made worse by the alcohol he drank to mute his pain and fear. A terrified Irish girl alone in her labor because the doctor wouldn't come and none of the honest Irish matrons in the neighborhood would touch "the likes of her and her fatherless baby."

In the face of all that desperation and need, Miss Addams and her friends and their donors added a nursery and a kindergarten to Hull-House, so little kids didn't have to stay home alone while their mothers were trying to earn money. They added a free school next, with a gymnasium and a cafeteria. There's an auditorium now, and a theater, and an art studio with a gallery, and a music school, and a library, and club rooms—all for people who never had such things in their lives, who never imagined they could live in such a community.

The most exciting part for Eva was reading about how Miss Addams and her friends fixed up another building to make a co-op residence with a communal kitchen where single working women could stay. It was called the Jane Club, and it was based on a little book called *Coöperation* by an English lady named Beatrice Potter Webb. The idea was that if everyone pooled their money for rent, the girls could take a chance on striking for better wages. Because there were others who'd stand by them while they went without pay.

That's where I should be, Eva thought when she read all this. I am just the sort of person who should be working at Hull-House.

She is already earning her keep. She helped Carla put in the new garden and she helps with the cooking and she looks after the Caretto cousins, making sure they get to school on time and do their chores.

In April, the strike babies began arriving, so many that Lucia couldn't handle them all, so Eva started going out on her own. The Carettos want her to stay in Calumet, to be part of their family, and she's grateful to them, but her heart is set on Chicago. So she found work scrubbing floors for a lady in Laurium, stashing the nickels in a cigar box, counting them every night.

When at last she has accumulated enough money to buy her own train ticket to Chicago, she decided to write to Miss Jane Addams. She got that idea from Jack Kivisto. Just write a letter. Ask for a job. See what happens. And for that idea she is grateful to him. It's like a librarian told her once: "If you learn something from each person you meet and from each book you read, you will be the best-educated person in the world."

She labors like a trammer over that letter, rewriting it a dozen times. When it is as good as she can make it, she brings it to that sympathetic librarian, who makes sure the spelling and grammar are correct before Eva copies it out in her best handwriting.

Dear Miss Addams,

I am an orphan, fifteen years of age, but I do not ask for your aid. I have been cared for during my childhood by the Women's Auxiliary of the copper miners' union in Calumet, Michigan. I am sure you have read of our recent battles here. Now that the strike is over, I answer to no one and may live my life as seems best. Mrs. Ella Bloor kindly sent me your book about Hull-House, which taught me that there was a world beyond the Copper Country where I can be useful.

I have grown up among good but poor people from many nations. I speak Polish, a little Italian, a little Slovenian, and a little Finnish (very little), which skills I hope may be of help in your work with new immigrants who have come to Chicago. I know how to "wash newborn babies, and prepare the dead for burial, and nurse the sick, and mind the children," as you wrote in your book. And now, as you once wrote, "I am through with everlasting preparation for life, however ill-prepared I might be."

I do not have much schooling, but I have learned from many people. From Father Horvat, I learned Jesus's warning "The poor you shall always have with you." From Ella Bloor, I learned that we will always have rich men who never willingly share a penny of their wealth. From Annie Clements, I learned that if we work for the common good, we can make a good life more common. Annie also taught me how to organize a group to do what a single person cannot accomplish alone. From Mother Jones, I learned that when you lose one battle, you find another and fight on. From Moishe Glass, I learned that what you do when you've been defeated is important and that to improve a single life is to improve the world.

From your own book, I have learned that one woman and a few friends can provide education, good food, and decent housing to those who need it most.

I want to be part of that, if you will have me. Please tell me if I may come to work with you and your friends in Chicago.

Sincerely,
Eva Lucyna Savicki

She rereads it twice, folds it into an envelope, buys a stamp, and mails it to Miss Jane Addams, Hull-House, Chicago, Illinois. The answer comes by return post, just one week later, in the hasty handwriting of a woman with too much to do and not enough time to do it.

Yes, my dear. There is a place for you here. Come to us as quickly as you can. The need is great.—J. Addams

There is money for the train fare in the envelope.

For a time, Eva sits still, the note clutched in one hand. She does not cry—not from happiness or sadness or relief or grief. She stands up as tall as she can and holds her head high and says it aloud, to make herself believe it: "I will make you proud, wherever you are, Annie. I will carry the flag for you."

Author's Note

Most of the events and many of the characters in this novel are known to us with varying degrees of historical detail. Those seeking comprehensive nonfiction accounts of the 1913 Michigan copper strike would do well to begin with *Cradle to Grave* by Larry Lankton (New York: Oxford University Press, 1991), a scholarly study of the Michigan copper industry. Steve Lehto's *Death's Door* (Troy, Michigan: Momentum Books, 2006) focuses on the Italian Hall disaster in both legal and social terms. Both of these books have extensive bibliographies.

The Italian Hall disaster is said to have been the event that inspired Justice Oliver Wendell Holmes's dictum that free speech does not extend to shouting "fire" in a crowded theater. President Wilson did bring together the Commission on Industrial Relations to scrutinize labor law; Mother Jones, Samuel Gompers of the American Federation of Labor, and the famous attorney Clarence Darrow testified to the commission during its consideration of ideas like a minimum wage, paid overtime, and a national prohibition of child labor. Those reforms were not codified until the end of the 1930s, after the National Labor Relations Board came into existence under Franklin Roosevelt. However, the Clayton Antitrust Act did pass in 1914, after which courts could no longer rule that strikes and other union activities were illegal conspiracies or trusts in restraint of trade; the Clayton act was called the Magna Carta of Labor by Samuel Gompers.

This progress was lost to view in August of that year, when head-lines about the war in Europe replaced those about labor strife. The Great War's pointless slaughter scythed through a generation of young men not much older than the children of the Italian Hall, bringing death in unimaginable numbers: thirty-seven million casualties in four years. Even before that carnage drew to an end in 1918, a lethal influenza began its sweep around the globe, killing some fifty mil-lion people. By 1920, the Italian Hall disaster was forgotten by the world beyond the Copper Country. In 1984, the building itself was torn down, apart from the stone archway that once led to the staircase where seventy-three people died. A plaque now commemorates the disaster. The strike itself and its contribution to Calumet's decline remain controversial.

For this novel, I have loosened the time line to allow for character development and to clarify the narrative. Some events have been taken out of sequence. Annie Clements's time in jail reflects the experiences of suffragettes and labor organizers of her time, not her own incarceration, about which we know little.

Dialogue and inner lives are the province of the novelist, but where possible, I used direct quotes from Anna Klobuchar Clements, Governor Woodbridge Ferris, President Woodrow Wilson, Mother Jones, Ella Bloor, and Jane Addams. As theatrically villainous as James MacNaughton may seem, the portrayal is accurate—including the dedication engraved on the gold watch he demanded from the miners who went back to work after the strike. A ledger in the ar-chives of Michigan Technical University contains the list of men who "contributed."

The photographer who documented life in Calumet and the af-termath of the Italian Hall disaster was John William Nara. Michael Sweeney is a fictional character based on Frank Shaw, Annie's second husband and the father of her only child. Shaw was a journalist rather than a photographer, but I wanted to reflect the importance of photog-raphy to the work of social reformers. I have given Annie a consider-ably better fictional relationship with Michael Sweeney than she had with Frank. At the end of the strike, she divorced Joe and joined Frank

Shaw in Chicago, where they were married shortly before the birth of their daughter. Like Annie's first and third husbands, Shaw became a dangerous drunk; Annie divorced all three. She opened a millinery shop in Chicago and treated her own employees well, although according to members of her family, she never spoke of the Calumet strike or her own role in it.

Tom Fisher is a composite character, representative of the men who ran private armies of strikebreakers hired by company executives. As one of his men suggests, these criminals eventually infiltrated labor unions around the country. That's a story for someone else to tell.

Major Henry Van Den Broek is loosely based on Major Roy Vander-cook. Eva and Kazimir Savicki are entirely fictional, but the Kivisto family and their situation in Calumet were real. (The family surname has since been changed to Kewest). Solomon Kivisto was the last man to die in the mines before the strike; his widow was offered the deed to their company house in exchange for fifty years of labor. Solomon's son John was the grandfather of my friend Rivkah Tobin. Her personal memories are of a violent, angry old man whose unhappiness echoed down three generations of her family. Like Annie Clements, John Kewest never spoke of what happened during the strike. The closest he came to that was in 1966 when he drove up to Calumet with Rivkah, who was thirteen at the time; when they passed the Italian Hall, her grandfather pulled the car over to the side of the street and sobbed. He never explained why.

I am also indebted to Joyce Minks for details of her father's family history in Calumet; Joyce's father, Henry (Andrej) Zagar, was a child who survived the Christmas Eve disaster. Thanks also go to Elaine Petrocelli, who shared memories of her great-grandfather Moishe Glass, whose family ran several general stores in the Upper Peninsula of Michigan during the years of the strike.

Charlie Miller represents two real people—Charles Moyer and Guy Miller; they were the leaders of the Western Federation of Miners and a Local 15 official, respectively. At the end of the strike, Charles Moyer was shot in the back by Sheriff James Cruse's deputies; Moyer survived the assault, barely.

A strike is a collective action, and by focusing on Anna Klobu-char Clements, I have not given other union organizers and leaders in Calumet the attention they deserve. That said, the central role of women in the 1913 copper strike and in the labor movement in general was remarkable and has been underrepresented in most historical accounts.

A number of people generously shared their expertise with me: Dr. John P. Beck (Michigan labor history); Amy Cooke, Ann Hoffer, Susan McMullen, and Jean Lightner Norum (genealogy research); Carey Granger (early mining technology); Eugene Frank Hodal (union history and politics); Alice Margerum (strikers' songs); James Reichardt (legal practices); Steven Porter and David Selcer (tactics used during labor-management negotiations); Dina Rossi and Bob Price (early camera technology); Kathleen Valentine (union social welfare work). Special thanks go to those who helped me with Finnish history and culture and who related family memories: Kathy Grzedzinski, Erika Koskinen-Koivisto, Kristi Manninen, Antti Pesonen, Marjaana Pilvikki, Paivi Trip, Marjaana Voutilainen, and Kate Willette. Michigan Technical University generously offered a grant to underwrite my research in the strike archives.

As always, I benefited from a team of early readers; they provided me with encouragement, criticism, and personal reactions to the developing story over a period of nearly three years: Bob Price, Gretchen Batton, Frank Hodal, and Joyce Minks. Early versions of the complete manuscript were much improved by the corrections and suggestions of Miriam Goderich, Vivian Singer, Rivkah Tobin, David Selcer, John P. Beck, and James Reichardt.

A 1913 miners' strike in the Upper Peninsula of Michigan is not an easy sell. I am so very grateful that my extraordinary agent, Jane Dystel, simply would not give up on this novel and found the perfect editor for this story. Tara Parson's enthusiasm for the manuscript gave me the determination to push through three more drafts. Her clear and specific suggestions made this novel far better than it was when it first landed on her desk.

Bonnie Thompson has copyedited all seven of my novels; I rely on her meticulous care and attention to detail. If any errors remain, it's because I reintroduced them in galleys!

Jane Dystel, Miriam Goderich, and Bonnie Thompson are the only fixed points in my wandering literary life. We four are coming up on our twenty-fifth anniversary now. It has been a privilege and a pleasure to work with you all these years. Thank you.

About the Author

Widely praised for her meticulous research, fine prose, and compelling narrative drive, Mary Doria Russell is the *New York Times* bestselling and award-winning author of *The Sparrow, Children of God, A Thread of Grace, Dreamers of the Day, Doc,* and *Epitaph.* Dr. Russell holds a PhD in biological anthropology. She lives in Lyndhurst, Ohio.